THE UNANOINTED

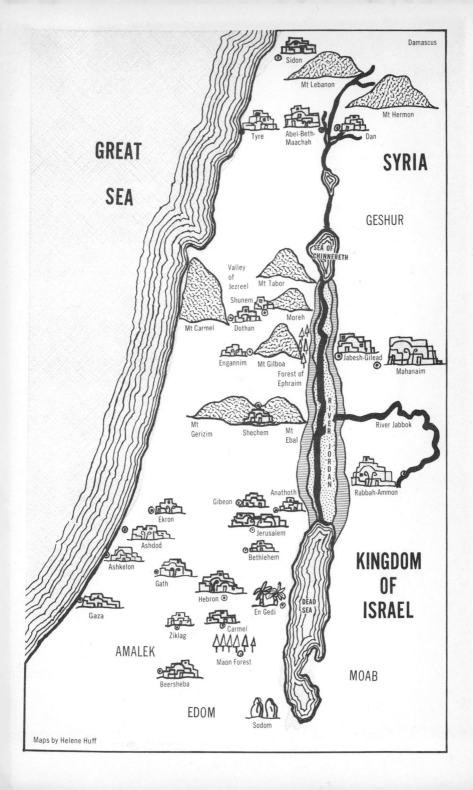

THE
UNANOINTED

A NOVEL BY

LAURENE CHINN

CROWN PUBLISHERS, INC.

NEW YORK

*To Harry, Elizabeth, and Wanda, who each in a
different way contributed so much to the
writing of this novel.*

Foreword

OF THE THOUSANDS of men and women whose lives were bound up in the career of David of Israel, none touched him more closely than Joab, his kinsman and commander. Joab it was who enabled David to capture Jerusalem in a single night without a major battle. In addition Joab led David's armies, killed four public enemies, and interfered frequently and memorably in the affairs of David's sons. Of Joab's public life much is recorded. Of his private life almost nothing is known.

Many characters found in these pages lived in David's household and served in his armies. Some are completely fictional. A few familiar figures were omitted and their essential acts ascribed to others in the story.

Since many major characters in David's period bore similar names, Asahel, Abishai, and Ahinoam are here called Asa, Seth, and Reba. Readers will have to do the best they can with Abigail, Abiathar, Absalom, Abishag, and Adonijah. The term "cousin" is frequently used in its more general sense of "kinsman." It may mean cousin or, as in the case of Joab and David, nephew and uncle.

In the Jerusalem scenes the locations of the Dung Gate and the fountain En Rogel were shifted to opposite sides of the lower city. The location and description of Millo follows one of several contradictory sources. The building program ascribed to David was in part the work of Solomon. With these exceptions, the topographical and historical references will be found to agree with modern atlases and commentaries, at least insofar as they agree with one another.

LAURENE CHAMBERS CHINN

Borger, Texas

PART ONE

The Wilderness

I

JOAB STRAIGHTENED SLOWLY, still gripping the knife. He relaxed his hold on the bone handle with conscious effort. He felt the fading of hatred, the sharp onset of remorse.

You're dead, Joab told the huddled figure. In death as in life, Lem's jaw hung slack.

Remorse mounted. Life is good in the Bethlehem pastures. The sun in the face at dawn, the shine of stars by night—these are good. And after the sheep have been driven into the fold—when their silly bleating ends and silence begins—this moment is very good.

Lem too had known the sights, the sounds, the earthy odors of the pastures, and the arid, acrid breath of the wilderness stretching south to the Dead Sea. Lem had known the caves and sandy wadies of the wilderness, the thorn bushes, the scant, wiry grasses. Life had been good, even for the witless, treacherous Lem.

I did not mean to kill him, Joab thought defensively; he leaped on me while I lay dozing at the door of the fold. I did not plan to kill him. But that was not wholly true. In the moment when he struck, Joab hated the pesty fellow with his foolish babble and his sulky silences, with his sudden attacks from behind and his long, strong, twining, strangling arms. I wanted to kill him, Joab thought, accepting guilt honestly. For one moment I wanted to kill him.

He looked at the misshapen figure on the ground. Lem wore the same filthy cloak often for weeks at a time. The unbleached wool was daubed with mud and spittle and sop, and now it was smeared also with blood. He twitched the torn skirts so they covered the body and then he closed the sagging mouth. He had never before seen Lem with his mouth shut.

Blood was drying on the knife. Joab plunged the blade into the earth and he scrubbed it with sand. The knife had entered Lem's body below the fifth rib, in the spot David had taught Joab to find in the body of a lion. Even now, Joab could feel in arm and shoulder a memory of the yielding of flesh under the knife's thrust. Well, he had known the sensation before. Killing Lem was no different from killing any other beast. Joab

[1]

shoved the knife into its sheath. I will not fret about it, he told himself. A beast sprang on me. I killed the beast. It is done.

But Lem was not a beast. Lem was a boy who had grown strangely powerful during the months of this spring. Lem was a boy with a brother who would welcome an excuse to avenge his death. Elhanan, thought Joab, and shivered though the night was warm. Elhanan will kill me. The law gives him the right.

A picture of Elhanan rose to blot out the sprawled figure. Hairy of face, hairy of body, quick to anger, slow to forgive—Elhanan was a braggart, winner of many encounters with raiders from the Negeb, to hear him tell it. Lem is dead and Elhanan is my enemy, thought Joab in rising panic. Killing is a family matter and vengeance is a family matter. I must go home. My mother and my brothers are involved in this.

Joab turned now to stare at the close-meshed walls of the fold, fighting his battle with habit. When you have placed the welfare of a lot of silly sheep above your own safety since the age of nine it is not easy to leave them untended. Well, here was the body of Lem to distract any beasts prowling up from the wilderness tonight. Joab set out over the hills, his long legs consuming the miles.

The low house of gray stone had been built more than two hundred years ago by an ancestor of Jesse the patriarch. Rooms had been added as the family grew. Jesse had fulfilled for many years the duties of elder in Bethlehem, as his fathers before him had done. He judged causes and performed marriages in the city gate. On feast days he presided over sacrifices and burnt offerings at an altar of heaped stones on a high hill near the Hebron highway. He owned the threshing floor east of Bethlehem, and the oxen and the sledge by means of which the grain was separated from the straw. He was hospitable to strangers and Levites and visiting priests or prophets. He gave bounty to the needy at sheepshearing time and the harvest season. But in recent years, since David's flight from the murderous anger of King Saul to hide in the wilderness, Jesse's family had scattered. Now only Zeruiah and her sons remained.

The house spread its blank face along the narrow cobbled street. Joab went around to the wide gate at the back. The gate was barred at night, but it could be opened by day to admit carts and donkeys or camels into the paved court. Joab climbed over the wall at a place known to the sons and grandsons of Jesse, where a gnarled old sycamine tree grew close against the wall and a couple of stones could be pushed inward to make toe holds for the climber. Nobody knew how old the tree was, but the fine black mulberries it bore had been used for generations to make a red wine sweetened with honey. Joab dropped lightly from the top of the wall and crossed the court to rap on the door of the women's quarters. Behind this door slept his mother, Zeruiah, eldest daughter of Jesse.

Zeruiah emerged quickly, winding her girdle over the sleeveless white tunic she wore.

She was a neat, small woman with deft hands. Her dark hair was brushed back smoothly from her oval face. She had brought a lamp from the inner room, and she went to the fire at the back of the court to light the three wicks in the spouts of the brown clay vessel.

Joab never looked at his mother without feeling pride and respect and a little fear. When all the others fled, she remained in Bethlehem, keeping her three sons with her. She was Jesse's daughter and David's sister, but her loyalty was to the family's land and possessions, not to its scattering members. She wasted no motions and few words. She lived here with her sons and a scant dozen servants, keeping the house in order and the flocks together, observing the customs of hospitality and the giving of bounty. In her capable hands she held together possessions gathered by generations.

Zeruiah held the lamp high, looking anxiously into his face. "Why did you leave the sheep?"

"I have killed Lem."

Joab's eyes fell before the fear which leaped into Zeruiah's face. He said defensively, "He sprang on me. He would have strangled me. He is—was—strong."

"You could have cut him a little. Why did you kill him?"

"He would have waited his chance. He would have killed me, sooner or later. He has attacked me many times, and each time he has been stronger than before. For just the little time it took to kill him I—I was so angry I wanted to kill him." He hung his head, ashamed to have caused his mother to feel such fear.

Zeruiah went to the low table under the old sycamine and set down the lamp. She said resolutely, "You did what you had to do. Now we must plan what is to be done next."

In the corner of the court a wall of stones and mortar enclosed an open cistern, which provided water for the household. Joab sank onto the stone curb, feeling deep exhaustion now that his mother had taken over the responsibility of decision.

Zeruiah said, "Wash yourself, my son, and put on clean clothing. Roll a change of garments into one of the mats."

Joab drew up the earthen bottle which hung in the cistern and splashed water into a basin. He carried the basin to his room and stripped and washed himself. When he returned, food was set out on the table. He spread a small rug and sat down to eat. A shallow dish held a cold knuckle of roast lamb, and an earthen bowl contained sop into which to dip his bread.

Zeruiah sat on a rug near him, the lamp lighting her face. "I depend on you more than on your brothers," she said earnestly. "Asa means the

[3]

best in everything, but his eagerness outruns his judgment. As for Seth, though he is the eldest, he is gone when I need him. Seth will always be a better soldier for David than son to his mother. Remember, Joab, I depend on you. When you can, return to your mother and your home and this land which is yours to share."

Joab moved restlessly. Zeruiah made it sound final, and the pain of parting was sharp in him. He choked on the bread, swallowed painfully, and asked, "Where shall I go?"

"You could go to Hebron. The law would protect you if you went to stand trial before the elders there."

"I don't want to go to Hebron." He hated the city of refuge with its walls that shut out the sight of the land. He hated the people of Hebron —men with furtive eyes and women whose mantles did not conceal their calculating glances.

"Very well," Zeruiah replied. "You will not go to Hebron. You will go to David."

Joab laid down the knuckle of lamb. "I would rather go to Hebron."

The trembling had returned. Even his voice shook. It was easier to battle any bully or beast in the fields than to withstand Zeruiah. But Zeruiah had never understood the quality of Joab's feeling toward David, the golden boy of Bethlehem.

David was the family hero, the family legend. Even in hiding, an outlaw, hunted by Saul's army, his exploits were the subject of tales which continued to filter through Judah and all Israel. David had welded the fugitives he found in the wilderness into an army which kept at bay Judah's traditional enemies, the Edomites and Philistines. Men were drawn to him from everywhere. His name was on the lips of women who danced and sang in the streets.

Joab averted his eyes from the determination in Zeruiah's face. "When David was seventeen he killed the Philistine giant. I am seventeen, and I have killed the pasture idiot. I cannot go running to David. Let me go to Moab. When I have proved myself—"

"How do you propose to prove yourself while you are hiding? Elhanan goes to Moab now and then."

Joab gulped the wine his mother had set out to wash down the meal. He rose and rolled his rug and set it against the wall. He had no answer for Zeruiah's question. He felt the walls of the court closing in. The wine had been tasteless, but he had swallowed it anyway because a journey lay ahead.

Zeruiah's fingers traced on the low table a pattern of two triangles superimposed to form a six-pointed star. It was a figure she used often in her embroidery, a figure David had carved on the arm of his lyre and on his sling. Joab watched the tracing finger, and longed to lay his face in his mother's breast and wail as a child does, and have his troubles kissed away.

Zeruiah said, "I will tell you of this brother of mine. David was the youngest of the seven sons of Jesse, and errand boy for all. He stayed with the sheep when the older boys were busy with feasts or courting, wars or journeys. David climbed up into the branches of the old sycamine tree to pluck at the strings of his lyre for hours on end, making up little songs about flowers and birds and stones and stars. In spring when our little bulbul bird was nesting in the tree he would sit nearby and talk with the bird as if it understood and replied. He was a pretty little fellow, and pleasant, and we were all very fond of him.

"Then a day came when the prophet Samuel was a guest in the house. Before departing he offered his blessing to one of the sons of the house in return for hospitality received. With an insight peculiar to those prophet fellows, he saw the jealousy that exists among active, stalwart brothers. So he chose the youngest, the red-haired, lyre-strumming little fellow whom everybody loved and nobody envied. Samuel anointed David and gave him a seer's blessing."

Joab closed his eyes, waiting for Zeruiah to finish. Her words could not change his feeling about David. But he listened dutifully, as a son must.

"The anointing oil must have got in the child's eyes," Zeruiah said, smiling a little, "because from then on David saw himself wrapped in a cloak of destiny. When he made songs the songs told how God had made the stars and streams for David's delight. When he killed a lion in the field he sang of how the Lord had strengthened his arm. On the day when he went to the Valley of Elah to carry bread and cheese to his soldier brothers, the memory of the oil blinded him to the size of Goliath and to his own gangling awkwardness. Fortunately, his luck was good that day and he got a stone right through the visor of the giant's helmet. The stone blinded Goliath, and he fell, clawing at his eyes and bellowing with pain. Once he was down under the weight of all that brazen armor, even David could hack off his head."

Joab smiled. "Even David." Zeruiah missed the whole point of the Goliath episode. David was a strategist. For days the armies of Israel had gazed on the boastful, posturing giant, and had seen only his size, his armor, his great iron sword. But David had seen the open visor of his helmet, and had known he could put a stone through it and that the clumsy braggart would have no defense against his own surprise and pain.

Zeruiah said, "So David became the darling of Israel, as he had been the darling of this house. He married Saul's daughter. He became a captain. Eventually Abner himself was jealous for his own standing with the soldiers and especially with Saul. Of course David made a good soldier. The best soldiers are the believing fools who haven't sense enough to be afraid."

Women, thought Joab, are stupid about military matters. He went to the cistern and sank down on the curb, leaning his head back against the rough stone wall of the house. The best soldiers, he was thinking, are the strategists. I could be a good soldier. For almost four hundred years the people of Israel have lived in Canaan. They have taken every city but Jerusalem, and it stands there atop Mount Ophel, with ravines dropping steeply away below its walls, strong in its walls as Goliath was strong in his armor. But I have found a place in those walls like the visor of Goliath's helmet. I know how a small army could take the city in a single night. With the few hundreds David commands in the wilderness he could take Jerusalem, if I told him how. With such a prize, David could dictate his own terms to Saul and Abner.

Zeruiah said, "And that is your David. Abner roused the king against him and David ran for his life. David is an outlaw, dependent on the bounty of the householders of Tekoa and Maon and Carmel. And he has dragged down his family with him. He owes us this small favor. He will protect you from Elhanan. You will march with David against Edomites and Philistines, learn to fight and to defend yourself. When you have made for yourself a reputation for strength and courage you will find Elhanan and tell him the truth—how Lem leaped on you and how you defended yourself. After that you can come home to your own people in Bethlehem."

Joab rose. "I will go." He would take his plan to David. Once David had captured Jerusalem with Joab's help, his fame would spread as David's had, and fame would be his protection from Elhanan.

Zeruiah came to where he stood in the center of the great court, with the moon shining down upon his strong face and his thick sandy hair. Joab was tall, not yet accustomed to the length of his legs and the width of his shoulders. Zeruiah raised her hands to his shoulders in a gesture that was almost a benediction.

"When, at seventeen, you have nightly risked your life in the pastures, when you have matched your strength against the strength of a hungry lion, matched your short sword against his claws and teeth, you learn where courage ends and folly begins. You would never walk out in cold blood to attack Goliath with sling and stone. I thank God for your good sense. When need arises you do what must be done, and you don't make songs about it afterward. Don't underrate the boy who goes to David. David has need of a kinsman with your gifts of common sense and reliability."

Joab touched her hands. He smiled down on her with pride and deep affection. "I will go to David. Now tell me what to take."

While Zeruiah stuffed hampers with cheeses and bread and oil for David, Joab searched the house for weapons. He strapped half a score short

[6]

swords under his cloak, out of sight. To go bristling visibly with knives would advertise his destination.

Joab lifted the hampers to his back and slung across his shoulder a full goatskin of Zeruiah's best mulberry wine.

"God go with you," Zeruiah said, and stood on tiptoe to kiss him. She watched him stride away through the alley and disappear. Then she turned her mind to what must be done about the sheep.

2

THE SUN WAS high and hot when Joab turned east from the highway to avoid Hebron. The road followed the crest of hills which formed the backbone of Canaan. Eastward the land sloped sharply into the deep Arabah which embraced the Jordan River and the Dead Sea. West from this crest the land sloped gently down into the green Philistine plain and on to the Great Sea.

Exhausted by the night's emotions, Joab had stopped before day to sleep for an hour, and had slept until the sun wakened him. He was making slow progress, burdened with the hampers and the wine and the weight of his own thoughts. The region was a refuge for outlaws, and the food he carried made him a tempting target. He entered the shade of the oak forest which clothed the highlands south of Hebron, and felt grateful for their shade until he remembered that in the forest danger can leap upon you from overhead or from behind any clump of underbrush. In the pastures you can see danger before it is upon you, but not here. Moreover, what chance have you for defending yourself all cumbered with hampers and wineskin and bedding?

I could have planned some other way, Joab thought fearfully. I could have gone through the wilderness. I could have found some of David's men at En Gedi or one of the other oases, and gone to David under escort. Seth came and went continually among David's men, serving as courier between the outlaws and the sons of Jesse who were in Moab. Seth moved through the forests and through the wilderness unafraid. I could have hidden at home and waited for Seth to come and take me to David, thought Joab. But Elhanan moved through the caves and forests as freely as Seth did. And if Elhanan found him unprotected by either David or the law, Joab was finished.

No plan is perfect, thought Joab, consoling himself for his hasty flight. But I don't even know where I'm to find David's stronghold. Everyone knew David was in the Maon Forest, south from Carmel. But where? Finally Joab resolved to go first to Carmel, skirting the town, and then south by some trail. He would find a place where he could watch and wait until some of David's men came along to take him the rest of the way.

During the afternoon, Joab's fear and weariness increased. I will never reach David, he thought. I will have to sleep in the forest tonight. But how could he sleep in the forest, unless he found some sort of shelter from men and from beasts as well?

Joab resolutely turned his mind from anxiety to other journeys he had made. He had gone to Hebron to buy the wares brought by caravans from Egypt or Damascus. Before the shrine at Nob was destroyed, he had gone there with his mother at feast times, circling round Jerusalem. Samuel was often at Nob, and his presence made the festivals a solemn occasion. Zeruiah was deeply moved by any solemn occasion. But Joab took more interest in the sharp hills and sharp faces to be seen in the Benjamite country than in the ritual of burned flesh and ascending smoke. Now he wished he had paid more attention to matters of religion. His courage needed bolstering.

Joab hitched up his burden of food and weapons and wine, relieving the drag on his shoulders. Who could tell whether he would live until the day ended?

If he were David, he would put his trust in the Lord. Joab muttered, "I will fear no evil for Thou art with me."

Empty words, composed by David in the quiet Bethlehem pastures. Joab was alone. He would not deceive himself. Still, he wished he had paid more attention to David's songs. There was something in those songs that lifted the heart.

"The Lord is my—something—of whom shall I be afraid?"

If only he could remember, he could pray to the God of David. He thought, not considering it a prayer, "Deliver me into the hand of thy servant David. I know not how to serve the Lord, but I will serve David while he attends to serving the Lord. Deliver me and I will serve David with my life."

Samuel always spread his arms to pray. You cannot spread your arms when you are carrying hampers of cheese and oil and a full skin of wine. And you do not fall on your face when you are girded about the middle with short swords.

Joab moistened his lips, fearing the God of David almost more than he feared the dangers of the forest. "Deliver me," he mumbled.

A blow caught him behind the ear. He did not sprawl upon his face. He rocked on his feet, felt his knees fold, felt himself sink. The wineskin was jerked from his shoulders. He was reaching to clutch it when he lost consciousness.

Even before he opened his eyes, Joab knew that the voices above him were quarreling in the idiom of Judah. He lay on the hard earth, surrounded by tattered, bearded men. They were quarreling about the distribution of the food and the wine.

They must be David's men, he thought with a sweep of relief. They had not killed him. Thank God for that. But what ruffians they were! Most of them wore no cloths on their rough sunbaked hair. Most of them had an unwashed look and odor. But at least they were men of Judah, and they would surely take him to David.

A wave of superstitious fear washed him. This God of David had answered his prayer, but with what violence! He reached gingerly to touch the lump behind his ear.

Joab scrambled to his feet and stood swaying. His head throbbed. The men's laughter roared and eddied and he felt the redness rise in his cheeks because he was the object of their laughter. With the toe of his sandal he traced the six-pointed star of David in the hard earth.

The nearest man was a dark-faced giant not two years older than Joab. His skirts were gathered high on his sinewy, scratched brown legs. His hand clutched a short length of oak. His tangled black hair partially covered a strip of brown-smudged linen which had been bound about his head.

He shouted, "It is a beardless stripling. They come to join us with their mother's milk still in them, since we defeated the Philistines at Keilah!"

"And is that down on your cheeks a beard, Benaiah?" The quiet drawl was a cooling breeze to Joab's flushed cheeks. The speaker was a man whose curling brown beard and woolen robe were clean. His heavy-lidded eyes smiled on Joab, so that Joab knew with a surge of relief that here was a man who would listen.

A third man said, "Nabal has repented and sends bounty by this boy."

Benaiah snorted. "Even Nabal would be ashamed to send the niggardly offering this fellow carries."

The older man drawled, "Since you struck the boy before we could question him, you shall carry his offering to David. I suggest that you persuade these men not to tell David how you attack before asking whether a stranger is friend or enemy."

Benaiah ducked his head. "Fair enough, Ira," he muttered. "One holds to lawless habits, forgetting one is a soldier of David. Here, boy, I'll carry your hampers."

Joab said, "I carry the wine." He seized the wineskin from a man who was gulping from its nozzle, and slung it once more upon his shoulder.

Ira asked, "What brings you here, my boy?"

"I seek David."

"What do you want from David?"

"I will tell my business to David himself."

Ira laughed. "If you have come to join us, let me warn you that David already has more men than he can provide with food and weapons."

[9]

"You tell me this, not knowing whether I am David's friend, or perhaps a spy for the Benjamite king?"

Ira's heavy-lidded eyes crinkled into deeply-marked lines of laughter. "You will go with us to David. If you are not for David, you will carry no news to his enemies. Benaiah is a soldier who is willing to double as executioner."

Benaiah spat into the dust not far from Joab's left sandal. "That's the truth."

Joab eyed Benaiah with distaste. His head throbbed. A trace of weakness remained in his knees. He needed food and sleep and he longed to see his cousin David. He said, "David's sister Zeruiah is my mother. And I am as old as David was when he killed Goliath."

He saw with satisfaction the look of sullen discomfort which settled over Benaiah's face with his announcement of kinship to David. Benaiah lifted the hampers, grunting at their weight.

Joab said, staring hard at Benaiah. "As for the blow you struck, I have had worse from a half-wit named Lem in the Bethlehem pastures. Lem also had a trick of springing from behind."

Ira said, "Come along, men. We'll be on the road after dark as it is. Let's move right along now."

There were ten men in the band. Joab and Ira strode together at their head. Benaiah with his hampers brought up the rear. Joab felt fine now, free of fear. The day's events had turned out very well, after all. He was grateful that Ira, not Benaiah, was in charge of these ruffians of David's. Still, the memory of his prayer haunted him. Would the God of David hold him to the promise he had made, that he would serve David with his life? After all, a promise made under stress of fear should not be taken too seriously. Remembering with what violence the God of David had answered his prayer, Joab shuddered.

To escape the confusion of his thoughts, Joab inquired, "Who is this Nabal your men are so gloomy about?"

"Nabal is a sheik of Carmel. A fool and a drunkard, but a sheik. He has refused us bounty at the time of sheepshearing."

Behind them someone muttered, "I wager we let the Edomites plunder his flocks hereafter."

Another man said, "Uriah's men wait only for permission to loot Judah's herds. We'll take for ourselves what Nabal owes, and a little more to salve the itch of his insults."

Benaiah said savagely, "David will destroy Nabal, root and branch! We'll teach these people a lesson before others take it into their heads to ignore the obligations of hospitality as Nabal has done."

Ira said mildly, "Very likely we will. And we will live to regret it."

Joab was piecing together the scraps of information. Nabal was a householder of Carmel whose herds grazed in the wilderness. David's men protected the wilderness from Edomite raiders. In return, David expected bounty from all the sheiks of the region.

Ira said, "Nabal owes us bounty. Others sent gifts, but Nabal sent nothing, though he is among the richest. We have taken no tribute from the shepherds. We have stolen not so much as a tired old ewe. Nabal has never before known such prosperity as he has had during our stay in Maon. I had it from Hezro, who is chief of his shepherds, that Nabal boasts of the increase in his flocks these three years since David organized the outlaws of the region into a united band."

Joab nodded impatiently. Did Ira think he had to explain to a grandson of Jesse what a sheik's duties are? He owes bounty to the needy of his region, whether they serve him or not. A humane and sensible arrangement, it holds robbery in check because the needy receive as a gift what they might otherwise steal.

Ira said, "When no bounty came we went to Nabal to ask for it. Nabal was in the midst of the feast of sheepshearing. He was muddled with wine and gluttony, as is usual with him at such times. He sent us away with insults."

Joab's cheeks were hot. "He ought to die! With his family!"

"To be sure. David must vindicate his honor. Then we who are at war with Saul in the north, with the Philistines in the west, with Edomites from the southern desert, will be at war also with the people among whom we have found holes to hide in. What is honor to a band like ours, lad? We are ragged, often hungry, always dirty. Most of us sleep under the sky. We have come to David for our private reasons, some from choice but more from necessity. Some come for love of Judah, some for love of David, and some for love of danger. But all have come because we are safer in hiding than at home. Do you think we ought to endanger ourselves further because a man who was muddled with wine has insulted David?"

Joab's cheeks were cooling under Ira's reasonableness. "It would be better," he said thoughtfully, "to pass it by, and hereafter pillage the man's flocks until he learns to respect us."

The "us" slipped from him neatly. Already he was one with David's men, and the huddled body of Lem was part of a past which was farther away than Bethlehem.

Ira said, "And do you think because we are outlaws we care nothing for honor? It is precisely because we are outlaws we cannot dispense with honor."

Joab turned this over in his mind. He said uncertainly, "Well, then—"

"On the other hand, these forests are full of runaway slaves and wanted criminals. Nabal made a sound point when he said he cannot feed all the riffraff of the wilderness."

"David is no riffraff! David is—" Joab paused. Precisely what was David? The Lord's anointed? The hero of Israel? Or an ambitious young man who had made enemies in high places, both in Saul's court and in the wilderness?

Ira answered his unspoken questions. "David is the greatest hero Israel has produced since Samson. He is a man of Judah like Nabal, hunted by the Benjamite king. David has taken the riffraff of this region and made of it an army. He has destroyed more enemies of Israel and of Nabal than Saul and Abner together. Yet Nabal called David riffraff, and so Nabal must be destroyed, with his family. And before many Sabbaths we will all be dead or scattered. How long will it be, when we have destroyed Nabal's household, before one of his neighbors betrays our stronghold to Saul?"

Joab said, "You veer from one view to another till I cannot tell what decision you would make if it were for you to decide."

Ira said soberly, "You are just coming to us. You will return to your home, now that you know how precariously we cling to the ragged edge of existence. You cannot be expected to know that Judah's last hope of finding safety in her hills will die when David dies. We are outlaws, but while David lives we have a dream and a purpose. When David dies we will scatter, risking our skins at thieving to keep alive, and our dream will be dead."

Joab said, groping for the gist of the problem, "But suppose David has a—a special destiny—as a leader to save Judah from her enemies? How can his people follow him or honor him, if he cannot defend his honor from a drunken chieftain?"

"How can we follow him if we cannot save his skin?"

Joab nodded. This was ultimate reality. "Life is more precious than honor." He was pleased to have phrased it so neatly.

But Ira had an answer even for Joab's final truth. "Boy," he said soberly, "there are many kinds of honor. Nabal also has his honor. Hezro tells me that Nabal's wife Abigail speaks often of David's past exploits, his present misfortunes, his glorious destiny, and also, Hezro declares, she speaks of David's curling red beard and warm blue eyes. If my wife gazed after David as he passed about the camp as do the wives of some of our men, no doubt I would be tempted when drunk to speak bitterly of David. Fortunately, I left my wife at home in Tekoa where she belongs. This is a bitter business, boy. I love David and will serve him all my life, but I could wish he pleased the women less."

3

TWILIGHT ROSE FROM the undergrowth of the oak forest, mounting to the treetops and finally to the sky. In starlit darkness, eleven men pushed through a growth of vines among the oaks and entered a rocky ravine along which they continued their way.

Presently Joab made out ahead a thrust of blackness where one peak rose higher than its neighbors. As the band rounded this point they came upon a space sheltered on two sides by bluffs and elsewhere by the forest. Several pits held campfires. A scattering of women hovered at the fires, roasting small game or baking cakes of meal and oil on slabs of rock. Joab knew he could never have found this stronghold alone. He shivered, remembering the violence of the answer to his prayer to the God of David.

Ragged black tents hugged the shelter of the cliff's base and the shadows of the trees. One tent was spread to face the largest of the campfires. Toward this tent Ira led his band. Men joined them until their progress became a crescendo of angry voices. Ira led his augmented column to the campfire.

The figure beside the tent was illuminated by firelight. David waited quietly for his men to come to him. David was no physical giant. Joab himself was taller. David had reached only to the shoulders of King Saul. Yet there was in him a kind of articulate force, so that the women of Israel had looked at David and Saul, had compared them, and had sung their disastrous song:

> Saul has slain his thousands
> And David his ten thousands.

Ira had said, as they walked the forest path today, that Abner probably incited the singing of the song, because it served his purposes so well. But whether the song started in the envious mind of Abner or in the admiring mind of some sentimental woman, the song had caught on till hundreds of women in dozens of towns were singing it. And the song had been David's undoing.

Joab had seen little of David these past years. He had ventured twice to the oasis of En Gedi carrying wine or mutton or oil. But after David moved on south into the forest, Joab had not seen him again. David would remember Joab as a gangling, half-grown youngster. Joab shrank from the meeting. His childhood love for the comrade and mentor of the pastures had been fed by years of pride in David's heroic service in Saul's armies. Now David was head of a band of tattered outlaws in a wilderness stronghold. Today David had been spit upon by a boorish patriarch. Joab

[13]

was ashamed for David. With all his heart he wished he had not put in an appearance at this particular moment in David's career.

"Ira?" David's voice had grown thinner. Anxiety robbed it of the joyous confidence Joab remembered.

Ira said, "Aye, David. We return empty-handed, as you see, except for a lad we encountered on the road. He says he is your cousin, and he brings gifts of food and wine. Step up, boy. Benaiah, set the hampers in David's tent."

Bearing his wineskin and roll of bedding, Joab stepped into the firelight. David's quick glance recognized and immediately dismissed Joab and returned to Ira and Joab remembered with a wave of love David's trick of shutting out the extraneous, of concentrating on whatever was at hand.

David said urgently, "Is the bounty to be brought by Nabal's men?"

The outlaws crowded around David. Joab was jostled in the shouting crowd. The hubbub of angry voices roared in his ears.

Joab was young and resilient, but the mob-voices raised in threats and irresponsible anger reminded him that he had been upon the road all day, and with the sheep much of the preceding night. He had killed Lem, and fled Elhanan, and he had prayed a prayer which committed him to more than he had meant it to, and his prayer had resulted in his being knocked unconscious. He had come to David in admiration and expectation, and found David beset, humiliated, desperate. It was enough. Joab would find a place to rest while this mob had its way with David.

He went to David's tent. He found that the hampers had been laid against its posts. He set down the heavy wineskin and loosened his girdle. His skirts tumbled about his ankles. Stepping into the shadow of the tent's curtains, he let fall the cloak and untied the band which held the daggers against his tunic. After a day of sweating against their leather sheaths, the relief to his flesh was exquisite. He spread his bedroll and stretched upon it. In spite of the violent, quarreling voices at the campfire, Joab fell asleep almost at once.

He was wakened by a hand shaking his shoulder. Joab tossed back the hair from his eyes and sprang to his feet, his hand on his knife. Then he laughed, feeling foolish to have awakened full of fear in the safety of David's tent. David stood near him, a compact figure outlined against the dying campfire. The clearing had emptied and was quiet.

David embraced Joab. "Welcome, cousin. Forgive me for waiting until now to greet you. I was occupied with other matters. How is Zeruiah?"

"She is well." Joab felt about in the dark. His hands found the wineskin and the knives and the hampers. He had not been robbed while he slept. He said, "Mother sent wine, and cheese, and bread, David. And I brought all the short swords I could find in the house. It isn't much, but I was in a hurry and brought what I could lay hands on."

[14]

"We will try the wine. I have had no Bethlehem wine lately, nor any as good as what we make at home. You came alone?"

"Alone." Joab hesitated. "What will you do about this Nabal?"

David's face was a blur. His voice was somber. "I must destroy him, with his household."

So the violent ones had won the quarrel. David was not a leader of men. He was the tool of whichever men shouted the loudest.

"You're making a mistake," Joab said. Never in his whole life before had he spoken that way to David.

David said, "I'm doing what must be done. Joab, go back home. Before long I may be finished."

"I can't go back. I've killed a man. I fled the avenger."

David uncorked the wineskin, raised it to his mouth for a long draught. "Even at Saul's table," he said, "the wine is not as good as this that we make at home. So you have killed. How many avengers do you think are numbered among my enemies? I am a refuge to all Israel. I am harried on all sides, and no wonder. Why should anyone trouble to befriend David and his band of cutthroats and thieves and absconding debtors?"

Bitterly Joab wished he had gone to Hebron. Or to Moab. Nothing could happen elsewhere as terrible as this toppling of David from his pedestal. David was done for, and Joab would be on hand to watch the end. What would he do then? Why, go to Hebron, naturally!

David said, "If you can kill your own enemy you can perhaps kill enemies of David. God knows there are enough of them." He took another draught of wine and passed the skin to Joab.

Joab drank deep. The wine bolstered his courage. He wiped his mouth with the back of his hand and said, "Ira spoke of this affair with Nabal as we marched today." Marched? A word of dignity and importance unsuited to these tattered outlaws. He said boldly, "David, the hotheads among your men urge reprisal. Cooler heads, like Ira, would urge you to wait for a more favorable time to take vengeance on Nabal. Where will you go, if you have to flee Judah?"

David said shortly, "There are other places. We have tried them. We can try them again."

Joab did not press that point. He knew David had fled to the Philistine king at Gath, in the beginning, and had been befriended for a short while by the king who came after Goliath. David had also hidden in the southern desert, among the Edomites. But since then he'd fought more than one hard battle with both those peoples. Joab urged, "Forget Nabal. Take what he owes from the flocks by night. Let Uriah and his men plunder Nabal if you are unwilling to let your men do it. Nabal will think he has been robbed by Edomites. Nabal is of no importance compared with your need to stay here in the wilderness. Life is more precious than honor." The words had seemed impressive when he spoke them to Ira. Here in David's tent they were flat. Something had gone wrong with his logic, though he couldn't tell what.

"Not honor," David replied. "I don't kill for honor. To forgive an affront is better than vengeance. But to shrink in fear and call expediency forgiveness is to deceive myself and my men. I tell you, Joab, we cannot afford a magnanimity that could be construed as cowardice. If Nabal calls us riffraff and goes unpunished, we become riffraff in our own eyes. Nothing is left us here but the human dignity we carry, each in his own breast. We must cherish that dignity or we are no better than the beasts."

Joab muttered, "I would rather stay alive for now, and search about later for my dignity."

David laughed and laid his arm about Joab's shoulders. "Like your mother, you are endowed with much fine common sense. I am glad to have a kinsman with me, now that I have reached so low an ebb. You have come far today and carried quite a load. For the gifts I am grateful, cousin. Sleep where you have spread your mat for tonight. Hereafter you will do better to sleep among my men, in Ira's tent perhaps. Ira is in charge of supplies, and you shall be assigned to help him, for the present. When we march at dawn, stay in camp. I don't want your first taste of fighting my battles to be that dirty business tomorrow."

"David, I wish times were better for you."

"Aye, cousin. I wish with all my heart a time would come when I could cleanse my hands of blood. Well, it may come sooner than we expect. God knows. And we are in His keeping."

4

REBA HUNCHED HER long body on the thin rug, hugging her knees to warm herself. She wished the night would end. She hated lying here, closed in by the frayed curtains of her tent. She hated the odor of the goat cheeses, corn, and oil which were stacked against the tent walls. If she were a boy she could go and warm herself by the embers of a fire, or run about the clearing to stir up the sluggish blood. But she was not a boy. She was a fourteen-year-old girl, an orphan since Philistine arrows had killed her father at Keilah. She was alone and cold and lonely, and thoroughly tired of living in the outlaw stronghold.

There is no warmth in the curtains of a tent. They serve only to hide you from curious eyes, and to contain the musty odors of corn and oil. The curtains serve as a reminder to the wild young bucks that David's protection is promised you as long as you stay inside the tent at night with the curtains secured.

If her father had not died he would have brought a warmer robe, a thicker rug, perhaps even a whole new tent, as spoil from Keilah. But her father had died, and she was alone, except for David's protection. She could not go to David to ask for the things she needed. David had too many pressing needs of his own.

Her knees pressed against her breasts and she thought, "I am becoming a woman."

The thought held mystery, and fear, and the longing to talk to someone about what it means to leave childhood behind and move on into womanhood. Once she was a woman, with a husband, she would not sleep so cold. How would it be to have a man who brought you spoil taken in battle: warm clothing, thick blankets? How would it seem to have strong arms holding you against a hard, warm body? The thought brought memory of how her mother had died at the hands of a Philistine raider. Into her mind came the sequence of fearful pictures. There had been the tearing off of the cloak and tunic, revealing the thin, shrinking body, followed by a strange and awful struggle. Then the man had stilled her mother's struggle by plunging a knife into her naked breast, and after that the mauling of the poor corpse had gone on and on, until Reba ran and fell fainting in a distant olive orchard. Her father found her there, next day, and they never returned home after that. They came here to join David's outlaw band, and here they had stayed.

What was the mystery which changed men into panting beasts? Reba's curiosity held much dread, but also a certain fascination. What was the mystery which altered her body, so that men watched her with predatory eyes as she moved to and from the campfires or the springs?

I hate these wild young men of David's, she thought. But hate was not exactly the word for what she felt. Hate was for the Philistines, who came storming up from their green plain every year at harvest time. What she felt for David's men, who fought Philistines, was merely a shrinking dread. Sooner or later she must go to one of them and accept him as husband and protector. She would put on the white veil of the bride, if such a thing could be found in this place. The priest Abiathar would murmur words, and lay her hand in her husband's hand, and she would not sleep alone any more. She shivered with cold, but also because of mysterious stirrings in her body, stirrings to which hope and wonder belong, a portent of what it means to be a wife and belong to a man.

A procession of faces of the men of the camp passed before her eyes. Benaiah was the most aggressive and persistent of these men. Benaiah was violent and lustful, yet he was a man of consequence in the company. He was a good man in battle, and his household would never lack spoil. He was also truthful, honest, unafraid.

Still, there had been the times when Benaiah caught her in the edge of the forest at dusk, when she had been careless about David's edict for her protection. She remembered with aversion the panting struggle, the ugly set of Benaiah's mouth when she bit his hands or spit in his face and broke free to flee to her tent. Benaiah was not the man she would choose.

There was Abiathar, the gaunt young priest. Abiathar was alone and lonely, just as Reba was. Reba pitied Abiathar, remembering that his father and grandfather and uncles and brothers had been killed by Saul's soldiers in the massacre at Nob, because the priests at Nob had given David food and a sword when he fled from Saul. Of the entire family of the high priest of Israel, only Abiathar escaped alive. Abiathar was descended from Aaron, was hereditary high priest and second only to David in the camp. Abiathar had dark, somber eyes and a black, tangled beard. He took no care of himself at all but lived only for religion and scholarship. Abiathar was a writer, a man of wisdom in bookish things. He was different in all ways from other men. In all ways but one. Reba feared the avid intentness of Abiathar's eyes more than she feared Benaiah's lust.

There was Seth, the huge, thick-bodied kinsman of David, in camp from time to time but often in Moab with the sons of Jesse. Seth had a home in Bethlehem, far enough east to be out of range of Philistine raids, and far enough north to be safe from Edomites. Seth's home was David's home, a fine stone house, the house of a patriarch. It was presided over these days by Zeruiah, of whose courage and sense Reba had heard wonderful tales.

If she married Seth she could leave this camp and go to live in Bethlehem. Seth was the least objectionable of those who eyed her. Yet even a girl could tell that women meant little to Seth. He was a man who would come and go, leaving his wife lonely. Reba had known too much loneliness to be willing to offer the mystery of her ripening body as one offers cakes beside the fire. She had known what it is to be part of a closely knit family, to be cherished and companioned. She had known the richness of giving all the heart's burden of love to those with whom she shared the daily bread and common shelter. She would bide her time and contain her loneliness. When she found a man she could love, then she would marry.

David had promised she would be safe so long as she stayed in camp by day and in her tent by night. But it is not good to be always in the chill shade of the stronghold and never on the slopes at the top of the bluff. She used to go with her father to those rocky, barren slopes, and take off her cloak and let the sun beat down on her through the wool of her tunic. She used to stare with her father at the distant sea and the purple hills of Moab beyond the sea. She used to be so warm and content in the sun on the hills that she forgot even the black memories of the Philistine raiders. Thinking of those days, and of her father who could never be with her again, Reba wept.

In the dusk before dawn she heard the shuffle of feet, the confused and subdued voices of men preparing to march off on one of the endless errands of war or forage which engaged these outlaws. David's scouts were everywhere. They came by day or night with word of Saul's movements, or to call out one company or five to go against Edomites or Philistines. Reba felt no curiosity any more as to the destination of these dawn marches. She shivered on her thin rug, and wished the dawn would come to set her free of her curtained tent.

Someone was beside the campfire when at last Reba emerged. She glanced curiously at the stranger. He had noticed her briefly, then turned his brooding gaze back to the fire. He was a boy little older than herself, with thick, sandy hair which hung smooth and clean about his shoulders. The cloak he wore was of bleached wool, not as white as linen, but finer and whiter than anything Reba possessed. Even seated on the ground she could tell that he was taller than herself, though she was tall for a girl, as tall as many of the men in camp. The boy's face was marked by the soft beginnings of a sandy beard. The knowledge that he was shy of her warmed Reba more than the fire.

Reba held out her hands to the crackling blaze and studied the downcast face of the boy, and felt contentment in what she saw. This was a strong, brave face, the face of one who knew little of the fears the renegades and outlaws know. It was the face of one who had no part in the coarse talk one overhears at the fire, who would never sneak away on a night of the full moon to join with the men of Uriah's company in their revels to Baal. These uncircumcised natives of Canaan served David by day, but on the nights of the full moon they went to their high places to revel before the Baalim. And all too often wild young bucks like Benaiah went with them, treating it all as a holiday, a break in the monotony and hardship of life in this bleak stronghold.

Reba's eyes followed with pleasure the long, strong lines of the boy's body in the clean cloak. When the boy's gray eyes strayed to meet hers she smiled.

"Welcome to camp," she said.

Joab's glance held the indifference of a youth who has not yet found time for girls. He nodded curtly. "Thank you."

She said cheerfully, "I am Reba. My father brought me here after the Philistines destroyed our vineyards and stole our herds and killed—my mother." She faltered, then hurried on. "My father used to say only David cared enough about Judah to protect it from the Philistines. King Saul is a Benjamite. He resists the Philistines only when they raid in Ephraim and Benjamin."

Joab grunted. He didn't need a girl to tell him about King Saul. A woman's loose tongue had brought David into today's peril. No doubt this talky girl with the dark, wide eyes and the soft, wide mouth was one of those whose eyes followed David as he moved about the camp. To which of David's men did she belong? Which of them would she stir up against David with her prattling tongue? He glanced at her again and decided she had not given herself to a man. Yet a talky woman was a troublemaker however young. A girl has no business going alone among the men of a camp, making herself free with a stranger at the fire. Women, he thought. They are more dangerous than all David's enemies. But his eyes strayed back to the girl again, and when she smiled warmly he felt the hot blood wash up into his neck and cheeks.

Reba watched the boy's shy face, while warmth glowed in her and curved her mouth. She left the fire and went to her tent, then returned with meal and oil and began patting out cakes. The odor of the food reached the boy. She saw the twitching of his nostrils and knew he was hungry. Well, who wasn't hungry in this place? She smiled as she saw him covertly watching her hands. Her father often remarked on the grace of her hands when they were busy with small, homely tasks. She rounded the cakes carefully and laid them on a flat rock among the embers.

"Since you are a newcomer," she said, "you shall be my guest this morning."

Joab's tongue flicked over his lips. He remembered that he had eaten nothing since Zeruiah made a meal for him in Bethlehem a very long time ago. He was ravenous, but he would not betray his eagerness to this free-and-easy girl.

Reba said, "You are younger than most of the men. Did you come alone?"

Joab nodded. If he was to eat her cakes he would have to endure her chatter.

"You are of Judah, aren't you? You haven't told me your name!"

Clearly, thought Joab bitterly, it was nothing to this girl that David had gone with his men to destroy Nabal. Obviously she did not have sense enough to know that David's world would fall apart once today's violence was accomplished.

He swallowed his irritation. "I came from Bethlehem. I am Joab."

"Bethlehem? Then you know David!"

"He is my cousin." Joab rose and took a stick and stirred the coals to hasten the baking of the cakes.

Reba saw the tall strength of the boy, the awkward power of one who has grown fast and matured young. He is a cousin of David! The thought brought a growing excitement. His home is in Bethlehem. And she thought, this is a man I could choose. She trembled and felt the blood pulsing behind her eyes. With this boy she could be warm and safe and content in a strong stone house in Bethlehem.

I would like to touch his face, she thought. I would like to make him look at me and smile at me. I would like him to hunger for me as he hungers now for the cakes.

She said breathlessly, "Then you know Zeruiah? And Seth?"

"I am a son of Zeruiah. Seth is oldest. I am next. Then there is Asa, my younger brother, who is fifteen."

Reba said, "Seth comes now and then, but he never stays. Will you stay?" She held her breath, waiting for his answer.

"Perhaps."

Bitterness curled his mouth. He is troubled, she thought. Oh, I would like to touch him, to comfort him. I would like to make him happy.

"You will stay. David will keep you here."

"I will stay as long as David stays."

Words tumbled from her lips like water over stones. "David will not leave Judah! Here are his own people! He will stay and protect them. My father had a vineyard and olive trees and a small barley field. Year after year the Philistines came raiding, always at harvest time. David would never go away and leave us to the Philistines again. I hate Philistines! I saw one of them kill my mother."

Reba rushed on, wanting desperately to pour out her heart to this boy. She had never before spoken to anyone but her father about the things she felt closely. "I hate them so much—it is like a sickness. My mother's body was thrown into the flames of our burning vineyard. Now my father is dead, killed by Philistines at Keilah."

She bent to turn the cakes, hiding her face. She felt so strange. Grief was an old and familiar emotion, but not this turbulent wish to weep and sing and laugh and to touch this boy and be close to him. I want to cry against his shoulder with his arms to comfort me, she thought.

Joab saw the tears drip from her face to sizzle on the coals. He said roughly, "You are a girl. You can weep and make your troubles grow less. Why don't you weep in your tent?"

Reba said softly, "Tears do not make trouble less. If they did, I would be free of trouble by now."

"Why do you stay in a place like this? David has his hands full without bothering to look after a useless girl." What would become of her, if David fled? The devil take her! Why should he care what became of her?

Reba said with dignity, "Whether I stay or go is my affair, and David's." She was angry now, with a veering of emotions like the veering of winds in changing weather. "A kinsman of David should not be so rude. I have been kind to you. Why are you rude to me?"

[21]

The boy's gray eyes took on a look of shame. "I did not mean to be rude. Are the nights always so cold in this clearing?"

"Always. Even in summer." Her anger vanished as quickly as it had come. "But it is warm on the bluffs. See that path that zigzags to the top? I used to climb it with my father and lie in the sun and be warm. We can go there, if you like. Now the cakes are ready and we will eat."

Joab gulped the first cake and the second and third. He did not notice that Reba was giving them all to him and eating nothing herself. He did not notice that her eyes glowed as he devoured the food she had prepared. "You make cakes as good as those my mother makes in Bethlehem," he told her. He felt suddenly very kind toward the girl who had fed his hunger.

Reba said gently, "If I had somewhere to go, I would leave this camp. But I have nowhere to go. David says I may stay for my father's sake until I choose a husband."

Joab laughed aloud. "A husband! You are too young to talk of choosing a husband!"

"I am grown. Men have asked for me. Even Benaiah, who is of the council."

"I have met Benaiah." Joab spat into the fire.

"I did not say I would marry Benaiah. Still, he is better than many of the young men. David depends on him. He is strong, brave, and honest." Joab was looking at her at last. Even his mockery was pleasant. There was companionship in quarreling with a boy like this one. She smiled secretly, content with the derisive scrutiny of the boy's gray eyes. She said, "I will marry when I am ready, and to the man I shall choose."

Joab said curiously, "You *want* to marry?"

"Why not? A girl does not like to be alone. I have nobody to bring me spoil from the battles. I have nobody to cook for, nobody to talk to. I am forbidden to leave the clearing by day or my tent by night. David says he can protect me only if I stay where people can keep an eye on me. Of course I want to marry! To be alone as I am is no better than to be a prisoner."

Joab watched her with growing interest. Naturally she ought to live with someone. But not Benaiah! Joab felt a stirring of the pulses, as he thought how some man would touch her, hold her, feel the lithe softness of her body against his own. What is it like to hold a girl and know her in the privacy of your own tent or room?

Women are the devil, he thought. He was angry again, because of the emotion which so disturbed him. You look ahead to death or at the best to a life of fleeing or hiding, or to the alternative of imprisonment in Hebron. And you know that an amorous woman has brought disaster to David, and in consequence to you, and yet you find your head spinning because a girl with a soft mouth and smooth, dark hair speaks of becoming a wife to one of David's young men.

Joab jumped to his feet and strode off toward the bluff. He climbed the path Reba had pointed out to him. He would warm himself in the sun and forget the nonsense this girl had put into his head.

He reached the slanting, rocky land which dropped away to the blue depths of the Dead Sea. This was the wilderness, a country on whose edge he had lived all his seventeen years, a country which stretched between the farmlands of the north and the shifting sands of the southern desert. The mystery and the color and the tantalizing odors of the wilderness beat on him, as always when he entered this land. He found a bit of sand where he could sit with his back against a warm brown rock, and let the sun burn through his woolen clothing.

This was the wilderness, rough with boulders, blinding with the glare of sun on golden sand, prickly with thornbush and cactus, riddled with large caves and small ones, threaded by dry, sandy, winding stream beds. Beyond the deep blue of the sea rose the purple mountains of Moab. In the middle distance a single palm tree rose to a considerable height, where a spring found its way up out of the earth to mark with green the golden land. On the slopes at this time of the year patches of bright flowers bedecked the earth, a riot of red poppies, white anemones, vivid yellow daisies and tall blue lupines. And Joab sat quiet, pleased as always with the springtime riot of colors and odors of the wilderness.

But thoughts of Reba disturbed his pleasure. Life is crude and dangerous in a camp of outlaws, and women make it ten times more so. Women, he thought angrily.

A stone dropped at his feet. He turned and saw Reba standing nearby. Her cloak was girded high on her straight brown legs. She pushed back her headcloth and dropped it to the ground with a gesture full of grace and freedom, and he noticed with a sense of sharp annoyance how level the brows were above her smiling eyes, and how feathery the hairline above her forehead.

She said, "When the nights are long and cold in the clearing, it is hard to believe it could ever be as warm as this."

With the slow grace of a courtesan she loosened her girdle. The skirts of her cloak tumbled about her ankles. She held the girdle in her finger tips, then dropped it with her headcloth on the sand. She kicked off her sandals and curled her bare toes against the earth. Then she opened her cloak and let it fall in the heap with the other garments. She stood with arms stretched wide and eyes closed, her face raised like that of a pagan sun worshiper.

Joab watched her in mounting fury. The tunic she wore was one which had fit her when she was still a child with a straight, unformed body. It

[23]

was too short, too tight, quite threadbare. The thin wool stretched taut across her belly and breasts.

He said harshly, "David told you not to leave the clearing."

She opened her eyes and smiled at him lazily, then came close and dropped into the sand near him. "You are David's cousin. I came with you. David said I must not come alone."

He sees me now, she thought with pleasure. He really sees me. He wants me, at least a little. Joab, Joab, you are angry because you are greatly troubled. But you will not remain angry. You will love me, and I will love you, and we will make each other happy. Then you will take me to Bethlehem to live in the house with Zeruiah, who is not afraid of beast or devil or Philistine.

She said softly, "I have been kind to you, Joab. I welcomed you and baked cakes for you." She touched his face softly with her finger tips, smoothing the lines above his eyes.

Joab jerked free of her touch. "You are a pagan, a worshiper of Ashtoreth! A girl like you makes nothing but trouble, just as Nabal's wife Abigail has made trouble for David and all of us!"

"Who is Abigail? Who is Nabal? Who cares about them? Who cares about them, Joab?" She rose. Joab could not tear his eyes from her. Yet even while his tongue stuck in his mouth he wondered, how old was David when the girls of Judah and Benjamin first offered themselves for his delight?

He said, gagging on the words, "You are a pagan and you stand here without shame for all the world to see."

He stood near her, not touching her. She was quiet. Her head drooped. "What shall I do, Joab? How can I please you?"

"Go away from this camp. Go away from these men who hunger for you."

She raised her eyes. "I have nowhere to go."

"You stand here shameless though you have told me you mean to marry one of David's men. You will share his tent and bake his cakes and— sleep under his blanket and—"

"Do you want me, Joab?"

Joab said thickly, "Perhaps I will die tomorrow. But today I will tumble a girl in the sand and forget this troubled Judah of ours."

Yet even as his fingers fumbled with his girdle he was wondering in panic whether this wench would laugh when she learned how lacking in practice he was at the game she seemed determined to play.

5

HEZRO RUBBED HIS shoulder against the boulder to relieve its itching. The shade cast by the rock was scant now, but would grow longer as the sun moved west. He stared through slitted eyes at the tilted golden world which dropped abruptly into the Dead Sea.

"Hot," he muttered. "Praise God for a little shade."

Below him and near enough so he could hear their incessant bleating, the sheep fed. There was this small green patch which sprouted at the edge of the wadi where a tiny spring lived. Hezro had built up the edge of the pool with stones, this year as every year, but the sheep were already trampling the stones apart so that much of the water escaped to run down the wadi and lose itself in the thirsty sand.

"Poor naked sheep," murmured Hezro, smiling at the splotched backs of the newly sheared animals. Well, Nabal had trained the cutters at Carmel to get all the wool, even if you had to nick the skin here and there. Hezro pulled his headcloth lower over his eyes against the golden dazzle of sun on rocks and sand. He breathed deeply, filling his nostrils with the dry pungence of the sparse wilderness shrubs.

Abruptly he sat erect. Here came the priest! No wonder the fellow was addled. He never knew whether it was noon or midnight when he came galloping over the hills. He'd cooked his brains in the midday sun. He looks like the front end of an ambitious camel, thought Hezro, with his head thrust forward and his thin shanks flying. Hezro settled back into the shadow of his rock. It exhausted him merely to watch that crazy fellow.

The far side of the wadi was a steep hill, strewn with small stones which rolled under a man's weight if he didn't watch his footing. Halfway up the hill was a patch of black where a small cave nestled under a flat ledge. The priest was climbing toward the cave, losing his footing when the stones rolled but always scrambling on again. In his arm he carried something which looked like a mud pie. When he reached the cave he squatted on his heels and stared around suspiciously. He stared down at the sheep as if wondering whether they were spying on him. He glared across the wadi at Hezro, and Hezro waved his hand languidly, then obligingly turned onto his stomach and pillowed his face in his arms. The priest and Hezro had met at this cave half a dozen times. Surely the priest no longer feared Hezro!

Hezro had watched the priest crawl into that cave many times, carrying his mud pies. And he had seen him back out again after a while, carrying nothing. Hezro had gone a couple of times to investigate, but he never found anything. Hezro had concluded that the priest's purpose in entering the cave was to perform some kind of hocus-pocus which would spirit the mud pie away into air. One never knew what a mad fellow like this Abiathar had on his mind.

Hezro sighed and thought sleepily, Why doesn't he rest in the heat of the day and play with mud pies in the cool of the evening? Hezro would have slept, but for a troubling memory of a thing he had seen in the wadi at an earlier hour today.

He'd come down the wadi, leading his sheep to this oasis, when he'd seen the boy, and a moment later, the girl. These outlaws, thought Hezro, fill the wilderness till you can't follow your sheep to water without stumbling over a brace of them. Six hundred men, David had now, not counting the women and little ones.

He'd seen the boy when he rounded a bend in the wadi. The boy was watching him covertly, so you knew he was on guard for some reason. A moment later Hezro saw the reason. A girl lay asleep on one cloak, covered by another, while the boy himself wore only a tunic. The girl slept so soundly she did not hear the commotion the sheep made. Hezro had caught the bemused look on the face of the boy. The boy spoke a few civil words to him, but all the while his eyes wandered back to the sleeping girl as if he'd never seen one in his whole life before today.

Perhaps he never had, thought Hezro. These men of David's lacked many comforts, and women were chief of the comforts they lacked. Some of their wives were dead. Some were at home in distant towns. Some of the men contented themselves with the favors of harlots when they could afford that, or with the goodnatured wenches from the villages, or with sneaking off at the full moon to join in the revels to Baal. There were a few women in the camps, a few wives, a few daughters. No doubt those few were a great comfort to their own men, and a great temptation to the others.

Hezro smiled gently, remembering another girl and boy who had known love in the wadies for half a summer. For half a summer they had played together in this wilderness. They had loved moderately, as befits the young who have not known the gnawing of unfed hunger. Then Nabal came to buy the girl with his gold and his goats. Abigail had wept and stormed. Nabal had already divorced three wives because they failed to give him children. Nabal was an old man, a glutton and a drunkard. But nothing could change the stubborn avarice of Abigail's father.

Well, thought Hezro, stirring angrily against his boulder, I am comfortably married and my fourth child will be born before harvest. I need not be disturbed by the bedazzled eyes of a boy whose girl sleeps in the wadi, wrapped in his cloak.

Hezro rose and stared down at the sheep. He wished one of them would be silly enough to stray from the green bit of oasis into the hills so he would have to bestir himself to fetch it back. But the sheep fed quietly, or stood in foolish content while their lambs butted and suckled and cavorted against them. Hezro sighed, and sank into the lengthening shadow and pulled his headcloth over his eyes.

He wished he could forget Abigail's tender eyes and the full, deep curve of her lower lip. He had watched while the years robbed her of the radiance which had enthralled him on summer afternoons long ago. Abigail was possessed by a sour-faced old curd who had not even sap enough in his vitals to give her a child on whom she could spend her wealth of tenderness.

Now Hezro's mind went to a thing he hated above all things to contemplate. There had been the harvest festival last autumn, when David was invited to share the feast at Nabal's house. Hezro was nearby at the moment when Abigail first caught sight of the red-haired young man. What a figure he was, with his athlete's shoulders and his warm, intelligent blue eyes! How Abigail had fluttered that day, while Nabal grew drunk and drowsy. Nabal must have seen, as Hezro saw, how the radiance rose again in Abigail's dark, tender eyes. Too bad, thought Hezro restlessly, that so promising a young fellow must fall under the displeasure of the vindictive sheik. Too bad Abigail must love again and lose again, must live once more through all that agony. Hezro wished restlessly that he could forget the sun-browned face and bemused eyes of the boy in the wadi this morning, wished he could forget how Abigail had delighted him on those long-ago afternoons. No matter how good the wife a man marries, he never utterly forgets that first delight.

Hezro opened his eyes, disturbed by the racket made by rocks rolling downhill. The priest was emerging, rump first, from the cave. He scrambled upright and glanced suspiciously at Hezro, and Hezro sighed to think of the energy the gaunt young man was wasting on anxiety and suspicion. Who cared what the fellow did in that cave he had adopted for his own?

And yet, thought Hezro, with a pang he could not banish utterly, if I had not lost Abigail, I might have been one of the eager ones instead of the drowsy creature I have become.

He sighed and rolled over on his face in the shade of the boulder. A lizard scuttled from under a rock near his hand, and he watched it rush away to disappear in the roots of a stunted acacia. Then he closed his eyes and slept.

6

ABIATHAR CLIMBED THE wadi while the wind whipped his skirts about his sweating shanks. His head ached and his lips were dry and feverish and one of his nails had been broken to the quick in handling the rocks with which he had covered the linen- and mud-wrapped scroll he had buried in the cave. But the pain of the body is nothing. The anguish of the mind drove him faster, up the steep sandy wash. Today David had marched with his men against Nabal's household, as Saul's soldiers had marched against Abiathar's family on an unforgettable afternoon.

David had set out for Carmel without consulting Abiathar, without inquiring of the Lord by means of the sacred dice which Abiathar had risked his life to recover from the murdered body of his father at Nob. That is the worst of giving yourself to another man's cause, thought Abiathar bitterly. Gratitude is something David will never feel toward me. He remembered how, on the day of the massacre, he had crawled back at dusk to take from around his father's neck the pouch containing the Urim and the Thummim, those two blue stones with which, for Israel's leaders from Aaron's time until now, the high priest had inquired of the Lord concerning Israel's affairs. The leather thong from which the pouch hung had worn a groove in the skin of his neck, for he wore it always, never laying it aside day or night.

Well then, it was not for gratitude that he served David. David was both strong and weak, both wise and foolish. But David had been anointed by Samuel. He was one of the great ones, possibly even the one for whom Israel waited, the one who would make her strong and secure in her hills, a nation to be reckoned with.

For David's sake, thought Abiathar, my father, my uncles, my brothers all died. He recalled with a writhing of the spirit the monstrous destruction at Nob. Abiathar had ceased to grieve for his family. But more than men had died that day. Soldiers of Saul, drunk with destruction, had burned the scroll which Abiathar had been reading on that blood-red afternoon, the Book of the Wars of the Lord. Men are born to die, but those who destroy scrolls destroy wisdom learned through the struggles of uncounted lives.

Abiathar had huddled in the cistern, armpit-deep in the cold water, waiting for night. When darkness fell he returned to the scene of slaughter to rescue the scroll. He had managed to save a few charred fragments of parchment; with them he had gone with horror and shrinking to the body of his father, the high priest, and had taken from his neck the pouch which contained the sacred dice, and hung it upon his own neck. Then he had fled south to find David.

From that day till now, Abiathar had been writing from memory the stories he had read in the Book of the Wars of the Lord, that the heroes of the Lord might continue to live, today and tomorrow and for a thousand years after that. The thought of the great ones of old, Moses and Aaron and Eleazar, and all the nameless scribes who had not troubled to sign their laborious works—histories, allegories, poetry and law—brought tears to his eyes. A rich burden of meaning lives in the written word; the past and present mingle when living men know again what was in the minds of men long dead. Abiathar himself was one of the immortals, set apart to write down words on skins. This was the driving destiny which nobody understood. Not even David knew of these scraps of painfully garnered parchment which he filled with tales he had read, songs sung by the priests, and new songs which David sang by night at the campfire. Not even David knew with what painful care Abiathar had dredged up from his memory the tales of Samson, who had fought the Philistines—of Deborah and Barak, who fought the Canaanites—of Gideon, who led a coalition of northern tribes against a federation of nations from beyond the Jordan. With these tales Abiathar also wrote the stories of Samuel, of Saul, of their wars against the Philistines, and of David, the latest hero to rise among the people and the first man of Judah among all the heroes.

Someday, thought Abiathar, with the exalted sense which came now and then that he knew the mind of the Lord, Israel will be one people, ruled by one king, and all will war together against the enemies which ring them round. It will no longer be left to this tribe or that to fight each alone his local foe. Someday Israel will be one people, and one leader will rule all the tribes, and when that time comes, Jerusalem will cease to be an enemy fortress dividing Judah from the northern tribes. In such a time, Jerusalem will be a dwelling for Israel's rulers. The sacred writings will then be gathered together and made safe in the strongest and most beautiful city in the land.

It had been Abiathar's faith that David might be such a leader. Because of this faith, Abiathar had comforted himself after the massacre at Nob. But if now David began shedding the blood of his fellow tribesmen, how could he ever again lead Judah, let alone Israel?

Abiathar plucked at the skirts which stuck to his legs. He raised his face and gazed about dazedly. What am I doing here? he wondered. Why have I climbed this mountain when there is so much I could be doing in my tent?

He turned, leaving the wadi, heading north. There was a boy newly come to camp, a kinsman of David. I will ask him to tell me about David's years in Bethlehem, thought Abiathar. I will add this to my records, for David is as great a hero as Samson or Gideon, if he never again fights a battle for Israel. David is a hero, anointed of the Lord, and I am sent to be his conscience, his priest, his historian. To this end was I born, and to this end was I spared when my family died at Nob.

Somewhere in the hills rose the peal of a girl's full-throated laughter. Abiathar sat down suddenly in the shadow of a rock and rubbed his cheeks with the torn tail of his cloak. I am going mad, he thought. Even in the hills I hear her laughter.

I am a man to whom nothing is small, he reflected. The desires of the spirit and the desires of the flesh consume me. The love of God and the love of David and the love of the written word are great within me, but no greater than this hunger I have for a girl to sleep beside me in my tent. How many times had his flesh melted at the thought of possessing the tall girl with the straight brown thighs and the supple, curving back? How many times had he watched her mending his cloak or baking his cakes, and felt himself utterly consumed with longing to possess her and dwell with her?

The laughter came again, and he thought, It is the beginning of madness, when her laughter follows me through the hills.

Now he remembered the thing which had slipped from his mind when he reached the mountain top. He had intended to search the peak for the newest shrine set up by Uriah the Hittite and his uncircumcised horde. Abiathar meant to find and destroy the shrine before the next full moon —the day the pagans called Shabbatum.

"Let them alone," David had urged. "They are not children of Abraham. Leave them the consolation of their high places."

David was not driven by the zeal which would not let Abiathar rest. Still, David would not be the leader he was if there were no zealots dedicated to serving him. Yet more than zeal drove Abiathar in the will to destroy the local shrine before the next full moon. He remembered a day before the last rains when Benaiah had derided him because he never went with the young men of Israel to dance with the Canaanites.

"Come with us," Benaiah had urged, and had laughed and told Abiathar upon which hilltop the revels would be held. "You'll shrivel to a cinder if you don't do something to break the monotony. Come along, man. You'll serve the Lord better tomorrow for having a bit of fun tonight."

Abiathar spoke to David that day, knowing his own weakness and the hunger of the flesh and the senses. He asked for Reba to be given to him as his wife. But David was evasive. Abiathar saw the evasion and knew that David was saving the girl for himself.

The priest lay in his tent that night, tormented, longing to renounce the things of the spirit and satisfy the hunger of the flesh, longing to go and dance before Baal, make himself naked with those others, find among the pagan women one who would not care that he bore in his flesh the seal of circumcision, and so loose himself from the mandates and prohibitions of Moses.

The night ended at last. When morning came Abiathar spoke to David of how men of Israel joined with Uriah's men in observing the Shabbatum.

"How can we ask men who live as we do to forego the pleasures of the high places?" David asked. His face was ravaged by discouragement.

Abiathar asked, "How can I inquire of the Lord for you in a camp where men worship the Baalim?"

David sighed. "Do not ask me to punish my men more than they are punished already. As for Uriah and his Hittites and Jebusites and Amorites and Perizzites, they serve me, not because they love me but because they hate Saul, and the Edomites and Philistines. They serve me because together we are a better match for our enemies. I can do nothing about their private affairs. They served their Baalim in this land long before we came into it, bringing our tabernacle and our ark and our difficult faith in a God who cannot be seen or touched."

Abiathar said stubbornly, "If they follow David they ought to worship the God of David. They waste enough vigor in these carnal revels to win twenty battles."

"Do what you think best," David said at last. "They do not bring their Baalim into camp. They do not raid our people. They fight only on my orders. More than that I cannot ask of them. But you are our priest. Do what you think best."

Abiathar went into the hills that day, and found the high place last used by the men, and overturned the Masebah and chopped down the poles and scattered dung about, defiling the spot. But other full moons had come and gone, and the men cleansed their shrine and set up their sacred stone again and Abiathar knew he could not contend with them, since he was one and they were many. And he bore the rigors of chastity with patience, knowing his hunger increased his zeal for David and for the writings which he wrapped in linen and packed with mud and buried in a cave in the wilderness.

The laughter came again, very close, and suddenly Abiathar saw that the laughter was not a fiction invented in his tired mind. Beyond the rock beside which he had fallen he saw two figures running. A girl and a boy were chasing one another from shadow to shadow in a childish game of tag. Their laughter rang across the hills as if they were alone in some Eden all their own.

Abiathar's eyes filled with the ready tears of a man sick with exhaustion and longing. The tears were for the happiness and childish simplicity he saw in those two. The girl Reba had come to play on the slopes with this young cousin of David. How good it was that there were two of them so young, to enjoy the fragment of childhood which remained before they took on the mantle of maturity. Reba had been too much with anxious and desperate adults. She had missed the joy which is a part of youth. To play in the wilderness as lambs play in the pasture, forgetting danger and privation—to be lighthearted for no reason except it is spring and the sun shines—this belongs to youth, and the boy had brought this to Reba.

He watched her elude the reaching grasp of the boy, pivot lightly and dart toward his rock. He saw the smile light up her face when she recognized him. She ran to Abiathar, jumped into the shadow in which he sat and cried, "I'm out of breath, Joab. Enough is enough."

Abiathar passed his hands over his face, rubbing away the haze that came so often before his eyes.

Reba cried, "Abiathar, you look exhausted. You look as if you had forgotten to sleep and eat, and had come too far in the sun today."

Abiathar said to the boy, "You are David's cousin?" He liked his face. Joab's eyes turned continually to Reba, and the priest knew that here was someone who would not think of the girl in the lewd way of those men who went to romp in the high places with the pagans.

He ought to love her, thought Abiathar. He ought to marry her, when they are a little older. But he will never marry her. David will never give her to anyone, for David is keeping her for himself.

Abiathar rose, conscious of the ache in his head. "Joab," he said, "I meant to seek you out today, and ask you to relate a few tales of David's youth in Bethlehem."

Joab pulled his eyes away from the bright face of the girl. "Why?" he asked politely.

"I am writing a record of David to keep with the records of Samson and Gideon and others. Heroes have come—" Abiathar paused, listening. From the clearing came a noise of laughter and shouting, mingled with the braying of donkeys.

"David has returned," he cried, and set out at a run toward the bluff overlooking the camp.

Joab cried, "David has returned." All this day he had forgotten David and David's fearful errand to Carmel, and had thought only of this girl who could transform his every mood and motion into tenderness. Joab seized Reba's hand and they raced together after the gaunt-faced, burning-eyed priest. From the bluff they stared down at the long queue of laden donkeys and men. The late afternoon sun glimmered on fruits and hampers and wineskins, and on sweating, laughing faces.

"There has been no massacre," whispered Abiathar. He raised his face to the hot blue sky. "David has forsworn his oath. He has accepted bounty. He has not shed Judah's blood." Tears rained down his gaunt face. "I feel the hot breath of the Lord upon my cheek."

Joab stared at the priest, amazed by such an outpouring of emotion, pleased that the priest had looked on today's affair as he had himself. From the clearing someone shouted, "Abigail brought us bounty! Look at the gifts!"

Joab laughed aloud. "It is the hot breath of an amorous woman you feel upon your cheek, Abiathar," he cried, with all the authority of one experienced in the ways of amorous women. "David was saved by his own blue eyes and his curling red beard."

Abiathar turned dazed, reproachful eyes on him, but Joab did not notice. He was running, nimbly as a young goat, down the path which hugged the face of the bluff, and Reba was right behind him.

Love, Joab was thinking, is the greatest force in the world, for love can conquer all else. What wisdom was this which had come into his mind? He had been gone from Bethlehem only two days, yet he had learned many things. I am a man, he thought. Wisdom belongs to a man.

He leaped the last ten feet and turned to catch Reba in his arms. But she shook her head and darted around him. Above them on the bluff Abiathar still stood, his face and arms raised to heaven, his lips moving silently.

7

JOAB WAS KEPT busy in the days that followed. He helped tally and distribute the bounty Abigail had sent. This involved trips with donkey trains to the companies stationed at En Gedi and Adullam. When that was finished, Abiathar kept Joab talking of David for three endless days.

Not once did Joab speak privately to Reba. He saw her often at the campfires. But after he returned from the donkey trips her dark eyes no longer smiled on him. By the end of the first day with Abiathar she deliberately turned her back when he caught her eye.

He finally escaped Abiathar at the end of the third day. As he approached Reba's tent he saw the dark, scowling face of Benaiah. The bandage was gone from his head, but a new wound had appeared, a deep slit in one ear. Benaiah was talking urgently to Reba. Joab ran to the tent but Reba was already closing the curtains. Benaiah turned a darkly mottled glare on Joab and strode away. Joab lingered, speaking through the curtains, urging Reba to come out for only a moment.

"I haven't had a chance to speak to you," he said. "But I thought of you constantly." She must know how much he had thought of her, these lonely, busy days. She must know what a confusion of longing and happiness and remembered joy suffused all his thoughts. "You weren't afraid of me that other day," he pleaded. "Why are you afraid of me now?"

"Why did you stay away?" Reba's voice was low and close, as if she were pressing her face against the curtain which separated them.

"Do you think I wanted to stay away from you?"

"You could have come. You could have managed. A man can come and go. A girl can do nothing but stay in her tent and wait."

Joab was scandalized. "Do you think I am one of the lewd fellows who crawl under the curtains of a woman's tent in the night? I am a grandson of Jesse! I am David's kinsman. And David is your protector."

A hand was laid on Joab's shoulder and he was spun round to face David. David's face was flushed and angry. "This is the last thing I would expect of you, cousin," David said. "To come peeping and whispering at the curtain of a young girl's tent! What kind of man do you call yourself?"

Joab stood speechless with mortification. The curtain of the tent was lifted. Reba stepped between them. "David, don't be angry with Joab. He came because—because—" She hesitated.

Joab said, breathless with self-discovery, "I want her to be my wife. Give her to me, David. I will take care of her. Somehow!"

David's anger vanished. He smiled the affectionate smile Joab knew so well. "You are impetuous, cousin. You have been with us ten days, and you are ready to make twenty men your enemy by marrying our little Reba." He ran the back of his closed fist gently along the soft fuzz of beard on Joab's jaw. "Let's not be hasty. We will discuss the matter again when you are a man. After a year or so." David's eyes crinkled in laughter.

Reba pleaded, "I want to marry him, David. I want to go to Bethlehem with him, and live with Zeruiah. I have thought about it, and I have made up my mind."

"Would you like to go to Bethlehem without him? Suppose he does not choose to go to Bethlehem just now."

Reba's eyes were downcast. "Wherever Joab goes, I will go."

David's amusement was gone. "Forget this childishness," he said curtly. "I'll hear no more of it. Close your tent, Reba. Joab, I have an errand for you. Ira will tell you the details. As my kinsman you will represent me at Carmel tomorrow."

David strode away. Reba had already vanished behind the black curtain of her tent. Joab stood, miserable and irresolute. From the tent came a whisper of longing. "Take me to Bethlehem, Joab. Now. Tonight. I'm—afraid of what will happen if I stay longer in this place."

"No." Joab spoke the one word abruptly, ashamed of his helplessness to do the one thing Reba asked of him.

He walked away fast, but not fast enough to leave behind the shame which possessed him. He had caught a glimpse of the poverty of Reba's tent. He remembered the thinness of her tunic. She needs so much, he thought. And I can give her nothing.

The crooked figure of Lem seemed to dance ahead of him in the shadows. If I could take her to Bethlehem, he thought, I could give her everything she needs. A dream of the rambling house in Bethlehem, a dream of sharing it all with Reba, of being able to supply all her needs, burdened his spirit. Lem, he thought, how gladly I would have spent my life with you

[34]

in the pastures, if you could be alive now and I free to take Reba home to Bethlehem.

Next day Joab marched with Ira and eight others to Carmel. Their errand was with Nabal. "Make it clear to him we accept no more bounty at second hand," David said. "Get his promise, in the presence of witnesses, that there will be no more insults. If he is drunk, wait until he is sober and speak with him then. Tell him we will not wait until harvest to learn whether he is ready to deal justly with us in the future."

Ira had plenty to talk about as they trudged the forest path north to Carmel, but Joab was not listening. He was too deep in his own despair to think of anything else. I am responsible for Reba, he thought. He had never before in his seventeen years been responsible in this way. He had been a good son to his mother, obeying her orders with intelligence and discretion. He had been a good shepherd, following a pattern of action in which he had been instructed by the sons of Jesse. Life is simple for an obedient, capable boy. Except for trouble with Lem and the occasional bullying of Seth, he had faced no serious problems. But now David refused his request that Reba be given to him. David's word was law in the stronghold. Joab was helpless. And it was not pleasant to be helpless when you were a grandson of Jesse, patriarch of Bethlehem.

At the edge of the village Ira halted their little expedition. "We will not go to Nabal in force. We are to talk with him. We are not to compel him. Joab and I will go to Nabal. The rest of you go round by the camel gate and wait in the courtyard among the servants until I send for you. If you hear any talk about how it went when Nabal learned that Abigail sent bounty to us, do not close your ears."

The village of Carmel was a collection of circular huts built of mud bricks and plaster. The huts clustered around the imposing stone-and-brick dwelling of Nabal and Abigail. Nabal's shepherds and servants lived in the huts. As Joab, with the squadron of men, passed through the unpaved street of the town he noticed that the houses seemed deserted. From somewhere came a sound as of many voices lamenting. The nearer they came to the house of Nabal, the louder the wailing became.

"Somebody has died," Ira remarked. "And it is not a shepherd or a servant. The whole town is lamenting in Nabal's courtyard."

"Perhaps Nabal is dead," Joab said indifferently. The death of an ill-tempered old man seemed of small importance to Joab that day.

The house of Nabal presented a solid wall to the street. Joab noticed complacently that the masons who built this house had cut the stones less evenly and fitted them with a greater waste of plaster than had those who built the house of Jesse. Small slits under the projecting roof served as windows. A single barred door was set in the wall. The eight young men followed the wall around to find the camel gate at the back, but Ira knocked loudly on the street door with the handle of his sword.

"How fortunate," he remarked, "that a kinsman of David is here. We have come, mind you, to offer condolences in a time of bereavement. Let us hope it is Nabal and not the lady Abigail whose death is the cause of all that caterwauling. I am a brave man, friend Joab, but—" Ira was interrupted by the sound of sliding bolts. The door was opened inward by a maid.

The customs which govern mourning are practical, Joab reflected, as he observed the correctly disheveled appearance of the girl. With a rent cloak hanging loosely from her graceful shoulders, with ashes to mar the curly dark hair, with her face streaked by tears and soot, she gave every evidence of having suffered a great loss. That she had held her own in the lamentations was apparent from the hoarseness of her voice.

Ira said kindly, "We come from David, my girl. This is a time of distress in the household of Nabal—" He paused, waiting for more information before committing himself further.

"Alas for my master," the girl said hoarsely but with composure. "The light of his smile will gladden our hearts no more. Please come in."

They entered the reception room beside the passageway. Ira said, "This is Joab of Bethlehem, a kinsman of David. He speaks for David." He paused politely, waiting for Joab to take up the burden of meeting a situation for which they had not been instructed.

Joab cleared his throat. "We bring a message to your mistress, my girl."

"She is prostrate. However—since you come from David—I have no doubt that she will receive you." The girl glided from the room. Her hips rocked gently, setting the tattered cloak to swinging.

"'The light of his smile,'" mused Joab, who had an ear for a neat phrase. "I like the expression."

"If you had known Nabal you would like it even better. That girl has imagination." Ira smiled, as if contemplating the girl's pleasing qualities. "I am free to say," he continued, "that I shrank from encountering Nabal today. If I add my voice to the volume of hubbub in the courtyard yonder before we depart, it is testimony to good manners, not to grief."

"This girl—you know her?" Joab studied Ira speculatively. Love in the wilderness, he was thinking. There are surely many who have known it. The wilderness invites lovers as it invites outlaws.

"I know her only by reputation. Her name is Dinah. When you see her with her face washed and her curly hair combed, you will understand why she carries herself with so much—uh—charm. Abigail has surrounded herself with a remarkably attractive collection of serving maids."

"She has?"

"Aye. Hezro's opinion is that she hoped to distract her husband. But

Nabal never took a concubine. Abigail bore the brunt of his devotion alone."

Joab glanced around the room with curiosity. The floor was liberally covered with thick rugs of the kind which come from beyond the Euphrates, rather than the cheaper rugs made by the Amalekites of the southern desert. On a low chest along one wall stood a single ornamental urn. Obviously the urn held oil to which spikenard had been added, for the delicate fragrance filled the room. The reception room at home had fewer rugs, but the chest which held Zeruiah's urns was more handsomely carved, and her three urns were smaller but of a better color than Abigail's single one. Moreover, Zeruiah had caused a pair of carved cedar benches to be set in her reception hall, while here the guests, if they sat at all, would sit upon the rugs.

Carmel was near to Hebron, where caravans passed bringing objects from the whole earth; but though Bethlehem was only an hour's brisk walk from Jerusalem, Zeruiah could never bring herself to barter with the Jebusites in the city of the uncircumcised. A shelf which projected at shoulder height held an alabaster lamp with seven mouths which must have come from Egypt. I should like to buy such a lamp for Zeruiah, he thought, and swallowed, for thoughts of Zeruiah brought loneliness. So far he had done absolutely nothing which could serve to bring nearer the time when he could return to Bethlehem.

The scrape of sandals on stone came from the passageway. The woman who entered was small and delicately made, as was Zeruiah. She also had Zeruiah's air of determination and purpose. Her clothing was not rent, nor was she disfigured with ashes or any other signs of mourning. Her cloak was of fine quality, made of linen which had surely been dyed by the merchants of Tyre. Her mantle was scarlet, and decorated with a rich pattern of golden embroidery.

I wish I could give such a mantle to Reba, thought Joab with longing. He was surprised, but not displeased, to see Abigail so richly dressed, in view of the fact that the entire village was in her courtyard mourning the death of her husband. Abigail's eyes were clear and serene. Her mouth, Joab thought, was her best feature. The lower lip was full, with deep indentations at the corners.

Abigail is a woman of beauty as well as purpose, he thought. She calculates her moves. She knows she will gain nothing by disfiguring herself in mourning, and so she sensibly leaves that to the servants, who are paid good money to do the right thing. Joab was pleased to recognize his firm grip on reality in Abigail. I like her, he thought. I would like to know her well and call her my friend.

Abigail bowed and motioned for them to seat themselves, sinking gracefully upon one of the rugs herself as she did so. "You have come from my lord David?" Her voice vibrated on the name, as if she could not speak it without emotion.

"David is my mother's brother," Joab said. "He sends sympathy in your hour of bereavement."

"My lord David is gracious. You may take this word to him: The Lord who watches over my lord David has seen the behavior of that worthless man who was my husband, and has smitten him for the insult he offered to my lord David."

Concealing his surprise, Joab inclined his head. "I will tell my cousin what you have said."

"Tell my lord David also that all I have is his, if he will receive it; all the wealth of this house, these fields, flocks, vineyards, orchards, and pastures. My servants are the servants of my lord David, and I am his handmaid." Her eyes held Joab's, awaiting his assurance that her generous offer would not be refused.

Joab smiled warmly. "I will tell David what you have said. And I will bring you his answer." He added impulsively, because he liked Abigail's directness, "You are gracious far beyond the merits of my cousin, my lady Abigail."

Abigail clapped her hands together, and Dinah appeared. "Bring refreshments for these guests," Abigail said.

While he tasted the rich cakes of dates and figs and almonds, and the fine red wine which Dinah brought, Joab was thinking that if Abigail and David were married, Abigail would befriend Reba. She could do for Reba the things Joab could not do. He could bide his time until David was willing to grant his request, if Reba were provided for. Joab felt a lifting of the weight of his responsibility. The weeks would pass, and the months, and there would be many days when he was not occupied with errands for David.

The courtesies were concluded, and Dinah went to tell the eight young men in the courtyard where to meet Ira and Joab for the return. Joab found himself outside the house once more, walking through the village with Ira.

"The lady," Ira mused, "wishes to buy herself a husband who plays the lyre and makes poetry and has a curling red beard."

Joab smiled. He was feeling extremely pleased with the turn events had taken. "David's luck is beyond belief. If I had not heard the lady's words myself, I would find this development incredible. David will be lord of this wilderness, the richest sheik south of Hebron." He felt a gust of warm wind blow past his face, as they left the village behind. How suddenly David's affairs had shifted from desperation to security, even comfort!

I feel the breath of the Lord God on my cheek, he thought, with a stab

[38]

of superstitious fear. Is it the God of David who brought it about? Or is it chance which turns the tide of David's affairs so unexpectedly?

Ira said, "With flocks and orchards Nabal bought Abigail, so Hezro told me. And now it seems the lady will use the same coin to buy David. In the end Nabal was swindled, or so it seems to me. Without meaning disloyalty to David, I venture to predict that Abigail will also be swindled."

"You forget yourself," Joab said sharply.

"I forget nothing, my inexperienced young friend. It is no slander to your celebrated kinsman to say that David will never love the lady Abigail as she loves him. He never loved Saul's daughter Michal as she loved him. He will never belong to a woman, though many women will belong to David before he is finished with living. Abigail will never rule David, or David's household, as she ruled Nabal's. When David takes other wives, Abigail will mourn for her lands and her flocks, and she will know that she has been swindled."

In the edge of the forest the young men were waiting. They fell into line behind Joab and Ira, heading south together toward the stronghold. One of them, a Reubenite named Obed, told of the manner of Nabal's death.

"How lucky," said Obed, "that we did not destroy Nabal when we marched against Carmel ten days ago. He is dead with no help from us. David is avenged, yet we have not shed Judah's blood. Nabal was smitten by the Lord," he concluded, rolling his eyes piously heavenward.

Ira said, "Aye. Nabal's follies included drunkenness and gluttony. The Lord often smites drunkards and gluttons suddenly."

Obed smiled. "It was suggested in Carmel that the Lord had some help from the lady Abigail in the smiting of Nabal."

"Watch what you say!" Joab said sharply.

Obed laughed lightly. "Abigail humiliated Nabal in the presence of his servants, telling him how David came to kill him and all his household, and only her presence of mind in getting together a generous gift of bounty saved his life. Abigail railed at Nabal, while his servants sat about smiling behind their hands. And Nabal fell down in a fit and was carried to his own chamber. He lay there for days, tended only by Abigail. Not even Dinah was allowed in the room. Presently Nabal was dead. And it is said that when he died Abigail washed her face and put on fine raiment and came from his room as one who rejoices."

Ira said quietly, "We will listen to no more scandal, Obed. If Abigail hated Nabal, so did we all. If she loved David, well, so do we. It takes a woman of courage to act without pretense or hypocrisy. Abigail is our friend and Nabal was our enemy. We will not forget it."

Obed's voice was smooth and pleasant. "As you say, Ira. You shall love your friend and hate your enemy. That is the beginning and the end of virtue. Still, you asked me to keep my ears open. I only repeated what I heard."

Joab served as friend of the bridegroom in bringing Abigail to the stronghold after her seven days of mourning were accomplished and Nabal had been laid in the tomb of his fathers. Joab led Abigail to David in the wedding ceremony, laid her hand in David's hand. Abiathar blessed their union. To the camp Abigail had brought a long train of donkeys laden with provisions, with tents and rugs and woolens, wine and fruit. Many sheep were driven to the clearing for slaughter and all the camp rejoiced at the wedding feast.

8

THE MARRIAGE CHANGED the complexion of the stronghold. Prosperity came with Abigail, as well as the pleasant sight of half a dozen pretty serving maids who moved from springs to tents to campfires, neat and useful and friendly.

Many men now sent for their wives and little ones to join them. Ira's responsibilities as provisioner multiplied, so that his company of one hundred men was constantly employed as muleteers, porters, messengers.

Joab came to know the wilderness thoroughly that summer, though he had known its northern extremities all his life. He wore out many pairs of sandals marching up and down the wadies and across the rocky hills at the head of a donkey train.

It would be hard to find another land where such contrasts existed. The wilderness fell away from the green, watered mountains of central Judah down to the deep Arabah which embraced the Dead Sea. The sea received drainage from the hills on three sides and from the Jordan River on the north. The sea receives all and gives up nothing, Joab sometimes reflected. Yet that was not altogether true, for the sea gave up moisture into the thirsty desert air, and the moisture formed cumulus clouds which hovered always above it.

The wilderness was dotted with oases, where springs rose in the rocky earth to water a small area before losing their moisture in the sand. Here patches of glowing color defied the golden sand and rock.

The largest of these oases was En Gedi, which lay, green and fertile, close against the mineral-rich waters of the Dead Sea. Here lived an entire company of David's men. These were men who had raised crops and tended orchards and vineyards before their exile from home, men who still preferred farming to fighting. At En Gedi there were date palms and sycamore figs, vineyards and gardens and grain fields. A herd of Abigail's goats grazed on the rugged hills above.

Near the end of summer, Joab led a dozen donkeys with their drivers up a wadi from En Gedi toward the stronghold. Laden with melons and dates and summer fruits, the donkeys rebelled against the ascent over the yielding sand. The muleteers alternately cursed and prodded the beasts. They sang songs and told ribald stories about Abigail's maid Dinah. Joab took no part in their singing or their talk. He had grown increasingly silent during the summer, brooding on his own affairs. Ahead of him, wavering in the glare of sun on sand, danced the image of Reba. Abigail had taken a liking to her. She gave the girl clothing as colorful as her own, a cloak of dyed wool, a blue mantle decorated with white needlework, a scarlet girdle with ends which hung to her hem, bracelets that jangled, and a heavy neck-band of silver. Abigail spent many hours teaching Reba to do needlework. Still, Reba continually plotted ways to escape and be with Joab on the hills. Joab knew with shame that if Reba did not arrange these meetings there would be few of them, for he had no skill at all in clandestine arrangements.

More and more, as summer passed, their time together was spent quarreling. When Joab went to her tent at night he was angry because of the need to go wriggling under the curtains, in fear that he would be seen and denounced. Joab did not know whether he was more afraid of David's anger or of the men's ribald laughter. He knew with what merciless hilarity the men would pin on a youth of seventeen the title Despoiler of Women. Yet the secrecy angered him less than Reba's perpetual plea, "Take me to Bethlehem."

He had never told Reba why he could not take her to Bethlehem. Nobody here except David had been told about Lem. In a camp where so many men were outlaws it was not the custom to speak of the past. Joab told himself angrily that Reba ought to know without being told that a reason existed why he could not go to Bethlehem. Anger helped him endure the fear he felt that if Reba knew the truth she would no longer love him. How many times, when she spoke of Zeruiah, had the thought come, It is not a husband you want but a mother! Once he spoke the accusing words, and Reba wept, and he comforted her. Thereafter he did not speak the words, but the thought came to torment him, and only anger could ease the pain of his self-doubt and his own hunger to go to Zeruiah and lay all his troubles in her capable hands.

Twice he had gone to David to ask that Reba be given to him. Somehow, he did not understand how, the conversation shifted to more urgent topics, and then almost at once David had other matters to attend to.

The next time he found David alone he spoke of something he had long had on his mind—a plan he had for taking Jerusalem in a single night. He asked David to let him come before the council and present his plan fully.

But David had only laughed and clapped him affectionately on the shoulder. "You want to tell my men how to fight? You want to be a hero, eh?"

Joab protested, growing incoherent with humiliation as David continued to laugh at him.

When he ceased to attempt to explain or defend himself David grew serious. "You have never fought in even a minor engagement. Yet you want to tell my men and me how to conduct a battle. You seriously suggest that I take my few hundred half-armed, ragged men up into the hills of Benjamin where Saul's thousands have their headquarters and there lay siege to a city that not even Abner with all his ambition would attempt! Do you understand how many of my men are deserters from Saul's army? Do you know how many are in hiding from an avenger? Are you yourself so willing to go marching past Bethlehem? Think what you are suggesting! Think, and listen, and learn!"

Joab did not again attempt to speak privately with David on any matter. His love and admiration for David were all they had ever been. He was convinced that David with his six hundred ragged outlaws could withstand Abner with his thousands. But he knew he would have to solve his own problems and must not go again to David for help. And the months of summer passed, and the land grew brown and sere and Joab spent his days as a leader of donkey trains.

Reba accepted everything Abigail offered except for giving up her ragged tent to move into one of Abigail's. Reba declared she would not part with this one thing which her father had left to her. And Joab knew she made this sacrifice in order to remain alone in a place to which he could occasionally come.

Now Joab let his mind dwell upon the last time he had been with her. He felt in memory the twisting of her fingers in the downy fuzz along his jaw. "I want you to be my wife," he told her, voicing the desperate longing which kept step with him on the long marches. "I want to know every day that when I return home you will be waiting in a tent which is our own. I want everyone in this place to know you're mine."

She had moved restlessly, turning her face from his kiss. "The nights will be cold when autumn comes. I don't want to go through another rainy winter in this clearing."

"I'll talk to David again," he promised, knowing it would do no good.

"Don't talk to David. Take me to Bethlehem. Take me now, before autumn. Don't ask David again. We don't need his consent. We'll be married by the elders in Bethlehem."

"Forget Bethlehem," he said roughly. "I'm here to serve David."

She began to cry, saying that he didn't love her. He became exasperated and struck her, and went back to Ira's tent.

He clenched his fist now, remembering in his palm the arch of her cheekbone where he struck her. The sweat ran down his legs under the thick folds of the girded cloak. Behind him Joab heard the bickering of the men. Most of the springs were dry now that summer was ending, and all the men were hot and thirsty. It made them more quarrelsome than usual. At the moment they were quarreling about the maid Dinah. If Dinah accomplished half what she was credited with, Joab reflected wryly, she would have neither time nor energy left for serving Abigail.

A muleteer started the song of David and Saul, and another responded in the antiphonal way of women who dance in the streets. Soon all were shouting the song:

> Saul has slain his thousands
> And David his ten thousands.

David had forbidden the song. Joab had the uneasy feeling that a more forceful leader than he would surely stop the song. But he let the matter be. A rumor was afloat that Saul had set out on another of his marches into the wilderness. The rumor made the men restless, but the song gave them courage. Anything which gave the men courage was good, it seemed to Joab, since it is not easy to hide and wait, a few hundred outlaws, while thousands of trained soldiers march to hunt you down.

These men had never yet fought Saul's army. The maneuver had been to hold back, hide in caves, or disguise themselves as shepherds or women. In a land so riddled with caves it was easy to disappear. Still, now that so many women and children and tents had been added to the companies, concealment grew more difficult.

Joab led the men up over the ridge at a point where the wadi twisted north. Beyond the next hill they would enter another wadi, one which rose in a hill near camp. Joab was thinking how many times during these past years Saul had led his men into this region, and then turned back because of the failure of his guides, or because of reports that Philistines were raiding the threshing floors of Benjamin or Ephraim. Twice Saul had turned back because David had come near and spoken to him, reproaching him, calling him "My father."

"Saul is swayed by every wind," Ira said. "And the strongest wind of all is Abner. Abner fears that David will supplant him as commander. Abner invents tales of David's plots to supplant Jonathan or even Saul himself. He reminds Saul of the tale that David was once anointed by the prophet Samuel."

"That tale is true," Joab interrupted. "Samuel had received hospitality from Jesse and—"

Ira brushed it aside. "A prophet's duty is to leave a blessing where he receives kindness. Maybe the anointing meant much. Maybe it meant little.

But Abner tells the story as if it were part of a subtle plot against Saul himself. Abner will never give up while David lives."

At the east portal of the stronghold, where a single sentry had drowsily watched their departure for En Gedi the day before, a troop of men from Uriah's company, Hittites, Jebusites, Perizzites, Girgashites, Amorites and Canaanites, were stationed. Their leader halted the donkey train. He patted the hampers and poked among the fruits in an officious, offensive way which irritated Joab. The muleteers grumbled over the delay. They were impatient to get to the storage tent, unload their burdens, turn their donkeys into the fenced valley, and get to their tents and their women and their food and wine.

"You know us," Joab protested. "What's all the fuss about?"

"Orders," the man replied self-importantly.

Another man came forward. Joab recognized the swarthy face and wide, white-toothed smile of Uriah. "Saul has passed Hebron, friend Joab," Uriah said. "He is camped nearby. Your brother Seth came today with the news. One of Nabal's shepherds has taken pay from Saul to guide him to our stronghold."

Uriah raised his voice to be heard above the uproar among the muleteers. "David and Seth have gone to reconnoiter. We have orders to guard this point."

Uriah's man said, "Pass, friend." Joab hustled his men and donkeys forward through the thinning trees into the clearing and across it to the tent Ira used for storing supplies. This tent was not far from David's council fire. Fifteen or more men sat about the fire, talking earnestly. Among them was a newcomer, one whose heavy beard, rapid gestures and urgent, loud voice made sweat break out on Joab's face and body, chilling him. Elhanan was here! David had admitted Elhanan into this camp!

Joab had been in haste to get to the fire himself and confirm Uriah's news. But now he did not wait to speak even to Ira. Keeping the tents between himself and the fire, he dodged into the shadows and back the way he had come. In his arms he held melons he had taken up in haste to complete the unloading. He clutched the melons and ran through the trees, tripping over underbrush and fallen branches but plunging on in blind flight.

Joab turned north when he was free of the trees. He climbed the ridges and descended swiftly into ravines. Off to the right he could see the glimmering sea by moonlight. Above him in the sky the moon lay, a crescent of silver, rocking on its back. The stars were bright. He ran on, keeping free of the forest. He ran until the breath sucked in his throat. At last he tumbled, panting, into a wadi.

The law of Moses was specific. If the avenger came up with him outside a city of refuge, he was to kill him at once. But if Joab reached Hebron and Elhanan found him there, Elhanan would have to take him before the elders in the gate and bring charges, and the judges would hear Joab's defense. If they found Joab guilty of murder they would hand him over to Elhanan for execution. If they found him guilty only of accidental killing or of killing in self-defense, they would sentence him to serve a term of years within the city walls. Joab thought of the years ahead in Hebron, the very best he could hope for, and he felt like laying his head upon his knees and lifting up his voice in a wail.

Then he remembered that Lem had been dead for a whole summer. Elhanan had waited until now, had given Joab this summer with David and his men, a summer with comrades, a summer to become the friend of Ira and Abiathar, of Benaiah and Uriah. He had had a summer to know and love Reba. If he died tomorrow, or if he lived a decade in Hebron, he had had a summer of happiness and Elhanan had given it to him by waiting until now to pursue him.

Yet he could not forget that David had loved him so little that he had let Elhanan enter the camp, not knowing whether Joab would escape to Hebron or be killed. I do not understand David, he thought with some bitterness. Even now, with Saul's army at hand, surely David should have driven Elhanan away. He needs the strength of men more than of boys, thought Joab, crushed under the burden of familiar self-doubt. Yet I am his cousin. Surely he owes me something.

I will not think of it any more, he thought. And he laid his palms against the earth and said good-by to this wilderness. He would spend the days and nights of the future inside the mouldering walls of Hebron.

Joab took his knife and split open the melons he had carried and ate them, refreshing himself and ridding himself of their burden. Rising, he stood for a while listening. There was danger in these hills. There was danger from Elhanan, danger of coming suddenly on the encamped army of Saul. There must be no more of this panicky running. Joab girded his cloak and climbed out of the ravine.

As he neared the top of the ridge he heard voices on the hill beyond. Two figures rose against the sky. Saul's sentries, he thought, and dropped silently behind a thornbush. While he watched, the figures came into full view, silhouetted against the bright sky. One of the men seemed a giant. The other was smaller, with a familiar grace and compactness. David and Seth!

Joab's first thought was to leap up and shout at them. Then, bitterly bewildered, he remembered that David had permitted Elhanan to enter the camp. He remembered the scorn he had received from David more than once during the summer. He flattened himself behind the thornbush and remained silent.

David made a trumpet of his hands. "Abner!" he shouted in a voice that filled the night, the mighty voice of a man who commands armies in battle.

Abner! Then the army of Saul was camped nearby. David alone was challenging the army of Saul!

David shouted again, "Abner! Are you afraid to answer me?"

A distant voice called, "Who is it that shouts at the army of the king?"

David shouted, "What a brave man you are, Abner! While you guarded your king, I entered your camp and stood over him. I could have killed him. I have his spear and cruse, which were beside him. You, Abner! Is this the way you guard the king of Israel?"

On the hill Seth held aloft a spear and water bottle. Joab no longer huddled on the ground. He was on his knees, listening. Abner had stirred up Saul against David. But tonight David had put Abner to shame in the presence of the king and all his army.

An uproar had risen in the far valley. Above the uproar rose another voice, trained also to be heard in battle. "Is it you, my son David?"

"It is David, my father. Why do you want to destroy me? Who am I that your army pursues me through the hills? Do the king's armies hunt partridges in the wilderness? Is it for sport that the soldiers of Israel serve their king?"

The clamor died in the valley. Only the voice of Saul was heard, humble, old, tired. "I have played the fool and have erred exceedingly. Return, my son. I will never forget that you spared me when you could have killed me."

A trap! Joab held his breath, waiting to learn whether David would be deceived. Return, my son! Return within our reach so we may destroy you by stealth when you are no longer on your guard against us!

David's voice was as sad as that of Saul. "I leave the spear and bottle here. When I am gone, Abner can send a soldier to fetch them."

The defeated voice of Saul came once more. "The Lord is with you, David, my son."

Long after David and Seth had gone away south over the hills, long after a soldier had come and carried off the spear and bottle, Joab lay on the earth, under the moon. Long after the camp in the far valley grew silent, Joab lay among the rocks and shrubs on his hill. He stared up at the moon, pondering the wisdom and destiny of David. All the half-formed impressions of childhood, all the tales that came to Bethlehem from Saul's capital, all the love and awe he had felt through the years of his youth came back to him, and he thought of David as of a star. Tonight, he thought, I have seen the greatness of David. Tonight I have seen his wisdom.

God of David, Joab whispered against the earth behind his thornbush. Lord God of David. He did not know whether he prayed or whether he cursed. David alone had routed Saul and his thousands. David had found the weak spot, the visor in Abner's helmet, and in Saul's, and had struck an unforgettable blow.

Suddenly, Joab was sobbing. Earlier tonight he had said good-by to the hills and the earth and the life he had known. Now he was sobbing because he had seen against the sky the naked sword of David's wisdom. He sobbed because years must pass before he would be again with the girl he loved, and all because David, with all his wisdom, cared not the turn of a hand for his seventeen-year-old kinsman. He is like the sea, thought Joab, not for the first time. He draws us all into himself. He gives back nothing.

And Joab rose and set out toward Hebron, skirting the camp of Saul. I am quit of my vow to the God of David, he thought. Yet the thought brought no comfort. For he had never loved David more than he loved him now in the hour of his rejection.

9

IN THE DAYS that followed David's routing of Saul, the tents and campfires echoed with the telling and embroidering of the tale. In his own ragged tent, Abiathar wrote the story in neat, careful letters on fresh parchment, together with other stories of other wars. When the parchment was full of his writings he wrapped it in linen and packed it with mud, and carried it to the cave above the oasis where Hezro often grazed his sheep. It was not the first story he had written down of how Saul marched into the wilderness and then marched out again without lifting a hand against David.

Abiathar was writing many tales these days; ever since Abigail's coming he had had an abundance of skins. He spent tedious hours scraping and pounding and rubbing the skins. He spent other hours searching beside the sea for reeds to make into pens, and mixing lamp-black with sheep's gall to use for ink.

The abundance of work for his hands comforted Abiathar, so that the lust he had felt for Reba during the spring and summer no longer troubled him. Her face came between him and his parchment, but brought only tenderness mingled with pity. During the autumn Reba had taken on an air of tragic womanliness. Abiathar had seen the baffled anger on Benaiah's face as he watched Reba dreaming by the campfire. He saw the change which came over her after Saul's army came and went, and Joab disappeared. He grieved because Reba grieved and there was no one to comfort her. Then he turned again to his parchments.

In Abigail's tents the tale of David's newest exploit was rehearsed admiringly by the maids. Yet, now that David called Abigail less often to his tent, she could no longer bring to the maids the firsthand news of David's affairs which had made up so large a part of their talk. Instead, the maids brought tales at second hand, rumors which floated through the camp. Perhaps it was because Abigail had lived too long with Nabal, or perhaps because she realized how small her influence was with David, that she was finding much to criticize in the stronghold. She talked of how much pleasanter it would be if they all moved to Carmel. She also spoke of Joab, who when he heard that Saul was nearby, fled in the night, back to his mother and safety.

"I liked that boy," she said. "He was sensible and reliable and I would have said he was brave. I am sorry to learn that he is a coward."

Reba endured these conversations in silence. If she wept, it was at night in her tent. But she spent fewer hours now with Abigail, and more hours brooding alone. How often she had begged Joab to take her to Bethlehem, yet when he fled there, he abandoned her. She grew thin and listless. Her dark eyes grew large and the bones of her face were sharp.

Reba's thin, brooding face sent Benaiah shouting to David three times during the weeks of autumn. If Reba would not consent to marry him, Benaiah shouted, let her be given to him anyway. He would soon bring her to her senses. Once she was a wife with child she would be sensible as other women are. Who ever heard of a woman giving consent to her own marriage? If you waited for that, half the women would never be wives.

Abigail heard it all. She saw the opaque curtain settle over David's face and knew too well why David seldom called her to his tent. An evening came when she went uninvited to David. She stood in his presence, well wrapped in her scarlet mantle. "I am troubled for my maid Dinah," she told him. "She comes and goes freely about the camp, as if she were a man. Tent life is no life for my maids. Dinah speaks to them about how they all can marry men of property and go to live in towns. Before we know it, I'll be without maids to help me make this wilderness life bearable. Will you speak to her, David?"

David looked long into the troubled eyes of his wife Abigail, then nodded. "Send her to me," he said. "Tonight."

Dinah was sent to David's tent that night, and she became his concubine. So it was Dinah who brought news concerning David's affairs in the following weeks. When a slender, finely-dressed young man with a silky brown beard and burning, bitter eyes came to camp, guided by one of Abigail's shepherds, Dinah told the women that the stranger was Saul's son Jonathan. The shepherd who brought him was the man who had been Saul's guide. Benaiah had taken the shepherd outside the camp, and had returned alone after a little while, whetting on his palm the newly polished blade of his knife.

Why had Jonathan come? Dinah did not know. In her opinion, Jonathan had come to reinforce Saul's invitation to David to join the armies of Israel in a march against the Philistines.

Another maid, Judith by name, had it from her friend Obed the Reubenite that Jonathan had come to spy out David's strength for Saul. "Benaiah will attend to Jonathan also, when David is through questioning him," Judith reported.

"Nonsense," Abigail said sharply. "David trusts Jonathan. It was Jonathan who first warned David of Abner's plot against him. I do not think he came to urge David to return, and I am certain he did not come as a spy."

Still the rumor persisted that Jonathan had brought an offer of amnesty for all David's men and of Abner's post for David himself if they would join Saul's army.

Among all the rumors one undeniable fact was known. Ever since Abiathar had brought the Urim and Thummim to David, Saul had been without any means whereby to inquire of the Lord for guidance. Dinah heard Jonathan speak of this to David. When Saul sent his troops to Nob to destroy the priests he did not remember to warn them to bring the Urim and the Thummim to him.

"Saul thinks the stones were lost," Dinah told the maids and Abigail. "He does not know David has them." Then all the women twittered together because David had triumphed over Saul in a matter so portentous.

"A man called Zadok is Saul's high priest," Dinah said. "But without the Urim and Thummim his advice is not to be relied upon. Saul goes to consult with witches and mediums and soothsayers. Afterward he kills them, either because they foretold disaster or conversely because they foretold good fortune which did not materialize. Saul is despondent, and Abner makes most of the decisions." Dinah's eyes were bright and the tale she had heard from Jonathan's own mouth gave the women material for many happy hours of gossip.

On another morning Dinah reported that the king of Gath had sent a messenger to David to offer a treaty of mutual assistance. Achish, the Philistine king, would give David a city on the border of Judah if David would come with all his men to live there and protect Achish from his enemies in the southern desert. Ziklag was the city, a good city with strong walls and houses of brick and stone.

Abigail was delighted. "We would live in houses, not tents. We would be able to protect Judah as well as Gath. We could prevent Philistine raids on Judah and strengthen our friendship with the elders in Hebron. Then Achish, protected by David in the south, could push his wars against Saul. Meanwhile, David would war on the Amalekites, who are far richer than Edomites since they raid the caravan route that connects Damascus with Egypt. They are rich in slaves and camels and blankets and tents. David could grow rich fighting Amalekites. Oh, if only David would listen to me—"

Then Abigail glanced about at the faces of her maids and grew silent. But Reba, horrified at all this talk of moving down to live among Philistines, ran from Abigail's tent to the accompaniment of her own jangling bracelets.

That night Reba saw the Philistine messenger beside the fire with the men of David's council. The door of her tent faced the fire, and she sat on the thick, warm rug Abigail had given her, and watched these men she knew and the two strangers, Jonathan the son of Saul, and Ittai the Philistine. She watched them and shivered, and when at last she closed her tent and slept, she dreamed of her childhood and of Philistine raiders who had killed her mother and destroyed her home.

Next day Reba went to find Abiathar. He was not in the camp, but she waited beside his tent. He came, after an hour, carrying a bundle of the reeds which he sharpened to make pens. Her hands plucked restlessly at the silver band she wore at her neck, while Abiathar told her which of the rumors she had heard were true, which false.

Jonathan had come to warn David that he must leave Judah. Abner would not rest while David remained within his reach.

"David has sent to En Gedi to bring the captains here for the final council," Abiathar told her. His dark eyes avoided hers, and his hands trembled as he worked with his knife, spoiling two reeds for every one he perfected. "David has made up his mind to go to Ziklag and serve Achish. But he must persuade all his captains and all his men. The league with Achish depends on the size of the forces he brings. Nothing short of the full six companies David commands will satisfy the terms of the league Achish has offered."

That night Reba watched again from her tent the men who sat in this last council in the wilderness. The sight of them held her spellbound. Reba had learned that you can live without warmth, without comfort, without those you love. But to see the men who had been her father's comrades turn now to make a league with the enemy that had killed him was a death of the spirit. David, Ira, Benaiah, Abiathar, Uriah, Seth and his friend Elhanan of Bethlehem, the captains from En Gedi—all were there. All were bidding farewell to hope, honor, courage. Or so it seemed to Reba.

Now at last Reba could believe the worst of Joab. If these men could make allies of the Philistines, every life spent in fighting Philistines was forfeited in a cause not lost but abandoned. If men could do this, a boy could abandon a girl who loved him, fleeing from a battle that was never

[50]

fought. There is, in the end, no courage, no faith, no truth in the men of Judah.

Reba sat in her tent while the fire burned low. The men talked on, sometimes disputing hotly, sometimes listening to long harangues from one man or another. A long silence fell, followed by a word flung into the silence like the sharp yelp of a dog. Then the argument was resumed. David spoke seldom. His head drooped. When he raised his face he looked as a man looks who is under sentence and will soon be turned over to the avenger.

One by one the men rose and left the fire. Defeat was in the set of their heads, the slant of their shoulders. Finally only David and Jonathan were left. They talked quietly together beside the fire. Soon Reba would close the curtains of her tent and shut out the sight of the fire which was dying, and of men whose spirit, whose courage was dead. If Joab had not abandoned her—there was Zeruiah, a mother who was afraid of nothing on this earth. But Joab had abandoned her and had not returned, though three months had passed. There was nobody to whom she could turn. Even Abigail, lost in her own disappointment and loneliness, had shut herself off from friendly confidences.

I am alone, thought Reba. I am all alone.

She raised her face from her knees. David stood in the open door of her tent.

"My dearest girl," he said in a voice which shook with strange tenderness, "you have not closed your tent. It is long past dark. You know better than to be careless about this matter."

He stooped to enter the tent. He sat on the rug Abigail had given her, and took her hand and laid it against his cheek. "Your hand is cold. What is troubling my little dove?"

"You are going to join the Philistines. You will fight their battles and spend the lives of your men to enrich them."

"Dear Reba, you have more reason than any of us to hate the Philistines. Tell me what I ought to do."

"Would you listen to me?" What nonsense was this? David did not seek advice from a young girl! Reba knew quite well that the decision had been made in full council, and no matter what she said, she could not change that decision.

David said gently, "I will listen. In the end, the responsibility is mine, and the decision will be made by me. But I want to know your thoughts." His arm went round her. She rested her head against his shoulder. The touch of his cheek on her hair comforted her. Some of the bleak loneliness ebbed in the comfort of David's affection and concern.

She said, "Joab used to talk of a plan he had for you to take Jerusalem. With your six companies you could hold Jerusalem against Saul forever until finally he would be forced to make a treaty with you. Joab says you could march from here in a night, and be inside the city before dawn. Joab says the Jebusites have no plan for defending their city because they trust in their walls, as Goliath trusted in his armor and his sword. Joab says—"

David's arm had dropped away. His voice was suddenly harsh. "Joab is a dreamer of fantasies. How would we feed ourselves in a city of Jebusites where not one of us owns an inch of ground? I have never believed in Joab's dream of taking the city so easily, and if I did believe it could be done, I could not feed my men if Abner came to besiege me."

Reba sighed. "Well then, stay here in the wilderness. Abner will not live forever. A Philistine arrow will reach him soon."

David sighed. "I cannot stay here, Reba. My companies have grown too large to live on the frugal bounty of the wilderness. The Edomites have long ago yielded up all we can hope to take from them. Besides, the women are sick of camp. They cry for a city, for houses, for protection from the coming rains. Jonathan warns me that Abner will soon march again if I stay within his reach. I must leave Judah."

Reba moved closer to him, feeling the bitter sadness of his mood, longing to comfort him, longing to be comforted as well. When his arm went round her again she felt the trembling of his body and thought how deep his grief must be. She said softly, "David, you could make a league with the Moabites. They have received your father and brothers. Surely they would receive you."

"The Moabites are at peace with Saul. They could not remain at peace if they received me. There is only one king who will receive me, and Achish is the one. Achish alone is not afraid of Saul's reprisals."

David's head drooped until it rested on Reba's breast. She cradled his head in her arms, longing to comfort him, forgetting her own grief in the longing to comfort David. He said, "If only I could go to Moab. Or stay here in Maon. But I cannot. I can never fight against Abner. Three times I have stood over Saul. Three times I could have killed him. But my hand refused. I cannot fight Saul and I cannot fight Israel. I have nowhere to turn. Why has it come to this? I obeyed orders and served Saul and Abner with all my might. Why am I brought to these straits where every man's hand is against me?"

Reba cradled his head, comforting him. "How can I answer?" she said softly. "I only know we all love you, all of us, your people. We trust you and look to you. You are the sweet singer of Judah, the protector and champion of those who have been abandoned. I have loved you since I was a baby. You'll find the right way. You have been desperate before."

David kissed the face that was so close above his, then rose, and Reba stood beside him. He said, "There is no way out for me. We are too many for this country, for we can neither hide here nor be fed."

His arm closed round her, pulling her to him, and she rested her head on his shoulder, proud that he had turned to her for comfort. This was the first time she had ever been of service to David, who had been her protector for so long. To be of help to one you love, one who is lonely and despairing, she thought, that is how a woman finds comfort in her own distress. "I wish I were wiser," she said. "I wish I could really help you, David."

David's lips brushed her cheek. "Reba, sweet child. You are so lovely, so young. You grow sweeter in this wild place, as if sweetness began and ended in yourself. Your father would have been proud to see how you have blossomed in this wilderness." His arms were so close about her now she could not breathe. His hand moved down her back, pressing her against himself. "You said that you love me," he whispered. "I have waited for your love. You can comfort me indeed, my darling. Only you can comfort me tonight."

Reba stood rigid and dumb with the shock of David's meaning. He loosened the fastenings of the tent curtain and let it drop. He said, "You were wrong to leave your tent open tonight." He knotted the curtains securely fast and in the darkness his arms found her, his hands found the knot in her girdle.

She pulled away from his touch.

"Don't be afraid of love," David pleaded. "Don't stand here stiff and unyielding. You are a woman, ready to give love and to be loved. Did you think I would let you go unprotected among Philistines? You will go as the wife of David. You will be safe."

She whispered faintly, "David, you have been my protector. Protect me now."

"Now and always," David replied, and pulled her rigid body to the mat.

After an endless time, when the cool air of dawn could be felt, David said, "I am glad you love me, Reba. I am glad you are finished at last with the nonsense about my young cousin. I knew you would forget him if I got him out of the way. That is why I brought the avenger to the camp. I knew he would flee to Hebron for a time. I did it for you, my darling."

"You brought the avenger? Joab—fled from the avenger?"

David's voice was the voice of one who speaks of trivial matters. "Of course, my darling."

"Joab was in danger of the avenger. Joab might have been killed." Her throat was tight with anguish.

"No, no. There was no avenger, except in Joab's guilty mind. My sister concealed his crime. When Joab has suffered a little for killing the other

[53]

shepherd, we will tell him all about it, Seth and I. Meanwhile, he shall sweat a little, so he will be in no hurry to kill again."

When at last David left her, she lay face down on the mat, exhausted, unmoving. David, she thought, you are too much for us, for all of us. We all serve you, David, she thought. And when you are finished with us, we wait until you need us again. Abigail, Abiathar, poor Joab. Even the lusty Dinah. And now me. I will be the wife of David. The third wife of David. First Michal, Saul's daughter. Then Abigail, Nabal's wife. And now me. Others will come, other wives, other concubines.

David's first two wives brought him power, position, wealth. I bring you a gift also, David, thought Reba. A gift you do not yet know about. A child. David's first-born child. I hope he will be a son. I alone will know he is not David's son. That will be my secret—and my strength.

David, she thought, I do not hate you. I do not hate anyone. I was a fool to choose as protector a boy who could not protect even himself.

Reba rubbed the place on her neck where the memory of the pressure of David's crisp beard lingered. She wanted to blot out that touch from flesh which had felt the downy beard of a boy. She turned her face to the earth and wept for herself, for Joab, for her son, who would come into the world as the first born of the mighty David, but with no heritage of David's greatness.

You draw us all into yourself, she thought sadly. Is it true, David, that you give back nothing?

10

JOAB REACHED HEBRON before dawn. He entered at the broken gate and lay down close by the crumbling wall, drawing his cloak around him. He did not want to sleep. There would be nights aplenty for sleeping inside these walls.

Ten minutes before he reached the gate, he had passed the cave of Machpelah, which Abraham had bought from the Hittites a thousand years ago as a tomb for Sarah, his wife. He thought of Abraham, and of Hebron, which had been a thriving city when Abraham migrated here from Syria. Abraham had pitched his tents outside the gate and had grazed his flocks on the abundant grass of the slopes both east and west. His nephew Lot had taken his wife and his flocks across a wilderness greener then than now, and had settled at Sodom, at the southern end of the Dead Sea. But the cities beside the sea had been blotted out by overwhelming disaster, and were now remembered only by the pillars of salt which had been flung up to mark their passing.

Joab thought of the many years Abraham and Sarah lived together. He thought of the meaning of race and family, and how its roots are in the strength of a man and the tenderness of a woman, and in the delight they have in one another.

I could live with Reba, he thought, as Abraham lived with Sarah, and love her no less after many years. He pictured himself standing with Reba before the elders of Bethlehem to receive a blessing on their marriage. He wondered how it would be after ten years, or twenty, or fifty, to know always that the place which is home to you is home also to the girl you chose in the exuberant vigor of your youth. Joab knew that morning that nothing would ever reach more deeply into the core of his being than the love he felt for Reba, the longing to share with her his home in Bethlehem. Men live and die, he thought, but the force that ties a man and his wife together is eternal, binding together families, generations, races.

At dawn Joab rose and found a spring where he could wash himself. Then he walked about, following the winding streets of the city.

Hebron was the metropolis of Judah, and in a sense the capital city of the tribe. Joab had heard Jesse speak of it as the oldest city in Canaan, possibly the oldest city in the world, though one could not be sure in comparing Hebron with Damascus or the cities of Egypt. Protected by its hills, fed by the fertility of its valleys and slopes, watered by a score of springs and two score wells, it was ideally situated as a dwelling for peaceful men. For men of war, the Jebusite city was better, being on a hilltop and easier to defend. But for men of peace Hebron lacked nothing. When invaders came, therefore, the people of Hebron did not resist. They adopted new ways and did business with the invaders.

The valley of Hebron was rocky and narrow, yet so well watered that vineyards and olive orchards abounded, testimony to the bounty of nature and the industry of men. The streets wound among low, gray stone buildings which hugged the contours of the eastern slope. The walls were crumbling, wholly gone in places where the terrain served to indicate the boundaries.

Accustomed to open fields, Joab was oppressed by the narrow alleys reeking with the strange odors of wares brought from Egypt and Nineveh and Phoenicia.

He had laid his plans during the night. He would not go to the elders himself. Nothing can be gained by going to meet trouble. He would find employment and wait for trouble to find him. He was hungry and had no resources but his two hands, his young strength. He had no intention of seeking out friends of Jesse in this town to make known to them his disgrace. So he followed the narrow streets until he came to the market.

There was in the market a booth where men could go who wanted to sell their labor, and Joab went to this booth. He found employers looking

[55]

for workers in vineyards and orchards beyond the walls, but he could not take the chance of being found in such a place by Elhanan. Men were wanted to go with camel caravans to Beersheba and on through the Negeb to Egypt, and Joab toyed with the thought that he could see the world if he joined a caravan. Then he remembered Zeruiah and Reba, and knew he must not delay any longer but must be here when Elhanan came, stand trial, and get the whole thing settled. The only employment he was able to find that suited his circumstances was with a wine merchant named Aziel.

Aziel's vineyards, like the rest, were above the city on the hill. But below the vineyards lay a stone trough, Aziel's winepress, and below that lay the vats where the wine was aged. Aziel not only made wine, he bought and sold it. He had shops in the bazaars of a dozen towns of Judah, from Beersheba north to Gibeah. Aziel was a very rich man, but he was not an elder in Hebron. Aziel thought only fools would waste their time on civic duties when they could be using it to make money instead.

When Aziel hired Joab he set him to treading grapes. He promised to give the boy more responsible and less tedious work after grape harvest ended. Yet Joab did not put much faith in Aziel's promises. He saw how Aziel measured him up and down, and was sure Aziel recognized the nature of Joab's sojourn in the city, and meant to enrich himself out of Joab's need. The wage he offered was a pittance, but food and lodging within the walls went with it, and Joab was in no position to barter.

Employment as a treader of grapes is no better than slavery. Even for a boy of Joab's strength the work was exhausting, as well as monotonous and humiliating. The food provided him was a slave's food, a dark, ill-baked kind of bread with sour wine and occasionally lentils. He was given a dark kennel-like shed to sleep in. He had brought nothing with him but the tunic and cloak on his back, nor was anything given him. So he slept on the dank straw he found in the shed, wrapped in his cloak. After the first day he could not wash the stain of the grapes from his feet. He walked through the city with the skirts of his unwashed cloak flapping in the dust, unwilling to gird them up and make a show of the purple toes thrust between the cords of his sandals. The purple stain became his badge of slavery. And the days went by, and Elhanan did not come to Hebron.

Grape harvest ended and the labor at the stone vat was finished at last. The vat was scoured and covered for another year. All this while Aziel refused to pay Joab the scant wage he had promised.

"When I return from Egypt," he would say. Or, "When the men of Beersheba pay what they owe me," or, "When I have paid off the muleteers who carried my wine to Jerusalem." And Joab realized that he would never be paid, because Aziel had no intention of giving a strong, intelligent, dependable boy money to lodge elsewhere.

At last Joab was given work with some dignity to it. He was set to tending the wine booth. "I will double your wages if you can show a profit," Aziel promised generously. But Joab reflected gloomily that double the wages he had had from Aziel so far would still be no wages at all.

Tending a wine booth in the bazaar is lazy work, with plenty of time for observing the merchants, the sheiks, the slaves, the veiled women, the priests, and those who, like himself, were refugees in Hebron.

Aziel came now and then to spend an hour in the shop. Aziel had discerned from Joab's manner that he was interested in David. Joab had no doubt Aziel had figured out long ago that he had taken refuge in the wilderness with David for a while before coming to the city. So now he talked often of David, praising David's courage and wisdom, and predicting a dazzling future for Judah's hero.

"When Saul is dead," Aziel said, "David will be welcomed in Hebron as first man of Judah. We'll give him a fine house. We'll make him our judge and protector—our king. We'd do it today, but if we did Saul would come marching to Hebron, and this city is certainly not adapted to wars. But you wait and see, young fellow. See if David isn't king of Judah, once Saul is dead. We men of Judah have no use for Benjamite kings, or for any other kings stemming from those northern tribes. We are a tribe apart, and we'll rule ourselves hereafter. But not while Saul lives."

There was little to do in the long days in the sunny bazaar, except listen to the merchants in nearby booths, watch the women as they bargained for provisions, and stare at the green hills above the city and dream of Reba. He wondered how Reba would manage when the rainy season came, how long Elhanan would wait before coming here to find him.

Toward the end of an afternoon in late autumn, the shadow of a man fell across the stone pavement of the booth. The shadow was broad, and the voice which shouted at him was familiar. "Wine," shouted Seth. "Wine, boy, if you please! Much wine for a wedding. Step lively!"

Joab pushed back the headcloth that shaded his eyes and blinked up into the bearded face of his brother. He leaped to his feet with joy. Then he turned away, remembering.

Seth exclaimed, "Well, if it isn't my vanished brother! I've come to fetch you, boy." He stepped forward to embrace Joab, but Joab turned his back.

"I suppose you brought Elhanan?"

"Elhanan? Not I. I'm not Elhanan's keeper."

"You are nobody's keeper. Mine least of all."

Seth's laughter roared through the bazaar. Heads turned, and Joab shrank back into the shadows of his booth, but Seth did not notice the heads, or if he did he enjoyed the stares of the city dwellers.

Seth shouted, "I have come to buy wine for David's wedding. But I have also come to bring you back to camp, for David insists he must

[57]

have you to serve as friend of the bridegroom. So here I am in all friendship, and you reproach me with Elhanan. Boy, will you ever learn what it is to have a brother who sees to your interests?"

"Don't add lies to your other sins," Joab muttered. "And in the name of God, lower your voice."

Seth dropped his voice, but the broad smile did not leave his face. "We have known for three months that you were here, and for two months that you were in the employ of that shrewd fellow, Aziel. Now the time has come to fetch you to camp again. David says you brought him good fortune once before as friend of the bridegroom, and he is more in need of good fortune now than ever before."

"David knows I cannot come. You know it too."

"You can go wherever you like, Joab. You are free as any man."

Joab stared at Seth's broad face, unbelieving.

Seth said softly, "Our mother told me a tale when I was last in Bethlehem. It is a tale you may enjoy, younger brother. It seems you had a friend in the pastures, a half-wit named Lem. Well, it seems that on the night you took it into your head to forsake your duty and run off to play outlaw with David, an accident befell this poor lad. He was torn by beasts and died."

Joab stood open-mouthed while Seth continued, "Our mother was herself obliged to go to the fold, because you had abandoned the sheep. She took young Asa with her. They found the mangled body of Lem, but the sheep were unharmed. Asa avenged Lem's death by killing the bear. He took the head of the bear, and went to fetch Elhanan, and all Bethlehem praised Asa for his courage in avenging the death of the hunchback."

Joab sank to the earth, overcome by the reversal in his fortunes. And Seth roared, "Now will you shut that idiotic mouth of yours and bring me wine? I swear, you look as half-witted as ever Lem looked in his lifetime."

Joab turned his back. If Seth saw the tears on his face he would never stop ridiculing him. He mumbled, "I will sell you all the wine you want." He began laughing. His laughter swelled, filling the bazaar, but Joab no longer cared how many of these hustling Hebronites stared at him. "I will not sell the wine. I will give it. Wine to celebrate my freedom. Wine for David of Judah. May he have a hundred wives, and may each enrich him as did Abigail. Wine for the wages my master did not pay me. Bring up your donkeys and we will empty the shop."

Joab was laughing to cover his tears. He was laughing because, beyond all banter, Seth took an interest in him and had come to Hebron to bring him back to freedom. Neither David nor Seth had betrayed him in permitting Elhanan to come to camp; only his own fears had betrayed him. Before night fell he would be in camp. He would see Reba. He would see Abiathar and Ira. He would have food to fill his belly after three months of slave diet, food provided as a wedding feast for David and his new bride. He bundled the wineskins onto the donkeys, bundled the bottles into the hampers, laid two of the largest skins over his own shoulders. In a few days now he would take Reba to Bethlehem, and she would be his wife in the presence of Zeruiah and the elders.

"We will leave word for my master in the next booth," he told Seth. "With nothing here to sell and nothing to steal, he cannot object that the booth is untended. Aziel is a scoundrel, but he loves David. We will leave word that he has donated this wine for David's wedding celebration. We will leave word that David will not hold it against Aziel that he made a slave of David's cousin, and cheated him of his wages. And now tell me, what is the name of David's bride?"

I I

JOAB STOOD AT the door of Reba's ragged tent. The curtain had been tied back and Reba was veiled and ready.

This was the first time Joab had seen her veiled, though he had seen many other women so covered. The veil she wore was of white linen, brought from Bethlehem. Zeruiah had kept it in a chest in the stone house for use by brides of the sons of Jesse. Seth had brought it here. The veil hung from Reba's head, covering her completely, held in graceful folds by the white linen girdle which Dinah had just finished winding about her waist. Dinah set a handsome silver chaplet on her head, touched the folds of linen here and there, and stepped back.

Zeruiah had sent all the garments Reba wore today, as her gift to a bride who came to David without dowry. The sight of Reba clothed in bridal garments sent by his mother sent waves of anguish through Joab's body, so that he trembled and clutched at a tent pole to still the tremors.

Dinah murmured, "Happiness, Reba, and many sons." The words were formal, but the tone held hostility. Abigail's faction would naturally feel hostility toward a wife taken by David before either Abigail or Dinah was with child.

Joab extended an arm stiffly. "Come. David is waiting."

Dinah took Reba's hand and laid it on Joab's. She held the curtain aside while Joab led Reba from the tent.

The customary procession of virgins following the bride had been omitted. Reba wanted it this way, since she had lived without friends of her own age in the outlaw camp. So Reba and Joab walked alone from her tent toward the council fire where David and Abiathar and the men of David's council waited.

Joab spoke softly, choosing formal phrases as befitted their formal attire but finding in the formal words an outlet for his heartache; "On a day in early summer I came to this place. I was welcomed by a girl of tender beauty. I was fed with cakes of her making. When she followed me to the hills she welcomed me in other ways, so that I loved her and would have shared my whole life with her. Now I repay her kindness. As cousin and friend of the bridegroom, I welcome her into the family of Jesse of Bethlehem. I bring her to my cousin David, the most distinguished of us. David says that she is shy as a young hind. I never found her shy. I found her one who gives love bountifully. I ask now that she receive my kinsman as generously as she used to receive me. And I swear by the God of David, if ever I find her playing the harlot or causing my cousin anxiety through the jealousy of any man, I will plunge a knife into her heart."

The last words were spoken through set teeth.

From the veiled figure came words softly spoken. "David has always been too much for us, Joab. We cannot help what has happened. But we must not hate each other."

Joab gripped her hand so hard he heard the sharp intake of her breath. He quickened their slow pace. Reba stumbled, unable to see the footing because of the white veil. But Joab gripped her hand, pulled her along.

Now they were with the others. While the men of the council looked on from the firelight, and all the men and women of the camp crowded into the nearby shadows to watch, Joab laid Reba's hand in David's.

Abiathar stood waiting. His gaunt face was pale, and his eyes seemed sunk deep into his head. He raised his arms in the familiar gesture of benediction:

"May the Lord bless you and keep you. May the Lord make his face to shine upon you and be gracious unto you. May the Lord lift up his countenance upon you and give you peace."

The benediction of Moses was fresh and new to Joab whenever he heard it. Yet to hear it spoken now for David and Reba turned his heart to stone and caused his face to grow rigid in an effort to conceal his anguish. He watched while David led Reba away to his own tent. David did not return to join the feast, as is the custom of bridegrooms, but followed Reba into his tent and the curtain fell, closing them in together.

Joab turned his back upon the tent. He moved stiffly, almost blindly, bumped against Benaiah, and they snarled at one another. Joab saw that Benaiah's dark face was suffused with much wine drinking and a length of smudged linen was wrapped around his left arm.

Benaiah shrugged and spread his hands. "Come," he said gruffly, and led the way to where the feast had been spread. Game, sheep, and oxen had been roasted. Shops in Carmel, in Ziph, in Tekoa, in all the villages of the region had been emptied to provide for the celebration. From En Gedi David's men had come to eat and drink, and this night marked the end of their living in the wilderness.

Tomorrow they would march, six hundred men plus women and children and beasts of burden, over the hills and down to the green Philistine plain.

The clearing was crowded and noisy. Joab ate and drank with the men but shared none of their mood of celebration. He kept beside him a skin of wine, and drank from it between each mouthful of meat. Beside him Benaiah also had a skin of wine which he offered to share with no one.

Joab had made only a little progress with his wine when Dinah bent gracefully above him. "My mistress sent me," she said, "to bring you to her tent. Come."

Joab followed her swaying hips, clutching his skin of wine. He ignored the laughter which rose after him. He found Abigail in the public room of her tent, seated on a rug. Her face was swollen from weeping. She looked as if she had not slept for many days. Joab sat cross-legged on the rug facing her and extended the wineskin. "Here is wine from the vats of Aziel of Hebron," he told her. "It is good wine, well fermented."

Abigail took a silver cup which Dinah brought and Joab poured wine into it. She dismissed Dinah and drained the cup, then took a second cupful and said, "I received Reba as if she were a sister. I brought her to my tent and taught her needlework. I urged her to abandon that tattered old tent and share my tent with my maids and me. But she would not. I gave her fine clothes made of dyed stuff, as costly as my own. I gave her bangles and a neckband of silver. I talked to her about her home, and about Bethlehem, and about the time when I went with Nabal on a caravan to Egypt. I told her all I have seen and all I have been taught, so that she came to know as much about the world we are in as I know myself. I showed her kindness. Now she has stolen the love of my husband."

Joab took a long draught from the wineskin, refusing the cup Abigail offered.

"David is still your husband," he said. "He is more your husband than hers, because you love him. Reba does not love David."

"All women love David."

Joab extended a cupful of wine to her. "You learn to appreciate the goodness of wine when you have labored in making it," he told her. "The sun and the earth and the mysterious germ of life which is seed—all go into it. But without the labor of a man enslaved there is no wine.

"And without the passage of time," he said brokenly, "there is no wine. I wonder who will drink the wine of my treading."

Abigail reached for the wineskin and took a draught from it. She did not use the silver cup again, but drank as Joab did. "I shall go to Carmel," she said, "and be mistress of my own household. Why should I live among Philistines? I do not want to live in a harem."

"Good," said Joab. "I shall go to Bethlehem and tend my mother's sheep. I am free, and there is no avenger pursuing me. I can live at peace in Bethlehem, and I need never again be at war with anyone. Why should I live among Philistines when I can live in the house of Jesse and Zeruiah, in Bethlehem?"

Abigail said anxiously, "You must go with David. The treaty with Achish specifies particularly that David must bring all his men to live in Ziklag and defend the southern borders of the Philistine plain."

"I was treading wine in Hebron when the treaty was made. I am not bound by it." Then, emotion filling him, he said, "Reba hates the Philistines. She does not want to live among them. She fears them so much it is a sickness within her. Reba ought not live in a harem. She will never know what it is to be the one beloved wife of her husband, as my mother was to my father, as Ruth was to Boaz, as my grandmother was to Jesse. Already David has taken three wives and a concubine, and he will have many more. That is no life for a girl like Reba."

Abigail patted his shoulder. "I will look after her. I know what it is to marry one man while loving another. I often barred my door against Nabal. Yet I shed no tears when I was Nabal's wife. Since I married David, since I saw how love for that girl gnawed at him, I have shed more tears than before in my whole life as the wife of Nabal. She has come without dowry. Michal brought him honor and dignity in Saul's city. I brought him the wealth of the wilderness. But this girl brings nothing to David, not even her love. Because I love him, David will return to me when his hunger for this girl abates. Yet I cannot bear to think that David married me only for my goods and my lands and my flocks."

Joab gazed at Abigail earnestly. "David respects your judgment. He listens to your advice. Ask Abiathar how it was with David before he married you. He had lost faith in himself. You restored his belief in his destiny. Ask Ira. Ask Uriah. Ask Benaiah. They know what you have done for David. And David knows. He trusts you and will turn to you when he has—has—" Joab could not go on. He turned his face from Abigail and drank deeply from the wineskin.

Abigail said, "I will rule David's household, in Philistia as in Judah. Wherever David goes, I will be head of the harem. If he marries twenty wives, I will be senior among them. David will turn to me again."

Joab nodded. He too wanted to believe it.

"This greatness of David," said Abigail. "It is like nothing else we will ever know. David's greatness comes from the Lord. He is the Lord's anointed. But it comes also from the labor of men, like the goodness of the wine. David will drink the wine which all of us have trod, but he will never know how we labored in the treading. This is not to say he wants to use us, but only that we are at hand. I will go to Ziklag. I will wait until he needs me again. You are his cousin, Joab. You will serve him too."

Joab rose, clutching the limp goatskin bottle. "You are his wife and cannot help yourself. But I will never again tread any man's wine but my own. I will return to Bethlehem and tend my mother's sheep. And when the Philistines, or Abner, or some other enemy, thrusts a spear into David's heart, I will walk with the mourners but I will not weep. I will go to his house and take Reba from among his wives and bring her home to Bethlehem. When that is done, I will no longer hate David."

"You do not hate David."

Joab sighed. "Perhaps you are right. Perhaps it is you I hate. David is your husband. Why didn't you stop him? A woman of your resource could have found a way."

Abigail said sadly, "I tried. I gave him my deepest love. I gave him also my maid Dinah."

"Dinah is a wanton."

"Dinah is a woman who understands men."

"I am a man who does not understand women." Joab left the tent, and set out up the trail which hugged the face of the bluff. When he reached the spot where, with his eyes bulging, he had watched Reba drop her cloak on the sand, he scooped out a hollow for himself and lay down in it and wept.

So now, he thought, I have given Reba to David. If I served him again, what more would he take from me? Never again, he vowed, will I go near David. The night wore on, and in the end Joab slept.

PART TWO

The Philistine Plain

12

FLEEING THE COLLAPSE of the Minoan civilization on the island of Crete, a tribe of wanderers reached the mainland of Asia to filter gradually around the end of the Great Sea. Passing through the narrow shelf of rocky highland where later the Phoenicians built a maritime empire, they moved south until they reached the richest land to be found between the three rivers and the Nile, the plain which stretched, green and fertile, along the coast from Mount Carmel to the desert.

The wanderers brought with them knowledge of iron, picked up from the disrupted Hittite empire. Settling in the fertile plain, they turned their backs on the sea and they neglected the fertile soil, which could have yielded grain in abundance. Instead they robbed the orchards and threshing floors of their neighbors; they made their iron into swords and chariots of war and built a civilization whose name is synonymous with all that is crass and destructive. This people, whose only boast was in their military might, vanished leaving a legend of how their greatest hero died of a stone cast by a shepherd boy.

Of the five cities from which kings ruled the people of the fertile Philistine plain, three lay on the coast of the Great Sea. These were Ashkelon, Ashdod, and Gaza. Ekron lay a little inland, on the main caravan route connecting Egypt with the cities of the fertile crescent. Gath, the most eastern of the five cities, was on no caravan route, beside no sea. Gath was the city nearest to the mountainous Hebrew country, and consequently Gath was the city oftenest at war with Israel.

Here in Gath on an autumn evening, in the court of the palace of Achish the king, was spread a feast of mutton and pork, of wine and raisins and dates and melons, of cheese and cakes and olives. At the head of the table Achish was seated cross-legged on a rug. On his right was Ittai, chief of his counselors.

Achish rose from his rug, groaning with the stiffness of his joints. He stretched mightily and belched, and stood watching his men relaxed on the profusion of striped Amalekite rugs, wolfing down the meats and bread and fruit, swilling down the wine. They were too busy to notice that Achish

[64]

had risen. Ittai noticed, however, and laid down a succulent knuckle of pork, licked the grease from his fingers, and waved a genial salute.

"A splendid feast, my lord Achish," said Ittai, and reached for a cluster of raisins.

Some of the men had finished gorging themselves and had fallen asleep on their rugs, their cloaks covering their faces. Achish looked them over, pleased with their pleasure in his bounty. He wished David had not refused the invitation to share in the feast. Still, a man's religion was his own, and the religion of David was peculiar, as is the religion of all who do not serve Dagon.

David's religion, however, was stranger than most. Imagine serving a god whose whim it is that his people eat the meat only of animals which chew the cud and have cloven hoofs! What a lot of good eating a man would miss who served such a god. Still, Achish was not the man to trample on the religion of others, for who could tell in what strange ways strange gods might take their vengeance?

Achish scratched his armpits and wished he could do justice to the feast as these others were doing, without suffering discomfort. I grow fat and lazy, thought Achish. There is no longer pleasure in war or feasting. Even women seem lately to require more exertion than the meager returns warrant.

Achish belched again, turned his back upon his noisy table and walked ponderously across the stone paving into an adjacent room. He sank, groaning with repletion, onto a padded couch. He ran his hands over the heavy pigskin covering. The leather had grown brittle. I will have thicker padding put on it, and a new and softer covering made, thought Achish, and yawned, and composed himself to sleep.

But Achish could not sleep. His belly rumbled and pains shot through his bowels. Turn and twist as he would, he could not be comfortable. I have been idle too long, thought Achish. Now that David protects our borders and conducts our raids, I do nothing but eat and sleep and quarrel with Ittai. I must bestir myself. I must make war again. But the thought of jouncing along the road to war in his great iron chariot made his flesh ache. And he thought, when neither women nor war nor feasting please a man, what is left?

Religion is the pleasure of the old, he thought. But religion also troubled Achish. There was a tale he had heard when very young, of how the god of Israel had been captured in battle and set as a trophy before Dagon. The god itself was a queer thing, as queer as the religion of the people who adored it. The thing was merely a box made of acacia wood, with an overlay of gold carved to show the figures of men with wings. The box held a few relics of stone and wood and sugar, wrapped in crumbling linen, but nothing of any value was in it. The box was set before Dagon and left overnight, and next day Dagon was found fallen from his place, with head and hands broken off. No doubt the tale was false, yet the priests of Dagon made it a crime to repeat it, and consequently the tale continued to be told. Somehow since hearing the story Achish had felt a little contemptuous of Dagon. Whenever he went to spread before his god any trophies taken in war, he felt the wish to comfort Dagon, who had once been vanquished by a box. Well, the box was no longer in Philistia, having long ago been set on an ox cart and sent back into the Hebrew hills.

Still, it was a comfort to know that David, who served and adored the box, was the servant of Achish, and had provided the very feast which was rumbling in the king's belly.

Ittai, thought Achish with a smile of secret triumph deep in his beard, Ittai will acknowledge at last that I have utterly vanquished David and have made him my servant forever.

All good things bring some discomfort, Achish reflected. This applied to religion and war and the feasts. It applied also to Ittai. Ittai was a pesty fellow, with his extravagant admiration of David and of the scholarly priest who dwelt in David's city. This priest carried a pair of dice by which to inquire of the god of the box. He had also an incomprehensible penchant for writing things down on parchment and hiding the parchment in caves. Ittai was obsessed with admiration for those two. Yet Achish knew he could hardly rule Gath without Ittai to counsel him and enforce his decisions.

Even the throne itself, Ittai had seized for Achish. Years ago this same David of Judah had killed Goliath, a cousin of Achish. When the demoralized Philistine army reached the gates of Gath, Ittai stood in the gate and rallied the army. They made a stand there, and turned back the pursuing Hebrews, and the Hebrews returned to plunder among the dead and to burn the abandoned Philistine camp. But Ittai stood in the gate and declared Achish king, and the people had accepted him.

Confound Ittai, he knew Achish was here in the anteroom. Why didn't he come to see whether he was wanted? Why didn't he come to compliment Achish on the abundance of the feast, and on having subdued David to make him his servant forever?

"Ittai!" roared Achish.

There was no answer except the gusty voices of men who had eaten much and would soon be asleep. Achish fell into a troubled doze, punctuated by memories of Ittai's praises of David.

"David was clever enough to see that size and strength could not avail Goliath, providing David got in a crippling blow from a distance," Ittai had said, when he heard the manner of Goliath's defeat. "He disabled Goliath before he ever came within reach of that huge sword."

And Ittai had profited by David's wisdom. He had set up a unit of archers in the van of the Philistine army. Thereafter the chariots swept in only after the arrows of the archers had disabled the enemy. In the chariots Ittai had placed javelin throwers to cripple the enemy further before the swordsmen came up. Because Achish had let Ittai have his way in all these matters, there was no other king in the five cities of the plain as rich and powerful today as was Achish of Gath.

Of the long quarrel between Saul and David, Ittai had also spoken. Saul marched against David again and again, and returned each time without striking a blow. Each time David contrived some new stratagem to change Saul's plans.

"David's political wisdom exceeds even his military brilliance," Ittai concluded admiringly.

Well, a time comes when a man has heard enough of his chief counselor's praises of another man. Achish sent Ittai as messenger to arrange a league with David. He offered David sanctuary and a walled city. In return, David was to bring the full complement of his six companies to live in the plain, guarding the Philistines from desert enemies and continuing the usual raids on Hebrew threshing floors and orchards at harvest time. The spoils were to be divided between Achish and David.

David had lived more than a year in Ziklag, and he had never been niggardly with tribute. The feast today celebrated the second year of harvest raids. He serves me well, thought Achish complacently. And he turned on the couch, groaning.

"Ittai," he shouted. "Come here."

"I am here, my lord Achish." Ittai leaned lightly against the stone arch. His spare body was erect and relaxed. His cloak was clean, unmarked by grease or gravy, a remarkable feat after a feast. His eyes creased in the familiar, unreadable smile, as if all the thoughts of Ittai were his own, and the words he spoke were measured and sifted.

Achish said querulously, "Why must I call? You saw me leave the table."

Ittai shrugged and spread his hands. His lips smiled within their silken frame of black beard. "I eat slowly, my lord. A bad habit, perhaps, but one which it pleases me to indulge."

Achish brushed aside Ittai's habits. "We took a wise step in summoning David to Ziklag, yes?"

"A wise step, my lord Achish."

"The credit belongs to you, Ittai. I called you here to express thanks for the way you have handled all our dealings with David. You have served Gath well, in this as in other matters."

Ittai came near the couch and sat on the rug. "Many thanks, old friend. Your praise is beyond my merit."

"No doubt." What ailed the fellow that he was unable to return compliments to his king? Old friend, was it? "You must admit that David serves me well," said Achish petulantly.

"Indeed, my lord, whatever David does, he does well."

Achish groaned. Anger was growing, and with it the unrest in his belly, for anger impeded the working of the juices on the heavy burden of pork and mutton and dates and oil cakes.

Achish said loudly, "I tell you, Ittai, David has done for me what he never did for himself. He has raided his tribesmen for me, though he never robbed them while he hid in their hills. At my command he brings grain from their threshing floors and fruit from their orchards. His people abhor him, so that he will be obliged to remain my servant for the rest of his life. Acknowledge it, Ittai. Acknowledge that I have subdued David forever."

Ittai said soberly, "Among David's people they have a saying, 'You shall love your friend and hate your enemy.' I wonder who is David's enemy? Saul? Or the Philistines?"

"Saul! Certainly Saul! He seeks to kill David. We saved David's life. And David shows his gratitude in these gifts he sends. You come from the feast David sent, and you ask whether he is our enemy!" Achish was churning with honest exasperation.

"I ask whether we are his enemy. There is a difference. My dear fellow, have you the testimony of a single Philistine that the food we have eaten came from Judah?"

The breath rasped in the king's throat. "What do I need of observers? I have the wine and oil, the barley and corn, the mutton and pork. Don't be insolent, friend Ittai."

"I spoke as in the old days. Forgive me, my lord, but tell me this, when did ever swine come from a raid on Judah?"

Achish rose on his elbows. It had become impossible to breathe while lying down. "I ordered David to raid Judah. That is how I know he raided Judah. Many border householders raise swine for the caravan trade."

Ittai shook his head. His eyes were somber, kindly, almost pitying. "The rumor is that David raids only the desert people. Far from raiding Judah, he splits the spoil three ways, one to you, one to the elders of Judah, one for his own people. Rumor says that from the beginning until now, David has made every change of fortune serve his own ambition. Rumor says when David is stronger he will march against Gath, coming up behind us when we go into battle in Ephraim or Benjamin. Rumor says he will destroy us, and then make his peace with Saul."

"Rumor!" Achish wiped away with his sleeve the spittle which had dribbled onto his chin while Ittai spoke. "Lies, rather. You invent them, because you want to see me dead at your feet. You come to me after a heavy meal with lies to destroy me. You—you—"

Achish would have fallen if Ittai had not caught him. Ittai eased the king's heavy body back onto the pigskin couch and summoned a servant who brought a basin of water. Then, while he continued speaking, Ittai bathed the king's face with a damp cloth.

"Forgive me, my lord Achish," said Ittai gently. "It is necessary to speak plainly of David, and to decide what must be done. Daily he grows stronger. Men flock to him, not only from Judah but from the northern tribes as well. Last week a company of Saul's own archers deserted and marched to Ziklag and placed themselves under David's command. This must mean that Israel loves David. Israel is not David's enemy.

"Up to now David has refused to teach his men methods of plains warfare. He does not use chariots or camels when he goes to battle, but fights still in ways suited to mountain warfare. This surely means that David does not expect to remain in the plain, but will return presently to the hills.

"It is said that David takes much spoil from the desert peoples and the farmers of the Negeb, and that the people of Judah grow fat since they no longer fear our raids but are enriched by David's gifts. I tell you this, my lord Achish. Five years ago David fled alone from Saul, in peril of his life. A year ago he marched to Ziklag, leading six companies. Today he commands twelve companies, with more men coming every month. Soon he will command more men than are in the armies of Gath. The very rivers flow toward David, turning in their courses whenever he moves across the land."

Tears flowed unchecked from the king's eyes. "David's god is too great for us. We must get rid of David, as we got rid of the box he adores. We must dispose of him before he comes upon us to overwhelm and destroy us."

Ittai rose and paced the floor. "You are right, my lord. David serves us, but he also serves himself, and our enemies. Yet it is said that his strength lies in the fact that he has never yet shed the blood of a single Israelite. Because this is true, his god loves him and strengthens him continually. With David it is as it was with Samson, whose strength lay in his uncut hair. Well, we cropped Samson's hair, and he became weak. We must force David to shed Hebrew blood with his own hand, and he will then lose his power and be as other men. Once his hands have shed Hebrew blood, his god will forsake him, and he will be your servant forever."

"You are my right arm, Ittai," said Achish gratefully. "Tell me how we are to do this."

"We will make war on Saul. We will gather the armies of the five cities and gather also every man of David's twelve companies. They will fight as your own bodyguard, and with your own eyes you will see and know that they fight for us, against Israel."

Peace flowed through Achish. He would sleep now, and rise ready to make war or do any great thing which the times demanded of him. "Make the arrangements," he murmured. "Send messengers to the cities and to David. You are my right hand, Ittai, my good friend, my sword. Make the arrangements." And Achish sank back on the pigskin couch and closed his eyes.

13

THE WALLS OF Gath were old and gray, damp with moss and splotched with patches of newly mortared fieldstone where sections had crumbled away and been repaired. In the shadow of the walls, two armies converged. At the order of Achish, David had marched from Ziklag, bringing every man of his twelve companies. David's men were camped south of the wall. Now that day had dawned they were covering campfires, buckling on breastplates, securing greaves, tightening girdles, bustling and rattling about in preparation for the day's march to Ekron. There they, with the army of Gath, would join the armies of the other four Philistine cities.

The iron chariot of Achish rumbled through the eastern gate soon after dawn. This was the largest and heaviest chariot to be found in the plain. It held, besides Achish himself and the driver, two others, each armed with both javelin and sword. Achish stood vast and gleaming in his brazen armor. Early though it was, sweat was already running down inside the heavy helmet. His shield rested on the floor of the chariot between his great braced legs. His sword hung on his hip. His sleeves were wet with sweat. Achish wished he could forget the whole disagreeable enterprise, leave it to Ittai.

Well, Achish comforted himself, this one last time he would march. After this campaign he could safely leave fighting to David and to Ittai, for after this campaign he would have David utterly under his thumb.

The driver halted his chariot at the junction of the two armies. Achish inspected the Philistine forces proudly. On his left were the chariots with their drivers and javelin throwers. The helmets of the men, the harness of the horses, and the polished tips of the javelins gleamed in the morning sun.

Beyond the chariots, drawn up in close formation, were the bowmen. Great bows and quivers of arrows hung on their backs. Their shields were small and light, attached directly to the body, leaving the arms free for the use of their weapons. On their hips hung the short, sheathed swords which would serve them in hand-to-hand fighting.

The swordsmen were chosen for strength of arm and fleetness of foot.

Their shields were slung over their shoulders during the march, but in battle would be strapped to the left wrist.

Achish looked them over with pride in the brightness of their metal, pride in their vigor and aggressive eagerness. These were men who lived fully only in the hour of battle, men who had grown weary of idleness and were eager to march, to kill, to pillage. These were the men of Achish, king of Gath. Achish gazed on them proudly while he waited for the messenger he had sent to fetch David of Judah.

David had not been summoned to last night's council of captains. David would receive his orders this morning.

David arrived promptly, trotting forward from among his men, quick and eager as though no weight of armor hung upon him. His manner with Achish was respectful. His blue eyes met those of the king of Gath, guileless, submissive. This was a servant it was worth a man's time to subdue, thought Achish with pleasure. That David was subdued who could doubt?—seeing the look of sleepless exhaustion which hovered behind the bright blue of the eyes and the taut lines of his mouth. This was a man, thought Achish with a stir of pity, whose god had chosen him for some high destiny and had then left him to the mercy of Achish. Dagon had defeated the god of the gold-crusted box, or at any rate would have done so by the end of this campaign.

Achish said kindly, "We march together at last, friend David." No use reminding the young fellow that he was no more than a servant to the men of Gath. His eyes noted the ruddy color under the weathered brown of David's cheeks and the curling, copper-bright beard. No wonder the women loved this fellow. He was of a remarkably handsome appearance.

"You shall be my bodyguard, David," he said. A clever thought, that had been. He'd observe the fellow's every move. There would be no tricks out of David in this campaign.

David bowed. "You shall know at last, my lord Achish, what your servant can do in battle."

From somewhere in David's companies a voice rose, high and clear, shouting a line of song Achish had heard spoken of but had never before heard sung. From nearer at hand a deeper voice answered, singing the second line of the refrain:

> Saul has slain his thousands
> And David his ten thousands.

A prickle of fear ran along the king's nerves. "Your men must not sing that song, seeing it speaks of the slaying of Philistines!"

David smiled ruefully. "I have forbidden the song. But the authority of a leader in exile is not all it ought to be. The men like the song. When they march against Saul it gives them courage. However—when they know it is displeasing to the king of Gath—"

"If it is heard again, I'll have the singers dragged from my chariot wheels!" Achish was shouting, ashamed of his anger but more ashamed of his fear. Before his mind's eye rose a picture of a ruddy-faced, beardless stripling casting a stone straight and true through the visor of Goliath's helmet.

David smiled. "You can understand that I hate the song as much as anyone, my lord. The song made me an outcast in my own land."

Achish was ashamed of his anger and fear before this candid young man. His voice was strong and steady, the voice of command. "Your archers will march and fight with my archers," said Achish. "Ittai will dispose them. Give me a hundred men skilled with the javelin to include among those who fight in chariots of war."

David nodded. "As you wish, my lord, although my men are not trained to cast the javelin from a moving vehicle. You may find them more useful on foot."

"We'll use them in chariots as needed," Achish said shortly. "They can practice throwing from moving chariots when we camp tonight."

David bowed. "As you wish, my lord."

Ittai whirled up in a cloud of dust. "Shall we move, my lord? The men are waiting."

Achish found himself strangely loth to part from David, restless in the feeling that much lay unsaid between the young captain and himself. "We will meet the others at Ekron," he said. "From Ekron we march north along the caravan route. When we reach Dothan we move east through the pass into the Plain of Jezrul. Somewhere beyond Dothan we will encounter Saul. After we defeat Saul we will pass on to the Arabah, cross the Jordan and take the cities of Gilead."

"My compliments, my lord. You Philistines have never before attacked us on so ambitious a scale."

Achish ignored the "us." "Our spies report that Saul is distraught. He has been deserted by hundreds of his men and also by his god. He turns to witches, but all predict failure and death. We shall win this campaign and henceforth draw tribute from all this land."

David bowed. "I have heard the stories of Saul and the witches. Saul expects to die in this campaign. He is defeated before he marches. Yet he marches, my lord."

Ittai said restlessly, "Shall we go, my lord?"

From the ranks the song rose, moving from this company to that, swelling in volume and receding. Achish shouted, "If the song is heard again, Hebrews will travel to Ekron chained to my chariot!" It was an empty threat. Not even brutality yielded Achish pleasure these days.

"I will stop the song if I can, my lord." David trotted back to his men, his brazen helmet on his arm, his copper hair gleaming in the sun.

West and north to Ekron moved the river of men. At Ekron the river became a tide, flowing north along the plain, out of the Shephelah into the Plain of Sharon, north toward Dothan and the mountains that clustered at the broad base of Mount Carmel. On the right rose the green hills of Canaan. On the left the blue waters of the Great Sea rolled endlessly in white froth against the shore.

The earth of this road had echoed for fifty centuries to the rhythmic beat of marching boots, marching sandals, and the tread of strong bare feet. Over it flowed the tide of invasion from three continents, for it was the land bridge binding a hemisphere. Over it now flowed the army of the five cities of Philistia, augmented by David's twelve companies. As ripples in a pool spread from a stone dropping, so whispers rayed out through the Philistine ranks before and behind and on either side of the marching Hebrews. Now and then, among the archers or among the javelin throwers, a song arose to be quickly hushed.

The army reached the narrow Dothan valley, where the road turned east to enter the Jezrul Plain, which pointed like a great, blunt thumb toward the vast ditch of the Arabah. In the Valley of Jezrul the army spread its camp.

Among the tents that night, as among the marchers during the day, uneasy whispers circled. "This is David, the man of Judah who killed Goliath of Gath with sling and stone."

"This is the shepherd who was once armor-bearer to Saul."

"This is the dearest friend of Saul's son Jonathan, who panicked our garrison one night at Michmash."

"This is David, who presented Saul with the foreskins of two hundred Philistines as dowry when he married Saul's daughter, Michal."

"This is David, whose tattered outlaws defeated us at Keilah."

"This is the shepherd of whom the women of Israel sang:

> Saul has slain his thousands
> And David his ten thousands."

Before midnight the kings of Gaza, Ashkelon, Ashdod and Ekron came in a body to the tent of Achish.

"Our archers are restless," said the king of Ekron. "They ask continually, 'What are these Hebrews doing in our company?'"

Achish spread his hands and smiled, though he was dead for sleep. "Is not this David, who has been with me now for more than a year?"

The king of Ekron replied angrily, "Is not this David who gave the foreskins of two hundred Philistines as dowry for Saul's daughter?"

Achish shrugged. "Who can say whether they were Philistines? All I

[73]

know is, he deserted to me from Saul. He has been a good servant. In all this time I have found no fault in him. He sends me tribute and holds back my enemies. He also holds back your enemies, my friends. All Philistia has been safe this past year from desert invaders."

The king of Gaza said, "That is true. We have had no trouble with Amalekites for more than a year."

The king of Ekron said, "Fighting Amalekites is different. How could this fellow better make peace with Saul than to attack us from within during the battle, and go to Saul bringing the heads of the five kings?"

Achish still smiled, though along his nerves prickled the fear of Israel's god. Surely that god was seeking now to save David from the shedding of Hebrew blood. Yet how could such a god guide the thoughts of these kings of the plain?

"David is quite a fellow," said Achish, smiling to hide his fear. "But he is hardly warrior enough to strike off the heads of the five kings in the midst of their bodyguards. Shall I call him here that you may look on him and see that he is only a man and no demon?"

The king of Ekron stood before Achish, arms folded, legs braced, black brows frowning. "You will fight this battle without these Hebrews, or you will fight it without the kings of Gaza, Ashdod, Ashkelon and Ekron. We are agreed on that."

"I will summon David," Achish replied.

"We have summoned him. He is outside the tent."

Achish stared about from one to another of his four friends. "You are four. I am one. I cannot stand against you." He raised his voice. "David. Come here."

David entered the tent. He was younger than any of the five kings, and of smaller stature, a lone Hebrew among the Philistine kings. Yet his blue eyes met the eyes of Achish without fear, open, submissive, trusting. "My lord Achish," he said, and bowed his head.

Achish felt trembling all along his limbs. In his mind he seemed to see Dagon, headless and handless, lying on the earth before a gold-crusted box. "You have been a true servant to me, friend David," he said loudly. "I have found no fault in you since you came to Ziklag to fight my enemies. However, these friends of mine, kings of Ekron, Gaza, Ashkelon and Ashdod, do not trust you as I trust you. They prefer to fight this campaign without your help. Don't be angry with them. They do not know you as I know you. They know only your mighty reputation."

David's gaze held nothing but obedience and friendliness, yet the lines around his eyes vanished as suddenly as if washed out with water. David said quietly, "What fault have you found against me, that I may not go to fight the enemies of my lord of Gath?"

"You are blameless, David. The fault lies with my friends here, who see evil where no evil exists." The fault lay rather in a box overlaid with gold. But Achish could not now or ever speak such blasphemy openly against Dagon.

David bowed. "What is your wish, my lord?"

"Rise early in the morning with your men. Start with the first light. Return the way you came. Take care that your men do not inflame these kings or the men who serve them, particularly in the matter of the song. Go to Ziklag. I will summon you when the campaign is ended and I am once more at Gath."

Ittai stood with Achish next morning and watched the last of the Hebrews march west toward Dothan. Ittai pushed up his helmet and scratched his head.

"There goes our Samson," said Ittai thoughtfully, "still wearing his hair."

Achish tried to shrug off the burden of defeat which had lain heavily on him all the long hours of the night. "We will attend to David another time. Today we must attend to Saul." Attending to Saul would be easy. The god of the box was not with Saul in the mountains. The god of the box was traveling with David south through the Philistine plain.

Ittai smiled. "Has it occurred to you, old friend, that we may be fighting David's battle today, even more than our own?"

Achish said irritably, "I am a simple man, yet you persist in your subtleties and riddles. Go and see to the marching orders. The day will be gone before we are ready!"

For some time after Ittai went away, Achish still stood beside his iron chariot and gazed after the cloud of dust which marked the departing Hebrews.

I wonder, thought Achish wearily, who started the rumors, the tales, the songs, which have set on edge the teeth of my friends the kings of Ekron, Gaza, Ashdod and Ashkelon?

14

A BATTLE MAY end in a day or two, but the aftermath of victory takes many days. There is the business of torturing the wounded, of dishonoring and despoiling the dead, of pursuing a demoralized enemy and looting and raping in the undefended cities. The armies of Achish had this to do both in the mountains of Canaan and in the plain of Gilead beyond the Jordan. There was also the business of gathering trophies to be brought to Dagon. There was the business of hanging the dead body of Saul upon the wall of a mountain town called Bethshan, and of hanging the bodies of his three dead sons on the same wall.

So more than a month had passed before the triumphant soldiers returned along the caravan route. Behind them they left garrisons to occupy the major towns and enforce the tribute. Behind them also they left the stench of uncounted dead. But the armor and regalia of Saul they carried with them, leaving a trophy from it in shrine after shrine in every city of the plain.

The returning men were laden with spoil, and their wagons and donkeys were laden as well. The men marched in triumph, and as they marched they sang a song.

> "Saul has slain his thousands
> And we have slain Saul
> And three of the sons of Saul."

The song brought no pleasure to Achish. The long ordeal of butchery had brought no pleasure. The campaign had left only exhaustion and a longing for home and a chance to rest on a padded pigskin couch. How can a man take pleasure in dismembering a people whose god has forsaken them? What pleasure would Dagon take in the armor of Saul?

So weary was Achish with his own thoughts that he sent for Ittai to make the journey from Ekron to Gath in his own chariot. Yet there was no pleasure in the company of Ittai, for Ittai wore the ironic smile which bewildered Achish, and spoke little of victory and much of David.

"You shall love your friend and hate your enemy," said Ittai, among other things. "Who now do you suppose is David's enemy?"

"I am a simple man," Achish said wearily. "Why do you plague me? We return from the greatest conquest in Philistine history. Hebrews will pay us tribute forever, so we need never again trouble ourselves with raids or petty forays. We are masters of the whole land, and David cannot afford to be anything but friendly toward us."

Ittai said, shouting to be heard above the rumble of chariots and the singing of soldiers, "While I was in the camp of David I heard many tales told by the priest, Abiathar, who had read the ancient records written by scholars among his people."

"What is this of reading and writing? What has that to do with our victory?"

"Would you not like to know, my lord Achish, that your children's children would be able to read of this great victory we have won?"

"My children's children will win their own victories." Yet in the tired mind of Achish the thought of his children's children reading with pride of the victories of King Achish held a certain beauty. To speak face to face with men of the past, with men of the future—even an old man, weary of war and of feasting and of women, could take pleasure in such matters. To commune with one's father's fathers, with one's children's children— this could give a man pleasure no matter how tired he had become. And to think that David, in exile, should have a resource so wondrous!

"I will send for this Abiathar," he said. "I will compel him to write of our victory, to tell the number of the slain, the number of the cities, the value of the loot."

"What would be the good? He does not write in our tongue. We would never know whether he wrote what we told him to write. Even if he did, our children's children could not read the tongue of the people we have conquered."

A long silence fell in the chariot of King Achish.

Presently Ittai said, "This priest tells a tale concerning the former adventures of his people which one does not easily forget. It seems that the Hebrews were formerly slaves in Egypt. But a mighty man came, a favorite of their god, Moses by name. Moses performed such magic before the Pharaoh that as a boon he was permitted to lead his race of slaves into the wilderness to sacrifice to their god.

"But the time allotted for sacrifice went by, and the slaves did not return, and Pharaoh sent his army to bring them back by force. Yet Moses did not yield, but led his rabble straight on until they came to the sea. And he led his people straight on into the sea and it parted to let them go through; but when the Egyptian army followed them, the sea came together and destroyed men, horses, and chariots. Is it not a wonderful tale?"

Achish said, "All people have their tales of gods and heroes."

"But not all people write down the tales, so they cannot be forgotten. I tell you, my lord Achish, in future times people will know of Goliath of Gath because of his death at the hand of David, not because of what he wrought in his lifetime. People will know of Achish of Gath because he befriended David when Saul panted against him. And people will know of this victory of ours because we destroyed Saul and set David free to return to his own land. All this comes to pass because David has a scholar, but the Philistines have no scholars."

Anger churned in Achish, together with the bitter taste of dust on the lips and the itch of flesh too long confined in armor. He shouted, "Be silent. Leave me. I will hear no more insolence about my servant David."

"As you wish, my lord Achish. Will you permit me to return to my chariot?" The ironic smile still remained on the mouth in its frame of silken beard.

"You will remain. But you will be silent. You will trouble me no more with talk I do not wish to hear. The king of the Hebrews is dead, and we have garrisons in the Hebrew cities. When I am at home, and have rested from the rigors of the campaign, I will bring David to Gath and destroy him and be done with him forever."

Outside the walls of Gath a small company of David's men were camped. They had penned up a few score sheep and had hobbled a score of camels. Beside the wall lay piles of tents and rugs and blankets.

One of the men came up to the chariot of Achish, bobbing up and down in an excess of humility which irritated Achish because he saw in it some of the irony he had seen too often lately in the face of Ittai.

Ittai said, "This man is Ira, who has charge of the distribution of spoils taken in battle and of goods given in tribute."

Ira raised his face. His heavy eyes were slits as he gazed into the glare of the king's armor and regalia. "Hail, O King Achish, and congratulations on your mighty victory, from David, my master."

"Thank you," said Achish.

"We too," Ira said humbly, "have won a small victory in your absence. David sends these few gifts in token of friendship for the king and people of Gath."

"David sends spoils so soon?"

"Aye, my lord Achish. A minor skirmish with Amalekites in the desert while you were winning great victories in the hills."

"David does well. He lost no time."

"He was obliged to lose no time, my lord. When we reached Ziklag after our march north with my lords of the plain, we found our city burned and our women and little ones stolen. We had marched north with every man, leaving Ziklag unguarded with disastrous results. However, we pursued the raiders, and found them feasting in their camp. We smote them by night as they feasted. We destroyed them utterly, except for those who escaped on racing camels. We recovered also our wives and little ones and all our goods, and took some spoil besides. We share the spoil with you, my lord Achish."

Achish nodded, glancing at Ittai, pleased with this new proof of David's loyalty.

Ittai was scowling at the man. "You heard of our victory and of Saul's death?"

"Aye. A man brought word that the Philistines had conquered all Israel, and that Saul and three of his sons were dead."

Ittai said mildly, "David also is to be congratulated. His enemy is dead."

Ira bowed and said nothing.

Achish said, "Go to David, my man. Tell him to come and feast with us, that we may enjoy the fruits of our two victories together."

Ira said humbly, "My lord, I regret that it will be impossible for David to come to Gath at this time."

"I order him to come!"

[78]

Ira bowed very low. "But David is no longer in Ziklag, my lord Achish. He has gone to Hebron on urgent business."

"Business? What business is more urgent than the wishes of Achish of Gath?"

"David is being crowned king of Judah, my lord Achish. You must know, my lord, how busy a king is during the days of his anointing and the setting up of his affairs."

"David is king? In Hebron?"

"Aye, my lord Achish. My lord David, king of Judah, sends his respects to my lord Achish, king of Gath, and hopes that the change in his situation will not alter the warm affection which exists between himself and the men of Gath. My lord David sends this further word, that he will continue to garrison Ziklag and to hold off the desert enemies of his kingdom and yours."

Ira bowed once more. "Is there any message to be taken to the king of Judah from the king of Gath?"

The words burst from Achish. "Who started the rumors, the tales, the songs which ran like fire through the Philistine armies so that our soldiers refused to march against Saul with David among them?"

For a moment the humility in Ira's face was splintered by amusement. "Who could do such a thing, my lord? Surely you have heard idle gossip or perhaps lies of soldiers who . . ."

"I have heard no Philistine lies. I have been cheated and lied to by David, who came to me with every show of submission and friendship, then went his way to serve his own interests at my expense!" Achish had said more than he meant to say. He had admitted here in the presence of Ittai that David had outwitted him. He swallowed past the smothering sensations in his chest.

Ira said softly, "David did not lie to you. He served you faithfully, my lord Achish. I did not hear the rumors you speak of, but I did hear the song, and I heard David silencing the singers. Yet if the song helped to save David from the need to shed the blood of his people, then it is possible that the God of David put it into the hearts of the soldiers to sing the song for David's sake. I am only guessing, my lord, for I march not with the soldiers but with the donkey trains."

Achish spoke a sharp word to his driver, and the chariot whirled abruptly through the gate.

But late that night, when the victory parade was concluded and the shouts of the people were subsiding into the sounds of feasting, Ittai found Achish in the anteroom, resting on the pigskin couch.

Ittai sat on the rug. His eyes held affection, regret, and also a certain determination. "I have come to bid you good-by, old friend," said Ittai.

"Good-by?"

"I go in search of immortality."

"I am a simple man, friend Ittai. Speak simply to me."

"I am a man who has only one life to live, old friend. I want to spend my life serving the one great man I have known. Above all, I want to make sure that this scholar and priest finds a place in his records to write down the name of Ittai the Philistine, who became a servant to David."

"Ittai! You are my right arm. You are my sword. How can I rule Gath without you? I beg you not to leave me, Ittai."

"I go, old friend. Let us trust that my lord David never chooses to send me against the men of Gath, but that I can use what small talents I have to ensure continued friendship between David and Achish."

"I will have you seized before you pass the gate. I will have you cut to pieces and hung on the wall." The threat had a strong sound, but there was only weakness in the voice. Achish lay on his couch, a tired, defeated man.

Ittai said kindly, "It will be worth your while to have a friend in David's court."

"Go then," said Achish brokenly. "Go quickly. Do not linger, lest I find the strength to send after you."

Ittai was gone. And Achish lay alone on his couch, and touched with his swollen fingers the cracked places where the leather had grown brittle. Tears rolled down into his beard, but he did not summon his servants, either to comfort him or to seize and torture Ittai.

All rivers, murmured Achish with a deep sigh, turn in their courses to follow David as he moves across the land. The tears rolled from under his lids, and dropped onto the pigskin in great dark splotches.

PART THREE

Hebron

15

JOAB RETURNED TO Bethlehem in the month Tishri, when the winds change round from the eastern deserts to the western sea, bringing the rains. Along the roadside wild pomegranates hung brown and ripe upon their bushes, and beside the courtyard at home the last of the mulberries had been gathered to make into wine. And Joab led the sheep south and east, down into the Arabah where winter came late. He built himself a booth of poles and tent-cloth and brush, within it found shelter for his fire.

When winter reached the Arabah he returned with the sheep to Bethlehem and sheltered them in sheds whose roofs of thatch sifted out most of the rain.

Spring came, and the grain fields and pastures were delicately green, and the winds shifted round once more, blowing off the desert. The streams and cisterns were filled and all over the wilderness flowers bloomed in a riot of color. Then the sheep were sheared, after they had borne their lambs.

And summer came, bringing harvest. Early grapes were gathered and made into wine, or laid upon the roof in the sun to make raisins. Summer passed, emptying streams and cisterns and baking the earth and the grass. And Joab learned that tragedy lies, not in moments of crisis, but in the long procession of nights which make up the cycle of the years.

On the night when Reba married David, Joab had glutted himself with wine and had slept at last. But hundreds of nights came thereafter, when he lay beside the fold living out his endless loneliness, tasting the bitterness of longing and jealousy. While the nights came, one by one, the down on Joab's cheeks turned into the crisp, sandy beard of a man.

All through the lonely months, as he led the sheep or lay on the earth while they grazed, he remembered words spoken by Ira and Abiathar and Uriah, words which cut through barriers that had hemmed him round. His horizon had broadened in the wilderness, and now the hills of Judah set limits which were too narrow for his spirit and restlessness often took hold of him; yet he did not know that he was restless for more than the love he had lost.

Another spring came, and in Bethlehem it was known that the kings of the five cities of the Philistine plain had defeated Saul's army on Mount Gilboa. Saul was dead, and David reigned in Hebron.

Jesse the patriarch died in Moab while David lived in Ziklag. The sons of Jesse came home from the purple hills, bringing the body of their father. They buried him in the Bethlehem sepulchre with his father Obed and his grandfather Boaz, and his grandmother Ruth the Moabitess. Here also lay the bones of Zeruiah's husband, a man with yellow hair who had wandered in from the distant north, remained long enough to beget Seth and Joab and Asa, then died of a fever.

After Saul fought his last battle against the federated cities of the plain, and was killed, hard times came to Israel. Every village and city paid tribute to the victorious Philistines. Philistine garrisons remained through all the northern and trans-Jordan tribes to enforce the tribute. Judah, however, was not occupied. David was king in Hebron. Through friendship with Achish, David was able to prevent the occupation of Judah, and by raids on desert peoples he was able to raise most of the tribute demanded by the five Philistine kings.

News that David was in Hebron came to Bethlehem by messenger within a week of the news of Saul's death. Messengers were running through all the towns and villages of Judah, summoning the elders from Bethlehem to Beersheba to go to Hebron for the ceremony which would make David king of the one tribe. Young Asa, who was swift as a gazelle, set out for Moab that same day to carry the news to the sons of Jesse.

Asa was seventeen when David became king in Hebron. Feeling himself a man, he clamored to offer himself to David, and Zeruiah, with the stone house she ruled once more overflowing with the sons and grandsons of Jesse, their wives and little ones and servants, sent him to Hebron willingly. Zeruiah was greatly impressed with David's altered circumstances. She began to tell again the story of David's anointing by Samuel, and to trace the strange pattern of his rising and falling and his rising again as a portent of greater glory ahead.

"David is like a wind blowing over the land," Zeruiah often declared. "He stirs us all from the petty daily round of duties to thoughts of glory. Go, my sons, and serve David. We suffered his disgrace. Let us have a part in his ascending destiny."

The elders blessed Asa, and he set out with a bedroll strapped to his back and a skin of wine on his shoulder to offer his swift young strength to David. He was made a runner. He stopped often at Bethlehem as he went and as he returned. Whenever Asa appeared the family sat long in the courtyard after the evening meal to listen far into the night to the tales Asa told of all that went on in Hebron.

Asa's first errand for David was to carry a message of conciliation to the elders of the town of Jabesh-Gilead. Gilead was a high land of green pastures and oak forests east of the Jordan where the tribes of Reuben, Gad, and Manasseh had settled when the other tribes crossed over to live in the hills of Canaan.

The men of Jabesh-Gilead had marched to Bethshan by night after the disaster of Saul's death to take down the headless, naked bodies of Saul and his sons from the wall of the city. They brought the dishonored corpses home to Jabesh and gave them ceremonial burial under an ancient oak. Then they fasted and mourned for seven days. Fifteen miles from Jabesh, in the strong walled city of Mahanaim, Abner and Ishbosheth, the only surviving son of Saul, had found refuge. To the men of Jabesh David sent Asa with a message of friendship designed to heal the breach in Israel.

Obed the Reubenite went with Asa on this errand. Obed was young, though not so young as Asa. He possessed swiftness of foot and the silver tongue of a royal messenger. Obed had been with David since he was a child and could offer his experience as a counterpoise to Asa's impetuosity. Further, Obed was a Reubenite whose relatives in Gilead might provide shelter for the king's messengers in case of trouble with adherents of Abner and Ishbosheth.

The two boys were dressed as Joab had seen no men of David's dressed before. They wore woolen cloaks girded for running, but carried in their bedrolls long linen cloaks which they would wear when they presented themselves before the elders in Jabesh. They wore scarlet girdles and on their heads they had bound scarlet headcloths.

They reached Bethlehem in the late afternoon to spend the night. They would rise well before dawn to make the long run to Jabesh the following day. After the evening meal Asa prowled about the court, restless with the gravity of his errand. The firelight and the torchlight played upon his sober face. "Who could guess," said Asa in wonder, "that David would seek the friendship of these people, after all they've done to him? He could easily defeat and destroy them now, for they are prostrate. David is friend of the king of Gath. He commands hundreds of deserters from the north, plus all the twelve companies he brought back from the Philistine exile."

Zeruiah exclaimed, "How does he feed them all?"

Asa shrugged. "The gifts from Judah have been abundant, since David is keeping Philistines, Edomites and Amalekites off the land. The raids on the desert people go on. And of course David owns property south of Hebron. He has an officer who manages it all very well for him."

Asa's young voice grew sweet and full, as David's had been at seventeen. "Listen," said Asa. Half closing his eyes, and chanting in solemn dignity, Asa spoke the words David had given him to speak to the elders of Jabesh, rehearsing them to impress his family and also to improve his delivery when he reached the city where he was to represent David.

"Blessed are you of the Lord, because you have shown this kindness to

Saul, and have given him holy burial. May the Lord show kindness to you. I will show you kindness also. Let your hands be strong and valiant, for Saul your king is dead, and the men of Judah have made me king over them."

Asa opened his eyes, smiling on his assembled kindred.

Zeruiah's eyes flashed admiringly. "Well, now, David is a true statesman, and perhaps he will not go through life making enemies in high places as he did in his youth. Still, who can see the ripe fruit when the bud is on the bough?"

Obed said soberly, "I doubt that David turns the men of Jabesh from Abner to himself. Of all towns, Jabesh has most reason to love Saul and to honor and protect Saul's son. The story is often told in Gilead. This town of Jabesh was the first which Saul delivered from their enemies. The men of Rabbah-Ammon attacked Jabesh, and besieged the town. If they had taken it they would have gouged out the right eye of every man, but Saul raised an army and marched to Jabesh and destroyed the army of the Ammonites."

But Zeruiah would not hear doubts spoken by an outsider. "So much the wiser then," she said firmly, "is David to direct his first act of conciliation to Jabesh. If only he could offer proof of his good intentions."

Asa smiled down on his mother. Her spirit and determination far outweighed her meager stature. "I have not given all the message," he told her reassuringly. "There is a song I am to sing for David beside the oak tree where Saul is buried. David first sang the song when he learned that Saul and Jonathan were dead."

Asa closed his eyes and lifted his face. His voice was sweet and true, as David's had been when he sang in this same courtyard.

"The beauty of Israel is slain upon the high places.
   How are the mighty fallen!
Tell it not in Gath, publish it not in the streets of Ashkelon;
      lest the daughters of the Philistines rejoice,
      lest the daughters of the uncircumcised triumph.
From the blood of the slain, from the fat of the mighty,
      the bow of Jonathan turned not back,
      and the sword of Saul returned not empty.

Saul and Jonathan were lovely and pleasant in their lives
      and in their death they were not divided;
   They were swifter than eagles,
      they were stronger than lions.
Ye daughters of Israel, weep over Saul!
How are the mighty fallen in the midst of the battle!

I am distressed for thee, my brother Jonathan;
      very pleasant hast thou been unto me;

[84]

Thy love was wonderful, passing the love of women.
How are the mighty fallen,
      and the weapons of war perished!"

Zeruiah's eyes were wet as she embraced Asa. "It is a good song, show-
ing in its beauty better than many spoken words the unity of Israel against
the uncircumcised. And your singing enhances its beauty."

Obed said, "We are to speak in every quarter of David's grief for Saul's
death, and of David's great love for Jonathan. We are to remind the elders
that David spared Saul more than once in the wilderness. We are to remind them that David has never shed Israelite blood."

Joab had listened in silence till now. He asked, suppressing with difficulty
the bitter jealousy he felt, "And what will you say when they mention that
David was serving Achish at the very time when the men of Gath killed
Saul and Jonathan?"

Asa smiled serenely. "David was not in Gath at the time, nor in the
plain. He was in the desert, chasing Amalekites. And nobody hates
Amalekites more than the people of Israel. They were our first enemies.
Abiathar has told me how they attacked our people when they first appeared in the desert after crossing the Red Sea. While our people made
the tedious journey through the desert, all unprepared as they were, without knowledge of war or reserves of food and water, fed on heavenly
manna and little else, the Amalekites skulked along for days and weeks,
torturing stragglers and raping women who fell behind the main body."

Joab hid the smile which rose when he heard these brutal words fall
so innocently from young Asa.

"Joshua organized a company of soldiers," Asa said earnestly. "Our
people knew only slavery. Yet they fought the Amalekites at last, while
Moses stood upon a hill the whole day with his arms upraised. When his
arms were weary, Aaron his brother and Hur his brother-in-law held up
his arms so the people could see that he did not falter. And the Amalekites
were destroyed. Those that did not die fled, though we were but rabble
while they were seasoned desert fighters. And these are the enemies David pursued while Achish marched against Saul."

Zeruiah said proudly, "You are a true envoy for David. May God bring
you success."

Obed said, as though he hoped to win for himself some measure of
Zeruiah's approval, "We will also tell how a young man came to David,
boasting that he was the one who killed Saul on Mount Gilboa, and ex-
hibiting bits of Saul's regalia which he had stolen to prove his story. He
expected David to reward him. But David had the man put to death, and
left his flesh to rot in the sun beside the burned and broken walls of
Ziklag."

[85]

Asa cried, "We will also tell how Achish ordered David to march against Saul, and of the strategems by which fear and doubt were planted in the minds of the Philistines, so that the kings of the other cities refused to proceed further until David had been ordered back south. David's wisdom in that affair was something marvelous, I can tell you. And we will talk of it in every quarter in Jabesh."

Suddenly the tide of talk about David's wisdom, magnanimity, and loving kindness was too much for Joab. He rose and left the house. He went to the pasture and sat with his back against the fold. He stared at the stars, and thought of David, who was a king, and of Reba, who lived in a king's harem and who had borne David's first-born son, and had called him Amnon.

She knew what she was doing, he thought bitterly, when she chose David over me. And yet under the bitterness he knew full well Reba had not chosen David. He sat there through the night, sometimes cursing, sometimes weeping, and within him the question grew and grew. David, David, you are the greatest of all. Why did you rob me of my only love?

16

THE GILEADITES RECEIVED Asa and Obed coldly. They returned to David no messages of friendship. Months later the two runners returned northwest, circling Gilead, to arrange a marriage between David and the daughter of the king of the Syrian city of Geshur. The girl, whose name was Maacah, was a strapping, swarthy lass of fifteen. Thus the land of Gilead and the northern provinces of Israel were protected from enemies to the north and east, since the king of Geshur was now David's ally. And so David strengthened his position and influence, protecting even the tribes which refused him friendship.

In the northern provinces the people suffered much deprivation from the occupying Philistines, while Abner and Ishbosheth skulked in Gilead. But in Hebron, David as king and judge was maintaining friendship with the Philistines, paying the tribute with spoil. So David and Judah grew stronger year by year, while in the north the tribes had no rest from the constant draining away of their resources.

"I feel the hot breath of the Lord upon my cheek," Abiathar had said, when David returned without bloodshed from his march against Nabal. And Zeruiah often said, "There is a wind blowing over the land, and the wind is David."

Whoever gets in David's way might as well throw himself under one of the Philistine chariots of war, Joab would reflect. Pride in David was never absent from his thoughts, as he wrestled with anger and resentment and loneliness.

Joab knew nothing of war, except at second hand. For a summer he had been a messenger for David and assistant to Ira. He had been a shepherd since the age of nine; the years went by and he remained a shepherd in spite of Zeruiah's frequent hints that now there was sufficient help about the place, in case he wanted to return to David's service. There were many nights when he hungered for savage destruction, remembering the godlike power he had felt in the moment when he plunged the knife into Lem's yielding flesh. He yearned to use his throbbing energies in struggle, not against a mean enemy, but against Israel's enemies. Love of Reba had opened his heart to a growing sense of family, of tribe, of nation. Again and again he rehearsed his plan to take Jerusalem, until he was sick with the frustration of knowing how easily it could be done if only he could persuade David.

Everyone loves David, he thought, except for those who envy him. Abner was one of those. Am I also one of those, he wondered? There were nights when he remembered only that he loved David and admired him. He recalled the songs David used to sing in the pastures, or sitting high in the sycamine tree above the court of the house in Bethlehem. He remembered how carefully David had taught him how to use knife and sling, how to kill with a single thrust the beasts which came prowling up from the wilderness.

There were many nights when Joab thought only of Reba, wondering whether life in David's harem suited her. And there were nights when he thought of Abiathar and Ira and Abigail and longed to see these friends. Yet he could not bring himself to come within reach of David or chance again the wounds a great man can casually inflict upon those dependent on his care and goodwill.

Then the choice was made for him. The Moabite wife of Eliab, eldest son of Jesse, had brought to Bethlehem a sister called Lisha. Lisha was only a child when she first came to Bethlehem, but the years changed that. Lisha had become a plump, vigorous young girl with hot dark eyes and a habit of wriggling and squealing whenever a male was about. Lisha helped in the house, grinding the barley and wheat, sweeping the stone paving, crushing olives to extract their oil and grapes to extract their wine. On the slightest excuse she was capable of girding her skirts to scandalous heights on her plump legs. It was thus that she went into the fields to carry messages or packets of food to the shepherds. When she was twelve any man would do as the object of her gigglings, but by the time she was fourteen she had singled out Joab.

She made excuses to come when he was with the sheep, and to linger into the night until he drove her away. She was careless with her garments, throwing herself onto the grass so her cloak fell away to reveal more than a man might wish to see. She loved to kick off her sandals and wade into the stream, folding her skirts about her hips and squealing about the coldness of the water or the slipperiness of the stones. She was never still and every movement served to remind a man of all that is lusty in a girl.

The hunger Lisha roused in Joab was no more like the love he had felt for Reba than the desert's parching summer wind is like the winter breeze which blows in from the sea. I despise her, Joab told himself, even while he could not forget the curve of her thigh or the pressure of her plump breasts as she threw herself against him when a lizard scuttled over her bare foot.

She measures men, Joab would tell himself, as if she were choosing merchandise in a bazaar. He had seen her kind in Hebron. He felt a certain compassion for her, remembering the energy with which she did her work. Lisha was not a bad girl, not yet. She was the victim of her own strong vitality. And Joab remembered Benaiah, in whom good and evil were tangled beyond separation. There were times when Joab hungered to take this girl and tame her and give her children on whom she could lavish her love-hunger. Yet he thought of the emptiness of her chatter and had no wish to be bound to her for a lifetime. He knew that no grandson of Jesse could afford to lust after the sister-in-law of Eliab unless he was willing to make her his wife. Yet he could not deny that he lusted. When he heard her laughter in the pastures his senses leaped and when she threw herself upon him he itched to drive his fingers deep into her flesh until she shrieked with pain or pleasure, small matter which.

On a night in summer when the moon was full, Joab found himself thinking of the high places of the Caananites, and of the revels the men of Uriah's band held on nights like this. Sick of his thoughts, Joab took his sling and a handful of stones. He chose as target a stunted acacia beyond the stream and set to work to improve his skill with the weapon which had first brought fame to David.

Again and again he whirled the sling and let fly the stone. Presently he heard across the stream the beginning of the giggle he had learned to know so well. But the stone had already left the sling. The giggle changed to a scream and the figure which had appeared suddenly from over a hill fell to the earth and rolled, as Lisha's screams filled the night.

Joab leaped over the stream and ran to Lisha and pulled her head upon his knee and her hand from the wound. The blood ran over his hands, warm and thick. Yet he saw that the stone had only opened the flesh along her cheek and slit the lobe of her ear. And Joab was burning suddenly with a savage wish to hurt this girl in ways she could never forget, to give her cause for her senseless screaming. He jumped to his feet, wild with the stickiness of her blood on his hands, the warm smell of it in his nostrils.

"Go to the stream and bathe your face," he told her hoarsely.

She rose obediently. "You bathe it, Joab," she whimpered. "It burns like fire. Wash away the pain, Joab." Her girdle had fallen from her and her cloak hung open and loose and Joab saw that her tunic was torn.

Panting with the tempest of his own hunger and revulsion, Joab pushed back her cloak. He dug his fingers into her bare shoulders, and the tunic slid to reveal the full circle of one plump, soft breast. The girl burrowed against him with a wantonness beyond imagining. Her panting and whimpering brought to mind a young ewe which had lost her lamb, and of the grunting and gurgling pleasure of the ewe when the lamb was found and could suckle the distended udder again.

Remembering the ewe, filled with his own tangled emotions, Joab bent swiftly and set his mouth on the breast, and clamped his teeth together so viciously that he tasted the blood on his tongue.

Lisha did not run from him. She stood before him, sobbing with her face uncovered in the bright moonlight.

Joab spat out the blood. "You," he said, filled with loathing. "You are of the family of Jesse, yet you run sporting and squealing through the pastures, uncovering your body. I am ashamed for my family, that you are one of us."

The triumph he had felt in the moment when hatred for Lem fused into the strength of the arm, the thrust of the sword, was upon him now.

"You hurt me, Joab," Lisha sobbed. "You hurt me." Her eyes held a queer shine.

Joab picked up her cloak and wrapped it about her so he need not look on her uncovered body any longer. "You want a husband," he said through gritted teeth. "You know that only a husband of the family of Jesse can prevent your being turned out on the roads sooner or later as a harlot. You want me to take you tonight for your pleasure, but also so you can go to Zeruiah tomorrow and tell her a tale such that she would take me before the elders and marry you to me. No, thank you, my girl."

Joab turned from her and started to Bethlehem, running to the great stone house, running to Zeruiah.

"I must leave this place," he told Zeruiah through pale, tight lips. "I will kill someone of this household if I do not go where I can kill someone in battle. The lust for blood or for women or for both is so hot in me I dare not spend another night in this place."

Zeruiah stared at her reasonable, sensible son, only half comprehending his desperation, but with perhaps some understanding of its cause. She wept a little, and gathered up gifts for him to take to David. And Joab

[89]

strapped up his bundle and shouldered his hamper. She gave him her blessing. Then he set out along the highway which runs from Bethlehem to Hebron.

I 7

THE HIGHWAY FOLLOWS the central watershed of Judah in such a way that at times Joab had a glimpse of the golden wilderness on his left, and at other times he saw the green valleys which are thrust like extended fingers westward toward the Philistine plain.

Beyond the plain was the Great Sea, which was a highway for the ships of Egypt and Phoenicia and far, mysterious islands. Joab had never yet stood beside the Great Sea, though he had heard Seth tell how the soldiers of David had marched along its shore. When Joab saw the glimmering blue in the distance, he thought how it would be to leave these hills and sail over the waters to far-off lands. He thought of the bold, hardy people who made the sea their path. He had seen in the bazaars of Hebron and Jerusalem the lumber and cloth brought by Phoenician merchants, the gold and ivory and grain brought from Egypt and the hot lands of the black men beyond Egypt, the iron of Cappadocia, and the tin and copper of the Sinai desert.

As the distance from Hebron lessened and the miles lengthened which separated Joab from Bethlehem and from Lisha, Joab forgot the savage emotions of the night. His mind moved beyond the bounds of the usual, to speculation about people and the ways in which they differ from one another. He thought of those who tend sheep, those who till the fields, those who fight the wars, those who dig in the earth to bring out metals, both precious and useful. He thought of tradesmen who travel on the seas and in caravans, and who chaffer over prices in bazaars. He thought of men like Abiathar who live for religion and the written word, and of David who led many men and was loved by many men. David was unique, a man for whom thousands were prepared to give their lives. And again he thought how simple life would become if only he could go willingly into David's service.

Joab was still half an hour from Hebron when he met Abiathar on the road. He approached Abiathar, smiling joyfully at sight of the old friend. After a moment of staring scrutiny, Abiathar's mind returned from its far journey. Abiathar's warm smile held all the affection of another summer, as if there had been no intermission of years since last they met. He laid his arms on Joab's shoulders and touched his cheek against Joab's sandy beard.

"My good friend," he said warmly, "we meet again after long absence."

Abiathar was well fed, clean, dressed in new linen which gleamed with

[90]

bleach. His girdle and headcloth were dyed blue. The tassels of his girdle hung to his cloak hem. His beard had been washed and combed.

Joab held Abiathar at arm's length. "I'll wager you are married," he smiled. "You have the look of a man who is well tended."

Abiathar shook his head. "I leave matrimony to David. He has wives enough to supply a troop, and troubles enough to warn us all. Nevertheless I am, as you say, well tended. Reba looks after me. I would not dare appear on the street without putting on a clean cloak and combing my beard."

Abiathar smiled, then sobered quickly. "Reba watches over me like a— a sister. She says the king's high priest must be a credit to him." He sighed. "Perhaps she is right. Though to me it seems she makes much of nothing. Yet I thank God for Reba, for she is a dear friend and has become a remarkably good and sensible woman."

Joab felt a trembling pass over him at the companionable intimacy of the priest's words. To be Reba's good friend—since one could never hope for more—to see her daily in the house of David—what happiness that could be!

Abiathar's gaze had wandered from Joab off into some urgent land of the mind. He turned toward the trees which were thickening along the eastern hills beside the highway. His brows formed a troubled frown. "I have found another of the abominations of the uncircumcised," he said. "Come with me, Joab."

"Where are you going?"

"To the camp of Uriah to protest once more. Uriah does not heed the warning of a priest of the Lord. Perhaps he will listen to David's cousin."

Joab drew back, unwilling to be drawn into Abiathar's wars.

"I will go another day. Today I am eager to report to David and see whether he has use for me."

Abiathar plucked at his sleeve. "You won't be able to talk to David today. He's celebrating the weaning of his third son, an infant he has named Absalom. David will be feasting all day and probably all night. David is an extremely domestic man."

"David has three sons? Whose—whose child is this one?"

"This is the son of the princess Maacah, daughter of the king of Geshur. A lusty, thriving boy. David is out of his senses with pride. All Hebron is celebrating today."

Joab smiled. The thought of David absorbed in Maacah and her lusty son made him strangely happy. He was willing to indulge the priest, and turned to follow Abiathar into the forest.

They followed a well-beaten trail. Presently they came to a hill which rose as high as the tops of the surrounding oaks. Abiathar led the way to its rocky summit. The gaunt face of the priest was agitated as he bent over a mixture of cold ashes and charred bones to which bits of scorched flesh still clung.

"God of Abraham," he muttered in a tone too agitated to be reverent. "Last night they were here again. Only last night."

Joab thought of his own restlessness last night, and how his thoughts had wandered to the kind of carnal debauch which the Canaanites called worship. Here, in this spot— He shrugged away the thoughts and pictures which came to mind.

Abiathar stirred among the ashes with a broken branch. He pondered one long thigh bone for some time. At last he remarked with a deep sigh, "I cannot say certainly that it is human. Come, Joab. We will take it along when we confront Uriah. You bring it. I cannot bear to touch the thing."

Joab had no wish to touch the bone either, but then, he had no wish to argue with the stubborn, single-minded priest. He picked up the smoke-blackened remnant and knocked off the clinging ash and stuffed it into his girdle beside the sheathed knife. Its touch seared him though its ash was dead, for it had been burned to Baal.

Abiathar and Joab found a sentry sleeping heavily beside the path at the edge of the Canaanites' camp. When they shook him awake he went, yawning and cursing, to fetch Uriah.

Uriah, short, powerful, pleasant-faced, with a great nose and a sensual, smiling mouth, was a man of fanatical loyalty both to his own men and to David. He greeted them with a wide smile. A tawny lionskin gave scant covering to his square, muscular body. His chest and face and legs were covered with coarse dark hair. He kicked at the dogs which slunk about his legs and cursed them in the Hittite tongue.

Abiathar hurried through the necessary courtesies. Then, pointing to the bone Joab held, he demanded, "Is this bone human?"

Uriah's smile gleamed. "Our cult does not demand human sacrifice."

Joab was surprised. "It doesn't?" He had supposed the pagan cults were a hodgepodge of everything obnoxious to pious Hebrews.

"Our worship concerns fertility and abundance—life, not death." Uriah smiled and yawned. "Forgive me, please. One sleeps sound, after a night of the full moon." His smile was for Joab now. "I am happy to see you, friend Joab. You have been long away. Have you prospered?"

Abiathar laid his hand on Uriah's sweat- and earth-caked shoulder, then jerked it fastidiously away. "Give me a straight answer about this bone, man. No evasions."

"It is the bone of a sheep."

"It is too long for a sheep."

"It was a long sheep, friend Abiathar."

Abiathar's exasperation did not abate. "You serve David badly in bringing pagan worship among his men."

"We do not invite his men to join us. Our priestesses complain of them. If you can keep them away, we will be grateful. They cavort among us like naughty children, without respect or reverence or knowledge of the sequence proper to the rites. We have too few women who are willing to serve as priestesses at the full moon, and your men discourage those who are willing." Uriah's dark eyes were troubled. "We, too, have difficulty in the service of our gods."

Abiathar's voice was tense with anger. "There is one God, and He is the Lord."

Uriah's shrug and smile held only tolerance for Abiathar's peculiar view. "We served Baal long before you brought your deity into our hills. Your deity is one I cannot understand. If we cannot see him or touch him, how can we worship? He is too subtle for us."

Joab envied Uriah, who believed with all his being in Baal. He envied Abiathar, whose faith in the Lord was a mighty hand gripping his hand and sustaining and leading him. Faith, thought Joab, is a grace of the spirit. I wish I possessed this grace. Aloud he said, "Nor can I understand this God of the Hebrews, though I am a Hebrew and a grandson of Jesse."

Abiathar cried in anguish at the stupidity of men. "If God were so small that a man's mind could contain Him, what would there be to worship?"

"Friend," said Uriah with a troubled sigh, "these questions are not for me to answer. My people serve David as best they can. We remain in camp on your Sabbath. We bring David a share in all our spoils. We refrain from marching north against Abner and Ishbosheth, though a week's work would wipe them out utterly. Leave us the consolation of our high places and do not be troubled about us."

Abiathar's full lips tightened over his teeth in an expression of outrage. "You ask the priest of the Lord to speak approval of your high places?"

Joab laid his hand on Abiathar's arm. "Uriah does not ask you to approve. He asks you to ignore. To tell the truth, I do not see how we can prohibit a worship as ancient as the hills themselves. Baal was god here before ever Moses brought the Lord down from Sinai."

Abiathar's look and gesture indicated utter discouragement. "Moses did not bring the Lord down from Sinai! The Lord brought Moses up to Sinai. The Lord brought Moses and our people out of Egypt, out of bondage, through the sea. The Lord gave our people the law by means of Moses, because Moses was a man who had an ear to hear and a heart to understand and a mind to obey."

Abiathar's sigh was profound. "Still, you are not to blame if you do not understand these mysteries. As for you, Uriah, you are not to blame that you were born a Hittite. You have served David well in all things except this one. I cannot stop you in this. Yet I can protest when such abominations are brought within reach of our men to debauch and contaminate them. And if ever I find a human bone among the ashes—"

"Now, now, you do not understand our cult any better than we understand yours, friend Abiathar. Human sacrifice belongs to cities and to kings. We are a mixed company of hangers-on made up of many peoples, with no roots and no homes. We are a conquered, motley group, and eventually we will intermarry with our conquerors and lose all tribal memory. Meanwhile, our simple revels help to make our meager life bearable."

Abiathar said bitterly, "Mixed peoples, mixed worship, mixed wines— these lead only to evil. Well, friend Uriah, we will meet on a happier occasion when the council convenes tomorrow. God bring you to an understanding of Himself."

Uriah saluted cheerfully, yawning. Abiathar turned and disappeared on the path by which he had come, but Joab lingered. He touched Uriah's arm, and did not mind the touch of flesh soiled in service of an honest faith.

"If it is true you have trouble finding priestesses—I know of a certain Moabitess who seems to have been formed for just such a purpose. Yet I would not want her identity known, if she served Baal in the company of your people."

Uriah's smile was broad and affectionate. "We will talk of it another time, friend Joab. I am dying on my feet."

Still Joab lingered. "Is it true that your men are eager to march against Abner?"

"Aye, Joab. We itch for action against our enemies."

"Can David be persuaded?"

"By a cousin, perhaps. Not by me."

Joab raised his hand in salute. "It was good to see you today, friend Uriah."

Joab followed Abiathar up the path among the trees. For every vessel, he was thinking, there is a use. Even for such as Lisha there is a use. And the thought washed from him the sickness of disgust he had felt toward the girl and eased his mind of its shame. I will attend to the matter before the next full moon, he resolved. With the resolve came something like respect for Lisha. Surely she was formed to serve the gods of her people.

Joab overtook Abiathar at the edge of the forest and plucked at his sleeve. By the surprise on the gaunt face he knew the priest had forgotten him completely.

"Do you still write the records of David?" Joab inquired as he fell into step beside the stork-legged priest.

"Not often. David has become so comfortable and content in his big house with his wives and concubines and his little ones that he forgets the work to which the Lord has appointed him. His companies are idle in camp and every day more men from Israel march to Hebron to join his forces. On every side men wait to march against Abner in order to strengthen themselves so they may meet the Philistines. Yet David is idle. What is there to say except that David dwelt in Hebron, and sons and daughters were born unto him?"

18

DAVID'S NEW HOUSE stood near the north gate of Hebron, which is the main gate of the city. It was in the north gate that David had sat in judgment from the day he was made king until the judgment court of his house was ready to be occupied. Today's feast was set in the great court, though workmen were still occupied with fitting stones in the walls and in the archway of the imposing entrance on Hebron's main street.

David's court calendar was light. Hebron, as a city of refuge, was a place where the judge would be in demand almost daily throughout the year. Still, on most days, David contrived to be finished before noon with his work as judge, and whenever domestic affairs were pressing, he was able to dispense with the work of the court.

Joab passed the big front entrance with its honor guard of soldiers in short cloaks, dyed girdles, and leather breastplates. He glanced through the open gate at the celebrating throng and went on around to the camel gate at the back of the house. This gate opened onto the courtyard which served the household. The harem opened off this court. A row of fireplaces where meals and even feasts could be prepared filled the back of the court, near the wall. Joab found an old comrade from Maon dozing beside the door. He embraced Joab and admitted him readily. When the man saw that the concubines were busy at the fires, he himself showed Joab the urns of water in a small anteroom. Joab slopped a little water into a brass basin, stripped off the dusty cloak and sandals, and scrubbed himself. He rubbed himself dry with a piece of linen and put on a clean white tunic and cloak with a girdle of dyed Tyrian linen, bought recently in the Jerusalem bazaar. The girdle was scarlet and brought sharply to mind the bright colors Reba loved to wear. He cleaned his sandals of the dust from the highway, combed his hair and beard, and thought a mouthful of the wine flowing in the front court would be welcome.

His mouth was dry and his throat was clogged and there was a strange feeling of pressure behind his eyes. The truth was, he dreaded seeing what the years might have done to Reba. I'll go away, he thought. I'll find Ira and spend the night with him. I will return tomorrow and pay my respects to David and his household.

He rolled up the mat, tucking his soiled garments inside. Now he was ready to leave the way he had come. But the flick of a rust-colored skirt in a far doorway caught his eye. He turned and saw Abigail. She saw him in the same moment and moved quickly toward him, both hands stretched out. She seemed quite oblivious of the disarray of her dark hair, of the way her girdle had come loose and hung, only half knotted, down about her hips. The rust-colored cloak flapped open as she walked, revealing a soiled white tunic below. Something had blurred the firmness of her mouth, and her eyes were vague even when she smiled. Yet her step was quick and light as ever, and Joab remembered with pleasure the deep-folded corners of her full mouth.

"Joab, my friend and kinsman!" Abigail laid her hands on his shoulders in a gesture Zeruiah often used, and Joab felt a rush of affection as he had with Abiathar and Uriah.

Abigail said, "Welcome to Hebron, Joab. Do rest here and talk to me before you join the celebration. How well you look! But older. Oh, much older."

"We are all older," Joab said somberly.

A film of tears washed her dark eyes. Joab took her hands and held them closely, ignoring the maids who passed across the court with platters and basins of smoking food for the feast in the main courtyard. How seldom Joab had thought of Abigail these past years, yet how very fond of her he was. How much fonder he was of all these friends than he had remembered.

"You must join David and the men of Hebron and enjoy the celebration! David has weaned another son. His third. A strong, beautiful, lusty boy! How he squalled, that one, on the day he was born! And when he was circumcised! You should have heard him, Joab." Abigail laughed gleefully, yet the laughter seemed unreal as if she might more readily have wept.

"You have a son, Abigail. How old is he?"

"He is five years old now, Joab. I do want you to see my little Daniel. Later, that is, when he is stronger. Such a pretty child, Joab. He has David's red hair and blue eyes." Sadness crept into her face. "I only wish he were stronger."

"Isn't he well?"

She looked up quickly with a smile that was too bright, too determinedly brave. "Daniel is fine. So affectionate, so dependent! Oh, he coughs. During the rains each winter he breathes harshly. But he will outgrow all that and be a second David. Oh, Joab, he is such a darling child. He has the child's gift of a loving heart. As David has—had—must have had when he was very young. If I could have borne this son for David when I was young—as Maacah is young—if I could have given him vigor and health—

the things he lacks. But he will find strength for himself presently. When he outgrows the harem and goes to live among the men, the active life of court and camp will make him strong."

"Tell me about this third son of David's." He wanted her to talk of Reba and her little Amnon. But he could not seem to bring the question out directly. If Abigail talked long enough of the sons of David she was bound to speak of Amnon and Reba.

"Such a beautiful boy! You never saw a child with such black hair! Maacah is his mother. Only a child herself, but so vigorous, so lively. She does us all good with her fresh, gay spirit. How often I say to myself it is no wonder Absalom is such a brute. If I could have borne David a son when I was her age—but that is so silly. I was just that age when I married Nabal."

She burst into a storm of weeping. Joab put his arm around her shoulder and pulled her head against him, and she clung to him. Joab waited for her weeping to subside, embarrassed by the curious glances of the servants, not knowing what to say that would comfort her. He became conscious of his hand, foolishly patting Abigail's shoulder. It was a gesture designed to comfort a child who has stubbed its toe, not a woman whose world lies in ruins. He doubled his fist to stop the foolish patting and waited for the storm to pass.

Presently Abigail wiped her eyes on her sleeve and turned the over-bright smile on him. "I can't think what got into me. I was awake with little Daniel much of the night. When he gets choked there is nothing to do but have him sit on my lap and sleep with his face against my shoulder. I wouldn't dare to leave him for a moment even when—even if David were to send—that is—forgive me, Joab. I can't seem to stop my tongue from wagging."

She went to the washroom and washed her face and returned. "Do forgive me." Her speech was the babbling, repetitious speech of an over-excited child. "I am so happy to see you, and I can't think what got into me to burst into tears like that!" She patted his hand vaguely. "You must get to know Maacah, Joab. We all love her. She has such zest. David forgets all his troubles, I think, in the pleasure of her youthful vitality."

"His troubles? David has a palace, a family, a kingdom! His men grow in numbers year by year. His people love and honor him."

"David enjoys Hebron, of course. But he cannot be happy while Israel is divided. It gravels his soul to be subject to Achish, to be unable to unite and defend Israel. And so he waits in Hebron, comforting himself with wives and concubines. As he comforted himself in Maon. Remember how he took first Dinah, and then that other young girl—what was her name? I never seem to recall it."

Abigail laughed merrily. "Love comforts David as wine comforted

Nabal. Only imagine it, Joab! Seven of the women of the harem are with child—three wives, four concubines. And little Absalom just weaned. Oh, David takes great comfort in domestic life." Abigail laughed as if she would never stop.

Still laughing, she rose. She tapped his shoulder in a merry gesture and moved toward the door whence she had first come. "I must see to my child. Do look in on us often, now that you have finally found your way to Hebron."

Joab watched her walk away with her quick, light step. The loosened girdle fell unnoticed on the pavement as she disappeared through one of the doorways. But Joab did not think of that. For Reba had entered through an adjacent doorway. She wore a blue cloak, a scarlet mantle, a girdle rich with silver embroidery. She clasped the hand of a small, sandy-haired, gray-eyed boy who was dressed in exquisite garments of blue linen. Joab scarcely breathed at sight of them, and of the radiance in Reba's face.

He moved toward her, holding out his hands. She released the child. Her golden bracelets jangled as she laid her hands in his. "When I looked to see who had sent Abigail off on one of her spells again, it was you! Oh Joab, why did you stay so long away from us all?"

Joab shook his head, unable to speak.

Reba freed her hands and pulled the child against her skirts. "Amnon, darling, this is your—cousin, Joab."

The child stared at Joab with eyes in which curiosity blended with insecurity. He bobbed his head. "Is he your cousin too, mother?"

"He is David's cousin." She hugged the child excitedly. "You don't know how happy I am to see you, Joab. You just don't know."

"I know." Joab felt lightheaded. He seemed to be surrounded, not by the walls of the court but by the golden stretches of the aromatic wilderness. When his eyes were on Reba he could not look away, yet when they went to the boy he could not look away from him, either. This was no son of David! He has my eyes, my hair, my arching brows! *When was he born?*

Joab saw hostility gather in the child's eyes at the intense inspection, and turned quickly to Reba. It was incredible that she should be both older and the same. Level brows, feathery hairline, dark, direct eyes—even the bangles and neckband were the same, except these were of gold, while those Abigail had given her were of silver and brass. It was incredible that the years had left her so like the girl he had loved in the wilderness. Only the sweet firmness about the mouth was new.

He blinked away the haze, cleared his throat and reached again to take her hands. "You haven't changed at all. Except to grow more beautiful."

"You've changed, Joab." Reba touched her palm quickly against his beard. "In all my thoughts you were still a boy with down on your cheeks. Oh Joab, why must we grow older?"

Joab left the stone bench and moved restlessly across the paved court. How could he talk to Reba with this child watching? He is my son! Does David know? Surely David must know! The servants came and went and Joab could not think of a thing to say that was fit to be heard by the servants or the child.

Again he cleared his throat. He said, "I saw Abiathar this morning. We visited the camp of Uriah. Abiathar looks very well. He says you are attending to his needs."

Reba smiled serenely. "It comforts me to sew for Abiathar. He has done more for David than anyone will ever know."

"Yes," Joab said. "Yes, of course."

He had to touch that boy. He could not keep back his hands. There was a lock of sandy hair that fell over the child's eyes as Joab's hair did when he did not wear a headcloth. He brushed it back and swallowed past the smothering sensation in his throat. "Amnon," he said, "my—my—Amnon, I'm glad to know you."

The child stared at Joab resentfully and dodged beyond his reach.

"He is having a bad day," Reba said in apology. "For years he was monarch of the household and unused to competition. Then Absalom came along, and now seven babies are to be born into the harem before spring. This court will be full of flapping linens and squalling small fry."

"Amnon was monarch? What about Abigail's little boy?"

All the brightness washed out of Reba's face. "Poor little Daniel. He will not be with us long. The wonder is he has lived till now. I sometimes think Abigail keeps him breathing by the sheer, desperate force of her longing."

"What ails her? She could not seem to remember your name."

"She has learned to forget the things which hurt her. She even pretends nothing serious is wrong with Daniel. I think she will be friends with me again, presently. She and I were—alone together—for so long, while David was fighting the battles of Achish, and while he was getting settled in Hebron, setting up a tax system, organizing border defenses. This feeling Abigail has about me came then. She loved David so much, and he—"

"Loved you," Joab said, low-voiced. He wished desperately the servants would go away and leave him alone with Reba and this child. So much was clamoring to be said. Yet even this was a thousand times better than to be in Bethlehem and never see her lovely, serene, compassionate face.

Reba said, "David has ten wives now and a score of concubines. Abigail cannot go on hating me forever." She drew Amnon against her and brushed back the lock of hair that fell over his eyes. "When my big boy gets to be seven years old, he will go to live with David in the men's rooms. Then

Abigail will remember that I am lonely and will no longer hate me. Abigail started by pretending that truth is only what she wanted it to be. Now she blames me for much that is not my fault."

Joab said, "Can we go somewhere, away from this hubbub?"

"Of course." Reba took Amnon by the hand and led the way out the back gate along a path to a nearby well. They sat on its rim.

Their eyes met and Joab thought, I can't bear to look at her and not be able to touch her. He said, "Marriage agrees with you, Reba. You are—beautiful."

Reba's voice was low. "I know nothing of marriage. Harem life is not marriage. David would be the first to say so. It is being the mother of my son which agrees with me." She held Amnon so tightly that he twisted out of her arms and went to sit on the grass nearby.

Joab said, "When will Amnon be seven?" He knew the answer. The boy's birthday would surely occur sometime during the early spring.

Reba's eyes met his serenely. "In the spring. A few weeks before Passover."

Joab's eyes wandered from hers. His lips trembled with this confirmation of the thing he had surely known from the moment he saw the boy.

Reba said quickly, very low, "David told me—once—that if I had loved him he would have wanted no wives but me, no home but ours. David would have been happiest with one wife and his children growing up around him. But his success prevented that. Once he was king, more marriages were made to strengthen our borders, to finance his great, useless army. Being lord of a harem is wrong for David. With all my heart I pity him."

Amnon rushed at Reba, beating with his fists on her arms and shoulders. His voice was high-pitched and hysterical. "You will not pity David. I will not let you pity David."

Reba took his hands and held them firmly. "My son is wiser than I. David is strong and wise and good. He is the king. He does not need pity."

"You do not love him." Amnon's mouth twisted with a strangely unchildlike bitterness. "You love—*him!*" Amnon pointed accusingly at Joab, and Joab thought sadly what incredible conversations a child must overhear in David's harem.

Amnon cried, "I hate you! I hate you both!" He ran sobbing down the path and disappeared through the gate into the house.

Joab would have gone to bring him back, but Reba held his sleeve. "Amnon gets these—impulses—and he is better if left alone. He turns from comfort and tortures himself with thoughts I cannot understand."

Her wide, dark eyes were raised to Joab's face. They were filled with tears. "David is Amnon's idol. And now David will have many sons and spoil them all, as he has spoiled Amnon for six years. Amnon will be one among many, and David will overlook him because he is a difficult, moody child. Amnon builds a wall around himself and we who love him cannot get through to comfort him. He needs his mother's love and understanding, but I can't comfort him because he knows my secret."

"Your secret?"

"That it is you I love and always have and always will."

"Come with me, Reba." The words burst from Joab, unplanned. "We will go to Egypt. Or Phoenicia. Or Damascus. Or to the islands of the sea."

"Joab, if only we could." For a moment only she rested quietly against him. Then she pulled away. "I can never take Amnon away from David. He adores David. I will not rob Amnon of his heritage as David's first-born. And I'll never go away and leave him behind."

Joab said, "You don't love me."

Reba said steadily, "I would rather live with you in a mud hut in the wilderness with Amnon our son and the other sons I could give you, than to live in that lonely house. But I am what I am—the wife of David, the mother of Amnon. And you are David's cousin, and you love him though you may not know it. We aren't children, Joab. We will do what must be done. We will spend our lives serving David."

Joab turned from her, unable to reply.

19

THE GREAT OAK gates to David's court of judgment stood open daily, guarded by a score of soldiers whose captain was Benaiah the Levite. These soldiers wore short white cloaks with dyed purple girdles and leather breastplates front and back, attached at the shoulders with brazen clasps. They wore greaves of leather on their legs and heavy-soled sandals on their feet. They were armed with swords and with stout bows which hung down their backs. Ten guarded the gate and ten stood beside the wide stone dais on which David sat in judgment.

Though a dozen or more men were still employed on the stonework and shrubbery, the pavement and walls were complete. David had been holding court in his own house for three months past. It was here that Joab caught his first glimpse of David the day after he reached Hebron. Staring about at the fine workmanship, Joab reflected with some pride that David's judgment court was a credit to Judah.

David himself was equally impressive. Clearly, David had a gift for the pageantry of kingship. His robe was of linen dyed with the rare Tyrian purple, costliest of all dyes. Six-pointed stars cut from gold cloth were stitched around its hem with gold thread. The robe was of a remarkable fullness and fell in heavy folds about the gold-painted leather and cords of his sandals and the gleaming onyx which inlaid his bench and dais. His girdle was of purest bleached linen, with golden threads worked into the deep fringe.

David wore a ceremonial headcloth of white, though the heads of his workers and bodyguard were bare. Over the headcloth was a chaplet of golden cords fastened with four large red stones called carbuncles. The chaplet with its carbuncles had been the gift of the king of Geshur, father of Maacah and grandfather of the infant Absalom. A similar gem, set in a wide golden ring, ornamented David's left thumb. Golden bangles clasped his arms below the hem of the wide purple sleeves. In his right hand he held a short staff or wand of office, made of polished cedar wood and decorated at the tip with the golden figure of a lion.

God of Gideon, thought Joab. If Zeruiah could see this!

More than the usual daily number of disputes had accumulated during yesterday's gala celebration of Absalom's weaning. Joab found an obscure spot in a far corner where he could observe without being conspicuous. David had put on weight since Joab last saw him in Maon, but the blue of his eyes and the red of his curling beard were as vivid as ever. The look of strain and exhaustion was gone. Yet Joab knew that David was not a happy man. What new quality had crept into his character? Evasion? Willingness to compromise? Or had David merely learned to bend with the wind?

He has become a realist, thought Joab with a thrill of recognition. At last! David the Dreamer is gone, and David the King replaces him. The man who sat on the onyx-studded bench would not risk his whole destiny by making a march against Nabal for the sake of something as imponderable as a man's trace of human dignity. This David would hold back from such a march and sing a song about the beauty of forgiveness and the glory of magnanimity.

David was a rich man. He had built Nabal's possessions into enormous holdings. That David had survived many compromises, Joab knew. He had married Nabal's widow while loving a very young girl whose heart had never opened to him. He had accepted the friendship of Achish of Gath and used his position to strengthen himself and weaken Achish. He had taken to wife a girl whose father was king of Geshur and could help him politically. He had taken other wives for political reasons. This man had come to terms with circumstances.

And Joab thought with satisfaction, Zeruiah would approve of David now, more than at any time before. This is a David even I can understand.

David's work as judge was commonplace enough. The elders of Bethlehem tried similar cases and with about as much wisdom. A man whose wife was barren asked for a divorce that he might take a wife who would give him children.

"Take a second wife," David said. "But keep the first, since she has nowhere to go if you send her away."

"This I would gladly do, my lord David," said the man humbly. "But the truth is, I cannot feed two wives and the children who will come."

"The wife you now have brought you a dowry?"

"Aye, my lord David. A small flock. Not enough to provide for a household such as—"

"Marry a second wife with a second flock, or one with a vineyard or field."

"But the girl I have chosen—"

"If you cannot afford the girl you have chosen without injury to the wife who brought you the means of your present living, choose a girl you can afford."

Crestfallen, the man departed. And Joab thought, he is a practical man, without sentiment. Why then did he keep Reba and Amnon, giving them the protection of husband and father, knowing, as he surely must know, that Amnon was not his son?

A farmer with a dense beard in which black and gray mingled came before David. He was bowing and scraping in a false humility which surely deceived nobody, David least of all. "In my barn are grain and oil and wine. Lately, since the soldiers newly come from Issachar and Asher built their camp nearby, the grain and oil and wine are disappearing."

"Do you accuse one of these soldiers of stealing your substance?"

"I accuse all of them, my lord David."

"All?"

"My lord David, all soldiers look alike—and smell alike—to me."

"You have seen soldiers enter your barn?"

"My lord David, these men are too clever to be caught in the act. But the stocks diminish and everyone knows that soldiers live by pillage and thievery, especially deserters such as—"

David rose. His face was dark with anger. The farmer backed away from the dais. He fumbled his hands together in a supplicating way. "My lord David, I mean no slander against the men who serve you, but the tax I pay for the support of an army which sits idle in its huts—I ask only for some rebate on my taxes. I—"

David's voice was a thunder of anger. "How many years have passed since your barns were raided by Philistines?"

"Many years, my lord David." The man bobbed to punctuate his words and demonstrate his servility. "The greatness of my lord David in protecting Judah is beyond praise."

David shouted, "My men do not rob the people of Judah. Yet if a man among them is robbing you and you bring him before me, with proof from witnesses, he will repay you fourfold. Until you can name a culprit, do not slander the men who risk their lives to protect you and safeguard your wealth. Next case!"

Eventually the last dispute was settled. Joab rose from his place in the shadow of the wall and moved toward the dais. David embraced him, unsmiling. "You have been long away, cousin," said David. "Welcome to Hebron." His voice was empty of welcome or, indeed, any emotion.

A heavy odor of costly ointments clung to David, reminding Joab of the last burial he had attended. David plays at being king, with all the pageantry of royalty, he thought. Actually he is only chief elder in Hebron by virtue of Abigail's wealth, and a glorified puppet of Achish of Gath.

Joab said, "You live magnificently, David. I wish Zeruiah could see all this splendor."

David's nod was perfunctory. "Are you in need of protection?"

Joab flushed. "I came to offer my services to you." It was plain how deeply David hated him. The thought of being hated by David brought sadness to Joab. Reba was right, as always. In spite of everything he loved David. Not because he wanted to but because he could not help himself.

David was moving toward the door to his inner quarters, followed by his bodyguard. "Let me consider the matter of your assignment, cousin. Come to the council meeting at sunset. I will assign you to one of my captains if that is your wish. Meanwhile, Benaiah will make you comfortable."

Joab said, "I stayed with Ira last night. I will return to his quarters."

"Very well." Without having once smiled on Joab, David left the hall, walking with an athlete's grace in golden sandals, while his flowing garments billowed about him.

20

THE HILLS OF Hebron were pocked with caves, many of them storehouses where Ira laid by supplies for the continually expanding army. Ira took Joab on a tour of the caves and the stone warehouses within the walls. He saw bales of cloth and tanned hides, huge earthenware jars filled with olive oil, honey, or cheese. He saw bins filled with wheat and barley from the recent harvest. He saw wine in vats and wine in skins. Dates and figs and raisins filled the air with their rich fragrance. And west of the city whole valleys were used to pasture David's camels and donkeys.

In spite of all the wealth he saw on every hand, Joab soon realized that morale had never been so low in the wilderness as here in Hebron where David was king. In the wilderness David had shared every hardship with his men. But in Hebron the men lived in huts and tents outside the city while David lived a soft life in the big house with the pillared court, sur-rounded by soft-eyed women. His men idled away the years with never a battle to provide the joys of violence and pillage.

"We need action," Ira apologized. "Idleness breeds discontent. Even I am filled with the fever of unrest. I find myself wishing I had never left my wife in Tekoa to follow David."

"Why did you?" Even in Maon, where nobody asked embarrassing ques-tions, Joab had known that Ira was no outlaw. He followed David from devotion, not from necessity.

The sightseeing tour had ended at Ira's tent, a large new one, and they sat upon the earth, grateful for the shade of the great oak under which the tent had been pitched. Ira said thoughtfully, "I hoped to help David fight his wars because his wars are Judah's wars. But the only fighting we have done during the past six years has been raids against desert peoples, where one or two companies suffice. All the while we are subject to Philistines. We have the strength to free ourselves from their rule, to drive them from Judah at least. Yet David sits in his court clothed in purple. He marries wives, begets children. And the army grows larger but remains idle."

Ira had aged during the seven years since Joab last saw him. His shoul-ders stooped. His body had grown more spare. Joab's heart was stirred by Ira's pain and longing. "Why don't you go home to Tekoa?"

Ira took a stick and traced in the earth the six-pointed star of David. "Here in Hebron we have grown so cynical it shames me to admit I have followed a dream all these years. Yet I know this, friend Joab. If we have no hope in David we have no hope at all."

Joab's pulses leaped at these words, as they had on a summer morning when Ira first spoke them in his hearing. "You say this still, after six years of submission to Philistines?"

Ira paced about in the shadow of the great tree. "David is ruled by one purpose—to unite Israel. When the men of the northern tribes have had their fill of sending tribute to those Philistine hogs, they will come to David and ask him to be their king. Their young men drift down to David con-tinually. Abner is even more idle than we, having not even raids on Amalekites and Edomites to provide diversion and pillage. A few com-panies could shatter Abner. But David has sworn an oath never to shed the blood of an Israelite. David's patience and the rapacity of the Philistines are his weapons, and in the end he will win over Abner if only because he is younger and can better afford to wait."

When the sun set, twenty men, most of them captains, sat on benches or rugs in the court of judgment. Flaming torches in wall brackets cast flick-ering shadows over the solid stonework and the somber faces. David did not ascend the dais. He sat among his men, dressed as simply as any of them. There was no need to play the king among these captains.

The captains of troops stationed in Ziklag and En Gedi and Beersheba were here. The Philistine Ittai, who had deserted Achish to serve David, was present. Seth was also here, to Joab's surprise. But then Joab knew little of Seth's comings and goings.

Seth, he learned, had arrived two days ago from one of his errands for David. Asa was useful as a messenger, but Seth was a liaison officer, circulating among the camps or moving through the towns of the north or the cities beyond the Jordan. Asa carried messages David formulated, but Seth represented David, giving advice, making decisions, using his discretion and above all, keeping his ears open for any change in sentiment among the tribes still loyal to Abner.

The meeting began with a discussion of the tribute. Achish had demanded more oil and wine, instead of cloth and camels and swine. Since oil and wine came from the orchards and vineyards of Judah, while cloth and camels came from desert raids, it was clear that Achish disapproved of Judah's current prosperity.

Ittai spoke. His spare frame and the easy grace of his posture were illuminated by a torch which flamed behind him. Joab looked curiously at this man who had exchanged the luxury of the palace in Gath for a hut in the forest near Hebron.

Ittai glanced around with a small half-smile. "May I speak to you of Achish?"

David nodded. "We are attentive to whatever you wish to say."

Ittai said, "I love Achish, but I know his weakness and his fear. Achish is doomed, whereas the star of David is rising."

A murmur went round the circle. Ira said with a smile, "You speak in riddles, friend Ittai."

"I speak of a man who is feared and of another man who is greatly loved. I speak of a man who lives only in the present time and of another who, because of the scholarship of Abiathar, lives in the past, the present, and the future. Circumstances at this moment seem to favor Achish, whereas David is subject to events he cannot control. But circumstances change, and so I say that David's star, which has risen and fallen and risen again, will continue to rise until it reaches the zenith of the world."

There was a stirring among the men. Only David remained sober. And Joab thought how heavy a thing it is to bear the weight of the love, hope, and longing of so many people. It was clear that whether or not David believed in himself, these men believed in him. The words of Ittai touched their ears and their hearts.

Ittai waved his hands in a graceful, negligent gesture, as if brushing aside discussion of his remarkable prediction. "We are concerned with the tribute. I suggest that Achish could be persuaded to accept the usual tribute if word were to reach him of a skirmish between our men and Abner's men. Achish must surely be troubled by every suggestion that an accord may be reached between the two parts of Israel."

David said somberly, "I cannot raise a sword against Israel."

Ittai sank down on his rug. Seth rose. He was a huge man and his robe made him seem even more imposing than God had made him. He folded his arms across his great chest. "We are balanced dangerously between Philistines and Israelites, so that we seem to be friends with one and enemies with the other. We long to be allied with Israel in order to turn our united strength against the enemy who bleeds us year by year."

A murmur went round the circle. Seth was surely speaking for all. He went on earnestly, "It is not Israel that is our enemy. It is Abner. Ishbosheth is nothing. Abner prevents him from renouncing the throne. The elders of the north look to Abner. I suggest therefore a maneuver which will so discredit Abner that not only the people but Ishbosheth himself will cast him out. I suggest we send an army marching through their cities—a small army—a show of strength. Three or four companies would be enough to show that we are not afraid to appear armed among their Philistine garrisons."

A smile lighted David's somber face. "To win their hearts, without shedding their blood!" His blue eyes gleamed in the torchlight. "How I have yearned to go to Benjamin, to the tabernacle at Gibeon, to worship the Lord!"

From the dismay on Seth's face Joab knew he had not expected David to give his suggestion such a twist. The tabernacle had been removed from Nob after the massacre of the priests. It had been set up farther north in Gibeon, a city of Benjamin. The priest Zadok—who like Abiathar was descended from Aaron, but by another line—had been made high priest in the tabernacle.

David rose, smiling. "I will send an offering to the tabernacle. I will send it by a kinsman."

Seth protested. "This is not what I had in mind. A band of soldiers, to demonstrate in the village squares or before the city gates—"

David continued as if there had been no interruption. "I will send one company of picked men, and with them a donkey train led by Ira."

Abiathar had sat apart brooding until now. He said, frowning, "What kind of offering is brought to the Lord by armed men?"

David said resolutely, "Each soldier will bring his own offering. When they have made their sacrifice to the Lord, they will march on through the provinces. Ira will return with the donkeys to Hebron, but the soldiers will march as you suggest, Seth."

Abiathar said gravely, "The plan is of the Lord." He returned to his brooding, and Joab reflected with approval that Abiathar was above rivalry, even when gifts were to be sent to the man named by Saul to succeed Abiathar's murdered father.

Seth cried in anguish, "A single company is not enough for such a march."

David said reasonably, "If we send more than a single company, we rouse both the Philistine garrisons and the soldiers of Abner against us. If there is to be any virtue in such a march, it must be made by a single company."

Joab understood: Seth's hope had been to arouse Abner to attack and to wipe him out with his three or four companies. But David saw through the ruse and circumvented it with perfect amiability.

Ittai said, "Achish would construe the march as unfriendly to Abner. Achish would be pleased."

David said, "The march must be led by a kinsman, since I cannot go."

"Not by me!" shouted Seth. "I will not lead one company! Four, yes. But not one!"

"Not by you," David agreed pleasantly. "You must go ahead and prepare the way. Make sure the elders in the towns understand it as an act of courage, not an act of aggression. My cousin Joab will wear the trumpet for the march." His lips curved in a strangely gentle smile. The eyes he turned on Joab were warm and kind but challenging.

Joab stumbled to his feet. "I have never in my whole life fought a single battle! I have never commanded anything but a donkey train."

"I have not ordered a battle. I have ordered a march."

"Let me march, then. Let someone else command."

"Do you refuse the commission, cousin?"

If I refuse, thought Joab miserably, I will have to go running home to Bethlehem and never trouble him again. But if I march and there is a battle and I am killed—either way, he wins. Except if there is a battle and by some miracle I destroy Abner—why then David still wins. We all win, he thought, and for the first time felt himself a part of this assembly.

He bowed without taking his eyes from David's face. "I came to serve you, cousin," he said. "I will lead the march." And with the words he felt suddenly years older and inches taller.

David's blue eyes held a brief gleam of respect and pleasure. Then he became cool and practical. "Raise your company, cousin. If one company is not enough, take fifty archers also. Choose only men of Judah. The expedition loses its significance if men from the other tribes go with you. Let each man take his own offering as evidence that Judah serves the Lord of Israel as do the northern tribes. When the sacrifices have been made, march on through the other cities. Benaiah will help you select and drill your men. Ira will attend to your supplies. Seth will go ahead and prepare the way. What else do you require, cousin?"

Joab glanced at the scarred face of Benaiah, the broad, sun-reddened face of Seth, the swarthy face of Ittai in its frame of silky beard. Ira's heavy lids concealed the mockery Joab knew was in his eyes. This is a desperate chance we take, thought Joab. If I fail and survive, I can return to Bethlehem and it will be none the worse for me. I have less to lose in this venture than these others.

He looked directly at David, smiling. "If there is anything else I need, I will send you word."

In the days that followed Joab worked day and night, choosing his men and drilling them, planning with Seth the line of march, discussing with Ira the provisioning. The words of Ira were often in his mind. If we have a hope, it is in David. "We" was more than Hebron, more than Judah. "We" was all Israel, now lying impoverished under the rule of Philistines. If I fight Abner for David and destroy him, David will surely become king of a united Israel, he thought. After that perhaps we can forget what has happened between us.

By day Joab worked with the others, but when work was done he paced among the tents alone, planning, rejecting, and planning again. I will find a way, he told himself over and over. If David could destroy Goliath, I can win a battle with my picked soldiers.

At last Joab found a plan which would give him and his men a chance. We will win, he thought, because we must. We will win in the name of the God of David, who is also the God of Israel.

Now he understood the meaning of David's choosing him. We cannot undo the harm we have done one another, he imagined David as saying. Our personal affairs have become tangled beyond repair. But I give you another gift, cousin. I give you the opportunity to serve our people. I give you the opportunity to prove yourself, to do for Israel the thing I am not free to do. Do not fail me, cousin. Do not fail yourself. Do not fail your people.

I will lift up my eyes unto the hills, Joab thought, remembering a fragment from one of David's songs. The hills around Bethlehem had closed him in for most of the twenty-four years of his life. I will lift up my eyes now unto the hills of Benjamin, he thought. I will take upon my shoulders the burden of this encounter with Abner, that veteran of many battles. The peace and prosperity of Israel have been placed in my hands by David. If the task is too great for me, he thought, surely the God of David will come to my aid.

He sent to Bethlehem for young Asa, wishing him to have a part in his preparations. Seth had suggested the original plan. Joab would lead the march. It was right that the third son of Zeruiah should also play a role in the event. Joab had, indeed, been wondering for several days what was keeping Asa in Bethlehem.

Obed the Reubenite returned from Bethlehem bringing word that Asa would be delayed for two more days. Asa, Obed reported, was taking a wife. He wanted Joab to come home and act as friend of the bridegroom in his behalf.

The news struck upon Joab's ears with a fearful sense of foreboding. Asa the impetuous was a perfect dupe to serve Lisha's purposes. Who but Lisha could rush Asa into a hasty marriage lest some general family alarm interfere with her design?

Joab left his painstaking preparations in the hands of Ira and Benaiah and set out that same evening for Bethlehem. If the bride was indeed Lisha, he meant to try to prevent the marriage.

I should have told Zeruiah all I knew about that girl, he thought in an anguish of self-blame. I should have foreseen that Lisha would find a way to get at my brother, having failed with me.

The first miles were covered at a desperation pace. Then Joab began to wonder how one goes about telling a beloved younger brother that he has played the fool. He was exhausted by that time, from haste as well as anxiety. And now as he continued north he began to ponder subtler ways of dealing with Asa. I will ask him to postpone the wedding until after we have fought this battle with Abner, thought Joab.

Joab reached Bethlehem late at night, and did not awaken till the sun was beating directly down upon him. By the time he had joined the family in the courtyard, Asa had already gone to wait at the gate with the elders, and Lisha with her train of maidens was ready to start. His suspicions were confirmed. But it was too late. He was quickly pressed into service as friend of the bridegroom. Heartsick, he had to join in the festivities which made Lisha a member of the family of Zeruiah, bride of bewildered Asa.

2 I

WHEN SAUL MOVED the tabernacle from the desecrated town of Nob after the massacre of Abiathar's family, it was natural to bring it to Gibeon in Benjamin. The Hebrews had made it a city of priests.

The town of Gibeon was celebrated for many things, chief among them its pool. Fed by eternal springs, the pool lay cool and deep, reflecting the great rock which shadowed it. The pool had been cut out of the solid rock, as had a circular staircase. This staircase with its handrail made it easier for the women to reach the water supply when it receded in the dry season.

The tabernacle was set on a hill overlooking the pool and the low gray houses of the town. Zadok, descended from Aaron through the third son, Eleazar, lived beside the court of the tabernacle and offered sacrifices on the brazen altar.

Israel's tabernacle embraced almost four centuries of Hebrew history in its tattered curtains. It was made, so the legend went, in the shadow of Mount Sinai from specifications given to Moses by the Lord God. Into the tabernacle went the most precious possessions of a people newly emerged from slavery—treasures of gold and jewels, linens and wool, silver and brass, oil and spices were brought as gifts. The finest artisans gave their labor to fashion a house of the Lord which could be transported when the people moved and set up when they camped.

The company which Joab led to Gibeon consisted of a hundred swordsmen and fifty archers. They left Hebron at dawn, marching in ranks of ten followed by Ira and his donkeys with their drivers, and with a flock of sacrificial sheep bleating behind.

The men bypassed Jerusalem and spent the night in the fields near Gibeon. They paused next morning at the pool to wash and refresh themselves and to refill their water bottles. Then, trailed all the way by chattering urchins, they marched toward the tabernacle on the hilltop and up the steps of the tabernacle court.

The paved court, worn smooth by the sandals of worshipers, faced east as did the open end of the tabernacle. Near the tent of meeting stood a great brazen altar, high as a man's shoulders, and hollow. Within the altar a perpetual fire sent smoke in a thin, pale thread against the blue of the sky, while beyond the altar was the basin where priests washed themselves after the sacrifice. Inside the sanctuary stood the table bearing the plate of shewbread with its linen napkin, and the brazen lamp with its seven mouths. Threads of old embroidery hung on the Veil that formed the back wall of the sanctuary. Beyond the Veil was the Holy of Holies, where once the sacred ark had rested.

The tabernacle was not large, and the wood of its walls was so shrunken that linen billowed through the wide cracks. Fresh skins and camel's-hair cloth had reinforced the roof. For the tent of the Lord had known the ravages of the centuries, and four hundred years is a long time for a tent to endure.

Joab looked now at the altar, the tabernacle, and the Veil, and remembered that Moses had stood within these curtains. Here to this altar generations of Hebrews had brought their offerings. This was the shrine holy to all Israel. I have come to this place, thought Joab, wearing the trumpet of command. Ahead of me lies the battle which may unite this nation at last. If ever I am going to pray to the God of Israel, now is the time and this the place.

A lone Levite knelt beside the altar. He had been polishing the brass corner post with its tapering horn, when the noises of men and animals interrupted him. He squatted there now, staring with open mouth.

Joab said briskly, "Are you the priest Zadok?" A foolish question. The fellow was as slack-jawed as Lem had been.

"I am a doorkeeper in the house of the Lord," said the man, meaning it was his duty to open the tabernacle doors by day and close them by night, to polish the brass, sweep the pavement, cart away the ashes, and mop up the blood.

"Will you fetch the priest?"

The Levite dropped his sponge and scuttled out of the court by a side gate. Nearby stood a house of stone with neatly timbered roof.

"Zadok!" cried the Levite as he ran. "Zadok! Sir!"

The door of the house opened. A woman looked out. Her eyes went wide and she ducked back into the house quickly, closing the door. She reappeared in short order to cry to the Levite, "Tell them to wait—Zadok will come. Only a moment."

Zadok did come in a moment, looking as if he might have spent an hour grooming himself for the occasion. His curling black beard gleamed with oil. His sleeveless linen cloak was a marvel of neatness, and Joab thought if Reba were to see it she would not rest until she had made one of just that cut and drape to cover the lank frame of Abiathar. The priest's blue girdle had been carefully folded and twined about his slender, graceful body. His headcloth was of the same blue, and a silver chaplet held it firmly atop the mass of black hair falling to his shoulders.

Zadok came briskly across the paved court. That he knew who his visitors were Joab had no doubt, for Seth had come through Gibeon ten days ago to speak of David's intention. He took Joab into a formal embrace.

"I, Zadok, priest of the Lord, welcome you, Joab, kinsman of David, to Gibeon and to this holy tabernacle." There was a pleasant odor of spiced oil upon the priest.

Zadok greeted Ira and Asa, then turned to the body of men and spread his arms. "Blessed are you of the Lord," he cried in a firm, strong voice which reached to the farthest donkey driver, "because you have come with your gifts to worship the Lord in His holy tabernacle."

Joab recalled that Zadok's descent from Aaron was as authentic as was Abiathar's, though in Zadok's line there had been no memorable priests while in Abiathar's there had been several, including Eli. Joab knew that in this tabernacle, denuded of the ark and also of the Urim and Thummim, service surely became a thing of form and appearance, lacking the core of holiness. He wondered whether Zadok, unlike Abiathar, might be a man to whom form and appearance were perhaps sufficient.

Joab bowed before this priest who looked the part of a priest. "We are

[112]

all men of Judah. We bring our offerings and the offerings of David, who is our king."

Zadok said warmly, "How does David prosper in Judah?"

"He prospers. As well as a man can who pays tribute to Philistines."

Zadok's dark eyes wandered to the offering. "He prospers," murmured Zadok. "Israel does not prosper."

Remembering that priests are fed by a set share of the offerings, Joab wondered whether Zadok saw on the hoof today the fat pieces to be burned to the Lord, or the joints and cutlets to grace the tables of the priesthood. Yet he could not smile at the poverty of Israel's priests.

Zadok said, "I will call servants to pen the animals and dispose of the other offerings until the hour of sunset. You will want to rest during the heat of the day. When you hear the sound of the ram's horn, it will be time to return for the ceremonies."

Joab bowed, and marched briskly down the steps with Asa beside him. His men followed by tens, moving smartly. They returned to the pool and rested in the shadow of the great rock, and ate their provisions of fruits and bread, happy that tonight they would share a feast to the Lord.

While the men rested, Joab took Asa and went to examine the terrain about the pool. He still had to complete his plan, adapting it to the terrain, for it was here within a few days that a battle with Abner would take place.

Joab dreaded taking Asa into battle. The boy's mood had been one of bravado mixed with desperation ever since he came back to Hebron. Joab had tried to persuade him not to make the march. "Return to your bride," he had urged.

But Asa had looked at him with pain in his bewildered young eyes. "I must get away," he said desperately. "If I can't go with you I—I'll—I'll run away to Egypt."

Today Asa was silent and brooding. He could not enter into the cheerful gaiety of the men, nor share Joab's absorption in plans for the battle. Asa had long been a prime object of Joab's love and protection. Now they were going into battle—the first battle either had ever fought—and Joab carried in his heart the guilty sense that Lisha had married Asa partly to revenge herself on him. He wished the boy would either unburden his mind or turn it to thoughts of the battle.

Presently Asa expelled a gusty sigh. "What a wife I have married, brother Joab," he said. "We live and learn. Let me tell you this—it is sometimes necessary for a man to escape from home to get his rest and find a little peace. The love that girl has for me is a bottomless well, and I do not think I will live to fill it."

Joab said uncomfortably, "When she has borne a few sons her hunger will abate." But he thought angrily, I should have killed her. The night I wanted to kill her, I should have done so.

[113]

Asa looked at Joab with admiration. "I tell you, Joab, I never planned to marry that girl. I don't know how it came about. But there was a hot night when she came to the rooftop where I slept and— Well then, it serves me right for getting mixed up with a Moabitess."

Joab exclaimed, "Don't talk like a fool. Our ancestress Ruth was a Moabitess. Many of the men of our family have married women from Moab. Lisha is—Lisha. There are such women in every race and tribe." He put his arm around Asa's shoulder. "Never mind. You shall divorce her." But he knew even while he said it that neither Zeruiah nor Eliab was likely to permit Asa to divorce Lisha and leave her to run wild among the shepherds of Bethlehem.

Joab said, "War is the best cure for domestic problems. Soon we will meet Abner and destroy him. When Abner is dead, David will unite Israel and start on a round of wars such as these hills have never seen, until our neighbors on every side are paying us tribute. We will be the greatest power between Egypt and the three rivers. When that is done, you will be such a man and such a hero that you can govern your wife."

Asa smiled a little at last. "Indeed, I am not in such trouble as I thought. Things will be better tomorrow. But first, we must destroy Abner."

During the afternoon Zadok came over the hill and sat on the grass beside them. "Tell me," he said, "how the men of Hebron celebrate the Passover and Pentecost and the Harvest Feast."

Joab said, "We celebrate the great feasts like the lesser feasts, at our own altar in our own town. When we have no priests, the elders preside. My grandfather Jesse used to preside in Bethlehem. Now my oldest cousin Eliab presides."

"In Hebron," said Ira, "we have an altar that is very ancient. It is said that Abraham built the altar ten centuries ago."

Zadok said sadly, "Every town has its altar, built on a hill as the natives of the land build their high places."

Ira said, "It is better to worship each in his own town than not to worship the Lord at all."

"How easily," said Zadok, "we content ourselves with what is good and forego what is better. Israel will be a people of parts and sections as long as the glory of the tabernacle is in eclipse, for the tabernacle is the source of Hebrew unity."

Ira nodded. "That is true. We are a scattered people. Yet we serve one God and keep one law."

"I pray," said Zadok earnestly, "that a time will come when the ark will be restored to the tabernacle and all Israel will bring gifts to this shrine. It cannot come about until Israel has one king, and it will not come about until that ambitious man, Abner, has been put down. This I would not say among Benjamites, since the priest of the Lord is the priest of all the people. Yet among the priests it is said that if in Israel there is one man capable of bringing together all the people and turning their hearts again to the service of the Lord at one holy shrine, David is the man. David is a man of piety and vision."

"He is a man of piety, all right," Joab said. "But long disappointment can blunt the vision."

"Has David ceased to hope for unity in Israel?"

"No," said Ira. "He has not."

"Is it true that the prophet Samuel once anointed David with oil?"

"It is true," Joab said. "It happened when I was very young, and I do not exactly remember it, but my mother has spoken of it so often I almost feel as if I recalled the look on the faces of all the brothers, and Jesse, and David himself."

Zadok rose. He looked pleased with the things he had heard. "This anointing is something the priests of Israel should be told about again and again, until there is no priest in all the north who does not know the story. The priests will tell the story to the elders. One obstacle remains, and that is Abner. As long as he moves among the people in the name of Saul, the priests can do little except talk." He gave Joab a quick measuring glance. "It is sometimes necessary to do evil that good may follow. Do you agree?"

Joab nodded. He understood perfectly. No prayer at the brazen altar, no benediction offered by a priest in full regalia could have moved him so profoundly as this unspoken benediction on the battle he had planned. The Lord is on our side, he thought. I will not fear the battle. Such words were not hollow when David spoke them. Joab's faith was in his plan and his men. Yet he was not sorry to be told that the Lord was on his side.

Zadok said briskly, "Well now, it is time to prepare for the evening's ceremonies. When you hear the sound of the ram's horn—"

Joab nodded. "We will come."

22

JOAB'S MEN SLEPT that night on the west side of the pool. Close by them, the spiral staircase led to the water which, at this season, was down a dozen feet or more. They rested there all the next day, wrestling and playing at dice and the other games soldiers invent to while away the hours of waiting which, more than battle and marching, make up army life.

Joab rested with his men. His plans were complete, his orders given. Spies had come to report that Abner was marching to Gibeon before the next Sabbath. He would have six or eight companies with him. Well then,

Joab's men were outnumbered five or six to one, yet this had been allowed for in Joab's careful plan. Abner would come expecting to be first at the pool, since he had been wrongly informed as to the time of Joab's march. Abner would expect to have the initiative because of David's long record of refusing to shed Israelite blood. By tactics of surprise, Joab expected to overcome Abner's numerical advantage.

Abner came the third day. Just as the heat of the day was beginning, he and his men appeared at the top of the hill, intent on the water below them. Their first view of Joab's men was the reflection they saw in the water. They raised their eyes to the men themselves, and their mouths fell open as they recognized the men of Judah, armed and waiting, here in their Benjamite land. Behind them others crowded over the hill, cursing them for blocking the approach to the water.

Abner stood on the bank. His gray beard was filmed with dust. His legs were covered with dust down which rivers of sweat had run. His shield hung apathetically from his sagging shoulder. He closed his eyes and shook his head, as if hoping what he saw would go away. Then he called, "Who makes free with the pool of Gibeon in Benjamin?"

"Joab, son of David's sister, has brought these few men of Judah to Gibeon's tabernacle with offerings for the Lord."

"Are there no altars in Judah?"

"There is only one tabernacle. David sent gifts to Zadok, high priest of Israel."

Abner's jaws tensed with anger. He had expected to intercept David's emissaries before the gifts were given. He well knew how such an act of piety on David's part could undermine his own prestige. But he was too late. He had made the long, hot journey to no purpose.

He growled, "You came in peace?"

"Did David ever approach the men of Israel except in peace?"

Abner nodded grudgingly. "My men," he said, "are hot and thirsty. Will you draw back from the stairway so we can fill our bottles from the pool?"

Joab replied boldly. "We also thirst. Let your men draw back to the brow of the hill until we have drunk from the pool and filled our bottles so that we may start our journey back to Hebron."

Incensed at this haggling, Abner roared, "Let your men draw back first, for they are fresh while my men have marched since dawn."

Joab said, "We reached the pool first. We will drink first."

Silent now, the men on both sides of the pool stood firm. Finally Abner shouted in exasperation, "Let the young men wrestle to determine who will drink first."

"Your men outnumber us five to one."

"Choose twelve of your men. Twelve of the young men of Benjamin will meet them to try their strength and skill."

It was a device as old as the hills around the pool of Gibeon, and it was the device Joab had counted on. For one champion to challenge an opposing champion, as Goliath had done in the Valley of Elah, was equally honorable but it would not have suited Joab's plans at all.

Joab beckoned to the ten men in the first rank, and to two in the second. Abner cried, "First let my twelve men slake their thirst."

Joab said, "The young men of Judah will also slake their thirst." He did not stir from his place beside the water.

Abner turned toward the horde which crowded thickly behind him. "Volunteers," he shouted angrily. "Twelve men."

From among those who moved out, Abner chose twelve. Joab's men were already trotting around the pool to meet the opposing champions. The rest of the swordsmen moved behind the twelve, emptying the space in front of the archers. But Abner's men did not appear to notice this maneuver. They felt themselves quite secure because of David's known policy. Their attention was all on their wrestlers.

The twelve Benjamites advanced, arms extended for the wrestler's grip. Joab's men edged forward, holding their pose until they were almost at grips, when they whipped out their swords and plunged them into the bellies of the unsuspecting Benjamites. Before the screams had formed in the throats of the dying men, the attackers had rushed upon another twelve, while those behind them crowded past to join the fray.

Meanwhile the archers had a clear range. Arrows flew across the water, striking men who stood so close together they had not even room to fall. And the screams of the wounded rose so loud that Abner's commands went unheard.

When the archers could no longer distinguish Benjamites from their own men, they dropped their bows and rushed around the pool, swords upraised. Before the men of Abner had disentangled themselves, Joab's men had slain more than two hundred. Some had already begun to run. The panic spread, and the thirsty, exhausted army fled from Gibeon, heading back the way they had come.

The first man on whom Joab seized was a bearded Bedouin from beyond the Jordan. The man was still struggling to unsheathe his sword when Joab's knife plunged through the sweat-streaked cloak into the flesh. The man fell without a sound, but the consternation on his face brought an exultant shout to Joab's lips.

"For David and the God of Israel!" shouted Joab. He was too busy defending himself from the Bedouin's neighbor to look back on the streaming blood his sword had drawn. The noise of shouting, the screams of the wounded, the turmoil of struggling bodies and clashing metal blurred the senses, so that Joab hardly knew the difference between the moments when his thrust went home and the moments when he was parrying a blow. When blood appeared on his sleeve he did not know whether it was his own or another man's.

One moment in all that turmoil stood out for him, and that was when one of those he struck cried out, "God of Israel," as he fell. In that moment Joab knew the sick meaning of striking down men who swear by the same God. We are brothers, he thought. We bring our gifts to the same tabernacle.

A sword ripped his cloak. The searing stroke of a blade at his shoulder brought Joab back to a sense of the hazard and challenge of the moment. He whirled, thrust his sword into the man's belly and with a strong turn of the wrist disemboweled him. The man gathered his entrails in his arms as he dropped to his knees, screaming.

Now Joab saw that the men of Benjamin were in flight. We have won, he thought exultantly. I have won! My stratagem has triumphed! It did not occur to him just then to assign any of the credit to the Lord in whose name Zadok had blessed his men. He thought only, We have defeated Abner and his army though they far outnumbered us. Now I am indeed a soldier and a leader of men.

Joab had been too busy fighting to remember the trumpet which hung at his neck. Now he raised the trumpet and sounded the pursuit. "For David and the God of Israel," he shouted. The shout was taken up by his men until it was a roar following after the fleeing army.

Already Ira and his muleteers had begun the work assigned to them —to dispatch the wounded and plunder the slain. Joab passed by Ira at his work, and Ira shouted, "God speed you, boy. David and all Judah will love you for this day's work."

Through the long, hot afternoon Joab's men had the advantage of freshness, but the Benjamites knew the lay of the land, and were able to lead pursuers into many a blind alley and there elude them. This knowledge saved many Benjamites that day.

The lust of battle is like a sickness, yet even a sickness runs its course. Long before the sun set, Joab was filled with abhorrence for the stench of spilled blood and the sight of his gory sword. There was no longer the exhilarating sense of power at the moment of the kill. Most of all he longed to shut out the sound of dying voices that called on the God of Jacob.

David is right, he told himself, and he knew he would never again shed Israelite blood if he could by any means avoid it.

The shadows were long and the breeze from the east was no longer hot. Joab found himself lost in a narrow, winding ravine into which he had been led by a pair of fleeing Benjamites. Now the men were gone and he turned back. He saw a saddle in the ridge on his left and began to climb toward it, hoping the next valley would be the main route followed by the fleeing soldiers. It was important, he remembered belatedly, for a commander to remain with his men, not go off on a mission of his own.

He was halfway up the slope when he heard from the next valley a deep voice heavy with exhaustion. "Leave me, boy. Go back and plunder among the slain."

The answering voice was shrill with excitement. "So this is the courage of the mighty Abner!"

Joab shouted, "Asa, go back. Stay with your comrades." He leaped up the slope, knowing he would be too late to save Asa from the mighty sword of the veteran commander. How well he knew the boy's zeal and Zeruiah's complaint, "His eagerness outruns his judgment."

Joab was crossing the ridge when he heard his brother's shrill scream. He scrambled down the slope, fell and rolled into some bushes, jumped up and leaped over boulders and plunged on. At the base of the hill he could see the writhing figure and around it the spreading pool of blood. He fell again in his haste, regained his footing and rushed on.

Abner was out of sight over the next ridge. By the time Joab reached Asa's body, it was still. While Benjamites streamed up the valley, he made no move to bring his men against them.

He heard the sound of a horn, and when he looked he saw the silhouette of a tattered figure, horn at lips, on a crag. Abner was sounding the call which would rally his scattered men to him on that mountain. The stream of Benjamites turned and disappeared, and their pursuers paused to cluster around Joab, staring down at Asa in consternation. Until this moment the slaughter had seemed to them one-sided.

One of the men took Asa's cloak and wrapped it round him, concealing the great wound in the belly, though blood still seeped out through the garment.

Joab now shouted, "After them, for David and the God of Judah! And for Asa, who is dead. We will surround their mountain and destroy them, root and branch." He raised his trumpet. With tears streaming down his dusty face he sounded the pursuit. They would charge into the very teeth of the enemy, up the very walls of the natural stronghold where Abner's men had gathered to make a stand.

But when they reached the hill they found that two sides were too steep to scale, and the Benjamites were so thick on the other two sides that to attack would be suicide.

From the crag Abner shouted, "How long will brother pursue brother? Aren't we all men of Israel?"

Men of Israel, thought Joab dully. Brothers. These men are my brothers, as Asa was my brother. And the heart went out of him utterly.

He raised the trumpet to his lips for the last time that day, sounding the recall. Then he led the way back to where Asa lay.

Ira was running up the valley. "We have triumphed gloriously," cried Ira, embracing Joab. "Three hundred sixty-five of the enemy are dead in their blood, in Gibeon and along the way. But of our own men only nineteen are slain."

"Twenty," said Joab.

He took up Asa's slight body in his arms and carried it down the valley till he came to where Ira had tethered the donkeys. Ira swept the burden off one small beast, and Joab laid the body of his brother across it. "We will take him to Bethlehem," Joab said. "We will bury him in the tomb of Jesse."

PART FOUR

Jerusalem

23

AMNON WAKENED TO the sound of bird song. Through the slit of window up under the flat roof he could see a sliver of blue sky with the bit of bough crossing it. Today! It is today! thought Amnon.

The thought made him shiver, as bird song made him shiver, or the music David drew from the lyre. Today I am seven years old. He said I would have breakfast with him today. I will sit beside the dais and listen while he tells people what to do.

People will look at me, thought Amnon. They will say, He is David's first-born. He is seven years old and no longer lives in the harem. They will stare at me and envy me because I am a son of David.

I am a son of David! I am!

Amnon jumped from the couch which was close beside his mother's. He looked at her and saw that she was still sleeping. I could ask her, he thought. She would tell me that I am David's son. That was the trouble. Even if she told him, he would not be sure.

Amnon ran out into the court on bare, silent feet, trying to forget doubt and pain. Every day I will be with David and see his beautiful clothes and his kind blue eyes. Every day David will see me and touch me.

In the harem David did not always see Amnon, since that great box of noise—that Absalom—entered the house. David would come striding into the harem with his robes swishing about his golden sandals, and his eyes slid right past Amnon to Absalom. When the boy ran forward, David seized him and tossed him into the air, laughing at his delighted cries.

I do not laugh, thought Amnon. Dinah has said so and it is true. These other people laugh so much. Why am I different?

Pain was in Amnon's heart. Then he heard the bird again and stared up into the big square of sky above the courtyard at the big oak tree that hung over the wall. He saw the small brown bird. It sang as if it owned the tree and the courtyard and the sky. Amnon remembered that his mother had said, "The plainest birds sing the sweetest songs."

Amnon was comforted a little, remembering the words. He blinked away the babyish tears which plagued him so often and shamed him so deeply.

I will never see Absalom in those other rooms, he thought. Absalom will not be seven for a long, long time. I am the eldest, the first-born. Today I leave these talky women and that fat, laughing boy, and the rest of these squalling babies. Today I am no longer the son of my mother. I am the son of David.

Doubt was sharp in his chest again, as always when he thought of himself in that way. David is my father! That other man, the man I hate, the man who brings gladness into the face of my mother—he is only my cousin. Dinah was lying when she told Maacah he was my father and not David. She said it because she hates my mother. David *is* my father! Today I will have breakfast with him, and sit at the edge of the dais while he gives judgment. Tonight I will sleep in a room near his room.

Amnon walked softly across the deserted court to the room with the great stone water jars. He poured water into a basin, spilling only a little, and carried the basin to the room he shared with his mother. He stripped off the scanty shirt and loincloth which are worn by children while they are very young. He washed himself all over and put on a clean tunic from the pile of garments which lay on a shelf, ready to be taken to his new room. His mother had made all these things for him. They were clothes such as men wear.

Amnon put on the fine linen cloak. There were dyed girdles to choose from. He chose a scarlet one, wound it carefully, and tied the knot himself. He would always dress himself from now on, and David would be pleased with him if he managed to do everything neatly and smoothly. When he looked up from his labor he saw that his mother was awake and watching him.

"My son," she whispered. Her eyes were bright with tears. She reached to pull him to her. "Oh, my baby," she whispered.

Amnon stood as tall as he could, sucking in his stomach to make his chest big. He could not bear to look at his mother just then. Having a room all your own to which your mother does not come is a lonely thing to think of. He would go to his bed tonight and she would not be there to put her arms around him. If he dreamed, as he often did, and waked up sobbing and terribly afraid, she would not be there to comfort him. Nobody would comfort him. He turned toward the window and stared out at the blue sky and the blurred bough. "How soon can I go?"

"Will you wait and eat breakfast with me, my son?"

"David promised I could eat breakfast with him." Amnon jutted his chin. If his mother was hurt it did not matter. She did not love David. Amnon wished he could go right this minute. Women turn a boy's heart to water. Every boy must go away to live among men. Still, he could visit her every day if he liked. If he had nothing better to do.

Amnon said, "I will have breakfast with you sometimes. But not today."

That is the way men talk to women. They are firm and sometimes rough. They do not cry and they do not plead. Well, not often. David had cried, one night. Amnon had heard, when they thought he was asleep. David had pleaded, "You do not love me."

"All women love you," his mother had replied, but the words did not sound loving.

"Not all women," David had said sadly. "Not you."

Amnon wished he had not waked up that night to hear secret talk not meant for him.

His mother now said, "Of course you will have breakfast with me sometimes. Comb out your hair, and you can go at once."

Amnon wiped his hand roughly over his wet cheeks and flung himself suddenly against his mother's breast. How warm she was. Soft and warm. "Mother," he whispered, pressing his wet cheek against her neck, "I love you, Mother."

David had not forgotten that Amnon was coming to share his morning cakes and wine. He was wearing a beautiful golden cloak with scarlet stars around the hem. A white and gold girdle was wrapped around him with the special smooth perfection his clothing always had. Amnon was so busy staring he could hardly remember the food on his plate. David was finished before Amnon had eaten even one cake.

David rumpled the boy's hair and smiled down on him. "Now finish what is on your plate, my man, and then you shall come with me to review the soldiers."

Amnon lost no time clearing his plate after that. To review the soldiers with David! That was honor! What can possibly happen in a harem to compare with standing beside David to review the soldiers?

But David did not review the soldiers after all. When Amnon had swallowed his cup of goat's milk and had finished the cluster of raisins which took so long because of the seeds, he found David on his bench of judgment. He was talking to a man whose beard was a great, gray bush upon his breast. He went close and waited to be noticed. But David was busy talking, so Amnon sat on the dais to listen.

David looked very strange. What had happened to his face? Suddenly Amnon knew. David was happy! He was happy enough to burst. Amnon had learned very young to read the passions, the disappointments, the hunger and resignation in the faces of the adults in this great stone house in Hebron. But he had seldom seen this kind of happiness in anyone's face, unless perhaps in his mother's face when that man had come into the courtyard.

There was a woman on a nearby bench. She was pretty but she was not the cause of David's happiness. Amnon had seen him with many pretty women and they did not bring this look to his face.

Amnon remembered something his mother had said a long time ago. "There is one thing David really, truly wants. That is to be king of Israel. Not just king of Judah, but of Reuben, Simeon, Dan, Asher, Gad, Naphtali, Manasseh, Ephraim, Benjamin, Issachar, and Zebulun."

Amnon had watched David as he spoke smilingly with the women in the harem. David loved them all. His mother had said so. But David had never looked then as he looked now. David was happy because of what the man was saying. And the man was saying a great deal.

The man's voice was deep and heavy but it was not happy. The man was saying that he had quarreled with another man. Suddenly Amnon was really listening to what the man was saying, because he knew who he was. This was Abner, and Ishbosheth was the man Abner had quarreled with. Abner wanted to be David's friend and make David king of Israel.

The tall priest was here—Abiathar. Abiathar wore his look of thunder, which meant he did not think the Lord was pleased with what Abner was saying to David. Abiathar saw, just as Amnon did, that Abner did not really love David but pretended he did because he had quarreled with Ishbosheth and he could not get along without some king for a friend.

Abner talked and talked, and the woman looked tired and unhappy, and Amnon thought if his mother were here she would take the woman to a room where she could rest.

The names of the tribes were rolling from Abner's lips. The words were like music when his mother spoke them, but they sifted through the gray beard like stones dropping on a wooden floor. The names were spoken arrogantly, as if all the people of Dan, Asher, Gad, Naphtali, and the others belonged to Abner. Abner boasted about how many friends he had and how his friends would be David's friends and would make David their king instead of Ishbosheth if Abner told them to.

Presently David said, "You are a man who has had a full life. It is well that you are ready to rest at last, friend Abner."

Abner's eyes grew very dark and angry, and he said, "I will not rest as long as there is a Philistine left in our hills. I will serve my lord David as I served my lord Saul. I will fight the enemies of my people while there is breath in my body."

Amnon thought this was a strange thing for Abner to say, because he had heard both his mother and Joab saying Abner did not lift a hand to help his people, no matter how bad the Philistines were.

A shadow crossed David's face. But his smile was just as friendly as could be. He held out his arms to give Abner the embrace friends give at parting.

"Then you shall march with me and command my army and your own, friend Abner," David said. "You shall be my commander, as you were Saul's. For I know well that there is no better soldier in Israel."

The man with the beard was gone. David turned to the woman. He said in a kind, happy voice, "Well, Michal, welcome to Hebron and to my home."

The woman did not smile. She said, "So I am the price you pay to inherit my father's throne."

"You are my wife, Michal. It is right that you live with me."

"I am the wife of Phaltiel."

"Saul gave you first to me. Remember that time, Michal? Remember how your father finally set the dowry at a hundred foreskins of the Philistines? He thought I would be killed."

The woman's eyes grew filmy and she shuddered. "I thought so, too."

David smiled and stepped down from the dais and moved toward the woman. "But I wasn't killed. I returned with twice the price Saul asked. And we were married. Michal, Michal, how young we were and how happy. You do remember, don't you?"

She stood up suddenly and David put his arms around her, but she turned away. Then David led her to another room. They were looking only at each other and did not notice that Amnon followed them. They sat close together on a rug in the room and Michal's face had a tortured look on it. "You could have taken me to the wilderness when you fled."

"To live in the holes that sheltered me?"

"You took other wives in the wilderness."

"But not at first. Not until I had gathered men about me—six hundred men, tents, weapons, booty from raids, and bounty from the sheiks."

"Now you have many wives. I am to be one of many wives and live in the harem of King David because I am Saul's daughter and can strengthen his claim to Saul's throne."

"Michal, don't torture yourself. You were the first. You were the first for me. I was the first for you."

"But not the last. David, I have learned what it is to be deeply, honestly loved. Do you know that Phaltiel followed me, weeping, all the long miles to Judah?"

David said gently, "We must forget all that, Michal. I have lived for the day when Israel could be one people. Let's not weep for what is lost, but rejoice for all the good that will come."

Michal said, "You left me without a backward glance. Phaltiel would never have done that. You sent not one message to tell me how you fared."

"I fared badly, believe me. Michal, do you know what it means to me to be able to unite Israel?"

"It is what you want. At any price."

David took her hand and laid it against his cheek. "You know I love you."

Michal cried, "Who is that child? Why does he stare so?"

David smiled and beckoned Amnon. He brushed back the straight, sandy hair. "This is my son, Amnon. My first-born."

"You have many sons now. Many wives and many sons." Michal looked at Amnon as though he were not there. "I have never had a son. Will you give me sons, David?"

"I will give you sons." David clapped his hands and a servant brought David's lyre to him. Amnon crouched on the floor near David. His breath came quickly because now David would sing.

David said, "Shall I sing one of the old songs for you?"

Michal looked at her hands. She did not answer. David sang:

> "When Israel went out of Egypt,
>   the house of Jacob from a people of strange language;
> Judah was his sanctuary
>   and Israel his dominion.
> The sea saw it and fled;
>   Jordan was driven back.
> The mountains skipped like rams,
>   and the little hills like lambs.
> What ailed thee, O thou sea, that thou fleddest?
>   thou Jordan, that thou wast driven back?
> Ye mountains, that ye skipped like rams;
>   and ye little hills, like lambs?
> Tremble, thou earth, at the presence of the Lord,
>   at the presence of the God of Jacob.
> Which turned the rock into a standing water,
>   the flint into a fountain of water."

David laid his lyre upon the floor. He smiled at Michal but she did not smile.

"You sing only of Israel," she said. "Even when we loved at first, you did not sing of love but only of Israel." She began to cry. "Now I know it was love of Israel and love of power that moved you to want me in the very beginning. You did not send for me because you love me but only because I am Saul's daughter."

"Michal, Michal." David pulled her close into his arms.

She cried in a shrill voice, "Send that child away!"

Amnon ran from the room, through the great court, ashamed to have seen David holding Michal that way. He could not keep back the tears, though he tried to hold them back till he reached his mother's room. They poured down his face as he went through the door into the back courtyard.

Absalom was on a rug near the door. He was playing with carved wooden soldiers that Hezro the shepherd had made for him. Absalom looked at Amnon and laughed and threw a wooden soldier and it struck Amnon on the cheek.

Amnon wanted to slap the child, but he knew he would be punished by both Reba and Maacah if he did that. He ran, sobbing aloud, to his mother's room. He was not sure what he was crying about but it had some connection with the way David held that woman. It had more to do with knowing how much Michal wanted David's love. Amnon knew how it felt to long for David's love, knowing all the time that you could never be more to David than one among many.

He threw himself into his mother's lap and buried his face in the cloth she was embroidering. His body was twisted with sobs and he could hardly get his breath. When she asked him urgently what was wrong, he could not answer.

Then Reba took him, big as he was, into her lap and comforted him, and presently he went to sleep.

24

JOAB WALKED OUT of the judgment court of David. His mind was rocking with the implications of the words David had used in dismissing him. "Go your way. Attend to your business, which is the business of destroying my enemies. Leave politics, cousin, to those who understand what best serves our people."

David had spoken those words. Did they mean what they seemed to mean? Joab knew very well that David's words often had a double meaning.

Joab turned north toward the city gate. When he came to Hebron after defeating Abner and placing Asa in the family tomb at Bethlehem, David had publicly denounced him for seeking a battle; yet privately he praised Joab's strategy and gave Joab permanent command of the company of picked men who fought the battle. They had drilled together month after month, all through autumn and through the winter rains. Now it was spring, and except for a couple of skirmishes with Edomites they had seen no action at all. As far as Joab could tell that battle might as well never have been fought. Asa had died for nothing.

Again and again Joab vowed he would go home, comfort his mother, tend the sheep. I am not David's man, he told himself. I will never be David's man. I will serve him for a little, while it pleases me. Then I will go to Bethlehem. The months drifted by, and he waited, dreading above all things to encounter Lisha. For now Lisha was Asa's widow. She was entitled to make certain demands.

Today Abiathar had come galloping out of the city gate and across the field to the drill ground. He had plucked at Joab's sleeve and whispered in a piercing tone which must surely have carried to the men, "David has made a league with Abner. He is turning his army over to Abner to command. In return, Abner will make him king of the twelve tribes."

Joab was stunned. How many hundreds of these men of David's were deserters from Abner's army? Treacherous as Abner was toward those he had a grudge against, who could tell how many men he would execute for his private revenge before marching against the Philistines? Who could tell whether he might not wait his opportunity to destroy even David? Who could tell what Abner might do? How dared David trust Abner with the lives of these men?

The city was in an uproar, some rejoicing because union was at hand, others denouncing David for giving Abner so much power. Joab had run all the way to David's house, then had cooled his heels for an hour in the court of judgment because David was occupied with Michal.

When David finally emerged from the inner rooms, he listened impatiently while Joab poured out all the angry protests he had rehearsed while waiting. David had brushed Joab off with the ambiguous words, "Attend to your business, which is the business of destroying my enemies."

Who were David's enemies? Abner headed the list.

Even as the thought crashed through his mind, Joab knew he had no authority to interpret David's order in this way, knew that David would never condone such an interpretation, no matter whether it was the true one or not. Joab knew how often in the past David's friends had done for him what he could or would not do for himself. There was no doubt at all in his mind that David had meant for Joab to fight the battle with Abner in Gibeon or somewhere in the north, though David denounced him when it was done. For nine months Joab had thought the battle was fought for nothing. Now he knew it had hastened the end of the long stalemate between north and south which for so long had kept both helpless under the Philistine occupation.

Still, to fight a battle is one thing but to kill a man in cold blood is another. It came to Joab then. I am Asa's avenger. Abner killed Asa. I can kill Abner and claim the right of the avenger.

Surely the time had come again to do for David that which he could not do for himself. In his joy at the prospect of uniting Israel, David would close his eyes to the fear and jealousy Abner had felt since the day David killed Goliath. For it had been Abner's duty to take up Goliath's challenge. What a craven fool Abner must have looked in his own eyes and in the eyes of Saul and the whole army on that long-ago day in the Valley of Elah. And how many times since had David made Abner appear ridiculous, even cowardly?

the Unanointed

by LAURENE CHINN

Of the Bible's great military leaders, few are less known than Joab, the kinsman of King David. Yet it was Joab who brilliantly led Israel's armies, it was he who was the king's confidant; only he had the courage to go against David's express commands and carry out the terrible killings of public figures so necessary to the kingdom's safety. Joab anticipated his cousin at every turn, often earning public reprimand in return; for David, Joab even sacrificed his beloved Reba, and his own son. Why? Because David was the anointed of the Lord.

Out of this stirring tale of devotion,

continued on back flap

continued from front flap

Laurene Chinn has fashioned an inspiring novel. Set on a vast panorama of the more than two-score years which saw Israel grow from a scattering of warring tribes to a unified nation ruled from David's Jerusalem, THE UNANOINTED is alive with the vivid color of the times. Here are unforgettable portrayals of the ill-fated lovers, Amnon and Tamar; ambitious Absalom, Bathsheba, Adonijah, young Solomon, hundreds of others. Here is the excitement of battle, followed by pastoral serenity as Joab returns to the peaceful fields of Bethlehem for the all too short hiatus between wars.

Sweeping in scope and conception, THE UNANOINTED introduces an extraordinary new writing talent. Towering even above the skill with which Laurene Chinn has blended careful scholarship with drama is the magnificence of her central theme and the stature with which she has invested those who devoted their lives to the Lord by serving His anointed.

Jacket design by John Alan Maxwell

David does not understand the depth of Abner's jealous hatred, thought Joab. But I do.

I'll do it, thought Joab. A coldness like stone seemed to spread and spread all through him.

And he thought, I must act quickly while I still have strength and resolution to carry it through.

He learned that Abner had already set out for Jabesh-Gilead to begin fulfilling his promises to David. Joab went to the camp where Obed the Reubenite had his quarters. "Go after Abner quickly," he ordered Obed. He licked his lips because they were so dry. "Hurry, before he gets too far on his way. Tell him David sends for him to return at once—today. Hurry, if you love David."

Obed went quickly, taking time only to gird his cloak and knot his head-cloth about his throat. Joab watched him go, thinking, You shall love your friend and hate your enemy. That was the essence of virtue, yet David broke the rule whenever it suited policy to do it. Any fool ought to know if you trust your enemy he will surely wait his chance to destroy you.

Joab paced the streets of Hebron, and as the day wore on he stood long at the north gate, straining for a glimpse of Abner returning. He had nothing to do until Abner came. He had nothing to say to a living soul, for how could he speak of anything except his intention?

I have killed before, he told himself. I killed Lem. I killed eight men in the battle of Gibeon. Eight or nine. I have killed Edomites.

His heart answered, I have never leaped upon a man and killed stealthily, having first planned how it would be done. This is a new thing.

And his mind answered his heart: this is Abner, who killed my brother. This is Abner, who stirred up Saul in his madness against David, bringing every hardship to my whole family, even untimely death to Jesse. This is Abner, who destroyed the peace of Israel for no reason at all except he feared and envied David. This is Abner, whose jealousy has so weakened Israel that for seven years we have remained under the heel of Philistines. It is my duty to kill him, for I am my brother's avenger. Yet within him echoed a reminder of another duty he owed to Asa, a duty he had chosen to ignore. He had a duty to his brother's widow, a duty quite as urgent as the duty of the avenger. For Joab knew that the law of the avenger does not apply to men killed in battle, while a childless widow has every right to expect her husband's brother to marry her and give her children.

Benaiah found Joab in the gate and sat beside him on the granite seat that had been used for centuries by the city elders when they sat in judgment. Benaiah had lost the uncouth, outlaw look. He no longer crouched when he walked or stared at strangers with suspicion. His hair was oiled and his beard also. But a cut over one eye attested to the fact that he had not lost his zest for violence.

Benaiah had worked with Joab's men before the battle of Gibeon, though he had not marched with them nor had a part in that battle. But he had drilled the men daily in the methods of attack which had proved so effective against Abner's Benjamites.

Now Benaiah remarked with a rueful smile, "This cousin of yours—after nine years in his service I still do not understand a leader who chastens his friends and rewards his enemies."

Joab grunted. He did not trust himself to speak on that subject lest he betray his intentions toward Abner.

Benaiah picked up a bit of splintered wood, drew his knife from its sheath, and fell to whittling. "You weren't here when we came to Hebron and the elders here made David king."

"No."

"It was a time of jubilation, I can tell you. Till one day an old fellow came in from Libnah to petition the king for redress. You know how it was with many of us—we had been outlaws in hiding from creditors or avengers in Maon till David joined us and called us together and made soldiers of us. The Libnite accused a soldier who was standing guard right there by David's bench of judgment, a man who had served with David in the wilderness, in the Philistine country, and in Hebron. We expected David to pounce on that man from Libnah the way only David can. But did he?"

Benaiah paused. His lips twisted in a bitter smile.

Joab said, "Knowing my cousin, I would say he gave his soldier to the man to serve as his slave until he had worked out his debt."

Benaiah chuckled. "It wasn't that bad. The soldier admitted having stolen a certain sum. The Libnite demanded four times the sum the soldier admitted. So David gave the Libnite an amount midway between, and kept back the soldier's share in booty from raids on the Amalekites until the sum was made up."

Joab said, "Who was the soldier?"

"A man of Libnah. He was one of the twenty who died at Gibeon. Yet I tell you he bore David no grudge, for he died a soldier, not an outlaw. It has been that way with all of us. You can imagine how the word spread that any who had complaints against David's outlaws could now come to Hebron for justice!"

"I can imagine," Joab agreed, his mind still preoccupied with Abner.

"I myself," Benaiah said, "stood trial for manslaughter, and was confined within the city walls for six years. But David made me commander of his bodyguard with a share in the spoil brought in from the raids, and I bear David no malice. Nor do the others. The important thing was, David gave us justice. And if confinement within the city was our punishment, he gave us employment at fair wages. That is how he got his palace built, and his storehouses and barracks for the palace guard. Yet as each man found himself finally free again and on the right side of the law, he was grateful to David. For we are a people who live by law."

The law, thought Joab. But the law of the avenger must be kept. The law that a man marries his brother's widow must also be kept. He rose and paced restlessly about the gate.

Benaiah had begun to speak of how he had gone on a recent night of the full moon to enjoy the revels of Uriah's men. It was the first revel of this sort he had attended since his confinement within the city. Though that was not to say he had been celibate for six years, Benaiah added, grinning, and went on to make much of the tale.

"They have a new girl among the priestesses. I had heard of her, to be sure, but the half was not told me. A Moabitess. If I could find her I swear I would bring her to my tent and you would not see me again for a month!" Benaiah made gestures of lascivious delight.

Joab was in no mood for this sort of talk. He started to walk away, when some word of what Benaiah had said penetrated his mind and he turned back and all but throttled Benaiah. "A Moabitess?" he shouted. "What does she look like?"

Benaiah laughed, loosing Joab's hands from his throat. "As to her face, I cannot tell. She did not remove her mantle. That is the only thing she did not remove, however. She is plump as a hen partridge and brown all over like a ripe pomegranate." Benaiah laughed gently now, as if the girl stood before him. His eyes held a faraway expression of longing that was close to sadness. "On her left breast is a scar, white against the brown flesh. I tell you, Joab, I could love that girl. I begged her to tell me where I could find her, but she giggled and burrowed against me until I could remember nothing but the joy she gave me. What I would have given to be a Joshua that night, to command the moon to stand still in the heavens! Afterwards I asked Uriah where I could find her, but he pretended to know nothing except that she appeared among his priestesses one night and has returned with each full moon." Benaiah groaned. "How can I wait for another to—"

But Joab was gone, walking swiftly out of town, north on the highway. If he stayed longer he would strike Benaiah, and if he did that he would never live to avenge Asa. I am to blame, he thought. For nine months Asa has been dead, and Lisha free to bring scandal on his name. I cannot continue to let Lisha run free through the land.

I will turn back from vengeance, he thought savagely. Let the dead bury their dead. I will not avenge Asa and I will not marry his widow. I will bring Lisha to Benaiah and after that it will be up to him to keep her in order. Yet he knew, even then, that he would do what must be done.

When evening was at hand and the shadows lay long across the road, Joab walked beside his enemy, knowing this was the time, that he would kill Abner when they reached the gate, and when it was done he would go to Bethlehem and marry Asa's widow. When he had claimed the right of brother in the one thing he could not escape it in the other.

Abner looked older than he had last summer when they faced each other across the pool of Gibeon. He was an old man, with the vigor of old men who retain their strength. The lines of his face were carved deep and the sinews of his hands were thick as cords. When he looked at the hands, Joab remembered that they had plunged the sword into Asa's belly, and he hardened his heart.

He was calm now, calm and sure. First he must talk with Abner as they walked, and by no word or sign warn this strong old man of his purpose. He said, "David asked me to speak with you of our armies. How soon can your men march to join ours?"

"As soon as the order is given. A week or two. The ceremony of David's anointing by Zadok and the elders from Israel must come first."

"Then if we withhold the spring tribute and let the Philistines come marching against us here in the hills, they will be at a disadvantage in their chariots, and we can meet them and destroy them."

"We can—perhaps. Though a little time to arrange—"

Joab interrupted, strengthened by his anger over Abner's suggestion of delay. As if there had been anything for seven years except delay! Delay is the policy of old men. Israel would lie prostrate while Abner lived.

Joab said thickly, "David asks you to tell me the number of men you have—the number of archers, the number of swordsmen. Also regarding chariots of war—"

He ceased speaking because they had reached the gate. Here in the gate of judgment he would kill Abner, and nowhere else. He stopped, blocking Abner's progress.

Abner said, "You are a man I will be proud to work with, Joab. You are a man of intelligence, of stratagems and plans."

Abner raised his hands then to speak of the number of his archers. When his hands reached chest level, Joab seized his sword and thrust it into Abner's belly, where Asa's death blow had been struck. Warm blood burst forth and bathed Joab's arm and spilled on his cloak. As Joab pulled out his sword, Abner fell.

Abner rolled his dying eyes on Joab. He disdained to rebuke Joab or to reveal his agony. "You are a man I could have worked with, Joab," he said, and died in his blood.

And Joab knew it was true, that he and Abner could have worked well together, providing Abner was not the one who had the last word when decisions were made. Both could kill without mercy if they deemed it necessary. And it came into his mind to wonder whether a day might come when Joab himself was called treacherous and ambitious, when he too might be put to death for the very qualities which made him decide that Abner was worthy of death.

Joab turned his back on the man on the ground and on the dogs which were already snapping and growling in the gate, and strode down the street toward David's house. Even after a battle he had never been exhausted as he now was. He wanted only to tell David what he had done, claim his right as avenger, then find a place to sleep.

2 5

IT WAS EVENING in the house of David. Servants were lighting torches and setting them in brackets high on the stone walls. Others were clearing away the meal from the long table at the end of the court of judgment. Tonight David had had many guests. Amnon's ears ached from all the talk and laughter. Everyone acted as if nothing bad would ever happen again, as if this were one of the stories Abigail used to tell, before she became so queer and went with Hezro back to her old home at Carmel. In those stories everybody lived happily forevermore.

Amnon watched and listened, lonely as a ghost since the men were too busy with all the fine prospects the day had brought to notice the small boy who wandered silently among them. Amnon had never found companionship, even with his mother. He was used to being an unnoticed child in a court full of people.

Amnon was near the great oak gate, which had been closed by Benaiah at sunset. He heard in the street a tumult of rushing sandals and shouting voices. There was a thunder of fists pounding on the door. Benaiah opened the door, and a crowd poured in led by that man, Joab, with the straight, sandy hair like his own.

The uproar was so loud Amnon could not tell what people were saying, except that anyone could see that that man was the center of it all. Joab was covered with blood in a way that fascinated Amnon even while it frightened him. Amnon was lost in the crush of people and shoved along with them. Then suddenly, there he was within touching distance of Joab and David as they faced each other.

Joab's shout was so loud everyone became suddenly quiet. "I am quit of the blood of Abner, son of Ner. I have avenged my brother Asa. Abner killed Asa, thrusting in the sword so it went right through and came out at the back and the very shaft was buried in his body. It was a brutal thing to see, and I saw it. Now my brother is avenged and the house of my father is avenged. I am clean, for I claim the right of the avenger in killing Abner."

Waves of pride surged through Amnon, setting his teeth to chattering. Abner had deceived David but he had not deceived that man, Joab. Now Abner was dead and Joab had killed him. Amnon pictured Abner lying dead, with blood on the great gray bush of his beard. He wished he could see it!

Now David was going to talk. David lifted his hands and Amnon saw with surprise that they were trembling. David's voice shook with his most awful anger. He said very loud, "Tell me what has happened."

"In the gate of judgment the body of Abner lies. The dogs lick his blood and the birds peck among his entrails."

Amnon stood entranced by the fearful words, the fearful picture. He stared at Joab, shivering with happiness. How wonderful it must be to be a man and do the things men do, thrusting swords, speaking great, bloody words.

The sound he heard next was coming from David's mouth, but it was like no sound Amnon had ever before heard, except when Abigail mourned the night little Daniel choked to death. The wail rose high and mournful. Tears streamed from David's eyes. His clenched fists threshed the air above his head.

"For many years we have labored and prayed for the unity of Israel. It came at last, but with one sword thrust you have destroyed it. You, Joab, you are guilty! I and my kingdom are forever innocent of the blood of Abner, son of Ner. May it fall upon the head of Joab and upon his house and upon his children and upon his children's children!"

Tears welled in Amnon's eyes at the terrible words. It was the second time he had cried on this strange and memorable day—his first day in the men's court. He rubbed angrily at his cheeks with his sleeve, but he could not stop the tears and he could not stop the terrible words David had spoken from eddying in his ears and echoing in his heart.

"I and my kingdom are forever guiltless before the Lord for the blood of Abner. May it fall upon the head of Joab and upon all his father's house, and may the house of Joab never be without one who is leprous, or lacks bread, or is slain by the sword!"

Mingling with the shouted words of David, Amnon was hearing Dinah's voice, cruel and malicious. "He is not David's son. He is the son of Joab."

David's curse is on *me,* thought Amnon in horror. David has cursed *me!*

Joab held his bloody hands before him, looking at them in a strange way as if he could not recognize them as his own. He said, very softly, so Amnon was not sure whether anyone else heard, "David, you need not curse me. I am already cursed, for I must marry my brother's widow. That is curse enough for any man."

David was shouting again. "Rend your garments, all of you. Gird on sackcloth and mourn before Abner. Let a company of priests go to the gate and take up Abner's body, and prepare it for burial. All of you who love your king will walk in the funeral procession and lament, for a prince in Israel has been shamefully slain. And Joab shall walk beside me, lamenting."

The big man was there now, standing beside Joab, his arm around Joab's shoulders. This was Seth, who was also David's cousin. Seth said, "I share my brother's guilt and I will walk beside him, David. Anything you have to say about Joab applies equally to me, for Asa was my brother and Joab has avenged his death for us both."

"So be it," said David.

David moved through the crowd and everyone made way before him. He came to the dais and sat on his judgment seat, taking up his lyre. His hands swept the strings, drawing from them chords which were a lament.

The uproar in the court died. Half a dozen priests left the hall, and Amnon knew they were going to the gate to attend to Abner's body. When they were gone, David sang a dirge for Abner. The music sent shivers all over Amnon, and he crawled behind the table out of sight so nobody would see that he was weeping. And all the people in the court rent their coats with a great, tearing noise.

David sang:

> "Died Abner as a fool dieth?
> Thy hands were not bound
> Nor thy feet put into fetters;
> As a man falleth before wicked men,
> so fellest thou."

But Amnon, whose ears had always been open for the voice of David and the music of his lyre, heard in the lament only a deepening of his own despair. He crouched against the wall out of sight, hearing over and over the sound of David's curse. He no longer wept. His despair was too deep for tears.

When at last the others were gone and the servants had taken away the torches, so no light was left in the court except the light of the stars in the sky high overhead, Amnon still lay against the wall behind the table, exhausted with his fear and misery. Nobody noticed that the child did not go to his own small room to sleep that night.

26

THE BABY ADONIJAH stirred in his sleep, then fell to sucking on his fists. Reba wakened and smiled in the darkness. The healthy gluttony of the sound was reassuring. After months of anxious care, it was apparent at last that David's fourth son would survive the hazards of infancy.

When Haggith died in childbirth, it had been a near thing that the baby Adonijah did not die with her. One of the concubines, a shapely wench with milk enough for triplets, had taken the infant to suckle with her own. But she was careless and did not trouble to coax the half-conscious baby to pucker its flaccid mouth and draw nourishment from her breast. If the baby wanted to sleep, she was willing.

This was the state of things when Amnon left the women's quarters to go and live among the men. And Reba in her loneliness noticed what was happening to David's fourth son. She went to David and asked that the baby be given into her charge. Thereafter she made it her business to sit beside the concubine when she suckled the baby, to waken him if he slept, to tease the little mouth and throat so they responded by sucking and swallowing. She kept a dish of honey and goat's milk handy, and whenever the baby wakened she dipped a bit of linen into it and laid it in the small mouth.

For weeks Adonijah lingered on the border between life and death, with too little strength to struggle for survival. Then suddenly the change came. Reba laid her hand on the baby's plump cheek, and he turned his face to her hand as if it were the breast of the concubine, making loud, sucking noises.

Reba gave him the honey-soaked linen, unwilling to waken the nurse when it was not yet daylight. Adonijah whimpered, dissatisfied with the substitute nourishment, and Reba rose and put on her robe over the tunic in which she slept. She held the baby against her shoulder, patting him soothingly.

She walked out into the court. Dawn had not come, but the sky had begun to brighten so the stars could no longer be seen. Shafts of red streaked the sky. Reba went to the corner where an oak tree grew against the wall, extending its branches above the court. Here a song swallow nested, year after year. The bird had been a favorite with Amnon. Reba paced the court with the baby dozing on her shoulder, and thought of Amnon who so far had failed to find much happiness in David's apartments. Amnon had always been a lonely child, rejecting love when it was offered. Amnon, she thought. My poor little boy. How passionately you long for love, yet how quick you are to thrust it from you.

Amnon had gone to David's apartments in a peculiarly difficult time.

David would have loved the boy and spoiled him outrageously had Amnon been put in his charge during the stagnant years. But Amnon went to David on the day when Abner came offering Israel to David. On that same day Joab killed Abner. The union had been within David's grasp, but it slipped from him, leaving him bitter. At such a time no doubt David saw, when he looked at the child, not Amnon his son, but a child who resembled the cousin who had killed Abner and brought on this present trouble.

Reba thought of the day she had found Amnon with a broken knife in his hand, chopping off his sandy hair in ragged chunks. "I hate my hair," he sobbed, when she scolded him. "It is an ugly color. If I had black hair like Absalom or red hair like David, he would not hate me. He looks at me and then he looks away, and it is my hair that he hates. It is my hair, my hair." Amnon seized two handfuls of the offending hair and pulled with all his might.

Reba trimmed his hair up as smoothly as she could, and made him a headcloth and a pretty little chaplet of gold cords, and sent him back to David.

David had been troubled over many things during the months after Amnon went to his court. Michal cried and lamented, taunting David with the fact that though he had brought her here to gain Saul's throne, he had lost the throne after all. "Let me go," she begged, in the presence of the wives and the concubines of David. "Let me return to Phaltiel."

Michal talked to David's wives, speaking of how Phaltiel had loved and honored her, inciting them to restlessness and dissatisfaction. Michal taunted David with marrying many wives to achieve a throne which Saul had kept with only one wife and the concubine, Rizpah.

Behind her back the women twittered together, gloating that they had children but Michal was barren. She had been David's only wife for a year. She had been Phaltiel's wife for seven years. Yet for all her boasting of the joys of such a life, she had no children.

The two Benjamites had come—that precious pair of brothers—bringing the head of Ishbosheth in a sack. That unfortunate young man had been unable to keep either throne or head after quarreling with Abner. The brothers thought David would reward them for killing Ishbosheth. But David sent them outside the gate under guard, and there Benaiah killed them. Then David gave the bloody head of Ishbosheth honorable burial in Abner's tomb, and Michal put on sackcloth and fasted and mourned for her youngest brother.

Negotiations began. David's runners kept the roads warm between Hebron and the north. The tribes sent their priests and elders to David, who consulted with men from all the tribes. Then came the day, three days ago, when Zadok came from Gibeon and in the presence of elders from

[137]

every tribe anointed David king of the twelve tribes of Israel. This was David's third anointing.

The court had been filled with notables from all over the nation. The women and children of the harem watched through the open doorways while the ceremony was performed. Most of them wept when Zadok and Abiathar spoke both together the words of blessing over David, king of Israel. And Reba thought what a pity it was that Abigail was not there to see it. Abigail had been so sure that the hand of the Lord was upon David, and that a great destiny awaited him. Even in the wilderness she had been sure. Now all had come to pass, but Abigail was in Carmel, knowing only the world of her own imagination.

Now Reba patted the baby Adonijah who cuddled contentedly against her neck. Amnon had never been a child you could cuddle and croon to. And she thought, How glad I am that this child has been given to me to love and tend.

Dawn was at hand. The servants were in the court, busy about the fires. Reba took Adonijah to be fed, and was in her room sewing when one of the maids came to tell her Abiathar was in the courtyard. Reba adjusted the golden necklace and fastened on the bangles without which she seldom appeared outside her room, and went out to talk with the priest.

Abiathar was sitting on a rug at the side of the court where the tables stood. He was eating a cake someone had given him. A small cup of milk stood beside him on the low table. When Reba appeared he turned with an awkward movement and spilled the milk. A maid came running to clean up the milk as Reba sat down on the rug beside the priest.

He had the unkempt look that meant he had stayed away from her too long, and she sent the maid to bring a new cloak she had made for him. She would see to it that he washed and combed himself before putting the new cloak on. But Abiathar did not notice either the spilled milk or the new cloak. He demanded, between mouthfuls of cake, "What is it Joab used to say about taking Jerusalem with a few men in a single night?"

Reba closed her eyes, breathing deeply. Here it was, the thing Joab had dreamed of doing since as a boy he had crawled about the great gray walls of the Jebusite city atop Mount Ophel.

She said, "David treated Joab shamefully. Why should Joab do this thing for David?"

Abiathar set down the bowl in which he had been dipping bread. He licked his fingers and wiped them on his cloak, rubbing his hand up and down his lean shank. He said, "It would be for Israel—if he could do it. Is it actually possible? Does he really have a plan? Or was it just youthful boasting?"

Reba cried, "It is as real as the stratagem by which he defeated Abner! You know Joab. He is no braggart!"

Abiathar ignored her indignation. "The council was ready to rend one another asunder at the meeting last night. The leaders from the north want to move at once against the Philistines. Those from Judah want to delay until we have a citadel to which we can retreat in case of disaster. There is no citadel in Judah, and those in the north are occupied by Philistines. Therefore the men of Judah say, take Jerusalem, make it our capital, and then march against the Philistines. Yet even they know that a long seige of Jerusalem, ending possibly in failure, can destroy the unity of Israel which has come at last."

Reba cried, "David has no right to ask Joab to help him. He cursed him and shamed him. If I were Joab I would not lift a hand to help David now or ever again."

Abiathar said sternly, "This is no petty personal matter. Jerusalem ought to be our capital. The tabernacle should be brought there and the ark restored. Jerusalem belongs neither to the northern tribes nor to Judah. It is God's will that we take Jerusalem and make it our capital and our citadel."

Reba said, "And Joab is a tool to be used when David needs him and cast aside when David becomes displeased with him."

Abiathar answered loftily, "You talk like a woman. David knows, as we all do, that it is fortunate Abner did not live to dominate the present councils. Joab's action in killing Abner was of the Lord. David knows this. Yet it was proper for David to mourn. How else could he face the northern leaders when they came? Joab did what was best for Israel when he killed Abner. He also submitted to shame for Israel's sake. Only a woman would be foolish enough to look upon this as a personal matter between two men who once loved her. Israel is the chosen nation of the Lord. We do what must be done for Israel's sake, and we do not think of petty quarrels among ourselves when the welfare of the whole people is at stake."

Reba smiled. "So now you want to make sure the Lord has the help of Joab in taking the city. Why do you not inquire of the Urim and Thummim?"

"We have done so. We invoked God's guidance, and the sacred stones confirmed what David was sure of already—that the plan to take Jerusalem is of the Lord. Yet the men of the north have been so long without guidance that they no longer put their trust in the Urim and Thummim. Zadok declares the stones are valid guides only if cast in the court of the tabernacle. They know of Joab's great victory at Gibeon, and if he led them in the taking of Jerusalem, they would follow him. They have more faith in the man who defeated Abner than in the sacred stones."

Reba wrapped her skirts about her knees and laid her head upon them. "I know that David has forgotten the past. He lives only in the present and in his plans for the future. So now he is ready to use Joab's knowledge and his stratagems. Well, I think Joab will come if he is sent for. But when he comes, David must not treat him as before but receive him with kindness and respect. Speak to David about that, Abiathar."

Abiathar said with a look of surprise, "That is not necessary. David respects Joab. Why else would he have let him live after he killed Abner? David put to death the Amalekite who brought him proof of Saul's death. He put to death the Benjamites who brought him the head of Ishbosheth. If anyone but Joab had killed Abner, he would have died for it. David did not lay a finger on Joab."

"No," Reba said sadly. "He only cursed him and sent him from Hebron in disgrace." She added wisely, "It is well he did not kill Joab, since he needs him now."

The irony went unnoticed by Abiathar. "David has sent scouts to study the citadel's defenses. He has spent countless hours in council, discussing ways to plan the assault. Nobody knows an easy way. Everyone wants to believe in Joab's plan. Yet if Joab fails in this matter, the kingdom will be in a worse state than it now is, for it will surely fall apart and never again trust in David."

Reba said quietly, "Joab has a plan whereby he can enter the city by night and open one of the gates. Once David and his army are inside the city, the Jebusites would be as helpless as Goliath when the stone flew through his visor."

"Has Joab told you how he would enter?"

"He has never told anyone. He wanted to tell David eight years ago, when we were in the wilderness. But David had no faith in Joab then. Now Joab is wiser. He will tell nobody his plan, lest someone else do the thing he has set his heart upon and rob him of his dearest dream."

Abiathar rose. "Well then, I shall urge David to send for Joab."

When he was gone Reba saw that he had not taken the new cloak after all. She sent a maid after him with it. Then she walked out into the alley which ran past the camel gate. She wrapped her mantle about her face and followed the path to the well where she had sat with Joab more than once during the months he had spent in Hebron. She sat on the stone curb and thought of Joab, and of how everything he had done in David's service turned out well for David but disastrously for Joab.

Joab, my poor boy, she thought, remembering both the man who lived now in Bethlehem with a wife he detested, and the boy who had come to David's camp at the age of seventeen, fleeing an avenger who had never actually pursued him. Love had been sweet in that distant summer. She remembered only the sweetness now, never the quarrels, never the endless longing she had felt to go with Joab to Bethlehem to the house of Zeruiah. She thought of the night Joab returned from Hebron with his purple feet and his angry eyes, ready to serve David as friend of the bridegroom.

What would have happened, she wondered, if we had run away together to Bethlehem that evening? Would David have let us go? Or would he have followed, killed Joab, and taken me with him to Ziklag? Remembering the love David had for her then, and the grief and anger when he knew she had never loved him and never would, she was sure David would not have let her go. It had taken David a long time to realize that the love she had for Joab, and Joab for her, was more than the foolishness of a pair of children.

So Joab had given his wife and his son to David. He had fought the battle against Abner which everyone wanted but which David could not have led or even ordered. Joab had seen his brother Asa killed, and had returned to Hebron to be publicly rebuked but privately commended for the battle he had planned and won. All Judah knew the battle had served to reduce their tribute to Achish that year; knew also that the battle had shortened the long stalemate, hastening the quarrel between Ishbosheth and Abner and the eventual submission of Abner to David. When David's unwise terms of peace with Abner had disturbed all his soldiers, only Joab had known what to do. Joab had killed Abner for Israel's sake and for David's, and in return he had suffered public disgrace.

This time, thought Reba, you will give David that pearl of cities, Jerusalem. This time you will be rewarded. Abiathar will see to it. And then she wondered, will Abiathar remember to see to it? And finally she thought, I will not leave it to Abiathar. I will speak to David myself. I have not spoken to David of Joab for eight years, but now I will speak to him.

27

THE MESSENGER FROM David reached Joab in Bethlehem at the end of summer, in the month Elul, when the dates were ripening on the palm trees in the wilderness, and on the sycamore trees the early figs were gathered. The streams were low in the pastures and in the courtyard of the house of Zeruiah the water bottle was dipped deep to find water in the cistern.

Joab no longer tended sheep, since that occupation is fit only for those with minds at peace. Instead Joab sought out every heavy, difficult job to be found. While the harvest season lasted he had tended the threshing floor, which belonged to his family but served the entire region. When the harvest ended he set himself to clearing stones from the nearest pasture land, making the stones into walls and plowing the crusted, virgin sod, preparing for the autumn rains and the time of the barley sowing.

Nor had he neglected Lisha, who had sorely needed the kind of strong discipline Joab was qualified to administer. In Lisha also the seed had been sown, and she was so bulky now she no longer needed to be watched and beaten to keep her in order. She was content to press the olives and grind the grain and help with the plowing by day, and to rest quietly when night fell. And if her chatter was as empty and her squealings as foolish as ever—well, one somehow learns to ignore these things. Joab's reward was that Zeruiah loved him doubly for the sacrifice he had made in the name of his dead brother. Zeruiah was fiercely partisan in the matter of Joab's quarrel with David. She was moreover delighted at the prospect of a grandchild of her own. If Lisha was not qualified to rear his children, Joab was confident that Zeruiah would make sure the job was well done.

When the messenger came Zeruiah spoke out sharply against Joab's placing himself again at David's disposal. Yet to Joab the invitation seemed to beckon him from humdrum confinement and boredom into a larger, fuller life. He had long ago realized that only one thing could free him at last from the confinement of Bethlehem. The taking of Jerusalem was in his mind now more than it had ever been in the past.

How many times had he gone to Jerusalem, walking the five miles at the end of a hard day's work to prowl about the ravines that ringed the city on three sides! The city had five gates, but only the north gate seemed to the Jebusites to need defense. The other gates, two on the east and two on the west, were narrow gates used in fetching water or carting out dung. Three were reached from below by flights of steps carved in the walls of ravines. A single man could enter the city as Joab had planned, open one of these gates to a company of soldiers, and moving silently in the night could overthrow the handful of watchers at the main gate, admitting an army. To a man who knew this, the capture of Jerusalem was simple.

Now at last the time had come when David sought Joab out, asking his help. And Joab set out for Hebron once more, laden with bedroll and wineskin. He had timed the eighteen-mile walk in order to arrive in Hebron after sunset, when the council would have convened. I did not sacrifice myself in vain, he thought as he walked the miles. Whatever David chooses now to do for Israel he can do without danger of Abner's treachery. If David needs me now he will take me on my own terms, for I will not be spit upon again by David or any man.

Joab found the great doors to David's court closed and barred. He pounded on them with his fists. And again it was Benaiah who opened the doors to him.

"Joab, old friend!" A broad smile lighted Benaiah's face. He embraced Joab warmly. "You are with us again. Welcome to Hebron and to this house. Your name is on every tongue."

The court held possibly forty men of Israel and Judah, though they made clamor enough for five hundred. Dissension was so hot among them there was the constant threat that it would go beyond words. Yet the clamor was music to Joab, so much had he longed to be again among these men who followed David.

Ira was beside him, embracing him. Ira's eyes with their heavy lids creased to slits as he smiled his affectionate greeting. "David has postponed the council meeting, awaiting your arrival, friend Joab. This is your hour!"

Zadok the priest was gripping Joab's hands. "My boy, my boy, we are one people at last. Who can tell how much your wisdom and courage have done to unite our twelve tribes? As for the death of that ambitious man, Abner, it was God's will, and I say you did well in that matter." Zadok had grown sleek and portly, the picture of all a well-groomed priest ought to be.

Joab had no words to reply to these friends. David's condemnation, when he was last among them, had been complete and all-embracing. Joab could not help hoping the next time God willed for an Abner to be destroyed, He would find someone other than Joab to accomplish it.

Zadok went on, smiling, "The whole north country is agog over you, Joab. You are both monster and angel of light. You defeated that man of many battles at Gibeon when he outnumbered you six to one. The story has been told and retold until now it is said that Abner outnumbered you ten to one, or maybe it was twenty to one at the last telling. And the story also circulates that you slew Abner in the Hebron gate before he could draw his weapon. My people are giving David trouble in the matter of sending the next tribute to the Philistines. They will listen to you."

Joab laughed aloud. "So this is how fame comes to a man!"

Obed the Reubenite was tugging at Joab's sleeve. "Go home, friend Joab," he urged, "while you still have the strength. They are telling such tales about you that you'll be safer in your own pastures. If you disappoint these northern soldiers when they demand the impossible, who can answer for your life?"

Joab smiled, far too happy to take any such warning seriously. "What tales are they telling, Obed?"

"They say you can take Jerusalem singlehanded. When you fail, they will stone you."

Joab said, "Friend, I can take the city. Not singlehanded, but it can be done in a single night. Have no fear."

A brightness like the glow of lamps appeared in Obed's face. "I have not dared believe it, but if you say it is true, why, then I would follow you to take the city if there were only the two of us!"

Joab put his arm about the shoulders of the slim young man who had been Asa's comrade on so many journeys.

Now Abiathar was tugging at Joab's girdle. His face held a look of peace. "When you have opened the gate, David with his army will enter and take that stronghold, and it will be our citadel. I will dwell in that city, and gather to it the documents which tell Israel's story, and the record of the laws laid down by Moses, and all the forgotten songs of our people. I will find scholars to help, and we will put it all together to make the story unified and complete. A man could ask no greater happiness." The joy in Abiathar's face was something Joab knew he would never forget.

Benaiah was urging Joab steadily toward the dais on which David sat. He spoke into Joab's ear, "To use Jerusalem as a citadel from which we march against our enemies—we could wish for nothing better. Yet I cannot quite believe it is as easy as you say. And if we try and fail, we will be split asunder so that the Philistines can continue to plunder us forever. Be advised, friend Joab. Do not cast your influence in favor of a course which, if it fails, will utterly ruin us."

Joab had reached the dais. David rose to greet him. David's smile was warm with love, as though there had never been misunderstanding or anger between them. It was the affectionate smile Joab had known so well as a boy.

"Joab, my cousin," David said, and embraced him. "Welcome to Hebron." He led Joab to a place on his bench. "We have asked you to come," David said, "because we need your advice in a matter of grave importance."

Joab said soberly, "My advice is yours for the asking, David. I am at your disposal in any matter whatever."

David said, "Will you tell me how to take Jerusalem?"

Joab shook his head, smiling. "No, cousin. I will open the gates for you, but I will not reveal my plan to any man."

David's eyes went over Joab. His smile was courteous though it had lost some of its warmth. "You have changed, cousin."

"I have changed. Hereafter I will not be spit upon and cursed and driven hence for that which I do in the service of Israel and of David."

The color rose in David's cheeks above the copper-red beard. "Your terms, cousin, are just."

Joab said, "I will march with the army as long as Israel has an army, except when I am called home to Bethlehem for any reason. I will command my own company, and they shall have the honor of helping me take the city, entering first at the gate I shall open." Yet even while he spoke so boldly Joab was thinking, If David refuses, how can I bear it? I would take Jerusalem if it cost me my life—as indeed it may!

David smiled. "If you open the gates of Jerusalem for the armies of Israel, cousin, you shall command them thereafter. You shall be to David what Abner was to Saul."

Joab swallowed. He closed his eyes for a long moment against the impact of David's promise. When he opened them he saw the half-teasing, half-affectionate smile in David's bright blue eyes, and knew with deep happiness that the love of his kinsman had been restored to him.

Joab said firmly, "You are generous, cousin. Zeruiah will be delighted."

David rose and beckoned to servants who brought from an inner room armloads of rugs. They passed through the crowd, spreading the rugs on the flagging, and the men, seeing that David was ready to speak to them, sat on the rugs, ceasing or at least reducing the volume of their arguments. David raised his great voice above the subsiding clamor. In a moment all were still with their faces turned expectantly toward the dais.

David said, "We have been at odds among ourselves for many days in the matter of tribute to the Philistines. Some say withhold the tribute, and when the Philistines march against us, destroy them and plunder them and seize their walled cities. Yet those who counsel thus choose to ignore the results to us if we should try to conquer the Philistines and fail."

A clamor broke out, but David raised his hands and it ceased. "Others say," he shouted, "pay the tribute one more time. Buy a year, and use the year to secure a citadel for ourselves. Then in case of disaster we will not have to flee over the Jordan to hide in Mahanaim or Jabesh-Gilead. We will find safety, in case of disaster, in our own walled city, the strong citadel of Jerusalem. Buy a year, I say, and many say the same. Use that year to invest and take Jerusalem."

The uproar was very great. Men leaped up; fists were flourished.

Joab jumped upon the bench. "Let me speak!" he shouted. "Hear me! Let me speak to you!"

The hush was only partial, yet by shouting Joab made himself heard. "Take Jerusalem now! I myself know a way to open the gates to you. In one night with a little street fighting you can conquer the Jebusites. You can take it at once. You will then have months to strengthen the city and prepare for war against the Philistines."

Laughter arose, derisive, unbelieving. Joab made a trumpet of his hands. "Twice," he shouted, "I have entered Jerusalem by night. Once when I was a lad of twelve, again during this past summer. I have gone inside the city and roamed at will. The Jebusites sleep like fat toads, secure inside their thick walls. The north gate is well guarded, but there are four gates where never more than two sentries can be seen, and both of them asleep. Everyone sleeps during the third watch, even those who guard the north gate and those who are upon the walls. We can take the city easily."

His voice thundered in the sudden stillness. Abashed at the loudness of his own voice he concluded quietly, "Once we are inside the city, the people who have trusted only in their walls will fall upon their faces, begging to be spared."

The last words were received with a roar of joyous laughter. These men, idle for seven humiliating years, were tasting already the joys of looting.

A long-limbed Benjamite leaped upon the dais. "This man can be trusted. He is Joab of Bethlehem. He killed Abner in the Hebron gate with one thrust of the sword. At Gibeon he defeated Abner in battle though outnumbered ten to one. I personally saw him kill twenty men in that battle. I fought with Abner that day, and before the day ended I would have traded sides most willingly. I tell you this, men of Benjamin—if Joab says he will open the gate, I will be waiting outside the gate if I wait alone."

Joab felt a tug at his skirt and looked down into the anxious face of Amnon. The boy had grown taller during the summer. He wore a blue headcloth over his hair, though at evening most of these men bared their heads. The boy's mouth was tense, as if he did not know how to smile.

Joab stepped down beside him. Amnon said, "Can you really get into Jerusalem?"

David was shouting, "Shall we take the city?"

Shouts of "Aye, take the city!" echoed through the court.

Joab pushed back the blue headcloth, caressing Amnon's sand-colored hair. "I can get into the city," he said.

"Will you climb the wall?"

Joab smiled. "No."

"Is there somebody there who will let you in?"

A wave of love swept Joab. This boy is David's heir, he thought. If we can build Israel into a mighty nation, this boy will one day be its king. He put his arm about Amnon's shoulder and bent and spoke softly. "Can you keep a secret, Amnon?"

Amnon's gray eyes never left Joab's face. "I keep many secrets."

Joab whispered in his ear. Amnon's eyes grew big with excitement. He nodded eager understanding. A wide smile spread over his thin face, transforming it. When Joab would have moved away, he tugged again at Joab's cloak. "I was glad, that night when you killed Abner. He was not David's friend."

Joab's hand gripped the thin shoulder. He had seen from the dais a group of women, David's wives, clustered at the doorway which led to the harem. Holding Amnon's hand he made his way toward the women.

Reba was among them. She held out her hands and Joab took them in his.

"Your day has finally come," she said. Her eyes were bright. "At last our people will know what you can do."

"I will be David's commander, second in the kingdom," Joab said, savoring the thought which he still could not quite believe.

Reba's lips trembled, and she pressed them firmly together. Presently she said, "So now you are to be a man of war. Will you like that, Joab?"

Joab wanted more than all else to tell the truth to Reba in this one moment they had together. Who could know whether they would ever talk together thus again? He said slowly, "Israel's welfare means more to me than Bethlehem, more than my life. In this matter David and I are united. Whether I want to be a man of war I do not know. But Israel needs men of war, and so if I live after Jerusalem is taken, I will be a man of war. It is good to have found, at last, a purpose to live for. David has given this to me."

Joab noticed that Amnon was glancing from Reba's face to his as they talked together. The pallor and tension were returning. He pulled the boy close against himself. "I once prayed to the God of David," he said, "vowing to serve David with my life. For many years I thought I was quit of that vow. Now I know that this God of David was merely waiting His time. Now He has decided to hold me to that promise. Well then, in serving David I also serve Amnon, who is David's first-born son. I am content."

He felt the tension go out of the boy's thin body. A smile that was almost radiant touched, for a moment, the gray eyes that were so much like Joab's.

Joab did not march to Jerusalem with David's troops. He went to Bethlehem instead to spend a few days setting all his affairs in order, for he knew he might not live in Bethlehem again for many years.

David's troops marched north, past Bethlehem, following the highway west of the ravines that cut into the highlands close to Jerusalem. There was only one place where a besieging army could camp. That was north of the city. Here a plateau rose to a peak called Mount Moriah. Here they spread their tents or made huts of crossed poles and brush, settling down as if for a long siege. The Jebusites, confident behind walls twenty-seven feet thick and fifteen feet high, confident also in their gardens and their water supply, congregated on the north wall to hurl insults at the encamped army.

In the evening of the third day Joab left Bethlehem. An hour's walk brought him to the southern tip of the city. Here three ravines united to flow away east and south till they reached the Dead Sea. The wall dipped low above the juncture of these ravines. On the Kidron side, at the lowest point in the wall, the Dung Gate pierced the thickness of solid stone, with steps carved in the face of the cliff. Here in the Kidron wadi cedars grew thick, offering concealment to waiting troops. The Dung Gate offered the best concealment and the shortest ascent, and this was the gate Joab had determined to open.

He followed the Kidron wadi north, past the Gihon spring and out onto the plateau where the army was camped. Darkness concealed movements as long as one stayed away from the campfires. He found his hundred men ready, wearing sheepskins and armed only with daggers and several spare sandal cords. He changed his cloak and tunic for a sheepskin, bound a leather belt about his middle and thrust a short sword into the belt. He bound some sandal cords about his ankles and embraced David and Ira. With his men he set out back down the Kidron Valley. At the Gihon spring they left him, passing silently on down to the southern end of the city to wait for his signal. And now beside the spring Joab waited for the beginning of the third watch.

Water from Gihon was channeled along a conduit carved in the side of the valley just below the city walls. When the guard changed at the beginning of the third watch Joab removed his sandals and tied them to his belt behind him. He walked into the cold stream, stepping carefully and quietly on the mossy stones for a distance of fifty feet.

He reached the place where the conduit passed beneath the thick wall, for the dip at the southern end of the city had been constructed to receive this stream inside the wall. Here Joab lay flat on his stomach and crawled on elbows and knees, squirming along in the narrow channel.

The water was cold beneath the walls. His body was so numbed he did not feel the pain when he scraped against jagged rocks. He came to places where mud was so deep it almost swallowed him. Yet by reaching above to the rough base of the wall he kept himself moving forward down the channel. There was scarcely room here to lift his face out of the water and draw breath. He inched forward at a snail's pace. Rocks bruised his body. Weeds dank with slime raked his face and shoulders. Ooze crept about his ears. With every breath he inhaled the fetid odor of rotting reeds and sour earth, for into this pitch darkness the cleansing sun never entered.

The journey was not long, yet so slowly did Joab move that it seemed endless. The bruises were nothing, and the slime and cutting rocks were nothing, for his company waited below the Dung Gate, hidden among the cedars.

At last Joab crawled out of the slime, emerging into the reservoir. The water was shallow here since it was the end of summer, reaching not far above his waist. Stone steps had been carved into the wall of the reservoir to enable the people to get to the water when it was at its lowest ebb. Joab paused to rest on the steps above the water level, and to daub himself with mud wherever the water had left him clean.

Presently he ceased to shiver. Pain stabbed from gashes on his elbows and knees, but it did not matter. He touched the sword at his belt, put on his sandals, took two cords from around his ankles and gripped them between his teeth where he could seize them quickly when needed. This was the best time for the work at hand. Two hours remained before dawn, the time when sleepers slept soundest, when watchmen, bored with the emptiness of the hours, nodded off to sleep also.

He moved quietly down the narrow, cobbled street, staying close to the houses to keep in shadow. He moved east then south, keeping close to the wall. Twice he heard the sound of sandals above, and huddled down as if he were one of the sleeping beggars to be found in any town. At last he reached the Dung Gate.

Two sentries squatted against the great oak door with its brass studding. Joab crouched in the doorway of one of those caves in the walls which serve the very poor as homes. He tossed a stone which fell at the feet of the nearest sentry. The man jerked awake and stared around. He shook the other sentry, but the fellow slept soundly. Joab tossed another stone, this one into the street just beyond where he was hidden. Gripping his spear, the man trotted toward the sound. When he had passed, Joab leaped upon him, strangling him with a sandal cord before the sentry could emit more than a startled grunt.

When Joab had dragged the body into the shelter of the cave he crept toward the sentry who slept, and dispatched him with the second cord. So silently had the whole affair gone that nobody had been roused in the nearby houses or upon the walls above. Then Joab went to the gate and lifted the heavy bar which was like a weaver's beam, and set it in its place against the gatepost. Then he swung wide the gate.

Softly his men entered, scattering as they had been instructed, not more than two or three in one group. Joab had started north along the pathway nearest the eastern wall as soon as the first of the men entered. He did not hurry, lest he stumble over basket or beggar in the dark. Close behind him came others, moving quietly. By the time Joab reached the bazaar in the square before the north gate, he had heard several muted sounds of struggle, but there had been no general alarm. He waited now in sight of the gate until the altered shadows of the bazaar indicated that a sizable portion of his company had reached this spot. As signal that the time to rush the gate had come, he cast a spear taken from one of the sentries at the Dung Gate, sinking it in the body of a soldier on the wall, so that he fell screaming into the square. Then with wild cries his men rushed the gate.

It still lacked an hour to dawn when the gate swung open and the army of David marched into Jerusalem.

PART FIVE

The Ark

28

FOR MORE THAN a year after the city was taken, Jerusalem was a bedlam. Against the advice of his captains, David had spared the Jebusites when he captured their citadel. Now he and his captains and his priests were moving their families into a city already crowded by a subject people. As many as four families sometimes lived in a single room, with dispossessed relatives and neighbors camping on roofs and filling courtyards. New housing was badly needed, but space was lacking within the walls.

The city David captured was built on a thumb-shaped ridge. Sharp ravines dropped down east and west, joining at the southern tip to surround the city on three sides. North of the walls the land dipped gently, then rose to Mount Moriah, atop which was the threshing floor which served the region. The threshing floor was the property of Araunah, king of the Jebusites. By custom it should have been forfeited to David when he took the city. Grain was paid to Araunah during the threshing season for the use of the great flat stone mountain top, and for the use of the oxen that trod out the grain. David laid no tax on this income; it was Araunah's, as it had been before David took Araunah's city. In return, Araunah ruled the Jebusites, supplying labor levies from among them or soldiers or household servants, as David required. Araunah gave loyalty as well as service to the conqueror who had spared him and his family and his people.

As the months went by, the wisdom of David's policy toward the Jebusites became increasingly apparent. A new city was to be built, north of the walls of the old city. While David and his soldiers fought and conquered the neighboring nations which ringed the kingdom round, the work of building the new city went on. Eventually, new walls would be built, encircling Mount Moriah and all its plateau, and connecting with the corners of the old wall. But houses were needed more than walls while the army of a united Israel was the city's protection.

From the old north gate up the slope toward the crest of Moriah, new houses were rising, built of stone brought in from the hills of Benjamin and Ephraim. The northern stone was whiter, much preferred for the houses, while the gray stone from Judah was broken into pieces small enough to pave the streets and courts.

Next to the old wall the houses of the priests were built. Farther north were houses for the captains and heroes of David's army. At the northern end of the new city rose David's palace, the highest building of all and standing on the highest ground.

The first of David's many wars was fought against Israel's perpetual enemy, the Philistines. The war was not of David's seeking. He would have been content to pay tribute for another year or two, meanwhile strengthening his newly acquired citadel. But more important than the need for peace was the need to strengthen the union between the scattered segments of his nation. The Philistines were peculiarly the enemy of both north and south, and elders from north and south alike were insistent that the long years of tribute must end. So the word went out and the tribute was withheld. The Philistines marched up into the hills of Ephraim, and the army of the twelve tribes marched out to meet the common enemy.

Many young men of the Philistines had deserted to David during the years when he was king in Hebron. David was unwilling to order them into battle against their own people. He formed them, instead, into his palace guard and left them in Jerusalem. It was these Philistines who had in charge the laboring Jebusites, with Ittai directing all.

Year by year David's conquests continued, while in Jerusalem the building went on and on. No house had walls thick enough to shut out the sound of hammer and chisel, the grind of sleds hauling stone, the squeal of timber-laden carts, the shouted orders, the thud of stone blocks being set in place, the whistle of overseers' whips, and the curses of men who found the stones too heavy for their strength.

As soon as men could be spared from building houses, they were set to work on the walls. The old city (which Hebrews now called the City of David) was long and narrow. The new walls angled away to northeast and northwest, making the new city as wide as the embracing wadies permitted, three times the width of the old.

Wherever the walls turned, a tower was erected. From these or from the battlements soldiers could pour down arrows, stones, or spears upon attackers. So vast were the new walls, so massive their gates and towers, that the building of them was to continue throughout David's reign.

Now from all the twelve tribes the families and servants of heroes and priests began to move into their half-finished houses. As soon as half-a-score rooms and a courtyard were completed, David's wives and concubines and children came from Hebron and settled in the great stone palace with its polished cedar beams.

Amnon, Absalom, Adonijah, and Shephatiah, the eldest of David's surviving sons, were growing up. By the time the family and household of David moved into the new palace on the slopes of Mount Moriah, the boys had left the harem to live in apartments of their own which opened

[151]

off a long corridor near the hall of judgment. While David and Joab were off with the armies, subduing Israel's neighbors, the boys emerged into youth under the spasmodic authority of priests, clerks, court officials, and the concubines who ran the everyday affairs of the palace.

David came home between campaigns. His visits were a time of pleasure to the boys. He indulged them all, canceling the daily instruction of the priests, calling little Tamar, Absalom's sister, out of the harem to play with her brothers or to learn songs David composed for the children to sing while he strummed his lyre as accompaniment. All the princes sang well, though none so well as David.

Amnon loved to sing, and from the sweet soprano of his childhood his voice had passed into a clear tenor. Singing was his one talent.

At fourteen Amnon joined the Levite choir and sang with the men on the Sabbath and at the feasts. But it was not long before Absalom too donned the white linen and blue girdle of the choir. Amnon's pleasure in each change of circumstances the years brought him lasted only until Absalom attained it.

Absalom was a sturdy, handsome boy, and brilliant, a son of David whom everyone praised extravagantly. He was endowed with every gift a prince should have. And if ambition and the will to dominate were also part of his endowment, this was not counted a fault in David's second son. The hatred he felt for the spindling youth who stood between himself and the title of heir to David's throne was concealed from every eye but Amnon's.

Amnon was small and thin. His sandy hair grew thick and straight about his large flat ears. His gray eyes were capable of concealing unsuspected depths of both delight and pain. He was small for his age until, at sixteen, he shot up suddenly into a tall, spindly youth with little strength in the narrow shoulders and reedlike arms and legs. For the most part he went unnoticed, quite overshadowed by his hearty, handsome brothers. Yet out of the gray eyes peered devotion to David, ecstasy in the singing, and pain when, as was usually the case, Absalom occupied the center of the stage.

Absalom's brutality toward Amnon was both verbal and physical. Often he burst into Amnon's apartment uninvited, since it was next to his own on the long corridor. Of all his insults, the one which was sure to bring anguish to his brother's face was the taunt, "You are no son of David." Absalom had no inkling why this taunt cut so deep, why it sent Amnon flying in helpless rage to his bedroom where the oak door with its brass bolt made a safe haven providing he got the bolt in place before Absalom threw himself against the door.

Absalom liked to buffet all his brothers, pretending, if they were observed, that he was teaching them to defend themselves. He knew Amnon abhorred violence and had an overwhelming fear of physical pain, and so he continually assaulted him. Amnon's only defense was to put his arms over his face while the blows fell.

Amnon was bitterly ashamed of his cowardice. Again and again he resolved to strike out at Absalom, not to quiver and shrink from his brother's brutality. Yet no matter how hard he tried, the encounter was sure to end with Amnon running up into the trees of Moriah's slope to be sick.

All of Amnon's sensitivity he expressed in love which he poured at David's feet. The suspicion that he was not David's son aggravated his shame as he constantly watched for ways to avoid Absalom. Envy, together with hatred of his tormentor, consumed him. And added to all this was an aching hatred of Joab, who was somehow responsible, Amnon believed, for robbing him of his heritage as the son of David. Somehow, some day, he thought, he would distinguish himself, prove himself worthy of being called David's first-born. If he failed, then he must punish those who were to blame.

29

THROUGH THE CRUSH of people and the racket of building, the choking gray dust of hewn stone, and the penetrating smell of wet mortar, Abiathar walked immersed in his dream. Abiathar's house abutted on the old north wall, close to the eastern side of the city. A day might come when the house would be finished, but it would be none of Abiathar's doing. From the moment Ittai's men got a roof laid over the spacious upper chamber, Abiathar needed nothing more. To this room he brought the parchments he had buried in the caves of the wilderness. He plied Zadok with insistent questions until, to be rid of him, Zadok gave him names of priests and towns where Abiathar could apply for ancient records kept in northern Israel. Zadok also sent him two learned priests and a Levite to serve as scribes. Abiathar set the three of them to copying parchments that were rotted or broken or discolored with time, and to making additional copies of the laws of Moses which could be distributed to priests throughout all the tribes.

Zadok's house was an elegant, solid, handsome affair, much the best among the priests' houses. During the months while it was being finished, he and his wife and his two concubines and their little ones lived in such rooms as were ready. Zadok gave Ittai no peace, and consequently Zadok's house was not only the finest but also the first to be completed. High it was, with rooms for the family built above the main court with its galleries, and quarters for servants and concubines in the lower rooms.

Abiathar's house hardly would have compared with Zadok's if Ittai had not taken a personal interest in it. Reba also made it her concern, consulting often with Ittai, whom she respected though she could never bring herself to like any Philistine. She came often to the house and kept a firm supervision over the Jebusite servant whose duty it was to keep the learned priest's house in order.

Abiathar and Zadok shared the duties of high priest of Israel. Zadok served in most of the public functions, presiding over the feasts at the great altar high on Mount Moriah, while Abiathar was content to work in the privacy of his house or to travel through the land in search of the written words of Israel's history and laws. In the minds of the people it seemed that Zadok was high priest, but in the mind of David they shared the honor. They also shared the gifts brought by the people when they came to sacrifice and worship in the new city. In this matter Zadok, though his household was far more numerous, made sure that Abiathar received his full portion.

In one public ceremony only did Abiathar regularly appear. The Urim and Thummim were in his possession and none of the hints dropped by Zadok could pry them from him. He carried them inside his linen tunic in the small, sweat-caked bag worn by his father Ahimelech before him.

Perhaps some vague political intuition warned Abiathar that he must retain one public function that was wholly his in order to hold his own in competition with Zadok. Perhaps he remembered too vividly how he had crawled through blood to take the leather pouch from his father's mangled body. Whatever his reasons, both waking and sleeping, Abiathar kept the leather pouch about his neck.

Before David marched to battle there was always the public ceremony by which battle plans were confirmed or altered. At the altar on Mount Moriah the heroes and soldiers assembled. Abiathar stood up and made the sacrifice with his own hands, then raised his face and arms to heaven as the sweet savor rose with the smoke. Then Abiathar questioned the Lord, praying for guidance, and cast the two blue stones on the sacred cloth. If Urim rolled farther than Thummim, the answer was yes. If Thummim rolled farther, the answer was no. In those days most of David's plans were confirmed by the stones, and in everything he did David prospered.

For all their differences the two priests worked together peaceably, each respecting the other's functions and responsibilities. Nor could anyone know that Zadok felt at times the twinge of the envy that the truly dedicated always inspire in the breasts of the merely prosperous.

One morning during the second Philistine campaign, Abiathar was sitting at breakfast when his servant announced a visitor. It was Reba. As wife of David, mother of David's eldest son and foster mother of his third son, Reba was privileged beyond most women. She moved about the city freely, accompanied sometimes by one of her sons, or by a concubine or servant, but often going alone. She visited the homes of priests and heroes, a friend of all and companion of many a lonely wife whose husband was away at the endless wars.

Reba carried her tall figure with dignity. The years had brought serenity to her dark eyes and firmness to her full mouth. Her love of bright colors and jangling bracelets had not changed, and David's growing wealth gave her opportunity to gratify this vanity. Her sons and friends were never at a loss as to what to look for when they went into the bazaars to find a gift for Reba.

This morning she wanted to be sure she had Abiathar's undivided attention as she seated herself on the bench at the end of the table. She pushed the bracelets high on her arms and plucked at the golden chain she had wound about her throat, waiting while Abiathar told her with glowing joy of a new-found manuscript that must certainly have been written by Samuel himself.

When he paused to drink the cup of milk at his elbow she came to the object of her visit. In the houses of the heroes was a widow of one slain in the first Philistine campaign, a woman named Rachel. She was a little older than Abiathar, a woman of capability and deep piety. Her husband had left no kinsmen who might take a brother's place and make her his wife. If Abiathar would agree to marry Rachel, giving her his protection and the shelter of his roofs, Rachel would make a home for him. Reba concluded, hurrying to get everything said before Abiathar could interrupt with a refusal. "She has two young children. Their need is great and they are—they are the kind of people you would get on with, Abiathar. Truly this is so. You miss so much living alone, with no young children growing up in your house. Marry Rachel, Abiathar. Let me play the matchmaker in your behalf, and hers."

Abiathar's deep-set eyes rested on the graceful figure of Reba. He looked beyond the golden bangles and the vivid colors, seeing how she had grown in beauty and wisdom and in a quiet composure which many spoke of as queenly. It came to him with sharp pain that he had once loved her almost beyond bearing. But that was past. There was room in his heart now for only one passion—his urgent concern for the Lord's records. Yet to live in a home as other men did, with a wife to comfort him and attend to his needs as no servant ever would, to watch while little ones grew up about his knees—the thought of all this touched him with longing. Abiathar was stirred also by the wish to please this gracious woman he loved so well. How well she knew his needs, and how quietly and surely she found ways to supply them.

He said gently, "She would keep my house in order and save you the trouble of looking after me, Reba."

Reba's wide, generous mouth curved in a smile. "That is not why I make the suggestion, old friend," she said.

Abiathar rose from the bench, leaving much of his meal untouched. "Take me to the house of this Rachel," he said. "I will talk with her."

Through streets strewn with rubble they made their way, past gangs of sweating workmen in scanty tunics or, after the Egyptian fashion, double aprons and nothing else to cover their browned, muscular bodies. The bleached linen and blue girdle of the priest and the purple and scarlet of Reba's cloak and mantle proclaimed them as persons of importance. Men noticed these badges of rank and a silence fell over the shouting overseers and grumbling workers as they passed along the streets.

They left the main street and turned down an alley. Here they found the house of Rachel. Only two of its rooms were finished, and it was evidently a long time since workmen had been there, for vines grew up over the half-finished walls.

They crossed a grassy court in which only a quarter of the paving stones had been laid, and as they crossed Rachel emerged from one of the small rooms beyond and came to greet them. She bowed respectfully before Reba, and stood waiting quietly with downcast eyes.

Rachel was a small, plump dumpling of a woman. Her brow was low and broad. Her dark eyes were troubled and humble. She had apparently dressed in haste, though Abiathar was to learn that she always appeared so. The folds of her cloak and headcloth were never quite smooth, and there were little bulges in her garments as if she carried an assortment of articles casually tucked in and later forgotten. By the metal clasp on her headcloth Abiathar knew she was a woman of Issachar. He recognized her as one of the devout who came to every sacrifice at the city's new altar. His heart went out to her as he held out his hands to take hers.

She did not take his hands. Instead, she prostrated herself. "I am the handmaid of the Lord's priest," she murmured.

Abiathar glanced at Reba. His heart contracted as he relinquished for the last time the dream of his youth. He bent and grasped Rachel's hands and lifted her to her feet. "Where are your little ones?" he asked kindly.

Rachel's serving woman, formerly concubine to her husband, brought in the two children, Jonathan and Minna. They were shy and small in their clean but shabby clothing. He stretched out his long arms, and they came to him trustingly, recognizing a friend with the child's sure instinct.

Abiathar had meant to talk with Rachel and her children and reach his decision another day. But their poverty and need so touched him that he could not turn away even for a day. It was to the children that he addressed his proposal of marriage with their mother.

The wedding was a modest affair, performed in Abiathar's court by one of the priests who served as scribe. Even during the ceremony the hammering and shouting and the rasp of stonecutting continued in the street outside.

And Rachel of Issachar ministered kindly and willingly to the deep hunger the priest had kept under stern control for so many years.

30

MARRIAGE AGREED WITH Abiathar. Rachel saw to it that he took his meals regularly, that his garments were made of the whitest linen and kept clean and whole. She kept the children away from the upper room as well as she could, but brought them to him each day before the evening meal so they would learn to know him as children should know their father. When Abiathar refused to take the young serving woman as concubine but gave her instead to be the wife of his Jebusite servant, Rachel knew that the love her own heart held for the priest was indeed returned.

Love for Rachel's children bloomed in Abiathar's heart from the first. Minna was a shy, pretty little thing who buried her face in Abiathar's cloak whenever he took her on his knee. Jonathan was a solemn boy, and Rachel was obliged to call him constantly away from the upper room when the priests and Abiathar worked on the scrolls. The written words attracted the boy. One morning he stole silently into the room without his mother's knowledge. Abiathar was poring over several fragments of parchment and became aware of Jonathan only when he found the child leaning against his shoulder.

"What does it say?" asked Jonathan.

"There are three stories here," Abiathar explained, while one long arm went round the boy's sturdy shoulders. "I want them all copied on one roll, but in the order in which they occurred. Our people followed Joshua into Canaan a very long time ago. Since then the various tribes have fought their own regional enemies. Priests among them have written down the stories in bits and pieces, but it is often hard to know when these old battles occurred. This is something we must try to figure out before we put down the many stories on one roll of parchment."

"Tell me the stories on these pieces. What does this one say?" Jonathan laid his not-too-clean finger on the smallest of the pieces.

"This one tells how Moses' father-in-law, Jethro, came up into the Negeb and settled there, and of how the men of Judah went against the cities of the Philistines but could not take them because the Philistines had chariots of iron. So the men of Judah were content to take only the cities of the hill country, where chariots are useless in battle."

"Where does it say chariots of iron?" asked the boy.

Abiathar set his long finger upon the words. His heart stirred because his own love of the written word was shared by this child whose milk-tainted breath was warm on his cheek. He said, touching a larger fragment of parchment, "Here is the story of how Eglon, king of Moab, made a league with his neighbors the Ammonites and the Amalekites, and captured Jericho. And thereafter for eighteen years the people of Ephraim and Benjamin paid him yearly tribute. Then Ehud arose to be a judge among the Benjamites. He was clever with metal work, and at his own forge made for himself a two-edged sword a cubit in length. Ehud was a left-handed man, and he bound this sword upon his right thigh under his cloak. He went to Eglon the oppressor, carrying the yearly tribute. By a ruse he persuaded Eglon to send all his servants out of the chamber. When they were alone Ehud came close to Eglon as if to whisper secret information into his ear. Then with his left hand he reached inside his cloak and seized the sword and thrust it into Eglon's belly, and the hilt went in after the blade, for Eglon was monstrous fat. Then Ehud left the chamber, closing the door and telling the guards the king wished not to be disturbed. And so Ehud escaped before the murder of King Eglon was known to the Moabites."

Jonathan drew a deep breath and smiled. "Show me where it says Eglon was monstrous fat," he said. When Abiathar pointed out the words the boy asked, raising wistful eyes, "Could I learn to read and write? Could I be a scholar?"

It came to Abiathar what it could mean to a man to share the love of the word with his son. And so began Abiathar's school for boys in Jerusalem. He discussed the project with his scribes, with Zadok, with Rachel and Reba. When David next returned for one of his brief visits between battles, Abiathar discussed the plan with David also.

In the end, ten boys were chosen. They were between nine and twelve years old, old enough to profit by instruction, yet not old enough to begin military training. They came to the upper chamber six mornings of the week and were excused from study only on the Sabbath. Among them were David's third son, Adonijah, Zadok's son Ahimaaz, and Amasa, one of the grandsons of Jesse of Bethlehem and cousin to David and to Joab. Other boys were chosen from among the sons of the priests and the captains.

To these boys Abiathar read from the parchments, teaching them to recite the laws laid down by Moses and the tales of Moses and Aaron, of Joshua and Caleb, of Deborah and Barak and Samson and Gideon and Samuel.

"Surely nothing," he said to the boys, "is more characteristic of an age of turmoil and oppression than forgetfulness of the law. And nothing is so strong a proof of a people's strength as a revival of obedience and piety. Without the Word written on parchment, the same yesterday, today and tomorrow, we would grow to be like our neighbors, forgetting the laws God gave to Moses."

Often Abiathar was away from the city, continuing his search for records, or listening to tales which had been told by father to son through the centuries. These tales he would bring home and relate to the boys, and the priests would write them down in the scrolls.

When Abiathar was away the priests took turns reading to the boys and teaching them. Those who could write made copies of the laws of Moses for their families at home. Zadok also took copies of the laws and sent them throughout Israel to priests in every town. So it was that Zadok and Abiathar, each in his own way, worked to make the nation ready for the greatness David was winning for it on battlefields. Whenever David was in Jerusalem he expressed his pleasure with the way both scholarship and construction were going forward in his capital, even in the midst of war.

One day Abiathar read to the boys the story of the building of the tabernacle and the ark. While the wandering tribes rested near Mount Sinai, Bezaleel, grandson of Miriam the sister of Moses, supervised the building of a tent of worship which could be folded and carried on the shoulders of the Levites when the people moved on. Bezaleel himself made the ark, using the hard wood of the acacia tree which grew wherever springs rose in the desert. The ark was not large, about four feet in length by two in width and depth. It held the holy relics of Israel. Poles for carrying the ark were passed through rings made of gold and attached to the ark's four feet. Its cover, inlaid with gold, was called the Mercy Seat. Here the Presence of the Lord, the Shekinah, resided.

When he had read these things, Abiathar laid down the scroll. His eyes were intent on far-off visions and his hands trembled.

Jonathan came close, pressing against him. "Show me where it says that about the Mercy Seat," he begged softly. Awe and reverence were in his sober eyes. The other boys crowded around Abiathar. "Show us the part about the Shekinah," Ahimaaz demanded.

Then Adonijah, David's son, cried, "I have never seen the ark. Where is the ark? Why don't we see it when we bring our sacrifices to the altar on feast days and holy days?" Adonijah was a short, chunky boy with the modesty a third son would develop, especially with an older brother as domineering as Absalom. Adonijah was affectionate and even-tempered. His hair was red like David's and his face was a mass of freckles.

Amasa, son of one of David's sisters, was a strong, aggressive boy, the biggest of the ten students and therefore quick to treat them with scorn. He had left Bethlehem to come and live in the house of Seth. He followed Absalom everywhere, and his servile attitude toward his princely cousin was a source of many jokes. Amasa was not scholarly. He attended school only because Seth had ordered him to do so, saying he would send him back to Bethlehem unless he applied himself and learned to read. Seth felt he needed a scholar in his household.

Now Amasa cried scornfully, "Silly! The ark is in the tabernacle at Gibeon. In the Holy of Holies behind the Veil. Everybody knows that!"

Ahimaaz, Zadok's son, was neat, careful, proud like his father, and second only to Jonathan in scholarship. He shook his head in a puzzled way. "It isn't in the tabernacle. The Holy of Holies is empty. I—I peeked in through the curtains once, when I was too young to know better. And anyway the tabernacle is old and ragged and not fit to be used for worship. I do not think much of it."

Jonathan gently shook Abiathar's shoulder to rouse him from his dream. "Where is the ark?" he cried.

Slowly Abiathar's eyes came back to the boys. From the far table where two scribes were at work, one said, "The ark was carried into battle by the sons of Eli. Philistines captured it, and nobody knows where it is now. That was fifty years ago. The ark has disappeared."

Jonathan's dark eyes flashed. His voice was outraged. "It is not possible! If the Presence of the Lord is with the ark, it is not possible for a Philistine to capture it!"

Abiathar said reprovingly, "The ark was only wood and beaten gold which the Lord used and blessed. The Lord gave symbols to His people because they were weak and could not understand that God is neither flesh and blood nor wood and stone. Yet those who do not understand spirit need tangible symbols to which they can attach their thoughts. These symbols are not God! They signify God's presence, but the Presence, the Shekinah, is spirit. If it were not so, how could the tabernacle wear out with the years and the weather, and how could the ark be captured in battle?"

Abiathar rose, shaking off the clinging hands of the boys. "Here is the crux of the matter," he said, and walked to the end of the room and back. His face was raised as if he could see beyond the timbered roof the thing of which he spoke. "The Lord is one God, and He chose our people to be His people, not because we are wiser or stronger or better than others but because among us have arisen from time to time those who could receive His inspiration, men such as Abraham and Joseph, Moses and Joshua, Samuel and David."

A suppressed titter rose from one of the boys at the inclusion of David's name with the fabulous figures out of the past, and Abiathar glared at all the boys as if each had denied the truth he spoke. "David is one of the great ones, and our times are great times because David is our leader. Do not forget it! David has inspiration from the Lord God! Not day by day, nor is he perfect in all his ways. But he is the Lord's anointed, and it is his destiny to lead Israel to the fulfillment of the promises made to Abraham and Moses and the others. It is for the sake of our great men that the Lord has blessed a stiff-necked and unrighteous people and has taught us His law. Among us also have arisen those able to record His word that it may not die when the great ones die. That is the work we do in this room. But do not confuse what we do here with the meaning of the word we record, and do not confuse the tabernacle and the ark with the Presence they represented. People have ever confused the symbols of divinity with the reality. The tabernacle is worn and tattered, and the ark is gone and I do not know where it is. But God is with us still."

The boys had been too intent on Abiathar to notice the silence which had fallen in the lower court, where Ittai had been supervising stonemasons at work on a row of pillars which would support a gallery. When Ittai's voice broke the stillness in the upper room, the boys and Abiathar turned toward the doorway with surprise.

Ittai's voice was smooth and pleasant, though he spoke with a Philistine accent. He lounged against the doorjamb, his thin figure wiry and supple, his bearded face swarthy and respectful. He wore only the short tunic of the workman, but nobody could overlook the authority in his dark eyes. "I will tell you where the ark has been these twenty years," said Ittai, and bowed to the scholarly man whom he admired second only to David.

Abiathar stared. "Of course! You are one who would know of this matter. Where is the ark?"

"That I do not know. But I know it was captured in battle. The sons of Eli brought it against us and we won the victory, and when the Israelites fled back to their towns we found the ark in its linen wrappings. We took it back with us and set it before Dagon, since it is God who gives victory."

Like thunder crashing, Abiathar shouted, "Truly it is God who gives the victory, whether to Israel or to Philistia, according to our need for punishment or reward."

Ittai bowed respectfully. "The tale is told in our land, though the priests of Dagon forbid it and deny its truth, of how Dagon fell on his face in each shrine where the ark was placed."

Abiathar was seething with scorn for the superstitious nonsense which people would never cease believing. "Do not tell stories of the ark as if it were a piece of heathen magic! The Lord gives the victory, not a box made to serve as a crutch for crippled minds!"

Ittai's eyes held a look of surprised respect. He had not expected this type of response from the priest. "I do not vouch for the truth of the stories. They were told in the five cities, and the priests of Dagon made a great to-do over the telling of them, forbidding it and crushing to death those caught repeating it." Ittai shrugged, smiling. "All religions have magic tales concerning their gods. Even yours, Abiathar. You tell of plagues of lice and boils and darkness coming upon a pharaoh who was your enemy. You tell of seas rolled back, of fountains gushing in the desert! You have read such tales to these boys. I have listened whenever I worked close by." Ittai still smiled, and spread his hands in a gesture that was half respect, half apology. "I do not understand these things. To me, Abiathar, you seem the wisest man of our age. I abandoned Achish, who was my friend, and joined David's cause as much to be near you, a man of learning, as to be with David."

There was too little of the egotist in Abiathar for the compliment to register in his mind. He said sadly, "Every Philistine captured in battle has no doubt repeated this story, and those taken in future battles will do the same till all our people hear it and believe it. As if religion were merely a question of which god has the strongest magic." He sighed. "Understanding comes slowly. I shall write the story into the record. But I will say only that it is a story told by Philistines, and I will not say whether it is true or false, for I do not know."

Adonijah asked, "Is the ark still among the Philistines?"

Ittai smiled. "I don't know what has become of the ark, my young princeling. It was placed upon a new cart and two cows were hitched to it, cows with young calves. The calves were taken from them so that they would wander in search of their calves, and they were turned loose in the borders of Ephraim. More than that I cannot tell, except that they did not return to the Philistine plain."

A look of desolation settled over Adonijah's freckled face and blue eyes. "It's gone, then," he said, and sighed heavily. "It's probably gone for good and all."

The scribe who had spoken before said, "I've heard that it is in the Ephraim hills somewhere—a barn or stable or some place like that."

Jonathan came close and laid his hand on Abiathar's knee. "Why do you think that story about Dagon falling on his face isn't true? Isn't God greater than Dagon?"

Abiathar's eyes moved from one boy's face to another, loving them all, longing to make them understand. "God's greatness is beyond our minds to understand and know. Yet He reveals Himself to us whenever our hearts are open and our minds ready. Whether Dagon fell to the earth because the ark was set before him, and whether because God willed that the ark should not be kept in that heathen shrine, or because the earth trembled that night from some other cause—if indeed the thing happened at all— these are questions we cannot answer. Whether God sent plagues of darkness and frogs and boils upon the Egyptians, or whether those things came from natural causes and God used them to set free a people enslaved— this we do not know. Whether He rolled back the sea to let our fleeing ancestors cross, or whether He put it into the mind of Moses to lead the people to the place where winds and waves were mightily at work—how can we know such things? We do know that God wills that we love Him and seek His truth, that we bring our offerings to Him but give Him our hearts and our obedience as well."

Jonathan protested, "But the ark—"

Abiathar said firmly, "The ark is not the Presence. Still, I long for a time when it will be returned to the tabernacle again, a shrine to which our twelve scattered tribes can turn their faces at Pentecost and at Passover and at the time of the Feast of Ingathering."

Next morning early, well before the time set for the boys to come to their studies, Zadok was pounding on Abiathar's door. When Rachel brought him to the upper room where Abiathar was bent over his parchments, Zadok so far forgot himself as to fail in acknowledging the courtesy of his hostess. He could not settle on the bench offered him, but paced up and down the big room in agitation. Abiathar waited quietly for Zadok to speak, then returned to the scroll spread out on the table.

Zadok came to an abrupt stop opposite his fellow high priest, clasped his hands together as if to still their shaking. "I am the Lord thy God, who brought thee out of Egypt and out of the house of bondage with a stretched-out arm!" he proclaimed, and pounded on the table so that it shook. "Our sons are taught this one thing from infancy. You take the very flower of our youth, and tell them it was all coincidence, that they just happen to profit by unusual conditions in Egypt, that they just stumbled onto a parted sea! Why do you undermine the work of the priests of the Lord? Why do you undermine the faith of my son, and of David's son, and the sons of other priests? We chose these boys for your class so that they could read the law and the tradition in their several households, which are key households in Jerusalem, and you tell them the sacred words are lies!"

Abiathar had risen when the tirade began. He said sternly, "My son is among the boys also. Do not forget that!"

For a long moment the two glared at one another, the one so exquisitely neat, the other rumpled in spite of Rachel's conscientious efforts.

Abiathar's eyes softened. "If Israel's priests cannot work together, how can the twelve tribes hope to remain united, friend Zadok? Surely—surely you know that there has been a misunderstanding. Either Ahimaaz mistook my meaning, or you mistook his. Surely you know I would not undermine the faith of our sons."

Zadok's customary self-control was returning. He sighed and sat on the bench he had been offered earlier. "Is it true that you laughed at the story Ittai told of how the ark was brought before Dagon, and during the night Dagon fell on his face and was broken?"

"I did not laugh at the tale. I cannot put my faith in any tale which treats our ark as if it were merely another idol, with a stronger magic than the idols of our pagan neighbors. It sounds like a fable to me—such a fable as a subject people might tell their conquerors, hoping for favor."

"The story was told among the Philistines for forty years before we became their conquerors!"

[163]

Abiathar bowed, admitting the thrust. "I will say no more, then, if it is your wish. Also, I will write the story down in my records, Zadok. I will say it was told us in this way by the Philistines."

Zadok said, "If you write it in that way, it will be plain to those who read that you do not personally believe the story."

Abiathar smiled, and crossed to the table where the priests usually worked. "Come here, Zadok," he said, and the priests stood together at the table. Abiathar picked up a piece of broken and discolored parchment, handling it as gently as if it were an infant. "I want you to read this tale," he said. "It tells how Abraham our father first dug a well at Beersheba in the Negeb and of a treaty he made with a neighboring king."

"Certainly," Zadok replied testily. "I can read, friend Abiathar. I may not be as scholarly as you are, but I can certainly read this old parchment."

Abiathar said, "Now read the story as this priest you sent me has copied it. You see he has added the gratuitous information that the neighbor with whom Abraham dealt was a Philistine. There is nothing about Philistines in the original script, but in this copy—well, see it for yourself."

Zadok studied the two scripts. "I told you he was a remarkable scholar, Abiathar. Not only is his script neat, but he takes the trouble to watch for errors and to fill in the missing details. He is a true scholar, worthy of the position we have made available to him."

Abiathar smiled. "You do not get my point, friend Zadok. I have talked with Ittai about his people. It is doubtful they were in this land when Abraham sojourned here. Their coming was more recent. The fact that they are not mentioned in the oldest of our parchments corroborates Ittai's understanding of the traditions of his people. But this scholarly priest of ours did not trust the knowledge of the nameless scholar who first wrote down this tale. He wrote an error into the records. Now that is something I cannot control. The priest is, as you say, a scholar. I am grateful for his help, and I cannot ask him to give God less than his best effort. Therefore I do not reprove or remonstrate when it seems to me he is overly conscientious."

Zadok tried to interrupt but Abiathar hurried on. "I tell you this to show you I do not have the final verdict when I am choosing what to record and how to record it. If I make mistakes (though I do all that any man can to write only truth), God will find a copyist some day who, in transmitting my words, will see truth more clearly than I and correct my errors. For this I believe with all my heart—God's hand is upon me in this work. I am an imperfect vessel for God's purpose, though I search my heart and fast and pray, seeking the truth. But I am not the first nor the last instrument for the fulfillment of God's purpose. God's truth will prevail. Do not be troubled, then, but pray that God will open my eyes where I am blind and my ears where I am deaf, so that I shall record only such things as may serve to reveal God's plan for His people."

Zadok said restlessly, "Are you trying to make me forget the doubts you have instilled in the minds of these boys?"

Abiathar asked gently, "What do you want of me, Zadok?"

"I want you to find the ark and bring it to Jerusalem. I am occupied in the city with the rites of worship, but you travel through the land and talk with many people. Learn whether the ark was returned to Israel and where it is now. We must bring it here to Jerusalem, so that the devout will have the one shrine to which they will come, bringing their gifts."

Abiathar laid his hands upon the shoulders of the neat, portly priest. "Surely our minds are one in this matter. Surely the ark belongs to all, and would weld our people together as nothing else could. Yet there is a better way to trace the ark to its present whereabouts. David's army is drawn from every part of the country. If word were spread through the army that David wants intelligence concerning the ark, he would be told whatever is known. Let us send word to David."

Zadok smiled warmly. "Truly, Abiathar, you are a thinker and a man of wisdom. I will see to the matter myself." His face grew thoughtful. "When we find the ark I will take it in charge, so that it becomes a part of every rite. You have the Urim and Thummim. Therefore the ark shall be in my charge."

3 1

THUS AT THE end of the campaign Joab came to Jerusalem leading Philistine captives to augment the labor gangs and speed the work on the walls, and bringing word also that David had taken certain companies of men to the hills of Ephraim and would return with the ark in joyful procession. Zadok bustled about organizing a procession to escort David and the ark into the city.

The Levite choir marched out, clothed in gleaming linen with blue cloths upon their heads secured by golden cords and clasps. After the choir marched musicians with lyre and harp, trumpet and tambourine, castanets and cymbals. The streets of the city were cleared of sledges and carts, and the rubble of building was moved out of the way in preparation for the procession.

Abiathar did not take part. "It is Zadok's affair," he said to Rachel. Seeing her disappointment, he sent her with Jonathan and Minna to follow the procession. For his students a holiday had been declared and they had gone, each with his own family, to sing and dance in the streets.

The procession entered the old city, the City of David, at the Valley Gate. It wound through the streets and the bazaar to the north gate in the old wall, then up through the streets of the new city. From his room Abiathar heard the voices of the singers and the sound of the instruments, and he went to watch from his window. Following the Levite choir he saw the oxen drawing the cart, and the ark atop it wrapped in blue linen. And David's place in the procession was just in front of the cart.

At the sight of David, king of Israel and the Lord's anointed, tears streamed down Abiathar's cheeks. For David had made himself naked before the Lord, wearing nothing at all over his muscular, well-knit body except a double apron of white linen, while he danced as the heathen dance before their Baalim.

When he could endure the sight no longer, Abiathar left the window and went back to his table. He picked up the scroll written by Samuel, but the words were blurred before his eyes. David, though chosen and anointed king of Israel, was a man, and a man may be influenced by the circumstances in which his life is set, by the people who surround him. David was too much with his people and the pagans who served him. Naturally he would be influenced in some things by their beliefs.

Abiathar closed his eyes and bowed his head over the parchment Samuel had once held. His heart went out to the Lord God for David, that his error would prove to be a small thing, and that in all important matters David would listen for the guiding voice of the Lord and be led his whole life through in God's ways.

Through the window floated the voices of the singers, and Abiathar knew the song had been written by David.

> "Seek the Lord and his strength,
>> seek his face evermore.
> Remember his marvelous works that he hath done;
>> his wonders, and the judgments of his mouth;
> O ye seed of Abraham his servant,
>> ye children of Jacob his chosen.
> He is the Lord our God; his judgments are in all the earth.
> He hath remembered his covenant forever,
>> the word which he commanded to a thousand generations.
> Which covenant he made with Abraham,
>> and his oath unto Isaac;
> And confirmed the same unto Jacob for a law,
>> and to Israel for an everlasting covenant:
> Saying, Unto thee will I give the land of Canaan,
>> the lot of your inheritance."

The song went on and on, reciting the wondrous dealings of the Lord God with His people Israel, a narrative that passed through different lands and times but ended always with praise to the God of Israel. And Abiathar left his room and went to worship with the people. To himself he said, Surely David makes the songs that I record. Surely he wins the victories that I inscribe on parchment.

[166]

PART SIX

Amnon

32

FIFTY MILES EAST of the Jordan River the city of Rabbah-Ammon crowned the highest hill in a cluster of five hills. North of the city a great plain stretched away along the River Jabbok whose source, a fine, unfailing spring, rose within the water town behind and below Rabbah-Ammon. The water town was enclosed by its own walls and connected with the city by a single gate. The stream ran under the walls of the water town, curving in a great crescent before turning to flow down from the high plains of Gilead into the deep gash of the Arabah and the Jordan.

Within the great circle of the river stood the tall pointed huts and the wide black tents of Joab's besieging army. For two years the campfires had been consuming the available wood, and now dry dung from nearby pastures was used to supplement the fuel supply.

In the midst of the city of huts stretched Joab's tent. Before it was the council fire. Here on a night in early spring near the end of the month Nisan, the captains sat upon the ground, the short dyed skirts of their battle dress wrapped about their knees. Ithmah, Joab's spy within the city walls, had signaled today that the Ammonite army would sally from the main gate at dawn for the first battle of spring. Joab's plans were made, his orders given. With luck it might prove to be the last major battle of the war.

The council was concluded but the captains remained, loath to leave their companions by the fire and retire to their tents. For the most part the men were quiet. If tomorrow's battle was a victory, ten years of war would end. They were preoccupied, each with his own thoughts of the battle or of what peace would mean to him.

Presently Seth rose and stretched and yawned. He had never been one to sit long in meditation. Seth commanded a third part of the army, with ten captains taking orders from him. His battalion would lead against the Ammonites tomorrow, yet it was not of this that he had been thinking. He was pondering a certain order which David had sent by the hand of Uriah, a command it would be Seth's responsibility to enforce. Uriah's company would lead the assault. David's order might be unwittingly executed by the Ammonites. If they did not, Seth would have to make certain Uriah did not return alive from the battle. He did not know why the order had been given. At best it was a dirty business and Benaiah rather than Seth should have been given the job to do. But the matter was secret, shared between the two brothers, Seth and Joab.

He yawned and looked about upon his comrades, bidding them good night. "Tomorrow comes soon enough," he growled, and departed toward his tent. Several others left. Benaiah followed. Benaiah commanded the second battalion, while Joab commanded the third though he also ordered all.

Finally only three or four remained, the men closest to Joab by ties of love and comradeship. Joab sat among them, reluctant to be left with the pain of his thoughts. The years had matured Joab more than the others. They had been years of danger for all. But for Joab they had been years of responsibility far beyond his age or previous experience.

During the Philistine and Moabite campaigns David had marched with the army. Joab's responsibility had been merely to administer David's decisions. But it had become apparent that Joab could direct the battles, and the captains were opposed to David's continued exposure to the hazards of war. In recent years David had remained in Jerusalem while Joab made the decisions. If he had failed even once he would have lost his post. But the victories continued. After ten years of warfare every nation in the whole great oval of Israel's boundaries paid her tribute. Each nation furnished laborers to fortify her cities, build her roads, construct the tiers of tombs under the walls at the southern end of the Kidron Valley, terrace the hills, and work the farms belonging to David and his people.

Unlike the men he commanded, Joab had not moved his family to Jerusalem. Zeruiah still ordered the household in Bethlehem, and Joab had no wish to remove Lisha from Zeruiah's observant eye. Joab had taken no other wife. War was his life. If the Ammonite campaign proved to be the last Joab would be welcome, whenever his responsibilities kept him in Jerusalem, to make his home in the house of Seth or Abiathar or a dozen others.

Joab had lived his whole life in the open, in the Bethlehem pastures or marching with David's army. His skin was weathered with sun and wind, so that his face was darker than the thick short beard. About his eyes the creases were deep from scanning the distance for enemy movement. The gray eyes peered out from this network of creases, decisive, alert, responsible. There was ruthless strength in his face, yet it was not the ruthlessness of one incapable of pity, but rather the strength of one who has endured frustration, shame, agony, and expects no less from those he commands.

There was no one at the fireside to whom Joab could speak of the pain in his breast this night. The matter was between himself and David.

Two others knew of the order—the priest who had read the letter to him and Seth. But the priest was a humble, simple man who would never question his king's orders, while Seth's nature was of such an animal heartiness that Joab seldom confided in him.

Joab sat among these few friends, and across the fire, one of the oldest and dearest of these friends, sat Uriah. Joab could not withhold his gaze from him, though the sight clouded his mind with grief. He was seeing, not the handsomely groomed though square and squat figure of Uriah turned Hebrew, but the pagan Uriah he had known in the wilderness and in Hebron. Three years ago Uriah had turned Hebrew to marry the granddaughter of David's counselor Ahithophel. Uriah had changed in many ways. His hair and beard glistened always with the spiced oil he used. He bathed oftener than any other captain in the army. His helmet and shield and the greaves on his legs and buckles on his breastplate were burnished. His linen, both battle dress and undergarments, were as clean as a soldier can keep them. As for the laws of the Hebrews, queer though many of them must seem to a Hittite, Uriah kept them to the letter.

In all these things Uriah had become a model among Hebrews for the sake of Bathsheba his wife. But somehow Joab liked better to remember him as he had been in the wilderness and in Hebron. There he commanded a motley horde who, for various reasons, had chosen to throw in their fortunes with the uncertain fortunes of David. Uriah had been genial, earthy, honest, courageous. Well, he was still courageous, though marriage to Bathsheba had robbed him of his confidence. He seldom smiled the broad smile Joab liked to remember.

What has he done, Joab asked himself for the fortieth time, that he has to die? He thought, I never would have had the stomach to order the battle you are to fight tomorrow, friend Uriah, were it not for the incredible message you brought me from David.

Ira of Tekoa sat beside Uriah across the whitening embers. He smiled at Joab, yawned, and covered the yawn with his knobbed and sinewy hand. Ira had grown stringy and stooped. It was not his age which kept him a provisioner all through the ten years of war. It was the philosophic turn of his mind. He lacked the active response necessary to save a man's life in battle. He possessed instead the care for detail and the strong sense of responsibility and justice which make a man fit to receive captives and spoil and to distribute to every man his share when the battle ends.

Ira placed a hand on Uriah's shoulder and pushed himself to his feet.

"Our last war," he said. "And it is about to end. We are rich in arms and armor. Joab alone has a dozen assorted shields in his tent and more swords than he will ever carry into battle. Yet he wears the same old helmet with the three sword-cuts across the crest and the broken buckle held in place by a nail. To look at our commander in his battle array, one would never guess he commanded the most powerful army between Egypt and the Three Rivers."

Uriah smiled. "That helmet!" he said, and spat into the fire.

Ira walked over to an oak and rubbed his shoulders against the rough bark. "There is no job more rewarding or less dangerous than that of provisioning a victorious army. What becomes of us all when we must sweat to earn our bread? My old wife, Telema of Tekoa, is wise and shrewd. But still she is a peasant, nothing more. She refused to leave our low-roofed house and our two score sheep to become a city dweller. I have thought the matter over and I do not want to go back to a cottage in Tekoa and an old woman who has followed the sheep. The song of war is not a song of victory or defeat. It is a song of men who wait together, march together, fight together in mutual trust."

Joab rose, turning his face to the shadows. Uriah had been his comrade for half the thirty-five years of his life. He had never questioned Uriah's loyalty. Now he had ordered a battle in such a way that tomorrow Uriah would die. It was David's decision, Joab reminded himself as he walked rapidly away from the fire and the handful of comrades who remained beside it. David knows why Uriah must die. When I see David he will give me the reasons.

But Joab could not push the pain from his heart. I killed Abner for Israel's sake, he remembered. I was young then. Now, after ten years of war I do not forget Abner's death nor the knowing look in the keen blue eyes before the glaze of death covered them. I will carry the memory while I live. Now Uriah's death is to be added to Abner's, to trouble me on nights when sleep does not come.

And he thought, Uriah will go to his death because I order it. He obeys me. That's what it means to be a soldier. Well then, I obey David. This is David's responsibility, not mine.

Joab climbed to the top of the hill which shut out the sight of Rabbah-Ammon from his tent and campfire. It was spring, the time of year when trees are feathered with tender green leaves. The time of year when men's thoughts turn to war. This was the third spring of the war against the Ammonites, those ancient enemies of Israel. Surely the time had come to make an end of it.

Joab sat on the hilltop and looked toward the city, seeing the stone walls that followed the contour of the hill on which the city stood, the towers which marked its gates and winding turns. Behind the walls the houses and palaces climbed higher and higher, crowning the hill. By day the yellow bricks and creamy-white stone were brilliant in the sun. This was the loveliest city Joab had ever seen. Yet it was his duty to destroy it. The buildings and walls were shadowy in the starlight, but Joab knew their shape so well his imagination supplied what his eyes could not see. Behind the parapets the night watch would be pacing up and down, or sleeping perhaps if their captain was not a finicky man. The citadel was strong— second only to Jerusalem of all the cities Joab had moved against and entered during the past ten years. But the city had its weakness, not unlike the weakness which had given Jerusalem to David. Tomorrow Joab meant to probe that weakness.

The plan had been in Joab's mind for more than a year. But the cost in lives would be great. Joab was in no hurry to end the war and return to Bethlehem and Lisha. He had waited, hoping for the luck to recur at Rabbah-Ammon that had followed the armies of a conquering and united Israel. Luck! A stab of superstitious fear shot through him. He stretched out on the hilltop and folded his arms under his head and looked up into the starry sky. He ought not to call it luck—the smile of the God of David. Abiathar did not call it luck. David did not call it luck. Perhaps it was their piety which had given Joab so many victories. Joab pushed fear of the unknown and unknowable out of his mind. Strategy was responsible for the victories. He smiled in his beard, remembering how many prayers of David and Abiathar had been answered in the cutting sweep of Joab's sword, the strong and accurate cast of Joab's spear, the cunning devices of Joab's brain.

His mind pictured the citadel all around, not just the part that was visible from where he lay. Once more his mind revolved the plan he had formed for taking it. The city's water supply was the key. The spring, the pools, the stream, the gardens and sheep folds that fed and watered the people of Rabbah-Ammon were all in the lower town, behind the high, forbidding citadel and separated from it by a wall. In the same way the City of David was separated from the new Jerusalem by the old north wall of the city. To take the water town it was necessary that the main body of the Israelite army attack the main gate of the citadel in such force as to draw off all the guards from the lower town. A major battle must be fought tomorrow, when the Ammonites executed their sally from the gate. A major battle at the main gate meant the loss of many Hebrews. It meant fighting hand to hand against Ammonites on the ground while Ammonites on the walls rained stones and arrows down from above.

Well then, Uriah's company would be foremost among Seth's men when they advanced. With all Seth's men and all Benaiah's and all but three companies of Joab's massed against the main gate, surely the Ammonites would be deceived and bring all their own forces to the defense of their citadel. Then Joab would lead his three remaining companies around be- hind the citadel, keeping out of sight among the trees that bordered the Jabbok. They would take the undefended water town easily. Already fifty ladders lay hidden under earth and sycamore branches in the ravines close under the walls, waiting for Joab's three companies to carry them to the low walls and swarm up them into the city.

I am confident in matters like this, thought Joab. I am a good soldier. I never doubt the orders I give to others. Why then do I doubt myself? Perhaps it is always thus for the man who is second in any kingdom. Compassion for Abner, whom he had killed, washed through him in a choking wave. He knew so well how Abner had felt when David came to camp, a stripling of seventeen, won the instant and undying love of Jonathan, killed Goliath, and set all Israel to singing and dancing in the streets.

> Saul has slain his thousands
> And David his ten thousands.

The song had not been heard for years, yet it echoed in Joab's mind as if he had heard it only today. Supposing some gifted youngster invaded Joab's army and created the furor David had created. I would hate him as Abner hated David, thought Joab. For Abner, for me, for every man who must command an army and serve a king, there is this conflict. David has Reba, and he has Amnon. When I think of home I think of Lisha, my harlot wife who has been barren ever since she lost our first child in the sixth month by cavorting while I was absent fighting Israel's wars.

Yet in spite of all these things, my love for David is true and I serve him with my whole heart. Knowing that David could destroy me with a word, I still love and serve him. David was not always right, but he was a man of understanding, with depths of compassion beyond any other Joab had known. David had sung songs of mourning when Saul and Jonathan died in battle. He brought the only surviving male in Saul's family, Jonathan's crippled son Mephibosheth, to live among his own sons in the palace in Jerusalem. Any other king would have put Mephibosheth to death, lest he contrive to raise an insurrection and steal the throne.

David forgave even his enemies. Yet Uriah must be put to death. Well then, it was enough that David had ordered it. What I do not know, thought Joab, I will learn by and by. Meanwhile, I trust David.

And he thought, I took Lisha to be my wife in order to justify the murder of Abner, who killed my brother Asa. Having Lisha for my wife is the price I paid for killing Abner. Will I also pay a price for Uriah's killing? He shrugged the heavy foreboding aside. If anyone paid a price for Uriah's killing it would be David.

Only Ira remained beside the fire when Joab returned. He sat near the open flap of Joab's tent. In the dimness inside the tent there was the sound of the heavy breathing of the boy Naharai, Joab's armor-bearer and servant. Naharai always slept restlessly on the eve of battle.

Ira looked up as Joab strode through the night toward the fire. He wore a look profoundly somber. "I am anxious concerning the battle tomorrow,

Joab. Forgive me if I speak plainly. You were so very—explicit—as to Uriah's part in the attack on the gate. I have known Uriah for many years. Only recently has he found a woman he could love enough to marry. Let me fight beside him tomorrow. I am an old man, with nothing much to go home to. Let me have one real battle to remember when I sit on our doorstep with my old wife and listen while she talks of which ewe is going to have trouble at lambing time."

Joab sank down cross-legged beside Ira. "You have more reason than most to thirst for Ammonite blood."

Benaiah and Ira were two of the messengers David had sent to Rabbah-Ammon when the old Nahash died and his son Hanun became king. The old Nahash had been David's friend, protecting his borders on the east while David and Joab fought the common enemies west and south. When the Nahash died, David had peace in Jerusalem for the first time since his anointing by Zadok. David sent messengers to Rabbah-Ammon with condolences for the loss of his father and gifts for his coronation.

But the young king had chosen young advisers, men brash and bumptious and without understanding of the true strength of their neighbor beyond the Jordan. They had taken the messengers, cut off their skirts at the hips, shaved off half their beards, turned them out of the city to find their way back to Jerusalem. And Ira and Benaiah remembered the shame of that journey, remembered how they had been received at Jericho, and how they had hidden there for weeks, waiting for their beards to grow.

That marked the beginning of this war. For a time Syria had allied herself with the Ammonites, but only for a time. After Syria made her separate peace, Joab marched against the city and made his camp on the wide plain, within the circle of the River Jabbok. Inside the winding walls of Rabbah-Ammon the remnant of the Ammonite army was shut up, together with a few men from Moab and from Syria who preferred war to peace. Whenever the Ammonite soldiers grew restless within the walls they made a sortie out the north gate against their besiegers. Sometimes they managed to win a skirmish, at least to the extent of gathering plunder from the slain. Twice they had managed to push Joab's men back so far that they replenished their food supply from Ira's stores. But always they were driven back to their city before the battle ended.

Joab longed to confide all his plans and all his pain to his old and trusted friend. But Ira could not be told of this matter. Joab shrugged off the affectionate arm Ira had thrown about his shoulders. "You have your orders," he said harshly. Then he added, to make amends for having used such a tone, "Amnon is your responsibility tomorrow. David has sent the boy to learn what he can before the war's end. He is young, and I doubt he has any knack at all for warfare. He will be your responsibility. I cannot permit you the luxury of committing suicide in battle. At least—not just yet."

He hoped the smile he forced to his lips would conceal his real feelings from this old friend.

He added, "My brother will fight beside Uriah, sharing his danger."

Ira's searching glance turned into smiling affection. He said, "Do not be anxious about the boy Amnon. I'll see that he observes as much as he can without endangering his life. I went to my tent to see how he slept on the eve of battle, but he was not there. Perhaps he has taken his fears and nervousness to the priest. I'll go and see if I can find him."

Joab said, "I'll find him. I want to talk with him. Good night, Ira."

Joab strode off among the huts toward the highest point in this level plain, holding up his skirts to keep them from whipping about his long legs. When the night chill fell he had changed his battle dress for the long cloak he slept in, and it flapped annoyingly because of the nervous haste of his stride. Here on this knoll was the tent of the priest who had the ark in his keeping, since the ark now moved with the army into every campaign.

From the height Joab gazed over the dying campfires which spread afar in all directions. It was a camp without women, for the Israelite custom was to sanctify soldiers and officers alike for war at the beginning of each campaign. Once the ceremonial was accomplished, no pious Israelite would defile himself either by taking to himself a woman or by handling or eating anything unclean. But battle rendered men unclean by bringing contact with the dead. After the battle, then, would come pleasures of every sort, including the enjoyment of female captives. The abstemiousness which preceded the battle only made the men more eager for killing and looting and every excess which is a part of victory.

Joab's mind dwelt for a little on these pleasures. In Bethlehem there were three slave girls he had chosen from among captives in other campaigns. They had borne children, whether his or another's he did not know, and it did not matter, for they were slaves. He thought of Lisha. When she lost her child, the tolerance he had felt had turned to shame and loathing. I am no more eager to go home than Ira is, thought Joab.

And so at last his thoughts turned to Amnon, son of his youth, son of his only love. He is seventeen, thought Joab. When I was seventeen I found my love, and he is the fruit of it. Pity for the boy stirred him, but also anger, since Amnon had disappointed almost everyone who cared for him. Where is his courage? thought Joab. I was foolish in my youth, but never was I so afraid.

He's had every advantage, Joab told himself, angry at the thought of Amnon's failures in the role of David's first-born. I gave up everything, and Reba lives in the harem and goes about on others' errands to conceal the emptiness of her life. We could have been happy, Reba and I, but we thought first of the boy. He loved David—adored him, Reba said. Well then, he's lived his life in David's court while the rest of us fought to establish the kingdom for David and for Amnon, who is David's heir. Does he appreciate the sacrifice I made? Indeed, he looks at me as if I were the cause of his troubles. I cannot talk to him. I can do nothing for him. I wash my hands of him!

Thus did Joab argue with the voice in his heart, seeking by anger to assuage the anxiety he felt for a thin, sensitive lad unable to excel in any of the things expected from a king's first-born.

The black tent which held the ark was here on the hilltop, a darker shadow in a world of shadows. Above the tent spread a great oak which cast dancing, elfin shadows over all. A figure knelt in the door of the tent. At first Joab thought it was the figure of the priest. But something in the narrow shape of head and shoulders told him he had been right to come here to find Amnon on the eve of his first battle. He went up to him quietly, not wishing to rouse the priests whose snores came from within the dark tent.

Joab meant to speak gently but his voice was rough. "What are you doing here, Amnon? Why aren't you sleeping?" His hand grasped the thin shoulder. He felt the shudder that passed through the slight frame.

Amnon was tall but thin as a reed, and no more fit for war than David's daughter Tamar. He was a pinched, spindling, miserable figure of a boy whose eyes begged for affection even as his mouth curled in a sneer of hate.

Reba had begged Joab to take the boy to war this year, before Absalom grew so strong and tall that David would decide he was ready to learn soldiering, for Absalom's development, in contrast with Amnon's immaturity, was ahead of his years.

"Amnon shrinks from violence," Reba had said, "and I do not think he will be able to fight. But he must try. You must give him a chance to try, before Absalom gets any older. If only, just once, Amnon could do one thing for which David could honestly praise him, perhaps he would find peace within himself. Help him, Joab. Try to win his—love. I think he suspects the truth about his birth. He needs to respect and love and admire you, Joab."

I'm willing to be loved, Joab thought now, baffled by Amnon's needs and complexities. He cleared his throat, crowding back the knotting pain in his chest. "We aren't the only ones who do not sleep tonight. It often happens to soldiers before a battle. Shall we go to take a look at the city by moonlight? I wasn't so much older than you when I crawled among the ravines at the base of Jerusalem's walls, while David camped with his army where the houses of the captains now stand."

Amnon said, low-voiced, "You told me how you were going to do it. You told nobody else, only me."

"And you kept my secret," Joab said, remembering the wistful child who had crowded against him on that night. "I'd wanted to please David ever since I was a small boy. I suppose there's never been anything in the world that I have wanted more than to please David. He was like an older brother when we were children in Bethlehem. Then he went away and became a hero. People sang songs about him and he married Saul's daughter and lived in the king's palace. And I stayed with the sheep in Bethlehem and thought about David and was glad he was my kinsman. Then Abner became envious and turned Saul's love for David into hatred. David had to hide to save his life. I would have died for him then. I was torn all to pieces at the injustice of Saul's government after all he had done for them. But for years it seemed as if everything I tried to do for David went wrong. I thought I would never win his respect and trust. But I did. That night at Jerusalem I did. It was the greatest night of my life."

Amnon stumbled as they plunged into the ravine which had been carved in the high plains of the region by the River Jabbok. They followed the ravine, sheltered by trees from the eyes of watchmen on the walls. Their footing was uncertain in the shadows, and when Joab put his arm around Amnon's shoulders to save him from falling, the boy did not draw away.

Amnon said, "If only I could crawl through where this river flows out under the walls of Rabbah-Ammon, and open the gates for you, Joab!"

Irritated, Joab exclaimed, "The battle is all planned, Amnon. You—why, you've never even killed a man! I had to kill two sentries that night. Besides—you're the king's son! David would execute me if I exposed you to such danger!"

Amnon seemed to shrink within his cloak. He drew away from Joab's arm.

Joab said, "Besides, that trick can only be worked once. The Ammonites have a heavy grating across the channel of the stream." He was ashamed because he had spoken to Amnon as an irate father speaks, not as a captain speaks to the king's eldest son. He said, "You will stay with Ira tomorrow, ride in his chariot, handle the reins if he asks you to. Ira gave me my start as a soldier—he trained me. He can teach you too, show you the strategy. That's what David sent you here to learn—not to win the battle but to see how battles are fought. Have you ever driven a chariot, Amnon?"

"Certainly. I'm not a child!"

"Well, driving a chariot in battle is not like racing up the highways of Judah. But for everything there must be a first time. Tomorrow is a great battle."

"Will you really take the citadel tomorrow?" Amnon's voice held suppressed excitement.

"Perhaps." Then he added proudly, "And after this city is taken, we will be finished with war. David will reign in peace. When you are king you will reign in peace. It is well that you are able to observe this last great battle, for you will need to know how such things are done."

Amnon averted his face. "I will never be king. Everybody knows that David loves Absalom best of all his sons. Everybody knows it!"

Joab was carried away on a surge of anger. "You *will* be king! I have spilled too much blood for your sake, and for David's. You *will* be king. I'll see to it!"

"You'll do nothing!" The boy's anger matched Joab's. "I will win to the throne or not, depending on myself. If I am king it must be David's choice. You will not force me upon David against his will!"

Joab could not reply. This unexpected burst of pride pleased him, yet the pain of his own helplessness was sharp. He sank down on the embankment and stared down at the murmuring stream.

Amnon stood near. His voice shook with fury. "Because of you David hates me, pities me, is sad whenever he looks at me. Because of you!" Amnon's voice cracked. He threw himself on the earth and shook with sobs he could not suppress.

Like the whisper of the night breeze in the trees beside the Jabbok Joab seemed to hear Reba's voice as it came from behind the white veil on the night he led her to David. "David has always been too much for us," she had said. "We cannot help what has happened. But we must not hate each other."

So now it had come to this. Amnon hated him because he was his son, not David's. He hated him and blamed him, and it was something he could do nothing about.

Amnon ceased to sob. He sat up, rubbing his sleeve over his face. He said, "This I swear: If I do not become king, neither shall Absalom. Whatever it takes I will do, but somehow I will keep Absalom from the throne. Let Adonijah be king, or some other son of David's—perhaps someone not yet born. And if I cannot manage that by myself, Joab, then I will ask your help in that one thing and in no other."

Joab's arm went round the boy's thin shoulders. "If ever you ask my help, it shall be yours. And I will not interfere in any matter against your will. But I say you will be king, Amnon. And you will rule Israel better because tonight and tomorrow you will learn something about how wars are fought."

33

ITHMAH PULLED HIS thin cloak about him and rubbed his shoulders against the parapet at his back. He tucked his feet deeper under his thighs, trying to warm himself against the cold wind which blew across the city walls in icy gusts. He thrashed his arms to warm himself. An hour remained before dawn, the coldest hour of the night. The moisture from a late spring rain was in the wind to add to the misery of those who kept the third watch on the walls.

Tomorrow there would be a battle and he would manage, if he could, to get himself a warmer cloak. The difficulty was that too many of his fellows would have the same objective. The chief purpose of these sallies was plunder. Famine, pestilence, and the sword had taken their toll of Ammonites during the two years of siege. By now they were more eager to kill the enemy's horses and donkeys than the men, for horses and donkeys could be dragged within the walls and butchered and boiled. His mouth watered at the thought of meat. Food was on short rations and water doled out by the cupful. His body stank so that he loathed himself; he could not remember when he had last bathed.

Ithmah rose, gripping the pointed stakes of the palisade atop the wall. He turned to look toward the Israelite camp. He breathed in a great breath of moist spring air. Suddenly he was remembering the warm earth of Moab in the hills above the Dead Sea. He had hated the earth when, as a boy, his father hitched him to the plow because he was big for his years. He had sworn to leave the little farm and be a soldier as soon as he was big enough to escape his father's constant watchfulness. Well, he'd had two years of soldiering, and now he hungered for the dark earth of Moab, hungered for the musky smell of growing grain. The stench of this closed-up city was an unending horror.

When it is over, thought Ithmah with longing, I will go home to Moab. I will take a wife from among the girls of our village, and I will plow the land Joab promised to give me if I would be his eyes and ears in Rabbah-Ammon. I will sow barley, thought Ithmah. I will plant a vineyard and buy a pair of goats. Perhaps I will need two wives, or three, when my farm begins to prosper. There are girls in plenty in Moab because David killed so many of our men in battle.

Light from the east was lightening the dull gray of the sky. The stars grew faint. Ithmah looked north toward the spreading tents and booths of the Israelite camp, and west toward Moab. In the Israelite camp the fires were burning brighter now. Across the empty plain between camp and city came the clash of metal, and he knew the Hebrews were preparing for the battle. They will win the battle, he thought. Oh, if only they would win a victory so great that Hanun would surrender the city.

They are ready for battle, he thought. How different from the customs of the Ammonites was their strange custom of sanctifying themselves for war, of denying themselves women and wine, of cleansing their bodies and the food they ate. Famine and pestilence drove the Ammonites to seek relief in the one indulgence not even a siege can curtail, so that one stumbled over their entangled bodies in doorways and alleys, and heard their squeals and giggles by day and by night. The famished bellies of half the women of Rabbah-Ammon nourished unborn children, and those whose infants perished at birth rejoiced that their babies did not live to die of hunger.

The air was warmer now. In either direction, up and down the wall, Ithmah could see his fellow soldiers huddled in their thin cloaks, sleeping away their watch. I do not care who wins the war, he thought, so long as I can return to Moab and till my land and plant my vineyard and my barley. Whoever wins, Moab will pay tribute to someone.

The battle would give him a chance to loot among the slain. The helmet he wore was too large, and chafed his ears and neck. Perhaps he would be lucky enough to find one to fit his narrow head. If only he might be captured in battle by the Israelites, freed from his promise to Joab! But he knew that even if he were captured, the most he could hope for would be a bath and a meal, and then Joab would send him back to the city; for how could he wage a war without spies?

He gazed at the tents and fires of the Israelites. The family of their king had taken refuge in a village not far from his own, long ago when Ithmah was only a child. Israelites had been occupied with fighting one another in those days, and had paid tribute to their neighbors as Moab now paid tribute to Israel. One of the grandsons of Jesse had come and gone between Israel and Moab many times. That was Seth, a big fellow with a very loud voice. One could hear his war cry from any quarter of the battlefield. Ithmah had seen David only once but he would never forget the ruddy face, the red beard, the exquisite cleanness of the man.

There had been a battle, and David's soldiers had won. The women and children had hidden in caves or wherever they could, but Ithmah had escaped from his mother and crept through the brush to the edge of the plain, had scuttled up into a mulberry tree. From its sheltering branches he had watched.

All the men of Moab who had not been slain in battle were lying on the ground, side by side in long, long rows. Seth and another Hebrew had a linen line in their hands. They passed down the rows of figures, measuring with the line. After them came other Israelites with short, bloody swords in their hands. These men killed all the men included in two lengths of the line, and spared those in the third. Such was the length of the line that as a usual thing ten men were killed and the next five were spared. Ithmah remembered how his eye had leaped ahead of the two Hebrews with their line, how he had seen that his father would be either the last of a group spared or the first of a group killed. And because the man next to his father was so broad the line had ended at his shoulder, with only four men spared in his group. Ithmah's father was of the next ten killed. Ithmah's brother and one of his cousins were next to his father, and they, too, were killed. To the boy Ithmah it was incredible that anyone could kill his father, who had always seemed the strongest, toughest, harshest man in all the world. There he lay, with blood bubbling in the gash that crossed his throat, and Ithmah stared and stared, feeling no grief but only astonishment that such a thing could come to pass. His father had died without a word, but Ithmah remembered with shame how his brother had screamed, begging for mercy, begging to become a slave, clutching at Seth's skirts until one of the soldiers slashed his hands with his sword.

One uncle had survived to gather Ithmah's family about him. In his house Ithmah had learned to feel no bitterness toward David. If Moab had won, his uncle said, all the prisoners would have been slain, and the third of them which David spared had been evidence that David was merciful. Yet it seemed to Ithmah that David had shown more wisdom than mercy in sparing a third of the men, for how could he hope to collect tribute if there were no Moabites alive to plant and harvest the crops?

So Ithmah had learned to look upon life with realistic eyes. You live in the midst of wars, and you make terms with whoever wins, and you pay tribute and are thankful if enough remains to keep hunger from your family and your village.

Even in Moab's bleak poverty there had been laughter over the story of how Hanun had taken David's messengers and set them upon the road with their skirts chopped off and half their beards gone. Well, a joke grows stale after two years of siege. Hanun had long ago executed the clown among his advisers who suggested the act that started the war. Hanun had learned a good deal from this war. It was a pity he would not live to benefit from what he had learned. Hanun and all the Ammonites had learned there is no profit in a defensive war. Profit is in wars of aggression —profit in spoils and in tribute from a defeated neighbor; profit in slaves, both male and female, to augment the strength of the conqueror. Profit would accrue to Ithmah when the war ended no matter who won, since he would be on terms of friendship with either winner. However, it was difficult to see how the Ammonites could possibly win.

Along the walls the soldiers of the third watch were waking, cursing the cold of the night and the hunger of their bellies, cursing because their clothing was tattered and filthy and their arms and armor in need of repair. It was well that the men had slept out their watch. They would fight better when they sallied out against the clean, strong, well-fed Hebrews.

Ithmah could not but marvel at the wondrous brightness of the Hebrews' helmets and shields, at the hundreds of chariots, the strength of the horses, the bristling forests of their iron-tipped spears. Ithmah felt a thrill of respect at the sight of these men, massed now in the plain and shouting defiance toward the walls of Rabbah-Ammon. In the midst of all moved a small procession of white-robed priests, carrying the fabulous ark of which one heard whenever he heard of these people. Their god is stronger than the gods of Moab and Ammon and Syria, thought Ithmah with a shiver of superstitious dread.

Now the whole city was awake. Soldiers, still hastily fixing buckles and straps, were forming in the square below the wall. Women and old men and young children were swarming up the stone stairway, bent on finding places on the walls from which to watch the battle. Among them were archers whose battle post was upon the walls. The captain of the third watch was shouting to his squadron now, and Ithmah fell into place with the others, cursing as his foot in its shabby sandal struck one of the stones piled ready to be hurled down on the Israelites if they came near the gate. The captain of the third watch shouted at the people who swarmed on the stairs, "Out of our way! Make room!"

Ithmah had learned long ago if you make noise enough it sounds impressively official, and so he added his voice to the captain's, as did the other soldiers who were sufficiently awake. "Make room! Step aside!" they bellowed as they plunged down.

The women backed down or flattened themselves against the wall. Children leaped onto the pavement at the foot of the stairs. Everyone shouted when one of the young fellows paused to fumble at the cloak of a bold-faced wench with dirt on her cheek and matted hair. The captain grabbed the fellow by his helmet strap and shoved him over the side of the steps, so that he sprawled in the paved square, and rose rubbing a skinned elbow. Everyone laughed again. The coming battle had excited them, with its promise of change, of possible good fortune. The mood was explosive, and all were as ready to break out in blows and curses as in laughter.

Shamit, brother to the old Nahash and uncle to Hanun, was commander of the unit that included the third watch. One of his henchmen was waiting at the foot of the wall with a thimbleful of wine and a very small barley cake for each soldier, to give him strength for the fight. Those not in the third watch had had their meagre rations before leaving their quarters. And so the soldiers of the watch fell into step with their fellows of Shamit's company.

Now the heavy oaken gates were creaking back on their iron hinges. Ammonites were marching through by companies, ten in all, each with bowmen, chariots, and foot soldiers armed with javelins and swords. The first company had already engaged the enemy. The Ammonites, noisy fighters, had raised their voices even as the gates were opened. From afar came the roaring war cry Ithmah recognized above the Ammonite clamor as the shout of Seth. Dust rose thick as fog, blinding and choking all.

From somewhere ahead rose the scream of the day's first victim—

whether Ammonite or Hebrew, who could tell? And Ithmah prayed in silence to the gods of Moab that he might outlast this battle between two enemies of his people. One thing above all was needful when you marched into battle in close formation: you must keep your feet, lest trodden down by your own comrades you choke in the dust. So for the first launching of the attack Ithmah was not concerned with friend or foe, but only with keeping his place as the ranks pushed forward, driving back the Hebrews by sheer weight of numbers.

Yet as the wedge of soldiers pressed through the gate, the edges crumbled away like those of a barley cake. Men engaged the enemy, pursued and pursuing hither and yon, scattering over the plain each with the foe of his choice, soldiers against soldiers, heroes and captains against their peers. And ever Ithmah, from wherever he found himself in the midst of the massed men, kept hearing Seth's battle shout raised again and again, and knew that the Hebrew giant must be cutting down all before him. Twice he caught sight of Seth, bristling with arms as if he had picked up two bloody javelins for every one he cast.

Another man fought near Seth, a short, square-built man who looked to be no Hebrew yet whose heart was surely in the Hebrew cause, for a great smile split his swarthy face at every Ammonite scream.

Out of nowhere an arrow struck Ithmah's shield and stuck, quivering, in the thick oxhide. In front of him an Ammonite fell, clawing the dirt and screaming. Suddenly the press of his own comrades melted and an Israelite stood before him, bent over the dying man as he stripped off his shield, jerking the left arm to loosen the clasps that held it.

Ithmah's orders were to fight on the side of the Ammonites as long as the war went on. His sword now slashed down over the shoulder of the Hebrew, severing muscles and tendons. The man's mouth opened wide but if he screamed Ithmah could not hear it above the din of the battle. He slashed again with his sword, severing the man's head, catching it as it fell to rescue the helmet. He threw away his own helmet, which had chafed his ears, but the new one was even larger and he threw it away also. He stood there surrounded by flying weapons with no helmet upon his head.

Realizing the extreme danger to which he was now exposed, he set out running, leaping over the bodies of men and horses and donkeys, ducking to avoid flying javelins and arrows. Suddenly he was out of the battle, and ahead of him a man lay, a Hebrew, one whose body had not been despoiled. Ithmah yanked at the dead man's helmet; the strap broke and the helmet came away in his hands. It fitted snugly, and Ithmah grunted his satisfaction as he pulled the leather cheek-pieces into place and patted the whole thing down. Now he could fight again. He saw that the man's cloak, though short, was whole and thick and almost new, and that he was armed with a fine sword and two javelins. When he had finished despoiling the body he was clothed and armed as the Hebrews were. And it came to him that he had only to be seen killing an Ammonite or two to free him from any further duty within the detested walls.

Tonight I will bathe in the River Jabbok, he thought, while exaltation rose within him. Tomorrow—or the day after—I will return to Moab. Before he reached the thick of battle again he had sunk both javelins in Ammonite bodies. He was close to the walls, and ahead of him the short, square Hebrew who was not a Hebrew was tussling hand to hand with the powerful Shamit, uncle to Hanun, king of Rabbah-Ammon. Ithmah seized a huge stone, one of those which had been flung from the walls and, staggering under its weight, moved forward to crush Shamit from behind. It was presumptuous of a common soldier to attack captains and heroes, but Ithmah would have dared even Hanun in that moment. Summoning strength, he lifted the rock above his head and cast it. As it left his hands, Shamit fell, struck down by the sword of the Hebrew captain. The rock crashed into the chest of the captain. At the same moment an arrow from the walls entered his back. The man's mouth opened as he fell but instead of a scream, blood gushed forth. He fell face up, strangling on his own blood.

Seth was standing over Ithmah, sword in hand. Ithmah raised his face. "I am one of yours!" he screamed. "I meant to kill Shamit! I am Joab's spy, Ithmah the Moabite. I am one of yours!"

Seth turned his sword at the words, too late to stop the blow but not too late to save Ithmah's life. When he fell with the warm blood flowing over the new cloak, now rent from neck to elbow, Seth's great voice shouted for a chariot. When it came he lifted Ithmah into it. "Take him to Ira to have his wound tended," he shouted to the driver.

Ithmah lost consciousness in the jolting chariot but only for a moment. The driver propped him erect with an arm about him. "You were knocking at the gates of Sheol, soldier," the driver shouted, grinning. "But we'll get a poultice on that wound before the gnats gnaw you right to the bone."

The chariot was out of the thick of the dust now and heading across the plain. They passed a stunted oak and saw a spindling youth in a soiled red cloak with a purple girdle, retching with convulsive shudders.

"His first battle," grinned the Hebrew. "He has known only the king's courts until today."

Soon they were in the shade of the trees. A donkey train was nearby. The charioteer laid Ithmah in the shade, shouting to someone that Seth had sent this man in to have his wounds tended. The chariot whirled away and the next thing Ithmah knew his wound was being washed by a pale-faced Hebrew with ungentle hands. Someone held a cup of sour wine to his lips. As the clumsy hands probed his wound, Ithmah fainted.

Evening had come when Ithmah wakened. He could not think, at first, where he might be. Singing and laughter were in the air, and also voices of women speaking in the Ammonite tongue and of Hebrews speaking in their own language. Ithmah opened his eyes and saw above him the feathery spring green of an oak branch. Then he remembered. I have killed one of their captains. Desolation filled his heart. For two years I lived with the Ammonites and served Joab as well as I could. Now it is all for nought. They will punish me because I killed one of their captains.

Nearby Seth was talking. Ithmah turned his head painfully and recognized Joab standing with Seth. He listened, dreading to hear what his fate would be. But Joab was telling Seth that he had taken the Ammonite water town and would hold it for a week or two until Hanun was ready to surrender. Ithmah felt the clammy sweat break out upon his body at the thought of what the citadel would be like now, with no access to the water and food supplied by the lower town.

Seth was cursing because he had not been informed of the plan. "My men died by scores today, trying to break through at the gate and take the citadel! You might have told me, at least, that the water town, not the main gate, was today's objective."

Joab said sternly, "Save your curses for stratagems which fail. What happened to Uriah? Was he slain?"

Ithmah's head throbbed. Uriah was the name by which Seth had called the Hebrew captain as he fell under the stone. He tried to raise his head, tried to shout to Joab that it was Shamit he had meant to kill, not the Hebrew. But fear and languor held him and he could not move or speak.

Seth's big voice was pitched low. "This spy of yours, Ithmah the Moabite, killed him. With a great rock he crushed his chest. I have told it that an arrow from the walls killed Uriah, lest the soldiers fall upon this fellow while he sleeps. He claims he meant the rock for Shamit, and perhaps he did. I do not care much one way or another. Uriah killed Shamit, and Shamit fell as his fellow cast the rock, and it crashed into Uriah."

Joab seemed to sigh, as if from the bottom of a deep well. "It was fate," he said. "We can wash our hands of the whole matter. As for this Ithmah, he has been a faithful spy, and we will send him home to Moab. He has served us better than he knew."

34

THOSE WHO HAD hoped for sport with that young prankster, King Hanun, before he was hanged in the city gate, were doomed to disappointment. David came to receive the surrender of the citadel in somber mood. There was no horseplay, either at the surrender or afterward. David stood in his chariot before the gate when Hanun and his commander, his captains, and his counselors came out, haggard with famine and exhaustion. In less than an hour all of them were dangling from the great beam that had been laid across the top of the gate. Then Hanun's throne was brought out on a sled and set in the open square before the gate, and Hanun's heavy gold crown with its enormous emerald was placed in David's lap as he sat on the throne while the procession of captives was marshaled before him.

Most of them were sentenced to return to tilling their soil, grinding their grain, tending their sheep and goats, providing heavy tribute for Israel. Some were fettered together and sent to Israel to augment the gangs of laborers there. And some were put to the sword. The city itself was put to the torch when the looting was finished. The sick were carried out into the fields and left to die or recover as best they could. When the sun set, the bodies were taken down from the gate and heaped beside the wall, and the soldiers of David passed by, each with his stone to add to the funeral heap. So the dead were covered from the birds and the dogs, as was David's custom, for he was not one of those who left the bodies of his enemies to hang upon the walls of their cities as the Philistines and other uncircumcised peoples were accustomed to do.

The loot from the city was brought to the camp. Each man gave over to Ira all that he found, whether jewels or garments or lamps or kettles or coins. But those who had chosen women from the conquered city took them to their tents for their pleasure. Yet the law required that if they found no delight in their captives, the women must be set free and could not be sold into slavery.

The evening was brightened by flames from the burning city. Laughter and singing rose from all parts of the camp and from the trees and the plain and the ravines that marked the course of the Jabbok. Later, in Jerusalem, Zadok would arrange a religious celebration to mark the victory. But tonight belonged to men set free from the holy restrictions imposed upon warriors fighting the battles of the Lord, men free for a time to celebrate in worldly and carnal ways.

David would stay tonight in camp in order to be present tomorrow when Ira distributed spoil to the soldiers. David shared Joab's tent. Together they ate the meal prepared for them by Joab's armor-bearer. Afterward they sat on the hill looking toward the burning city. Some of the captains came and lingered awhile, then returned to their own tents and their captive women. At last only Seth, Joab, and David were left upon the hill, and it was dark except for the campfires and the burning city.

Joab moved restlessly against the stump of oak at his back. There had been no chance to inquire about Uriah's crimes, nor had it seemed appropriate to introduce so unpleasant a subject during the celebration of this great victory. Yet underlying the rejoicing there was a deep sadness in David's voice and manner. An air of profound solemnity was in every act of judgment. Not even the sight of Hanun's golden crown with its enormous emerald could bring a smile to the somber blue eyes.

Joab said, "So the city is taken, and the wars are ended. Congratulations, cousin. You have established Israel in the land. Joshua couldn't do it, nor Gideon, nor Samson, nor Saul. After four hundred years in the land, you have conquered it. Whoever would have thought such greatness could come out of the pastures of Bethlehem?"

David rose and strode up and down restlessly. The great folds of his embroidered blue robe swished about his sandals. "I wonder," he said, and sighed, "how it all came about? Did God really choose me for so much honor? Or is it as Zeruiah once said to me, that on the day Samuel anointed me ambition was born, and from then to now I have acted only as the shrewd and clever opportunist, making my own destiny? I tell you, I am a man so sinful in my own eyes I do not know how a righteous God could indeed choose me for his vessel."

This thought had occurred to Joab often enough, yet it shocked him to hear David express it, for even in his hours of deepest doubt he had depended upon David's faith in the hope that his own doubts were wrong.

David said, "Did I deserve the hatred of Saul, the suspicion and distrust of Abner? Did I deceive and betray my dearest friend, Jonathan? All through the years I have accepted every turn of events as God's will. The plans that came into my mind have seemed to come from God's inspiration. Perhaps if one believes all this, the strength comes not from God but from his own belief. Perhaps that was the source of my strength, and God was never really with me at all. Look what I did to poor old Achish, who was my benefactor. He died in his palace, not of wounds but of his own despair, after our first Philistine campaign. Look at the Moabites. When the house of Jesse was at its lowest ebb, they took my people in and gave them refuge. Yet war came and the friendship they gave when we were weak became hatred when we were strong. When the war ended, I put two men out of three to the sword. I killed men from the village that sheltered Jesse. I killed the brother of Eliab's wife! Today I hanged Hanun in his own gate and put his city to the torch. All these years, while you were fighting my wars, my cousins, I have sat in Jerusalem writing songs, building my palace, begetting sons and daughters."

Seth was never one to indulge for long in any form of self-examination. "I do not understand your mood, cousin. We have won a mighty victory. A wealth of spoil is waiting to be distributed tomorrow. Peace will be dull for some of us, but for you—David, no man ever had such opportunities to strengthen his people and enjoy the fruits of victory."

[186]

David faced away from the two brothers, toward the burning city. He said sadly, "I hope we can strengthen Israel and serve the Lord in the land he has given us. I hope we can enjoy the prosperity we have bought with so many lives."

Seth's thoughts seemed to be on his own affairs rather than on those of David. "Peace will be dull," he reflected. "I have no wife to go home to. I am already weary of the captive maids who serve me in my house in Jerusalem. Yet in every nation we have subdued the peace must be enforced and the tribute collected. I trust you will find ways to make use of me, cousin, without keeping me too close and too quiet."

Seth had brought a buxom Ammonite maiden to his tent after the surrender, a girl he found in the harem of Hanun. He had found pleasure in her earlier in the evening, after the long abstinence imposed by the laws of holiness. He rose and yawned and stretched his mighty arms.

"I have one question, David, before I return to my tent. Why were you so long in coming? We sent for you ten days ago. The city was ripe for plucking. Yet here we sat, with nothing to do but bury our dead and cleanse ourselves anew and heal our wounds, while we waited for you to arrive and receive the surrender. What kept you so long in Jerusalem?"

The moon, coming from behind a cloud, shone on David's handsome, somber face. "I waited for seven days while Bathsheba mourned the death of Uriah. Then I married her. I could not leave until I had married her, for she is already more than four months gone with child."

Joab said, "I can't believe it." He was shaking. Into his mind came the wish to thrust his short sword between David's ribs. Was it for this he had arranged Uriah's death?

Seth's laughter eddied across the valley and the plain. "What a thing it is to be a king! And I was ready myself to thrust my sword into that poor cuckold, thinking he had offended you in some mighty fashion!" Still laughing, he crossed to where David stood, slapped his back resoundingly. "I tell you, cousin, I am thankful I have never yet set my heart on any one particular woman, lest something befall her in the city while I am away at war! Bathsheba! So it was for her sake that our comrade died in battle! The mighty David, mighty in war and mighty in the bedchamber as well! And now that proud little wench is the wife of the king of Israel. She has come up in the world."

David said, "I will forget what you have said, cousin, because I know of the wine you have swallowed, and the other indulgences you have enjoyed today. You are my kinsman, Seth, and you are mighty in battle for which I thank God. Yet I warn you, do not forget again that I am your king."

Sobered, Seth ducked his head and walked away among the tents.

Joab said, "I can't believe it was for this we had to kill Uriah."

David said bitterly, "Of all men living, Joab, you are the one who should not find it hard to believe such a thing of me." He came and laid his hand on Joab's shoulder, but Joab turned from the friendly gesture, unable to endure David's touch just then. This was the first time there had ever been a direct reference between them to the event of eighteen years ago, the event which had severed them, making intimate conversation between them impossible. They had worked together through ten years of war, but their talk had been formal, not that of kinsmen who in childhood had been close as brothers. They had not even permitted themselves the intimacy of a quarrel since Joab took Jerusalem.

Joab swallowed the pain that clogged his throat. He could not speak. His heart was wrung with grief for Uriah and grief also for David.

David said, "What I have done, I have done. . . . Joab, do you know what it is to be a king and ashamed?"

"I do not know what it is to be a king," Joab said. He added, "Nor to be ashamed."

David said, "I can speak to you of this, for you have known the worst about me and have served me in spite of it."

Joab said, "It is not easy to be the instrument of destiny. I killed Abner. It had to be done, and you know I was right in that one thing at least. So I did it, and I paid the price. You have served Israel beyond our measuring at this present time. Perhaps you—and Bathsheba—will serve Israel in some way known only to the future and to your God. Do not torture yourself, cousin. The thing is done."

David said, "She should not have married Uriah. She was not willing. Her grandfather arranged it. You know Ahithophel, how he bends everyone in his family to his will. Uriah had achieved a coveted position in Israel. Bathsheba had no voice in the matter. She was young—only fifteen. Uriah—doted on her, as you know."

Joab said coldly, "Please don't ask me to regard the death of my comrade as of little importance compared with the happiness you will have with your—latest wife."

David said, "He was my comrade, Joab, even before he was yours. I will tell you what happened. You may think what you like, for you cannot think worse of me than I think of myself. I have—noticed Bathsheba—ever since she came to live in the house Uriah built for her. She has beauty, certainly, but she has pride, an air of knowing her own worth that goes beyond conceit. To me this seems more important than beauty. She also has intelligence—oh, many virtues. Yet I would not have you think I planned all this just to gratify the admiration, the liking, the respect I felt for Bathsheba. It happened. It was not planned. There was an afternoon last autumn when the weather turned warm as summer. I walked on the roof above the judgment hall outside my chamber. The builders had been at work on a parapet and I was looking at it as the sun was setting, having been busy in the court all afternoon.

"I was restless. You have been at war, these years. You do not know what it is to sit at home and write poems and judge the quarrels of our quarreling countrymen, and watch the hatred my—my sons have for one another, and the jealousy that is in the eyes of their mothers. Well, the court of Uriah's house can be seen from my rooftop. Bathsheba was—she was bathing in her courtyard that night. I saw her and—I sent for her."

Joab said scornfully, "You are the king. It was your privilege. You have only twenty or so wives. A king is entitled to his pleasures."

David said, "I am a grandson of Jesse. I grew up in Bethlehem. If I am king it has come about through strange and fortuitous events. I have no wish to be what you just said, a king such as Achish or Hanun or the others we have conquered. Yet you may think what you like, and you are not compelled to listen to my efforts to justify what I have done."

Joab said, "If you are willing to confide in me after so many years, David, I am willing to listen. I want to understand."

David said, "We make a difference in our law between a killing that is planned and one that grows out of sudden impulse. Well, I did not coldly plan how I could take Bathsheba from Uriah and have her for myself. On an impulse, one warm autumn night when I was sickened by the pettiness of my people's quarrels, I brought a proud, lovely girl to my chamber. It would have ended in a night but for the delight we had in one another. I had not thought ever again to find—I will not embarrass you, cousin, by speaking of it further. It is enough to say that I did not leave my chamber for a week, nor did Bathsheba.

"A morning came, however, when I awoke to an awareness of the frightful wrong I had done, not only to Uriah but to all soldiers who served Israel at the wars while I remained safe in Jerusalem. I sent Bathsheba back to her house. When she sent me word, after a time, that she was with child, I sent for Uriah. He had been gone from home for many months, bound by the oath of sanctity. It was necessary to conceal the evil we had done from Uriah, for he deserved no dishonor and no shame at our hands or the hands of any man. I thought surely he would go to his house when I brought him to Jerusalem, for he doted on his wife, as you know. But he did not. I made him drunk. I urged him to go home. I suggested that he could renew his vows before returning to the battle. But having made himself a Hebrew, Uriah was a stickler for the Hebrew ceremonies. He did not go home. He did not break his vows.

"So it was for his loyalty that I slew him." Joab no longer tried to check the tears that flowed for Uriah.

"Tell me how he died, cousin." There were tears on David's cheeks also.

"He was smitten both before and behind in the same moment," said

Joab, and told what had happened. "Perhaps it was this Moabite who slew Uriah, perhaps the Ammonite bowman. We have announced that it was the bowman, since the Moabite was one of our people. We have given him a good-sized farm in Moab in return for his services. He was well pleased."

David said, "Let us return to the fire, for the night grows chill. It does seem as if it was Uriah's fate to die that day. I could have withheld my hand from writing to you, Joab. And yet, I do not think the Lord would want me to be free of blood-guilt."

Joab entered the tent while David remained outside, sitting beside the fire. Joab washed his hands and face at the basin and took a skin of wine and drank from it. You have had your pleasure, cousin, he thought, glancing toward the bowed figure at the fire, and I will have mine. I will bring Reba to Seth's house in Jerusalem. It will be arranged with discretion, for I would not want to shame you, David.

The pulses in his throat and temples and wrists were pounding. He thought he had put love out of his heart long ago. He had never permitted himself to think that he could know its joys again. David would not dare to raise a hand against me, he thought. Or against Reba. His heart was thudding in his chest. He moved to the shadowed doorway of the tent and looked at the figure of his cousin.

David was praying in a posture of profound contrition. Joab went to the fire and squatted on his heels beside him.

"Uriah died while fighting," he said gruffly. "He would not have asked a better way to die. No soldier asks for more than to fight to the limit of his strength, and to die courageously while his comrades win the victory."

David did not raise his face from his hands. "What Uriah would have chosen does not concern me. What I choose—that is what I must live with. How can I govern my house from now on? When my wives and my concubines steal out of the harem to meet lovers in the shadows, what can I say? Their eyes would rebuke me if I spoke to them of such a matter. What can I say to my sons, how warn them or counsel them? I myself am chief of sinners."

While Joab sat beside him, David returned to his prayers. Joab was so moved by the words David spoke that he could not rise or leave the place.

> "Create in me a clean heart, O God;
>   and renew a right spirit within me.
> Cast me not away from thy presence,
>   and take not thy holy spirit from me.
> For I acknowledge my transgressions,
>   and my sin is ever before me.
> Against thee, thee only, have I sinned,
>   and done this evil in thy sight.

Purge me with hyssop, and I shall be clean;
  wash me and I shall be whiter than snow.
Deliver me from bloodguiltiness, O God,
  thou God of my salvation;
  and my tongue shall sing aloud of thy righteousness.
Do good in thy good pleasure unto Zion;
  build thou the walls of Jerusalem.
For thou desirest not sacrifice, else would I give it;
  thou delightest not in burnt offering.
The sacrifices of God are a broken spirit;
  a broken and a contrite heart, O God, thou wilt not despise."

The murmur of David's voice ceased, but he did not raise his face from the dust. Yet Joab was thinking, with an anguish of spirit that might almost have matched David's, "He defeats me once again. I am a man who loves David and I cannot find it in my heart to sin against him."

35

REBA'S LIFE HAD never been free of trouble. In her childhood there had been the Philistines who destroyed her home and murdered her mother. In David's camp she knew poverty, hardship and her father's death in battle. During the one summer when love for Joab had had its brief idyl, David's disapproval and Joab's fears had clouded even that happiness. In marriage she had watched the advance of David's fortunes, troubled by her own and Joab's loneliness, by her inability to return David's love, and later by Amnon's failures and misery.

Yet so long as her hands were busy and her heart could love, she remained serene. When she saw Joab's trouble in the wilderness, love for him bloomed, and she gave it to him in childish ignorance, but fully. When she could no longer give her love to Joab she poured it out on little Amnon. When he left her she found Adonijah's need and filled it, and was herself renewed.

So through the years love flowed from Reba as water flows from a living spring. Dammed up in one direction, it found new channels. She did not fret and she did not brood. If during the night she sometimes wept for the love she had lost, day brought work and a renewed serenity as she fulfilled the obligations and employed the influence which were hers in the harem of the conquering king of Israel.

Among the wives of David, only Michal or Abigail could have disputed her seniority, and Michal had no interest in such matters and Abigail was dead. Moreover, there was not a wife or concubine in the women's courts who did not respect Reba. Many gave her affection. A few gave her love.

As David's fortunes rose, love of Israel and love of the God who smiled on Israel became part of Reba's nature. There was always needlework to be done for her sons, for Abiathar, for the tent of meeting on Mount Moriah. There were always children to enjoy in the court of women and there were daughters of David who remained in the harem with their mothers until they should reach an age for marriage. Tamar, eldest daughter and Absalom's sister, Reba loved as if she were her own, and Tamar returned her love.

After twelve years it still seemed as if the building of the new Jerusalem would never end. The enlargement and adornment of the palace of David went on and on. The carpenters and stonemasons were followed by the artists who carved the cedar fittings and the sculptors who decorated the pillars and their capitals, the cornices and ledges and parapets. David seemed never so happy as when he was planning and directing the architecture and the ornamentation of his palace. The artist who expressed himself in poetry, song, and religion found expression also in cedarwood and stone.

David's interest in the arrangement and ornamentation of the great court of judgment was no greater than his interest in the practical arrangements of the court of women. Here there was no detail too small to excite his interest and stimulate his imagination. The back entry was widened when David saw that it was too narrow to admit donkeys laden with supplies. He supervised experiments with various sizes of grinding mills for the endless work of preparing meal. He devised cranes that swung inward over the cooking fires at the back of the court, or outward away from the fires for the convenience of concubines who attended to the meats simmering in the pots. The great stone kneading troughs were raised to ease the back-bending labor of bread making. The tile ovens that flanked the fireplaces were rebuilt half a dozen times before David was satisfied with their shape, size, and placement. A counter where fruits and vegetables were prepared for David's table was arranged with basins for water sunk right into the counter, with plugs in the basins so that the water could be drained down into wide-mouthed earthen jars underneath. He even talked of building a system of pipes and drains to bring water to the palace, but gave up the idea when he learned how much the maids and concubines enjoyed their morning and evening trips to the fountain.

The tables for the women separated the kitchen from the nursery. Here the younger wives congregated, tending their small children, crooning lullabies, hanging up or taking down newly-washed garments. The younger concubines had their work to do, but if their babies strayed into the nursery there was always a good-natured young woman among the wives to keep the child out of trouble.

Galleries had been built along the walls above the court. Here the older wives embroidered curtains for the tent of meeting. Some of the wives were not Hebrews, and for them to do such work would have been an impiety. But they came to the galleries nevertheless, and embroidered robes for David, for the children, for themselves and for the grown sons who lived in the men's apartments.

The tent set up by Zadok near the top of Mount Moriah was the only structure higher than David's palace. At first it had been a plain affair. Since the ark was then with the army more than it was in Jerusalem, the tent had not seemed important. Sacrifices were made upon the stone altar, and the tent merely formed a backdrop for the priest, sheltering the lamp with its seven wicks in its seven mouths and the table that held the incense and the shewbread.

But now the wars were ended. For two years the ark had been in Jerusalem. There was some talk that eventually David would build a splendid temple to house the ark and the other holy articles, with galleries where scholars could work and vaults where scrolls could be safely stored. Meanwhile, the ark rested in the shadowy recesses of the tent of meeting, and devout women worked with bright wools and glittering metal threads to make the tent a fitting place for it.

Michal often worked beside Reba on the gallery, though Reba was not always happy in her company. Michal's bitter temperament was not adapted to the quietness and serenity of needlework. Nor was Michal reticent in speech. She said whatever came into her mind, not once but repeatedly. She would sit at the great oak frame, pushing the bronze needle in and out and telling and retelling incidents from her childhood in Saul's palace in the hills of Benjamin, or from the few ecstatic months she had had as David's wife when both were young and full of hope. She talked of the happiness she had known in the house of Phaltiel, of how wonderful it is to be the one wife of a good man, the undisputed claimant to his love. Over and over she described how Phaltiel, when David had her brought to Hebron, followed her chariot mile after mile, lamenting.

It was not to Reba alone that Michal talked in the gallery over needlework. Maacah, mother of Absalom and Tamar, sat with them often, and Tamar as well. Abital and Eglah, mothers of David's fourth and fifth sons, were at the frames daily. Dinah also sat with them whenever she was not too busy.

Dinah, first of David's concubines, had been brought back from Carmel to be chief of the concubines and housekeeper in charge of all the servants. She had taken Abigail to Carmel from Hebron, and had remained there until Abigail died, during the first year of David's reign in Jerusalem. Dinah gave many vivid accounts of Abigail's final illness, but it was Reba's belief that Abigail died of anguish. She knew how Abigail must have suffered in seeing David go on to fulfill all her prophecies for him while she herself was not a part of his great destiny. Reba had seen fits of sickness come upon several wives who had passed out of David's favor, superseded by some newcomer. She could not fail to observe how often illness grows out of anguish of the spirit.

Michal alone, of all the women who worked at the linen frames, had no son. However, her nephew Mephibosheth had his own apartments in the palace, and she found some interest in attending to his concerns.

The mood of the women altered when Bathsheba came among them. For many months no one else was called to David's chamber at the top of the palace. Yet there was never a night during that period when a silent figure or two did not steal out through the alley gate to return the same way before morning dawned. Michal grew silent, bright of eye, and for a time her bitterness vanished. Reba did not fail to observe that this occurred at about the same time that Phaltiel was in Jerusalem, conferring with officials about contracts for building roads between Jericho and the larger towns in Benjamin.

Reba observed changes in others as well, both wives and concubines, a heightened gaiety in some, an air of secrecy in others. She read the meaning of these changes and her heart beat faster at the thought of what this new freedom in the harem could mean to her if ever she found the courage to use it. In the great court or in the houses of her friends she often saw Joab, who was in charge of constructing a great fortress at the angle in the west wall. Joab dwelt in the house of Seth. When his eyes met hers, Reba read the loneliness in them and knew his love had not withered with the years.

Bathsheba was the most troubling influence ever to enter the harem. Michal was not the only wife whose tongue lashed out against the woman who married David seven days after her husband died in battle, and five months later gave birth to a son. David loved Bathsheba; that was the trouble. In the court, his eyes sought her out wherever she might be.

When her child died, the women were ready to sympathize with her. But she held herself apart, as though she alone was David's wife and they were all intruders. Six months later she gave birth a second time and named the child Solomon. Even those who hated her most had to agree that Solomon was an attractive child.

Whether David sensed the tension in the harem or whether his passion for Bathsheba had ebbed, Reba did not care to guess. Tension had eased. A new wife, a niece of Hiram, king of Tyre, came to the harem. David was once more noticing his wives, speaking with them all in the court of women, occasionally calling one of them to his chamber.

Bathsheba continued to give far too many orders, prefacing them with, "The king desires . . ." or "The king prefers . . ." as if she alone understood David. But the women told one another that her officiousness grew out of her diminished claim on David. And so Bathsheba was becoming one of them, though as yet she made no close friend among them but sat apart with little Solomon, singing to him or playing games with his fingers and toes so that he gurgled with laughter.

As for Reba, peace had come with knowing David had given Bathsheba his love as he had given it to no wife since he married her in the wilderness. She hummed as she worked. Not even Michal could trouble her. She lived for the meetings she had with Joab. She dreamed for hours and days over such occasions, reliving every glance, every word.

There was a day in spring when she stood in her whitest cloak near the altar beside which Zadok had killed a great number of Passover lambs. The blood flowed down through a trough carved in stone, and priests carried the carcasses away to be prepared for sacrifice and feast. Throughout the prayers the Levite choir sang, both ancient songs and new ones David had composed. Now they were singing one of her favorites, a song of David:

"The Lord is my shepherd; I shall not want.
He maketh me to lie down in green pastures;
He leadeth me beside the still waters.
He restoreth my soul:
He leadeth me in the paths of righteousness for his name's sake.
Yea, though I walk through the valley of the shadow of death,
I will fear no evil: for thou art with me;
Thy rod and thy staff they comfort me.
Thou preparest a table before me in the presence of mine enemies:
Thou anointest my head with oil; my cup runneth over.
Surely goodness and mercy shall follow me all the days of my life:
And I will dwell in the house of the Lord for ever."

Reba's eyes had gone to the choir in their white cloaks and blue girdles, and the blue headcloths held in place by silver chaplets. She had singled out Adonijah and Amnon among the others. And she had seen Joab among the men who stood with David. Joab's eyes were on her long before she saw him. He stood taller than most of the men, no giant like Seth, but tall and lean, with the seasoned strength of the soldier. All the lines of the weathered face seemed to lead toward the intent gray eyes. When she tried to smile at Joab her mouth trembled and her eyes blurred and the golden band at her throat seemed suddenly tight.

That had been a year ago, the first peacetime Passover in Jerusalem. Now it was spring again. It was morning, and Reba awakened to the sound of bird song outside the window high in the wall of her room. Remembering the song swallow that had nested outside her window in Hebron, and how Amnon had loved the small gray bird, she was filled with a happiness she did not analyze. Without knowing why, she felt the strongest urge to visit Rachel.

She left the palace by the main gate. She was wearing her favorite red cloak with purple bands above the hem, and her favorite gold collar. Inside the long sleeves half a dozen bracelets jangled as she walked over the cobblestones down the winding street. She passed the house Uriah had built for Bathsheba, and beyond it the house of Seth. She met people bound for the palace and remembered this was the day David would hear a dispute between two soldiers over a woman captive. All Jerusalem would be pouring into the great court of David to hear the trial. Reba was half of a mind to turn back, but still the impulse that had sent her forth kept her going.

She reached the section of the priests' houses, and turned. Her eyes rested with pleasure on Abiathar's house with its facing of great blocks of hewn stone. Upon no house in Jerusalem had Ittai lavished more care than this one. One forgot that Ittai was a Philistine, though there had been a time when Reba would not have believed such a thing possible.

Reba knocked on the polished cedarwood door, her bracelets jangling. The door opened, and Joab stood in the entry. "Reba," he said, and pushed the door shut behind her. "They aren't"—he swallowed—"at home." His eyes burned into hers with a gladness surely reflected by her own. "They are at David's court," he said, and took the hands she held out to him. He kissed her forehead under the veil of fine linen, then kissed her mouth. They had not kissed in twenty years.

It did not occur to them to move from the dark, shadowed entry. After a time Joab said, "At home in Bethlehem I have four concubines and a wife. But I have no pleasure in them. I live as austerely as if I were still sanctified for battle."

Reba's fingers twined in his beard. "You haven't changed. Your beard is the beard of a man, but you are still the boy I took in my arms in the wilderness. I had forgotten how it is to be embraced by the one I love." She pressed her cheek against his. "And here with your arms about me I am only a foolish, ignorant girl who took her love in the wadies of the wilderness or on a thin rug in a cold, stale-smelling tent. Joab, have we wasted our lives? Have we lived for nothing?"

Joab pushed back the white veil. It fell unnoticed to the stone floor. He touched her eyelids with a tender finger, then crushed her close while his tears moistened the smooth dark hair.

She said, "Where does a queen go to consort with the commander of the king's army?"

Joab's voice was muffled in her hair. "That is treason—what you suggest. We would both be put to death if we were found out."

"David is not concerned about such things. He has changed since he married Bathsheba. Six months after Bathsheba came into the harem one of the concubines was with child. When David knew of it he came into the court and before us all he spoke kindly to her and told Dinah to lighten her household duties till after the child should be weaned. With his own hands he circumcised the son she bore, though he seldom does this for the sons of the concubines, leaving it to the priests. You see, he acknowledged her child, even though we all knew it could not have been David's. Since then I think there is not a wife or a concubine in the palace who hasn't comforted herself at one time or another. Even Maacah and Michal. I sometimes think I alone of them all have remained—lonely."

Joab led her to a bench in the nearby reception room. "Ever since David told me how it came about between himself and Bathsheba, I have tried to believe I now have the right to ask you to give me your love. Yet it is hard to go against David. How can I commit this treason against him?"

Reba drew away from his arms. "David does not treat this thing as treason. Isn't it a little presumptuous for you to decide you know more than the king about what is treason and what isn't?"

Joab smiled ruefully. "We are quarreling as we did in the wilderness. Remember? We were always quarreling. You wanted to go to Bethlehem and I couldn't take you there—or thought I couldn't, which amounted to the same thing in the end."

"To this day," Reba said sadly, "I have never been to Bethlehem. Now I think I will never go. Since I cannot go there as your wife, Joab, I think I could not bear to go at all. What a bright dream it was!"

She buried her face in her hands. Joab gathered her close, kissing the hands till she took them from her face and raised her mouth to his. She said urgently, "Where do they go, these wives of David? How are such things managed?"

Joab could not turn away, though shame fought with the hunger that suffused his whole being. "Seth's house is near the palace," he said. "A woman in the dress of a servant could find her way there. No clanking bracelets. No golden chains. No fine linen. A coarse, unbleached cloak and a thick mantle and rough sandals. Seth is often away. He is away now. The servants go to their quarters when daylight fades. I will leave the front door unbolted so you need not knock, but just walk in." His arms were tight about her. His voice was choked. "Tonight," he said. "Come tonight."

Reba found the court of women deserted when she returned. She moved silently across the pavement to the corridor which led to her room. There she paced up and down in agitation, shaken with the exquisite pain of longing for tonight, shaken with this upheaval of all the emotions she had held in precarious balance for twenty years. When she could endure the close confinement of her room no longer, she returned to the court and climbed to the gallery and picked up her long bronze needle with clumsy fingers. She heard quick steps approach and looked up, and Tamar was with her. Tamar carried in her arms a blue cloak she was embroidering for Absalom. She was not yet proficient enough with the needle to work on the Veil of the tabernacle, but was content to embroider robes for herself, for Maacah, and now this one which she hoped her brother would consent to wear when he sat on the dais.

Reba's preoccupation fled at sight of this girl whom she loved as if she were her own. Tamar's beauty, in Reba's eyes, was complete, something perfect and whole. The erect, graceful bearing of the girl, the lovely arms, the set of her neck and shoulders, the curve of her cheek, the dark, joyous depths of the eyes under the heavy brows were all part of her beauty. She was fifteen, and womanliness sat upon her as she worked, but childhood was also in her when she romped with the children or skipped up the steps to sit with her mother and Reba in the gallery.

"I saw you were not in the great court with the others," she said. "I thought it would be nice to come and sit with you alone." On an impulse she put her arm about Reba's shoulder and kissed her cheek. Then she sat on one of the thick rugs and straightened the blue robe and inspected it critically. She had sewed silver bells in a row at the hem, and they tinkled as she shook out the garment. The silver stars she had embroidered at the shoulders were heavy with metal thread. "Will he wear it, do you think?" she asked anxiously, and then she said quickly, "I have a good notion to give it to Amnon instead. He has no sister to make him fancy cloaks with foolish bells on them."

"You are his sister. All the girls in the court are his sisters," Reba said.

At the words a flush crept into the girl's cheeks, and she cast down her eyes.

She loves him, Reba thought, with a quick intake of her breath. Perhaps it was her own suddenly-released emotions which revealed the truth to her now. Tamar had talked of Amnon a great deal as they worked together in the gallery. Reba had thought the girl did it to please a fond mother's feelings, but now she realized that for several months the girl had spoken as one speaks of the object of her dreams. She said, "Tamar, are you in love with Amnon?"

The girl buried her face in the blue cloak, then looked up with eyes that shone. Her mouth curved sweetly. "He is sad, so often. I want to comfort him. I think he needs me. I understand him. I—I love him. Is it wrong? In the court of my grandfather in Geshur it is common for a king's son to marry his half-sister. Well, then, why would it be wrong for me to marry Amnon? Because, even if it is wrong, I must love him anyway. I cannot help myself. And he loves me. I know he does. I see it whenever he looks at me."

Reba took the girl in her arms. "To think that Amnon could have you for his wife," she said. "I never dreamed anything so wonderful could come to him. When I think of it I could weep for happiness. To call you daughter. To attend you in childbirth and fondle the grandchildren you would give to David! Oh, Tamar, you wonderful child! How happy you have made me!"

The girl raised tear-wet eyes. "Would David really consent?" Then, confidently, "He would consent if I begged him. David is fond of me."

David was indeed fond of the lovely child who was his eldest daughter. Reba said, "Amnon must be the one who brings the matter to David. A man must be strong, and we who love Amnon must make him strong."

The girl sighed. "How will he know, unless he speaks of love to me? I can't tell him to go to David. He doesn't give me a chance."

"Give him time, dear. You are both young. Wait a while. Then if necessary I will lead Amnon to tell me what is in his heart. It will come out right in the end. Only be patient."

It came to Reba then that the plans she had made with Joab would endanger Amnon even more than themselves. Her heart grew cold as a stone. A stillness went over her, and her hands would not obey her will. She left the needle in the white linen and leaned her head against the wall, closing her eyes.

Tamar sewed and chattered away, but Reba was remembering a summer when she had been young and in love and full of the wish to give herself and her love to a boy with troubled, downcast eyes that were so like Amnon's.

When evening came she called Dinah. She told her only what had to be told, though Dinah was a friend whom Reba trusted completely. Dinah left the palace in the darkness to go to Joab and tell him that Reba could not come because of an urgent matter concerned with Amnon.

"I will see him tomorrow at the house of Abiathar," Reba had said. She could say no more without weeping.

36

HAUNTED BY FEARS and hatred, depressed by a sense of his own inadequacy, Amnon moved through his days. He shared the dais with Absalom, Adonijah, and Shephatiah in the mornings when David sat in judgment. Afternoons at rehearsals of the Levite choir he was companioned most often by Mephibosheth, son of Jonathan and grandson of King Saul.

Mephibosheth was in the palace on David's sufferance, just as Amnon considered himself to be, and so Amnon's contempt for Mephibosheth equaled his contempt for himself and made him acceptable as friend.

Mephibosheth was shrewd, clever, the confidant of many but the conscience of none. It was Mephibosheth who first led Amnon to the Gihon spring. Here in the Kidron Valley, near the junction of the new Jerusalem and the old, the serving maids and the concubines came in long processions, morning and evening, with jars on their shoulders, to fetch water for the great urns in the palace and in the houses of the city. Here the lewd and the curious and the venturesome among the young men gathered to watch the descent of the maids down the long flight of stone steps in the east wall of the Kidron ravine. Their hoots and whistles of appreciation set many a maid to giggling. Some were not averse to girding their skirts a notch higher than necessary and a few might remain to dally among the trees of the ravine or higher on the slopes of Mount Olivet.

Mephibosheth the crippled, the envious, had been coming to the well in the evening since he was fifteen. On a day in April he brought Amnon, who was curious, shamefaced yet eager. Amnon asked, "How can you tell which ones to—to approach?"

Mephibosheth laughed. "Watch them as they descend the steps. Watch how they flip their skirts as they walk. Watch their eyes, if you can manage to glance so high. Some are modest; some are not. You will know."

Amnon waited in the shadows of the cedars, watching avidly as a group of three maids, first of the evening procession, emerged through the Water Gate and started down the steps. The maid who led the three brought laughter to Mephibosheth's throat. Her eyes sought them out in the shadows. Her mouth was touched with suppressed humor as her left hand swept her skirts high on her trim brown legs. She stepped boldly down the crumbling stone stairway, and Amnon thought he had never seen such an exposure of well-muscled thigh.

A chorus of hooting laughter combined with whistles and catcalls. The first maid set her pitcher beside the well and moved with swinging strides toward the trees. One of the young men rushed forward and seized her and carried her away, and Amnon felt a loathing go through him. The fastidiousness that made him hate himself made him also hate the lewdness of this sport. He reached for the wineskin Mephibosheth had brought, only setting it aside as another group of maids appeared upon the steps.

With the deepening dusk the crowd of young men thinned out, and so did the procession of women. But by then Amnon had drunk so much of the wine that he was drowsy. He crept deep into the shadows of the trees, lest any should notice the state he was in and the laughter be turned against him. He dozed off.

He wakened to the sound of laughter nearby. It was a man's hoarse, contented laughter and it was a harsh reminder to Amnon that his adventure had failed. He heard the coarse laugh again and suddenly, unaccountably, it sounded to him like Absalom's. He bounded to his feet. Mephibosheth had deserted him, gone off on adventures of his own. Before anyone should find him here with the empty wineskin beside him, he must get away. Amnon started running, following the ravine to its head. I cannot take a woman such as these who yesterday or tomorrow might belong to Absalom. Absalom, young as he was, looked more a man than Amnon.

Amnon stumbled and fell. Nearby he could hear the murmur of voices, the low laughter of a girl. Shall I ever know what it is like to be one with a woman?

There is one girl, he thought, who can never be taken by Absalom in such a way. Her image came before his eyes. He saw the delicate oval of her face in its frame of heavy dark hair. He was swept by awareness of her wistful, shy sweetness. He remembered how she looked at the time of sheepshearing this spring. There had been a feast at Absalom's plot of land (for each of the sons of the king received a gift of land when he moved from the harem into the court of the men). Amnon remembered that Tamar had been there, remembered the sight of her at the fire, patting out cakes to bake, laughing as she told him that this was the bread David and all the captains had eaten when they were outlaws in the Maon wilderness.

Amnon had watched the grace of her movements, the delicacy of her hands, and when she bent forward to lay a cake upon the hot stones he noticed the wide set of the hips in her slender frame. His mind pictured her as she would look in her own small room in the harem, and before he could banish the thoughts he was imagining her as she would look while bathing.

Such thoughts concerning many women came often to Amnon. But now, remembering that time, the thought of Tamar was welcome even though his body was suddenly wrenched with desire. He rose and fled on north, crossing the Jericho road. He did not want to pass through any gate, lest watchmen question him. Before setting out on tonight's adventure, he had removed every vestige of purple from headcloth and girdle and cloak; he had changed his golden chaplet for a common one of undyed cords with brass fittings. Now as he approached the soldiers' encampment that stretched north of the city, where there were no walls as yet, he moved softly.

Keeping to the shadows, he skirted the guards, climbed the north slope of Moriah, bypassed the wide, flat threshing floor of Araunah, and headed down the southern slope, past the tent of meeting.

He did not enter the palace, but went round by the alley and along the side wall where the rooms of the wives of David were located. He found the window Tamar had told him was hers and lay down on the earth, staring up at the narrow, vertical slit. He thought of Tamar sleeping, innocent and sweet, and his hands moved toward the thick walls as if to touch the girl, as if to brush back the dark hair and caress the smooth cheeks.

Tamar, Tamar. The word formed in his throat but did not find a voice. He longed to pull the girl out here into the shadows and take her as those men in the ravine had taken the bold maids who brought their pitchers to the well. Into his mind crept thoughts he could not banish, of every unlawful amorous adventure he had ever been told. David, he thought, so many women have loved you. Will a woman ever love me? Will Tamar love me?

If Dinah spoke the truth long ago when he was a little boy living in the harem, Tamar was not his sister and he was not David's son. If Dinah spoke the truth he had been conceived in the wilderness, in the unlawful love of his mother and that man who could be so stern, whose hands were stained with the blood of uncounted dead. They were younger than I am now, he thought. They love each other still, though my mother, he thought with pride, does not seek lovers as other women of the harem do.

A feeling of terrible loneliness went through him whenever he thought of the love his mother had for Joab. No matter who my father is, he thought, my mother's face has held that special gladness for one man only, and that man is Joab. David loved my mother, but my mother did not love David. That much I heard from their own lips.

If I go to David and ask for Tamar, he will remember the anguish my mother caused him. He will look at my hair, which is like Joab's hair, and he will say to himself, Tamar is not his sister and he is not my son. This is something I can never speak of to David, he thought with despair. For if he said yes, I would know it was because he knows Tamar is not my sister. And if he said no, I would know it was because he did not want to start people speculating and gossiping. If I went to David I could only profit Absalom, since whatever diminishes me enlarges him.

When dawn came he crept round to the men's side of the great palace. He found the door that led to his own quarters and stepped quietly within, having been seen only by a couple of early-rising workmen and a late-staying servant or two. He did not waken his own servant, a young Philistine captive named Jabneel who had been given to Amnon when he was only nine years old. He went instead to the anteroom where the water jars stood and washed himself. He threw his soiled garments into a corner under the bench. Then he crossed the court where Jabneel prepared his meals, passed through the richly furnished room where he received guests, and went on into his own sleeping quarters. He stood at the foot of his couch and stared down at it as if Tamar were there. But then, hearing

Jabneel stir up the fire in the court, he pulled on a tunic and lay down upon his bed and stared at the ceiling with eyes that burned with hopeless and helpless hunger. When Jabneel came into the room bringing a bowl with cakes and honey and a pitcher of goat's milk, Amnon cursed him and drove him away.

The days that followed were a torment for Amnon and for all who came near him. Nothing Jabneel did suited him. Mephibosheth came from time to time, and sometimes Amnon let him stay and sometimes he drove him out with curses. At first he pretended to be ill to avoid answering Mephibosheth's probing questions about what had happened at the Gihon spring. But after a week of sleeping little and eating less he did not have to pretend he was sick. His eyes glittered and his body was feverish.

In the end it was Mephibosheth who prepared a plan for getting Tamar to Amnon's house. She had visited him, of course, in Reba's company or Maacah's, on many occasions. But to get the girl here alone took planning, and Mephibosheth the wily came up with a solution.

That afternoon Reba came to visit Amnon, bringing a small skin of old wine and a fresh-baked loaf of bread. She leaned across the couch, smoothed the linen sheet and brushed back his tangled hair. "You need your mother to look after you," she said, smiling. "Jabneel is conscientious, but he is only a servant, after all." She sighed. "That's what it means to be reared in a palace. You give up so many things that make life good. I am glad David has served Israel so well, but I am not glad we must live this formal life. I see so little of my son." She bent and kissed the feverish brow. "Can I do anything for you, Amnon?"

Amnon moved restlessly under the burden of her solicitude. He said, "David is coming. I sent to ask him to come and see me."

Reba sat on a rug beside the bed, tucking her crossed feet under her. The voluminous yellow cloak with its wide purple bands fell in graceful folds all about her. She said, "Now, Amnon, please eat just a bit of this bread to make you stronger before David comes in."

Amnon's burning eyes glared at her. The bread truly smelled so appetizing he was tempted to try the chunk Reba had broken off for him. But he remembered Mephibosheth's plan, and turned his head away. "Take it out of here," he cried. He called loudly for Jabneel, and when the servant shuffled in shouted for him to take the bread away.

"Bring us a small cup," Reba said, smiling pleasantly upon the bewildered Philistine servant. "I think at least he will try the wine. It is very old, Amnon," she added. "And one of the best of the Hebron vintages." She smiled. "It could be wine of Joab's treading. It came from the storehouse of that miserly merchant he worked for before David went down to live among the Philistines."

"Leave me alone," Amnon shouted. "Why don't you leave me alone? I don't want your bread and I don't want your wine!"

The servant was back, bowing low and backing into the room, with David close behind him. David spoke pleasantly to Reba, then bent over the couch and touched the feverish forehead. He asked, "Can I do anything for you, my son?"

Amnon's anguished eyes went to his mother.

"Do you want me to go?" she asked.

"I can only stay a moment," David said, and sat upon the rug that was on the opposite side of Amnon's couch. "But I would like to see you take a sup of wine while I am here. They tell me you haven't been eating your meals. What can I send you that will tempt your appetite? Some figs? Grapes? The dates we are buying from the Edomites this year are excellent."

Amnon closed his eyes. He was very pale. "If my sister Tamar would come and bake some of those little barley cakes she makes—like those at the last sheepshearing at Absalom's farm—if she would bake them herself and bring them to me, I think I could eat. There is something about the way she makes them, or mixes the oil and the barley flour—"

He lay back, exhausted with the effort it had cost him to get out the words Mephibosheth had given him to speak. He closed his eyes because he could not face either David or Reba now.

David touched his hand, pressed it warmly. "Tamar shall minister to you, Amnon. She is better than any medicine. I shall go to the harem myself and tell her this is your wish. Now, tomorrow when I come, I'll expect to see you looking better."

Amnon's burning, unsmiling eyes followed David from the room. Then he turned his face into the pillow, away from Reba's loving, questioning glance.

"Leave me alone," he said, muffling his voice with an arm flung over his face. "You can't help me. Nobody can help me."

"What is it that troubles you?" Reba was pleased that the boy, in his time of trouble, would think of Tamar. It was a good sign, she thought. Yet something was wrong, something that went deep. "You can tell your mother what the trouble is, Amnon," she said gently.

He closed his eyes because he could not meet the dark, level gaze, nor bear the serene beauty of her face. How could she be so—so tranquil—as if she had never done anything bad in her whole life? He bit his lips. "I am going away," he said. The idea had just come to him, and he seized upon it.

"Amnon! You are David's first-born, heir to a mighty kingdom!" The words were a cry of pain.

Amnon showed his contempt for this argument.

She rested her palm against the down on his jaw. "Where would you go?"

"The world is vast. A Tyrian trader told me their ships go away beyond the far gates of the Great Sea, out into a vast ocean, following the coasts to north and south. He says you could not believe how vast the world is! This land we think so great, from Egypt to the Three Rivers, is only a hand's breadth in the vast reaches of the great world. It stretches away in three directions from these narrow hills which comprise our little kingdom. East, north, south—there is more land than you could imagine in all directions. Caravans cross deserts far bigger than the whole distance from Dan to Beersheba. And to the west there is a vast ocean which washes away clear to the edge of the world."

He sat cross-legged on the couch, pulling the sheet around his hips to conceal his nakedness, carried away by his own word-pictures of the far places of the earth. Reba laid her hand on his shoulder. His skin was hot and dry. Suddenly her eyes filled with tears. She said gently, "It is time you chose a wife, Amnon."

By the scarlet which dyed his face and even his shoulders and chest, Reba knew she had hit upon the heart of the problem. She said gently, "Do you love Tamar? Is that what troubles you, my son?"

His eyes met hers, inflamed, anguished. "She is my sister. If she became my wife it would be a scandal in Israel. It would hurt us all, David included. Only Absalom would gain from such an act."

Reba said, "Happiness must come through decisions that are based on love, not hate, Amnon. You love Tamar. And as for Tamar—she speaks of you constantly. Ask David to give her to you. If David consents, the people will consent. Go to David, Amnon. If he does not say yes to you, then let Tamar persuade him. He dotes on her. He would be happy indeed to be the grandfather of children you and Tamar might give him. The sure way to David's heart is to give him grandchildren to love."

Unable to reply, Amnon flung himself face down upon the bed. He did not look up again until he heard Reba quietly leave, after tucking the sheet around his shoulders.

During the hour that followed Reba's departure, Amnon could think only, Tamar is coming. Tamar will be here, in these rooms. He bathed himself, put on his finest linen tunic, and wrapped himself in the blue robe Tamar had embroidered for him, with the tinkling silver bells about the hem and the wide bands of purple above. Jabneel was kept running from room to room, putting everything straight, getting out the oil and flour and the sesame seed which Tamar liked to use in cakes she baked, stirring up the fire, smoothing the bed, rearranging the cushions.

Then, when he could not think of another thing for Jabneel to do, Amnon was suddenly overcome with his own weakness and cloak and all got back under the sheets Jabneel had straightened so carefully. Suddenly Tamar was at the door.

She took over the apartment and the servant with complete self-possession. There was a shine to her eyes when she looked into the bedroom to speak to Amnon, and pity as she saw how thin and feverish he looked.

"Thank you for sending for me, Amnon," she said softly. "I was so anxious when I heard you were sick." She brought a basket of choice fruits and set it on the stand beside his bed. He reached out and touched the red stuff of her cloak, and she smiled. "You must eat something or you'll waste away to nothing. Now I'm going to make those barley cakes you asked for."

Amnon moistened his lips. "Will you—will you bring them to me yourself?"

"Indeed I will. And I'll make sure you eat them, too!"

She was gone, and Amnon lay shuddering with the conflict of strong emotions. Through the door he could hear the clear, sweet tones of her voice as she gave brisk orders to the servant. Soon the smell of baking cakes came to him.

Presently she returned. She had removed the fine red cloak with its long full sleeves, and was wearing a clean new tunic of modest fullness. Her arms were bare, and the tunic came only to her knees. At sight of her Amnon's eyes grew large.

She carried a bowl full of the crisp little barley cakes. She bent to set it on the stand beside the bed, but he took hold of her arm and pulled her down, and so she sat there on the side of the bed, smiling at him though her lips trembled till she had to set her teeth on them.

Not letting go her arm he shouted, "Jabneel!"

The servant appeared very quickly, as if he had been listening at the door. Amnon shouted, "Close the door! I won't have you spying on me! Go on about your duties!"

Jabneel bowed and departed, closing the door.

Amnon's arm went round Tamar's waist and he pulled her toward him. She protested, "Amnon—the cakes—"

"Put them down." His voice was harsh. The blood was pounding in his ears.

Tamar set the bowl on the stand. When he pulled her down across his chest he saw that her eyes, though fearful, held only love and trust for him. The goodness in the dark eyes sent a shudder over his body. She bent lower, forced by his arm. The wide neck of her tunic dipped and he saw the childish, pointed breasts so near his face. He could not hold off from her any longer. She did not resist, though he knew from her moans that he was hurting her. Yet not even pain could dim the love her eyes held for him.

When at last it was over, leaving him spent beside her, she laid her head on his shoulder and her arm went round him and her lips found his cheek.

"I love you, Amnon," she said. "I will love you always."

Suddenly he was ravenously hungry. He pushed aside Tamar's clinging arms, took up the barley cakes and one by one gulped them down. He ate half the fruit she had brought, and swallowed cup after cup of wine. When he turned at last to look at Tamar her eyes were closed.

He was filled with a strange lethargy and wanted only to sit here on the bed, heavy with food and wine, and look down upon Tamar's face. Now that her eyes were closed he saw how closely she resembled Absalom. The thick, dark hair, the fringe of dark lashes, the shape of her mouth and nose and jaw—all were like Absalom's, though smaller and with a delicacy wholly feminine. Amnon picked up his cloak from the floor and drew it around him, feeling himself a man because of the love he had for Tamar and the love she had for him.

Beyond the closed door he heard a loud shout and remembered with a start of horror that he had not locked the door. Heavy and drowsy with all that had passed, he moved slowly and with effort. Before he could reach the door it had been flung open. Absalom was in the doorway and behind him, peering over his shoulder with avid eyes, Mephibosheth. Behind both of them, shivering in fear, was the servant Jabneel.

Absalom reddened as his eyes took in the sight of his sister in her rumpled tunic on Amnon's bed. "I'll kill you, Amnon!" he shouted. "You have used my sister as a harlot dragged in off the street! I'll kill you for it."

Amnon stood shivering. The frightful intrusion into his tender mood robbed him of any power of action or even of coherent thought. Mephibosheth had betrayed him into Absalom's hands! Beyond that single realization he could not go. If Absalom had raised a hand to slay him he would not have had will or strength to resist.

Tamar scrambled from the bed, gathering the sheet about her, tripping over it as she rushed to thrust herself between Amnon and Absalom. She looked up into Amnon's face, weeping piteously. "We will be married," she cried. "Tell him, Amnon. Tell him we will go to David. Tell him you want me to be your wife!"

Absalom looked from his sister to Amnon. He seized the bright cloak Jabneel had brought from the court and thrust it over her shoulders. "Get it on!" he shouted. "Cover yourself! Fix your hair! Make yourself presentable before we go into the street. I'm taking you with me to my own quarters."

He seized Amnon's unresisting arm and pushed him through the middle room into the court. Then he struck him below the ear, knocking him to the stone pavement. He stood over Amnon, kicking him viciously. Tamar, free of the encumbering sheet, with one hand holding the cloak together, ran at Absalom, screaming, "Stop it! Stop it!"

In the background Mephibosheth and Jabneel stood rigid with fear. Jabneel was wringing his hands.

Amnon rolled away from Absalom. "Get out of here," he croaked hoarsely. "All of you, get out of here. You, Tamar, take your brother and get out! Leave me alone!"

Sobbing, Tamar ran to the dead fire, gathered a double handful of ashes and rubbed them into her long, tangled hair. Her feet were bare; her mantle lay on the floor. Her girdle was on a bench nearby. She cast a final agonized glance at Amnon and ran sobbing into the street.

Absalom seized her mantle and ran after her, and Mephibosheth, with a shamed glance at Amnon, followed them. Amnon stood in the doorway and watched as Tamar stumbled toward the door that opened into Absalom's apartment.

Amnon turned from the door. Avoiding the shocked glance of Jabneel, he staggered back to his room and flung himself across the rumpled bed. It was still warm with the warmth of Tamar's body.

There he lay, sobbing until he could sob no more.

37

DINAH WAS IN the great court supervising the clearing away of the evening meal. She lighted the wicks in the many lamps, while a manservant went about lighting the torches on the walls. David had shared the evening meal with his secretary and two of his counselors and a handful of his younger sons. They still sat on the rugs beside the table, and David had taken up his lyre. Into the peace of this scene Absalom came storming to shout a shocking story.

"Amnon has violated Tamar!" he shouted. "I found them together in his bedroom, and Mephibosheth also was witness to Tamar's shame."

David laid down the lyre. His face had gone pale and his hands shook. "And do you hate your brother so much you will even lie to do him injury?"

Absalom ran to kneel on the rug at David's feet. He seized his father's hands. "It is no lie, my father. When she came to bring him cakes in his bedroom he laid hold of her. The servant Jabneel will bear witness. Tamar will not deny it. She went through the street weeping, barefoot, with ashes in her hair and her cloak rent. She was seen by workmen. She has taken refuge with me." Absalom fell upon his face, weeping. "Alas for my sister that she should be so abused by the heir to the throne of David!"

David said no word. Terribly angry, terribly pale, he strode from the court down the corridor which led to the apartments of his sons. Whether he went to comfort his daughter or to punish Amnon, who could tell?

Dinah hurried to the court of women, and taking Reba and Maacah aside she told both together the shocking news. Maacah's screams filled the house, but Reba made no sound. She fled to her room where she stayed for many days, unable to face David's other wives, unable to eat or sleep or do anything but wait to hear the word that Absalom or his servants had played the role of Tamar's avenger.

But a month went by, and the time of the Feast of Pentecost was at hand. Reba rose and bathed herself and put on a robe of coarse, unbleached linen. She bound sandals on her feet, and put on a heavy mantle which covered both head and face, and went up the hill with the other wives of David, exchanging no word with anyone lest they speak of her grief and so destroy the composure she had gained with great difficulty.

Amnon had come also to the feast, though he no longer stood among the Levites. Nor did the other sons of David sing with the Levites at this time, since all mourned for the dreadful scandal which had afflicted the household. When Reba looked on Amnon's face she knew that she had thought too much of her own suffering, and Tamar's, and too little of the torture and self-hatred through which Amnon was now living. He stood among the sons of David yet somehow alone. Even Mephibosheth had pointedly taken a stand close beside Absalom, as if to prove that he was no longer Amnon's friend. The other sons of David were also grouped about Absalom. Tamar had not come to the feast at all.

The voices of the Levite choir had never chanted more sweetly than on this day of Pentecost. A new song had been composed for them during the past weeks by David, a song which both admonished and comforted:

"Hear me when I call, O God of my righteousness;
    thou hast enlarged me when I was in distress;
    have mercy upon me and hear my prayer.
O ye sons of men, how long will ye turn my glory into shame?
How long will ye love vanity and seek after leasing?

But know that the Lord hath set apart him that is godly for himself;
    the Lord will hear when I call unto him.
Stand in awe and sin not;
    commune with your own heart upon your bed, and be still.

Offer the sacrifices of righteousness and put your trust in the Lord.
There be many that say, Who will shew us any good?
Lord, lift thou up the light of thy countenance upon us.

Thou hast put gladness in my heart,
    more than in the time that their corn and their wine increased.
I will both lay me down in peace, and sleep;
    for thou, Lord, only makest me dwell in safety."

Reba was comforted by the song. She watched while Zadok made sacrifice, and the odor of burnt meat wrapped in fat filled the evening air. But when the feast began she did not stay to share it, for she had seen Amnon walk rapidly away and she followed. She caught up with him in the palace vestibule. When she grasped at his sleeve he turned, with an angry scowl that thinly concealed the sickness of his spirit.

She said, "May I come to your apartment for a moment, Amnon?"

He said roughly, "I am not going to listen to anything about—well, David has said all that needs to be said about that."

She said gently, "We will not talk of what is past. You are alone too much, but so am I. I am your mother, Amnon. Don't shut me out."

Amnon did not answer. He strode down the corridor and did not send her away when she followed. The door to Absalom's rooms stood open, and he ducked his head as he walked past, for Tamar was there.

It came to Reba that Amnon needed to get away from this place for a time. He needed to go where he would not see Absalom every day, where he would not pass by the door behind which Tamar had taken refuge.

Reba spoke pleasantly to Jabneel, and followed Amnon into his apartment. She looked around the luxurious room, hardly knowing how to begin now that she was here. What excellent taste the boy had! The couches were of a wood so dark that rubbing had made them black. Over them lay the whitest of sheepskins. Cushions stuffed with down were strewn about on couches and rugs. The harmony of the colors pleased her, and she realized that Amnon's love of color was as strong as her own.

"Beautiful," she told him, smiling with the mixture of love and pity she had felt for this strange son from his earliest years.

"Tell me about Tamar," he said abruptly. "I looked for her at the feast. She was not there."

Reba bit her lips. "I don't want to talk about Tamar," she said. "I only know what Dinah has told me—that Tamar has remained in Absalom's house, that she goes nowhere and sees nobody. She loved you, Amnon. She told me so at the time of the last Passover." Reba covered her face with her hands. She could not look at the despair that had settled over Amnon's face.

Amnon did not speak.

Reba rose and paced up and down, clasping her hands together to still their agitation. "I—love that girl. Second only to you and Adonijah. She will be all right, after a time. She has too much good sense to grieve forever. She has had a terrible shock, and she will remain hidden until

[210]

she is ready to be seen. She will show no public grief, nor in any way arouse public opinion against you, Amnon."

Amnon went into the next room and came back with a length of rope he was braiding out of thongs. He set to work as if it comforted him to find a use for his hands. He kept his eyes on the thongs and did not look at Reba.

She touched the rope, feeling its firmness. "I kept the first rope you ever plaited, Amnon," she said. "It hangs on the wall in my room. So small your hands were then. Small and unsure. Even the rough places in that rope are dear to me."

Amnon's hands moved faster. "Women are sentimental," he said gruffly.

"Men are also, when they allow themselves to be. Do you ever play on your lute? Do you have it here?"

"Mother, you are years behind the times. I told you long ago I would not play an instrument again. David does it so well I sicken at the sound when I try to make music. Even my singing—"

"We can't all be like David, Amnon. Will his shadow always blot out yours till you have no pride in yourself at all?"

Amnon's mouth twisted with an ugliness that made Reba's heart contract. His eyes met hers bleakly, then were shadowed by the sandy lashes.

"Darling boy, my son," she said brokenly, "tell me how I can help you." She knelt beside him, trying to gather him into her arms.

He jerked free and ran nervous hands through his hair. He said, "Well, at least we know now who will be the next king of Israel. Absalom has triumphed over me completely. I have hated him from the day he was born and now I have handed him the one thing he wants. I have made him a present of my birthright."

Reba cried, "Who can say who will be king, or when? David is a strong, vigorous man. He will live for many years. It is whispered in the harem that Bathsheba means to make her little Solomon king. I am not the one to say she could not do so. Why poison your whole life with this terrible rivalry with Absalom? Perhaps he has as much to fear from Bathsheba and Solomon as you have to fear from him. Perhaps in the end all the older sons of David will be defeated by Solomon rather than by one another."

Anger flashed from Amnon's eyes. "People do not compare me with Solomon, or with Adonijah or Shephatiah or the others. They compare me with Absalom. Every day when I enter the court and sit on the steps of the dais I must face the people who look at us, the two eldest sons of David, and compare us with one another. And I must sit there beside Absalom, knowing all this, and hating him."

Reba said, "Amnon, you are a man, with a man's need for love and a life of your own. I will speak to your father, and he will find a wife for you. A wife who will please you in every way."

Amnon said harshly, "My father!" He stopped short, stepped out into the court where Jabneel was busily scouring the stones in the fireplace. "Go to the well," he ordered. "The water jars are empty. Go at once."

It was woman's work. Maidservants from the palace were accustomed to fill the jars in all the apartments. But the young Philistine took one look at the flushed face of his master and bustled out with a water pitcher on his shoulder. Amnon returned to Reba.

"My father," he repeated. "You mean David, I suppose?"

"Of course. David will give you a bride. There is the daughter of Zadok. She is young, but gay and very pretty and she has her father's knack for neatness and propriety. She would brighten your home and your life and teach you to laugh. You can live down this scandal. Tamar—Tamar would help you live it down. If she knew you were happily married she would turn her thoughts from you and marry a husband of David's choosing. These things will work out. It is no easy thing to be the eldest son of David. I have always known the burden you carry."

"It is too great a burden for me. You saddled me with it, and you did not consider that one cannot be a son of David if one is really the son of a liar, a cheat, a murderer." The boy's voice became shrill, then cracked.

Reba cried, "Amnon, what are you saying?"

"I know all about myself, Mother. I have always known. Did you think I would not hear the gossip in the harem, after Joab came to Hebron? It was easy to see what you felt for him. I hate Joab! I hate you for making me his son, then passing me off as heir to David's throne. Do you know how it is to be spoken of as the son of David who is not like David? People jeer behind their hands. I know the humiliation David feels when I fail at every form of training. I have no knack for statecraft or for giving judgment. I can sing a little. It is my only gift. A minstrel is not suited for kingship."

He dropped the rope and buried his face in his hands. Presently he continued, "When I said that, I was not sure—not quite sure that is. But the way you look is enough. I said I had always known. Well then, I had feared it. I spoke of it now, waiting for you to deny it. But you did not deny it. You cannot deny it, can you, Mother?"

Reba had sunk onto a rug and sat as if transfixed during the whole outburst. She shook her head. Tears rained down her face.

Amnon cried, "I wish I had never been born. After it happened—with Tamar—I thought Absalom would surely kill me. That would put us both out of the line of succession. In my shame I wanted it to happen that way. Then Adonijah would be next in turn. I think Adonijah could deal with Bathsheba and Solomon! For myself I do not want the throne. I want only one thing now, and that is to arrange matters so Absalom cannot inherit it. I know now he will never endanger his right of succession by killing me. He likes to see me ashamed and despised, knowing my life is a punishment worse than death."

Reba had sunk onto a rug, but now she moved toward Amnon, put her arm about his knees. "Amnon. . . ."

He pushed her away. "I hate you," he sobbed. "My own mother, and I hate you! If you had—told David the truth before I was born—I might have been a shepherd. I might have married a simple Bethlehem girl who would be content with her shepherd husband, and never expect him to be like Absalom, like David! I might have even grown up to love my father and my mother, and to honor them!

"I know what Zadok's daughter thinks of me! I know how—Tamar—pities me! I will not marry. I will have no wife to hate me because I am what I am. I will sleep with harlots or with the women at the well who are content with an hour's play and will not ask me to be what I am not! Your ambition has been my enemy always. I have been made a fool before all the world. To make you the queen mother in Israel when David is gone, that is what you wanted from me! Well, you can forget it. Forget it, forget it! Now will you go back to the harem and leave me alone?"

Reba moved backward till she was against a bench. Then she rose and sat on the bench with her arms out on its sides, propping herself erect in the face of Amnon's terrible anger. "My son," she said softly. "Oh my dear boy, how can I make you understand?" She walked the length of the room and sank again onto the bench. "David was no king when he married me. He was an outlaw, hunted by Saul. He said to me—that night when he came to my tent—'I have nowhere to turn. Every man's hand is against me.' You know nothing of those years, Amnon. The poverty, the danger, the desperation. Abner and Saul, that precious pair—if one wasn't seeking to kill David, the other was."

Amnon said quietly, "I know. They were jealous. I know what that means. Mother, I *know!*"

Her eyes met his. He was quiet at last, ready to listen. The outburst had cleansed him of the anger on which his heart had fed, seeking forgetfulness of his own shortcomings and wrongdoings. He could listen now.

"Of course you know," she said quietly, her eyes meeting his. "Do you also know how much we all loved David? All of us, even the most wretched. Even Joab. Amnon, I am going to tell you something that is known to few people—a secret kept all these years. When Joab came to David in his outlaw camp in the wilderness he fled from an avenger, having killed a fellow shepherd in self-defense. What he did not know was that his mother and brothers managed to conceal the crime, making it appear that a bear did it. David learned all this from Seth. But he did not tell Joab. Instead, he brought the avenger to the camp, knowing that Joab would flee at the sight of the man. I knew nothing of all this at the time, only that Joab had left. And then I realized that I had conceived. We had begged David during the summer to let us marry, but he refused. He was blinded by his—his love for me. He thought Joab and I were too young to feel anything deep and lasting for each other. And during those desperate days when I thought myself abandoned and did not know the reason, David offered me his protection. So I married David."

Amnon's face was very pale. "Then David wronged you! It was not you who wronged David. All these years I have thought—"

"David did not realize, at the time. I was very young. We cannot blame him for believing I would learn to love him. You must not blame David. David loves you, Amnon. I love you. Joab also loves you, though it is hard for him to understand you because he has not been with you much. You must not hate, Amnon. I do not blame David for what he did. Nor do I blame myself. I needed a protector. And David needed me. Child as I was, I sensed the depth of David's love and need. So I comforted him as best I could. And I did not shame him by telling the world that his first-born was not his son at all. Nor did he shame me by disowning you or failing even once in all these years to give you equal love and equal honor with his other sons."

Suddenly she was weeping, great, wrenching sobs torn from her as the memories returned. Amnon knelt beside her, took her head on his shoulder, held her close. "Don't cry, Mother. Please don't cry."

She pressed her cheek against his. "I had forgotten the agony of those days. I did not know why Joab had left. I thought he was a coward. I had begged him to take me to Bethlehem and make me his wife. He did not tell me it was impossible. He did not tell me about the avenger. Then suddenly he was gone, and I thought he had gone to Bethlehem and had not wanted to take me with him." She sobbed, remembering. "David was going to the Philistines to serve Achish because there was no other place of safety for him. We all thought we would spend many years among the Philistines, perhaps never see Judah again. I had nobody to turn to, except David. How could I know what I was doing to my son in such an hour? At fourteen one is not very wise."

She was pacing the floor now, wringing her hands, completely in the grip of remembered agony. "David never rebuked me, never accused me. Nor have I ever accused or reproached him. We could not believe you would not benefit from our silence, our protection of the secret of your birth. None of us was wholly selfish. Of the three of us, only Joab is blameless. He lost all, all. Willingly, because he loved David without taint from childhood till now. It is rooted in his childhood, his earliest memories. He would sacrifice himself willingly—even die—for David's sake."

Amnon's eyes were bright in the dimness of the room. Twilight had deepened and only one lamp was burning in the lovely room where mother

[214]

and son had at last spoken openly together. Amnon said, "I would like to know him better—Joab, my father. I would like to have him for my—my friend. I wish, oh how I wish I had known the whole story long ago. Hating is a poison, especially when you hate your own blood, your own father, your own self. I wanted to be proud of—of my father. So many times I have wanted to love him. He's really a remarkable person, isn't he?" Happiness was brimming from Amnon's gray eyes. "He talks back to David, sometimes. Nobody else ever does. And in the end he sometimes proves he is right and David wrong. He had to force David to accept him, but now he is the greatest in the kingdom next to David."

Reba was quiet, her grief spent. "My boy," she said softly. "How easily I sheltered and protected you when you were little. How often I quieted your fears and soothed your pain. How I loved to see you toddling about the court of the women. How lonely I was when you grew too big to stay with me and went to live with the men."

Amnon knelt beside her and kissed her tenderly. "I need to go away for a while. I need to get used to all you have told me. I need time to think about everything and learn to understand myself."

"Go to Bethlehem," Reba said softly. "To me it seems that nothing could be better. Joab is there now. He has been there ever since it happened. Go and live with Joab and Zeruiah. Tend the flocks and sleep in the pastures and find peace under the stars. Joab will welcome you. And because he is David's kinsman and second to David in the kingdom, nobody will think it strange that you go there to get away from the terrible thing which happened here. In the pastures of Bethlehem, Amnon, you will find your true kinship with David and with Joab. While you are gone I will pray for peace to come to you."

Many months were to pass before Reba would see Amnon again. The cycle of the years passed twice around, and it was early spring when Amnon appeared one morning in David's court. He had come, and Joab with him, to ask in this public place to be forgiven and restored again to his father's love and friendship. Absalom sat on the dais on one side of David, Adonijah on the other. If Reba had had eyes for any except Joab and Amnon that day, she might have read in Absalom's handsome face the anger he felt when David stepped down to kiss and embrace Amnon.

Reba's eyes were wet as she took in the altered bearing, the bronzed face, the steady gray eyes of Amnon. She was gazing upon a young man who might almost have been Joab in his youth. And when she followed the direction of his eyes when he took his place with his brothers, she saw Tamar, looking pale and thin. Yet Tamar was a king's daughter and carried herself with dignity, making no display of the emotion she must have felt at sight of Amnon restored to David's favor. One who knew her well, as

Reba did, could have read the darting glance she turned on Amnon, the smallest of smiles which briefly touched her mouth. She seemed to be asking, Why did you remain away so long?

Reba never saw Amnon alive again. He was invited, with the other sons of David, to a feast of sheepshearing on Absalom's farm in the hills of Benjamin. Later Adonijah brought back the fearful news. During the feast, after much wine had been drunk, two of Absalom's men set upon Amnon with swords. His body would be brought to the new tomb made for David and his family at the southern end of the City of David.

It was said that Absalom killed Amnon to avenge the wrong Amnon had done to Tamar, or perhaps to prevent repetition of that wrong. Yet there were many who asked why, if that were true, Absalom waited two years to set his servants upon Amnon. Some declared that Absalom's vengeance was dictated rather by fear of the changed person Amnon had become. Whatever his reasons, Absalom had done the deed, and had fled to the court of his grandfather, king of Geshur, lest David punish him for killing Amnon.

And so at last, after twenty-two years, Reba and Joab met by night at the house of Seth to comfort one another for the death of their son.

PART SEVEN

Absalom

38

As COMMANDER OF the army, with foreign affairs his chief responsibility, Joab had seldom found it necessary to attend David's court of judgment. Now, however, three years after Absalom fled to his grandfather's court in Geshur of Syria, relations between the two nations were in serious peril. Seth had brought the information back from a recent journey to Geshur. Seth and Joab had gone to David directly to urge that the young prince be brought home to Jerusalem.

"We have reached the point," Joab urged, "where it is more important to preserve the peace than to win wars. All our neighbors pay us tribute. We can gain nothing by drawing our men off the land to fight a new war."

Seth took up the argument, speaking at length of all he had seen and learned in Geshur and concluding, "Absalom's talents are many, his ambition boundless. His grandfather is an old man, unable to cope with him. Many young men dwell in Geshur who would follow Absalom gladly into any adventure. You are the boy's father. If any man can mold and discipline this son of yours, you are the one. Bring him home, cousin."

But David rebuffed them, reminding them that he had sworn an oath to keep Absalom in perpetual exile. He ended by accusing them of unwarranted interference in his family affairs.

Joab had nerved himself with utmost difficulty to take up the matter with David, for hatred of Absalom was a consuming bitterness within him. Yet for the sake of Israel's peace he had buried his private feelings and had taken upon himself the role of pleader for Absalom. Now he saw that David's rebuff was caused chiefly by his pain and grief over Absalom, by the longing he felt to set eyes upon the son he could not cease from loving, and by his reluctance to believe Absalom capable of this further evil.

The two sons of Zeruiah went out from David's presence, but only to confer together as to what other means might be found to bring Absalom within reach of his father's influence. "If we deal with him ourselves," Seth had concluded gloomily, "it can only be by violence, and that is something David would not soon forgive. David must take him in hand."

Thus it was that Joab now found himself standing among the counselors who flanked the dais at the front of the great court, to learn whether he could accomplish his ends by guile, having failed to accomplish them by direct action.

The time was summer and the air thick despite the lofty ceiling of the hall. David had not yet appeared, though the room had been filled for half an hour. Spectators came early to David's court, hoping for a place of vantage from which to watch the circus provided by the troubled and the quarrelsome of Israel. Alabaster lamps stood in niches on the walls, but the burning of their spiced and fragrant oil could not overcome the fetid smells of sweat and leeks and sour wine.

The judgment chamber had long since been roofed over, for the quarrels of the Israelites did not end when the rainy season began. The open court in Hebron had seemed commodious and splendid to Joab as a youth. Now he stood in David's great hall in Jerusalem and thought how small and crude that court had been. The dais there had been only a step up from the stone-flagged floor. Here a flight of six steps rose to the dais. Carpets of brown and rust and gold covered the dais and steps, and led down past the space reserved for family and counselors to end in a strip on which petitioners sat while waiting their turn. Linens of the same russet colors were draped over the stone wall behind the throne.

The throne was a high-backed affair of polished cedar, handsomely carved with geometric figures and inlaid with amethyst and gold. The amethyst in the throne was the only purple about the dais, for David wore purple when he sat in judgment and his purple robe stood out handsomely among the russet hangings and rugs.

Twenty soldiers stood stiffly along the walls, guarding the dais and the open space before it. Whenever prisoners were involved in hearings they also guarded the prisoners. Benaiah was commander of the palace guard, and could usually be found near the dais as officer of whatever group was on duty here. Benaiah wore a short brown battle-robe, a bronze-and-cowhide helmet, and a sword. He carried a spear in his right hand. Buckled onto his left arm was a light shield of cowhide and bronze. Benaiah carried his age well. At forty-eight he looked only a little older than the burly bully who had fetched Joab a clout behind the ear with an oak branch in the Maon forest so many years ago.

Joab had come to court wearing a splendid crimson cloak made by Zeruiah for this occasion. His only insignia of rank were two golden armlets, the curved ram's horn that hung by a leather thong at his neck, and the golden ring with his seal—the six-pointed star of David. This seal was used only by David himself, Jehoshaphat the recorder of the court, and Joab. Its imprint marked any document as having David's authority and approval. Joab had used the seal to mark peace treaties and the terms of tribute with which all Israel's wars had ended. Now, in peace time, he used it to authenticate documents concerning workers and materials employed in building Jerusalem's walls and gates and towers.

The strip of rug on which petitioners sat was crowded. There were always more petitioners than could be heard. Joab was gratified to see among the petitioners the old woman, Telema of Tekoa. Telema was Ira's wife, but she had not been away from Tekoa half a score times in her whole life. Now she wore a widow's homespun mantle, with hands and face darkened with walnut juice, and Joab had no fear that her identity would be known. Joab and Seth had gone to Ira for advice in the matter of bringing Absalom home from Syria, and together the three of them, with Telema's help, had formed the plan. Ira did not come to Jerusalem, since the plan would be spoiled if he were seen with his wife, and also because Telema would not agree to come until Ira promised to stay at home and tend the sheep and the vineyards.

Only Telema could carry the plan through. From here on, everything was up to the old woman who sat upon the rug among the petitioners, huddled in her mantle as if distracted by grief. She looked the part she was to play. Could she act the part, when her turn came?

Jehoshaphat entered, carrying the scroll listing the petitioners to be heard and their complaints. The innkeepers of Jerusalem did an excellent business with petitioners to David's court. The people of Israel loved David and were proud of his handsome appearance and his fine city. Moreover, David dispensed true justice. Tales of his judgments were told in the towns, so that only the very poor now took their cases to the elders in their own gates. All who could scrape together means for a sojourn in Jerusalem came to the king for justice. Fortunate were petitioners who had friends or relatives with whom to lodge while awaiting their turn. Jehoshaphat alone determined the order in which cases were heard, and Jehoshaphat could not be bribed. Rich and poor alike registered their names and complaints with the king's recorder, found a place to lodge, and settled down to await the king's justice.

Telema had taken lodging in an inn, since it would never do for her to accept hospitality from one of Ira's friends. Telema hated the city and longed for her own house in Tekoa. Today, with luck, the waiting would end and she would be called to enjoy her day in court.

Adonijah entered, quietly, modestly, followed by three of his brothers. The young princes took their places on the steps which led to the dais, and looked about at the people who filled the great court. Adonijah glanced at Joab with an expression of friendly confidence. The two had been much together during the building of the fortress Millo at the northern end of the city. Adonijah was a golden princeling, from the curling red-gold of his hair and the splash of golden freckles upon his face, down to the pale gold of his sandal straps. Adonijah's prospects had changed greatly after Absalom killed Amnon and fled to Syria. Adonijah was a good son, a credit to David, to Reba, to Israel. He had been a great consolation to his parents since Amnon and Absalom had brought tragedy and shame to the family.

On a low table at the front of the dais was Jehoshaphat's silver ink pot and a silver cup which held a freshly cut supply of pens. Jehoshaphat sat upon the rug cross-legged, fidgeting with his scrolls on their bronze spools. Standing near the dais, Joab was in a position to watch the old man's activities. He could not help admiring the exquisite neatness of the script while Jehoshaphat spread out the scroll and propped it open with burnished pieces of Egyptian porphyry.

Jehoshaphat was a small thin man with nervous hands and a great beaked nose. His soft lips folded together over toothless gums. He was perpetually touching something, moving something, adjusting something.

Still David delayed his entrance, and the low buzz among spectators and petitioners grew louder, together with the scuff of sandals on stone as people grew restless with waiting.

The two chief counselors had taken their places on either side of the dais. The one nearest Joab was Ahithophel, a man of Judah and grandfather to Bathsheba. Ahithophel was a small, vigorous man with sparse white beard framing his jowls, and piercing blue eyes beneath brows of a startling black. The hairs of his brows were an inch or more in length. Those beetling, black brows dominated his face so that one forgot to notice the stubborn set of his pinched lips, the determined jut of his chin.

Across from Ahithophel stood a counselor from one of the northern tribes, Hushai by name. He was a big man, one who lived well and enjoyed comfort. His beard was grizzled and his face unlined. The two old men attended David's court day by day, but they treated one another with a distant courtesy reflecting the watchful jealousy that existed between the northern and southern branches of David's kingdom. Their concern for Israel's welfare was the one thing they shared. If David were to take counsel of one of these two men concerning Telema, Joab hoped Hushai would be the one, even though Telema was from Judah.

A warning tinkle of a silver bell Jehoshaphat took from his desk brought a measure of silence into the room. David entered through a side door from the stairs to his chamber on the roof. He crossed to the dais and climbed the steps between his sons with quick, strong strides. Sweeping the purple robe out into graceful folds on either side, David took his seat on the throne. Then Jehoshaphat rose, cleared his throat importantly, shot an admonishing look out over the assembled Israelites, and shouted out the name of the first petitioner. The day's hearings had begun.

The third petitioner called was Telema of Tekoa.

Telema rose stiffly from the rug where she had been sitting bowed together as if with grief. Her cloak and sandals were disreputable. The widow's mantle covered her head and shoulders and much of her face. Surely nobody in this room could look upon the old woman and suspect that her husband had long been David's officer.

Pity sat upon David's face as the old woman shuffled forward and threw herself face down on the rug at the foot of the steps. Telema cried out in anguished tones, "Help, O King!"

David said kindly, "What is your trouble?" He motioned for Benaiah to raise the old woman to her feet.

She stood at the foot of the dais, wringing her hands, a picture of woe, and as she told her story she scarcely dared raise her eyes to the face of her king.

"Of a truth I am a widow," she said. Her voice broke as she added piteously, "My husband is dead. I—I had two sons, and the two of them struggled together in the field. There being no one near to part them, the younger son struck the elder in his anger, and killed him." Here Telema burst into a torrent of weeping. The whole court was silent until the old woman could collect sufficient composure to continue.

"Now all my kinsmen have risen up against me. They demand that I deliver up my only son to them that they may kill him for the life of his brother whom he slew, for he is the heir to my small plot of ground and my vine and my fig tree and my few poor sheep, which will come to these kinsmen when they have slain my one remaining son. Thus they will quench my last hope, leaving my husband neither name nor remnant on the face of the earth."

David waited for her weeping to subside. His eyes were moist with pity. "Go to your house," he said kindly. "I will send soldiers to your village with orders concerning your son."

Plainly David was in haste to be finished with the old woman. The theme of brother killing brother could not be one on which he cared to dwell.

The old woman did not stir from her place at the foot of the dais. She said beseechingly, "Upon me be the blame for all that my son has done, and let the king and his throne be innocent of any blood shed by my son."

David said patiently, "If anyone threatens you or your son, bring him to me and he will not trouble you again."

Still Telema lingered. "My lord, King David, I beg of you, let my lord the king remember the Lord your God, not to allow the avenger to destroy, and not to let them murder my son."

David was growing weary of the persistent old woman. She somehow lacked the quality of humility and the quick gratitude he had expected from so ragged a petitioner. He had granted her request, yet she was of a loquacious type which cannot cease speaking even when a matter is finished. Well then, she was having her day in court. He was willing to let her draw from it the utmost gratification. "As the Lord God lives," he said kindly, "not a hair of your son shall fall to the ground." He motioned to Benaiah to lead the old woman away so Jehoshaphat could call up the next petitioner.

"I beg of you, my lord David," Telema wheedled, though Benaiah's big hand was on her arm, "let your handmaiden speak one word more to my lord the king."

"Speak then." David smiled and Benaiah stepped back beside Joab.

"Why," demanded Telema, raising her voice so it rang through the hall, "has my lord the king acted against Israel? For in rendering this judgment in my cause the king condemns himself, since the king does not bring back his banished son. For we must indeed die, and are as water poured upon the earth that cannot be gathered up again, nor can God Himself take it up. Therefore my lord the king should devise plans to bring home the son who is banished."

David's ruddy face grew pale at this rebuke from a ragged old country woman. How old he looks, thought Joab, feeling a stir of pity. The years of peace in Jerusalem should have brought David nothing but happiness. Yet David looked like an old man.

Now David cast his eyes about to see what his counselors and his people had made of the old woman's rebuke. Everywhere heads were nodding in acquiescence with the old woman's suggestion. Ahithophel and Hushai were agreed, this once, affirming the logic of this strange petitioner.

Telema flung back the mantle and straightened her shoulders. "I would not have dared to speak thus to my lord the king, except that those who have the interest of Israel most at heart persuaded me. Then I said, 'I will speak to the king; it may be that the king will hear me and deliver me from the men who seek to destroy me and my son and take away our heritage.' And I said, 'Let the word of my lord the king be a comfort, for as the angel of God, so is my lord the king to hear good and evil.' And now, the Lord your God be with you, O King!"

She turned as if to go, having finished at last with all that she wanted to say. But David said, "Wait, Telema of Tekoa."

Once again David's eyes passed over the groups on either side of the dais. He took note of Joab's presence among the others and read what was in his heart, for Joab could not conceal his thoughts from David, try as he would. Joab felt the warm color mounting his weathered cheeks and brow, and he wished he had worn a headcloth into court to cover and shadow his telltale face. When he could face David's accusing look no longer he closed his eyes. He felt no triumph in having once again defeated David in a clash of purposes.

David said, "Speak the truth, Telema, and no one shall harm you. Did my cousin Joab give you the words you were to speak to me today?"

Telema threw herself once more upon the rug at the foot of the dais.

"As surely as my lord the king lives, one cannot turn to the right or to the left from what my lord the king has said, for your servant Joab indeed put these words into my mouth. But my lord the king is wise, knowing all things so that he is able to read the hearts of all who appear before him."

David moved slowly down to stand face to face with Joab. "You have done the thing you set out to do, and I am forsworn in the presence of all my people. Go then, and bring the young man Absalom home to this city."

Joab stepped forward and bowed low in the place reserved for petitioners. He had won only a bittersweet victory over David, since Joab had no wish for Absalom's return. Yet for the sake of Israel's peace he was more than willing to humble himself and save David's dignity before the people.

"The Lord bless and keep you, O King," he said, using words the petitioners used when their petitions were granted. "Today I know that I have found favor in your sight, because you have granted my petition."

David returned to his throne. "Arise, Joab," he said. "Telema, arise. Do not think that I am deceived in anything you have said or done here today. When you see Absalom, cousin, tell him he can live in his own apartments as before and enjoy the use of his own farms and flocks. But the doorway which leads from his apartments to mine will be walled up, and he will not enter my palace nor sit in my court nor come into my presence."

Yet for all the anger David showed before the people, Joab knew that the thing he had done pleased David even while he chose to redeem his prestige by pretending the favor had been granted in Joab's behalf.

With all the courtesy of one who has received a favor, Joab bowed himself out of the court, and Telema departed with him.

39

ZERUIAH DIED IN midsummer. Her sons were beside her at the last, and for their sakes she concealed her pain. When Eliab's wife announced that Zeruiah slept with her fathers in Sheol, the house was filled with the sound of lamentation and the odor of spices as they wrapped her body in white linen. Her sons and her brothers carried the bier upon their shoulders and their wives and concubines put ashes in their hair and walked before the bier lamenting. When they reached the tomb of Jesse her father, they rolled away the stone and carried her in and laid her in one of the niches in the wall of the cavern. They sealed the tomb against the jackals of the wilderness. Then they returned to their houses, and ate no food that day until after the sun had set.

Joab did not return at once to Jerusalem. Life in the capital had become difficult since Absalom came home from Syria. Absalom assumed that Joab was his friend, that he had brought him home because of friendship. Absalom followed Joab everywhere, persuasive, confiding, insinuating.

"You persuaded my father to bring me home," he reminded Joab, over and over. "Surely you can persuade him to see me. I don't ask much, cousin. Only to look on the face of my father. A son can surely ask that much, even when his father is a king, and old, so that his hands grow slack upon the reins of the nation and his mind grows cloudy."

All Absalom's talk of his father was of this kind, though he spoke suavely, as if out of pity for his father. And his assumption that Joab was one he could use for his own purposes annoyed Joab almost as much as the manner in which he spoke of David. Joab mistrusted his own impulses, fearing he might lay violent hands on Absalom and so bar himself forever from David's presence. It was a relief to be away from the city, among people and scenes familiar to him from childhood.

Eliab was head of the Bethlehem household now, the elder who made sacrifice on the nearby hilltop for the townspeople on their holy days. Between Eliab and Joab a warm affection existed, strengthened by the forbearance Joab had shown toward Lisha, his wife's sister. On the day after the funeral, when the other guests had departed, Eliab walked with Joab out past the fig and olive orchards to where the barley fields lay, waving and yellow, for it lacked only a few days till harvest.

"I always thought," Joab told Eliab, "that a time would come when I could live here at last, to comfort my mother in her declining years. We did not even give her grandsons, Seth and I. I have never told her how much of my strength came from memories of her never-failing strength and justice."

"She would have been proud to hear you say it," Eliab replied. "Though I think she knew it was true. She often boasted that her two sons had done more for David than all six of his brothers. Zeruiah had remarkable vision. Not many women understand that Israel is more than Judah, and Judah more than Bethlehem, and Bethlehem more than the household of Jesse."

They had come to the southern end of the barley farm, to a field which had special memories for Joab. When Amnon came to Bethlehem, Zeruiah requested that he take upon himself the task of clearing this land of stones, which he made into a wall to fence the field. Together, Amnon and Joab had plowed the land, turning under the pasture grass. They smoothed the earth with branches of sycamore from the fig orchard. After the autumn rains Amnon sowed the seed, then dragged the field again with branches to turn the seed under. Amnon watched the field until after the grain was up, driving away birds and keeping the land free of tares. How proudly he harvested the barley, cutting it with a sharpened sickle. He tied the sheaves into bundles and loaded them onto an ox-cart. Then he drove the ox to the threshing floor.

Zeruiah had been Amnon's particular friend, helping him to find his place here as one of the grandsons of Jesse. Whether Zeruiah guessed that this lad was indeed the grandson she had craved, Joab did not know. The boy resembled Joab. That was enough to endear him to Zeruiah. Amnon's need for friendship touched her heart, as did his love of the earth. And the earth and Zeruiah and companionship with Joab his father had combined to heal the boy's wounds.

"I'll never again sit with my brothers on the dais," Amnon said. "I will ask for Tamar, and if she is given me I will bring her to Bethlehem. We will bring up our children among their kinsmen of the household of Zeruiah."

It was after the harvest season that year that Amnon reached his decision. He had unloaded his sheaves at the threshing floor. He had watched the old man who tended the floor as he hitched oxen to the heavy moreg with its broad runners to which iron ridges were attached. The old man drove the oxen round and round the heaped barley. The smell of dust from crushed straw was heavy, and Joab and Amnon drew away lest they fill their lungs with chaff.

When the grain and straw were broken apart, the old man took his wide shovel and tossed the grain against the brisk breeze which comes up before sunset. Then Amnon took the broad, flat sifter and shook the grain through the coarse screen to clean it of sand and weeds and straw. He set the baskets of grain in the cart and drove home to the village to pour the grain into the family bins.

"A hundredfold," he cried excitedly of his harvest. "I sowed two measures of barley, and I have reaped two hundred measures. Why should any man work for wages or serve as a soldier when the land will repay his labor a hundredfold?"

Still Amnon lingered in Bethlehem, though he had announced that he was ready to return to Jerusalem. Joab did not urge him to go. He had seen how much the active outdoor life had done to strengthen Amnon's tall, lean body. Yet the boy must become aware of his power before he could use it. So Joab tramped the fields with his son. He watched the sallow face grow bronzed in its frame of sandy hair and beard. He showed Amnon how to use sling and stone, the timeless weapon of the shepherd. He showed him how to grip the knife and where to strike, just as David had taught him.

Autumn with its rains passed and again Amnon sowed the field with barley, this time using seed from his own harvest. Winter grew cold, and a night came when snow was on the ground and the sheep were brought to a shelter near the town. One ewe was missing, and Amnon went out to find her. When he returned near dawn he carried a newborn lamb in his arms, and the little creature was wrapped in the skin of a lion. He told how the ewe had taken shelter to give birth to the lamb, and how he had found her because of her cries, for the lion had attacked her as she stood over the lamb, licking it. Amnon killed the lion, but not in time to save the ewe.

So it was that at last Amnon found courage to match his strength. "I will return home now," he told Joab. His eyes met Joab's without wavering. "I will never again fear Absalom."

Amnon returned to Jerusalem. And Absalom, now fearing this brother he had once held in contempt, made his opportunity and caused two of his Philistine servants, men of great strength, to fall upon Amnon while he sat at a feast at Absalom's table.

All that had happened three years ago. In Bethlehem Zeruiah had mourned for Amnon, just as today Joab and the household had mourned for Zeruiah. Thereafter Zeruiah gave this field into the care of Joab's Philistine concubine. She called it Joab's field, since Joab had worked there with Amnon. Now the grain was tall and yellow, and another harvest only a few days away.

"Perhaps soon I shall come to Bethlehem to live," Joab told Eliab. "If a time comes when it is safe to turn over Israel's foreign affairs to some other man. For us now it is more important to avert wars than to win them. That young troublemaker, Absalom, would have plunged us into a new war with Syria, a war without profit since Syria now pays us tribute. Yet we could not bring him home until we got Tamar out of Jerusalem, for she was torn between love for her brother and love for Amnon."

"So that is the reason you made the Ammonite marriage for her," Eliab mused. "I wondered why David's eldest daughter should be given to a prince who is David's hireling."

"Shobi is more than a hireling. He is the son of the old Nahash, albeit the son of his old age. Yet when the Nahash died and Hanun made war on us, Shobi fled to Nineveh rather than take part in that war, for he remembered David's friendship for his father. After the war ended, Shobi came to David and offered his services. So he became king of the Ammonites with David's blessing. Giving him Tamar as his queen strengthens our position east of the Jordan."

Eliab smiled. "It is a pleasure to hear you speak of these matters. Our lives are circumscribed in Bethlehem, and the affairs of the kingdom seem far removed from our quiet labors. You would find this life dull, Joab. Yet if you do come home to stay we will make you welcome, never doubt it."

Joab broke off a roughly-whiskered head of barley and rubbed it between thumb and fingers, enjoying the feel of the plump, hard grain and the sharp prick of the husk. Life in Bethlehem would indeed be far removed from enemies and intrigue. But he was not at all sure he wanted a backwater sort of life. Moreover, he thought of Reba and knew he would not care to live in Bethlehem without her.

"I will stay for a little while," he told Eliab. "I will stay until I have harvested this field. Then I will return to Jerusalem, for that is where my lines have been laid."

He stood beside the stone wall Amnon had built and looked away to the south and east. The wilderness stretched away and away, much farther than the eye could see. As clearly as if Zeruiah had spoken he knew that life and death alike are the gift of God. Whether our years are few or many, one thing is required, that we take the gift as it comes from God's hand and use it as God gives us the opportunity and the wisdom, knowing that not every man is a David, nor does God require of others what he requires of David, asking only that every man use the powers God has given him.

Zeruiah had lived well. If she had lived twenty years longer, no more could be said of her than that she lived well.

Joab had never known God as David did, to speak to familiarly as friend speaks to friend. Yet if I knew Him and could talk to Him, it would not be to ask for any gifts, but only to say thanks for the gifts He has given—and I hope I have not used these gifts amiss. That is how Zeruiah would pray, he thought. Turning, he walked beside Eliab across the fields, to the house which had been the house of Zeruiah and was now the house of Eliab.

Amasa had come in while Joab was in the fields. He was a grandson of Jesse and companion and errand boy to Absalom. Amasa was the problem child of the household of Eliab. Brilliant he was, but erratic. Having no great confidence in himself, he was easily swayed to place his confidence in another. He was quick to anger, quick to envy and to hate, but slow to make decisions because he placed little trust in his own judgment. Since Absalom's return from Syria, Amasa had been his constant companion.

Amasa was arrogant today because Absalom had put into his mouth the words he was to speak. Yet he clothed his arrogance in a pose of confidential persuasiveness. "I have come to give you a little friendly advice, cousin," he said, speaking to Joab out of the side of his mouth and glancing frowningly at Eliab. "Shall we walk out toward the holy hill?"

Eliab shot a penetrating stare at the plump young man. "You have lost something in courtesy since you left Bethlehem," he remarked rebukingly. "Those who stand before kings can hardly afford to forget the teaching of their mothers. Never mind leaving the courtyard of your home for this business. I have to make arrangements for the threshing season."

Amasa watched the patriarch of the family as he strode out the alley

[227]

gate. Then he tugged at Joab's sleeve. "Hear me, cousin," he said. "You did a very clever thing when you brought the heir home to Jerusalem. He won't forget that you helped him when he is king. But now you ignore him, and he won't forget that either unless you take steps to correct the fault. Remember, you help yourself when you help Absalom. David isn't getting any younger. Now there is talk about the fact that five years have passed since he has begotten a child. When the king grows sterile the land grows sterile. It is an old saying, and a true one. So protect your future by helping Absalom. Go to David. Persuade him to call Absalom into the court of judgment and either punish him or forgive him. David must not go on ignoring the heir to the throne."

Joab looked with contempt on his plump, soft kinsman. "Let him go to Ahithophel. Ahithophel has the ear of David. Moreover, he has always had a fondness for Absalom. My responsibility ended when I got Absalom out of Syria. He is now the affair of David's counselors, not his commander. Go to Ahithophel."

"Ahithophel does not dare speak out. Nobody dares do that except you. Come with me, Joab. Absalom sent me to bring you. Remember, you aren't helping yourself when you ignore the heir to the throne."

Joab said bitterly, "Yesterday I buried my mother. Today you come, though neither you nor Absalom troubled to come to pay your respects or walk in the procession which carried her to the tomb. Tell that young man I will not come. Let him look elsewhere for a friend at court!"

Amasa's sandals slapped smartly upon the stone flagging as he turned and strode out of the court. His mule was tied beside the gate, and he mounted briskly and rode away. Joab watched him go, wishing he had not come. I would not put it past that pair, he thought, to set spies upon me. He sighed. He had become unsure, ashamed, now that there was something in his life that had to be hidden. Reba too was troubled. If he did not send for her she grew fretful, accusing him of growing cold in his love for her. Each of them was anxious, more for the danger they brought upon the other than for their personal safety. Reba had lost her serenity. I do not think we have wronged David, thought Joab restlessly, but I know we have wronged ourselves. We had learned to live with loneliness. Now we are growing older, and must learn to live with conniving and deceit. Yet it is worth it. And he thought with tenderness of the delight they had found in one another after so many years.

Joab left the courtyard to go to the threshing floor and find Eliab. He wondered who had started the rumor that David was impotent? It was foolish superstition—nothing more—to associate the fertility of a land with that of its monarch. Yet many Israelites were foolish and superstitious, and such a rumor could harm David. He shrugged the worrying thoughts aside. He was in charge of foreign affairs. This was the affair of Benaiah and his palace police, the affair of that wise pair of counselors, Ahithophel and Hushai, the affair of Jehoshaphat the recorder and Sheva the secretary. Joab had fulfilled his whole duty when he averted the threatened uprising in Syria by bringing Absalom home.

Eliab was not at the threshing floor after all. Joab wandered on, retracing his way to Amnon's barley field. Zeruiah was content with her sons, he thought, remembering Eliab's comforting words. What more can a man ask of himself than that he please his mother and serve his people and his king? What sharper pain can a parent ever feel than that which comes when a promising son goes astray?

David has other sons, he thought. He has a dozen sons, ranging in age from Adonijah down to the little Solomon. And they are good boys, or seem to be. Yet Joab knew that a hundred good sons could not blot out the pain David had suffered, and still had to suffer, because his eldest surviving son, the handsomest and cleverest of them all, had no thought for anything except his own ambition.

Before dawn the next morning one of the shepherds rushed to the house calling for help to beat out a fire that raged through the ripening barley.

It was the work of only a few moments to rouse all the young men of the family and the servants as well, and they ran to the field with their shovels and beating rugs. The fire was stopped at the stone walls Amnon had built, so that only Joab's field was entirely consumed by the flames. And when the sun rose they went their way, most of them, to wash away smoke and grime and to bind up their burns. But Joab and Eliab examined the field as well as they could, and from the traces of scorched cotton they found and the evidence the shepherd gave it was clear that the fire had been set by vandals in a score of places about the borders of Joab's field.

"It is a good thing," Joab said grimly, "that I was taught by Zeruiah not to blaspheme. For if ever a man was tempted to curse his own kinsmen, I am. Absalom is at the root of this thing. Absalom and the young ruffians who do his bidding."

"What does he want of you?" Eliab asked. He rubbed with his sleeve at the grime on his face, then touched with tender fingers a spot where his beard had been burned away.

"He wants me to make peace for him with his father, so that he may sit with Adonijah upon the dais in the hall of judgment and be acknowledged once more before the people as heir to the throne of Israel. He wants to be king. And he will be, unless David learns to meet guile with guile and trickery with punishment."

"Hebron is ripe already to rise against David." Eliab spoke reluctantly, as one who had withheld painful facts as long as he dared.

"Hebron?" Joab stared at his kinsman incredulously. "But Hebron loved

David when the rest of the country would have nothing to do with him."

"That is why they have clamored for special favors. They were affronted when David removed his capital from Hebron to Jerusalem, though that might have passed since Hebron is no citadel. But David is a great king, and an impartial one, and he gives his love to all the tribes. Taxes and labor levies and the conscription of soldiers fall alike on Judah and the tribes in the north. A clever and ambitious prince could find many in Judah who would help him make trouble for David."

Joab said angrily, "Absalom has this burnished chariot in which he rides through the land, with fifty men to run before him, shouting hs name. I have seen him in the Valley Gate, where travelers from Judah enter the city. He sits in the gate as elders sit, and when they bow before him—for he is a splendid sight in his royal robes—he raises them up, and kisses them, and if they have come seeking justice from David, he asks about their troubles. 'Your petition is just,' he says, no matter what they ask. 'You have a right to be heard, but the king will not be able to hear your cause for a month or more. If only he would make me a judge, every man who has a suit might come to me for justice instead of waiting in the city week after week, spending his wealth with the innkeepers and the rogues who prey upon strangers in this great city. Yet I cannot deal with your matter. You must take your case to the king and await your turn.' And this he does, over and over, turning men's hearts from David."

Eliab said, "The time has come for you to interfere once more between David and this son of his. To be with David is to love him. If he welcomes Absalom back into the kind of life his sons expect to lead, perhaps he can save the boy from the ambitions and treacherous plots he will otherwise hatch out."

Joab sighed. "Ahithophel is David's favorite counselor. Why should I do this thing? Ahithophel represents Judah at court. He is Bathsheba's grandfather, and a man of profound wisdom."

Eliab said, "David lay with Bathsheba while she was still Uriah's wife. He married her seven days after Uriah died in battle, and the son she bore was not Uriah's child. Ahithophel was seriously affronted by the whole thing. I know that old man. His sense of propriety is rigid. He is a man of Judah, and for him David is only a shepherd in king's clothing."

"These domestic affairs are not my concern," Joab shouted. "Why don't you talk to David? You are his brother and the head of the family. I am sick of intrigue. I have been cursed by David more than once for speaking to him of matters he did not wish to hear about, or for using the sword against enemies he chose to trust. You are his eldest brother and a leader in Judah. Go to him, warn him, give him the benefit of your rural wisdom. I wash my hands of his family and his follies."

Eliab smiled. "You had better wash your hands and the rest of your body as well, and put on clean garments before you go to Jerusalem to speak with these troublesome kinsmen of ours. Your destiny is there and mine is here, and I praise God that I do not need to exchange places with you or any man."

40

FOR HALF A year now little Solomon had been living in the court of the men. His apartment surpassed all his brothers' for lavishness of decoration and of furniture. Peacocks he had strutting about his courtyard, and apes on silver chains and other exotic possessions, bought in the ports of Tyre and Sidon or from the caravans between Egypt and Damascus, Nineveh, and Babylon. All his cloaks were made of expensive, Tyrian-dyed purple linens; the chaplets he wore over his headcloths were of many styles and colors, but every one had decorations of polished gems. The child was a living ornament in David's court.

How much the boy's extravagant tastes were his own, how much Bathsheba's, was a subject often discussed. In the harem of David, where every mother could not help comparing her own son and his prospects with Solomon, jealousy often colored the speculation.

On a day near the end of summer, six months after Solomon left the harem, Bathsheba climbed the stairway to the gallery where the older wives habitually sat with their sewing. Draped over her arm was an unfinished robe of purple with gold bands above the hem. Solomon was outgrowing his robes these days faster than she could make them. She was erect and impersonal as she asked, "May I join you?"

Reba's heart was touched with pity. Bathsheba had lost her first son. Now Solomon, beloved and beautiful, was no longer in her care. Reba had not failed to see how often Bathsheba attended David's court these past months. She knew the reason. Solomon now sat upon the steps of the dais with his older brothers.

Reba said cordially, "Welcome, Bathsheba. Bring your sewing and sit with us any time."

A little chorus from the others echoed her welcome. Reba glanced from Maacah to Bathsheba. One of us will someday be queen mother, she thought. Adonijah ought to be king, she thought with longing. He is a good son, and except for little Daniel, the closest in resemblance to David.

Reba could not but acknowledge that each of the three sons had qualities to admire. Even Absalom, ruthless and cruel though he was, had committed his crimes because he wanted so much to be king, and such a man might very well become a good king once his ambition was satisfied. I shall always hate him for killing Amnon, she thought. Yet I cannot avoid seeing in him the things Maacah sees. We have been friends for many years, Maacah and I. We did not cease to be friends because of what happened between our sons.

Adonijah never thought of being king, she thought, until Absalom fled to Syria. Both Amnon and Absalom had been ahead of him in the line of succession. Then suddenly both were gone. He could easily relinquish his ambitions if Absalom were king. But suppose David lived until Solomon was a man. It would be hard for Adonijah to yield to his youngest brother. It would be hard for me to remain in the harem, thought Reba, if Bathsheba were queen mother.

Adonijah would make a good king, she thought. If he lacked the driving force of Absalom and the elegance of Solomon, he was conscientious, considerate, circumspect. He sought advice in the right quarters, from Joab and Abiathar. Israel would be secure with Adonijah on the throne. Absalom would probably embark on conquests—Egypt in the south, Assyria and Babylon in the east. Solomon would waste Israel's wealth on elegance and luxury. Adonijah would be the wise choice, the safe choice.

Reba said kindly, "Our sons leave us while they are still so young. It is hard to be the mother of a prince."

Bathsheba said quietly, "It is glorious to be the mother of a prince."

After a short silence Maacah inquired, "Do you have any word from your grandfather? Absalom has sent me no message since he went with Ahithophel to the shrine at Hebron." She smiled. "I think David was pleased that Absalom is developing a streak of piety at last."

Bathsheba bowed her face over her sewing. "To many, my grandfather may seem like an angel of the Lord for wisdom, but he is not so beloved by his own family." She glanced up, smiling at the surprise she read on the faces of David's wives. "You think me disloyal to speak of Ahithophel in this manner. But in our home he was not as he is in the court. He ruled us all, even my father, with an iron hand. I have yet to see a living soul disregard or disobey him. He was"—she smiled as if begging for understanding—"fonder of my first husband than my second. We like to think that all men love David. I think my grandfather would have loved him more if he had chosen him for me. But he was not consulted, and he has never forgiven me. He serves David as counselor, but with reservations. I often think my son has inherited the wisdom of Ahithophel. I hope he has also inherited the compassionate heart of David. Yet I have dreaded to think of the influence Ahithophel will surely have upon him, now that he has left the harem and is often in his grandfather's company."

Does she confide in us because she is lonely, Reba wondered? Or does she say only what she surely knows will break down our reserve and endear her to us? Does she hope, in the end, to use us all in the advancement of her son?

I have become suspicious and faultfinding, thought Reba guiltily. Peace and contentment are gone from my heart since deceit and peril have entered my life. If Adonijah were king, Joab and I could marry. If David died now while Solomon is still a child, Adonijah would be declared king by Joab and the army, and Absalom would be defeated. I never had such thoughts before. Why do I probe behind every word, every glance, watching for treachery?

As if in answer to the thought, an outcry arose from another part of the palace. The harem door burst open and Dinah rushed in, her hair splotched with ashes and her face streaked with tears and soot.

"Treason!" she screamed. "Treason! Rebellion! Absalom is king in Hebron! He will kill us all. Blood will flow over the door sills!"

Reba heard the gasping cry from Maacah as she threw the skirts of her robe over her face. Then David appeared. He was pale and tense, but not distraught. From the open door behind him a great clamor could be heard. He turned. "Silence!" he shouted.

David's voice was clear and strong and could be heard in every corner of the women's court and in the corridors and chambers adjoining. "My son Absalom has been made king in Hebron. He is marching on Jerusalem at the head of an army from Judah."

Dinah moaned, "Lock the gates. Shut them out."

"Solomon!" cried Bathsheba. "Where is my son? They will kill him!"

David's great voice drowned the wailing of his wives. "My advisers are of conflicting opinions, whether to hold the city while Absalom besieges us or to flee across the Jordan."

"Lock the gates!" screamed several voices. "Shut them out."

David raised his hands for silence. "Our walls are not yet completed. Even if they were, walls are no protection from the enemy within. Joab is my commander and in matters of war his counsel prevails. Joab is for marching across the Jordan. Since I do not know who is with me and who is with Absalom I dare not remain. At a later time we will make our stand. If you are for Absalom—"

David paused. His eyes went from one to another of his wives as if reading their loyalties. He paused longest at the rocking figure of Maacah.

"—if you are for Absalom, then stay in the palace. He will be here before nightfall. If you are for David, gather up what you can carry and follow me to the Damascus Gate. Dinah, you will choose out nine of the women to stay with you, women who will take orders from you and behave circumspectly. Someone must attend to the household in our absence. Do not harm the young man when he comes. Do not speak out against him, for he would not spare you any more than he would spare his own father."

Bathsheba sank down on one of the steps of the gallery. "Who brought the warning? Was it—was it my grandfather?"

David's eyes were bleak. "Ahithophel is with Absalom. My cousin Amasa commands his army. You who have relatives in Judah can assume they are with Absalom, for my own tribe and kindred are against me. Perhaps my wives are against me also. Stay here if you choose. Each of you must decide for herself. Ira of Tekoa came with his wife Telema, bringing the news. Ira is one man of Judah who is for David. As for the others—I do not know."

David's shoulders hunched. His head bowed. In the deathly silence of the women's court his voice became a despairing whisper. "When I have reached the ancient shrine at the crest of the Mount of Olives on the road to Jericho, I will pause to let those who are with me pass by. Then I will know who are my friends and—who are not."

The original stronghold of Jerusalem was built upon a promontory between two ravines which joined below the city to form the Valley of Hinnom. On the Kidron side, cedars darkened the valley and the Kidron wall was a steep, stony precipice pitted with tombs. The Tyropoeon Valley was, by contrast, a garden spot. The slope was gradual and had been terraced and given to the king's sons for their vineyards. The fountain En Rogel was here, and conduits carried its water to the vineyards. The Tyropoeon Valley was a place of pleasure, a place for celebrations, verdant and lovely. But the Kidron side was dismal with its tiers of tombs on the cliffs, its refuse heaps and dung piles below.

In one of the tombs on the Kidron side Jonathan, son of Abiathar, and Ahimaaz, Zadok's son, were hiding. They had come here at David's order to wait for darkness and the messenger their fathers would send them; for David had sent his priests back from the Mount of Olives to be his spies as long as Absalom dwelt in the palace.

The young men waited in the empty tomb all the long afternoon. They heard the trampling and the shouting when Absalom's army moved up the Bethlehem road to enter Jerusalem through the Valley Gate. Jonathan and Ahimaaz did not dare even glimpse the army of rebellion. What went on within the city that day they did not know. Shouts were heard, "Long live King Absalom!" or "Huzzah, Absalom!" With darkness the southern end of the city grew quiet. At last Jonathan and Ahimaaz emerged from the tomb to crawl stealthily around to the terraced vineyards. Here they refreshed themselves at the fountain En Rogel.

They lay down under the shelter of the vines, which climbed the stumps of olive trees planted here to serve as trellises, making a network of vines from tree to tree, growing longer and thicker with the passing years.

"I hope," Ahimaaz said softly, "that whoever comes to bring a message will also bring a loaf or two. I'm starved."

Jonathan was also hungry. "Too bad the grapes have all been harvested," he whispered. He shivered but not with cold, for the night was warm. Life in the household of Abiathar had been peaceful. In all his twenty-two years the only warfare Jonathan had known had come to him from words neatly inked on parchment. What was happening in the darkened city above?

Beside him the regular breathing of Ahimaaz indicated that he slept. Will I ever be able to fall quietly asleep again, Jonathan wondered? He pushed aside the vines and looked up at the stars.

> "The heavens declare the glory of God,
> And the firmament showeth his handiwork."

David had written the song and the Levite choir often sang it. David had written many beautiful songs for the Levites to sing on fast days and feast days. Today, on the Mount of Olives, David had sent back the Levites who bore the ark out of the city to carry it with David into exile. "If God is with me," David had said, "I shall not need the ark. If God is not with me the ark will not help me." Jonathan had felt a prickling along his spine when he heard David speak those words.

How can a son rise against his father? Jonathan thought with love of Abiathar, who was his father in love and care since the father who begot him had died in battle. Absalom had killed his brother and now he sought to kill David.

Jonathan's hand fell away from the vine as a voice nearby called softly, "Ahimaaz! Jonathan! Are you here?"

Jonathan nudged Ahimaaz. "Someone has come," he said. "Dinah, I think."

They slid out from under the sheltering vines, dropped quietly over the wall which banked the terrace. Dinah sat on the masonry that walled the fountain. A pitcher was beside her—an unlikely excuse for a visit to this place by night since the Gihon spring was so much closer to the palace, but an excuse nevertheless.

"I could not come sooner," she said softly. She handed each of them a loaf and a bunch of raisins wrapped in a napkin.

Ahimaaz cried, "Tell us what's happened? Are they still in the city, or have they gone after David?"

Dinah whispered, "Sh! Do you want to be heard? I have much to tell you. Listen carefully so you can repeat it to David. They are still in the city, fortunately. David sent Hushai back to welcome Absalom and pretend friendship, hoping Absalom might follow Hushai's counsel rather than Ahithophel's and Hushai could thus gain time for David to muster his defense. Ahithophel wanted to take a detachment and march out at once, kill David, and bring all the others back to be servants to Absalom. But he was too anxious, too worried and nervous. Hushai flattered the young upstart, saying the troops could not march without their king at their head, and that Absalom owed it to himself and to his subjects to observe certain formalities at the palace before he set out. Certain—rites—he said, to reassure Israel that the young king was strong where the old king was weak. After that, Hushai declared, the army could find David wherever he hid. With Absalom to lead them, they could not fail to destroy David."

Ahimaaz grunted. "I'd have known better than to listen to flattery!"

"Don't be too sure, my young friend." Dinah patted his shoulder patronizingly, and Ahimaaz shrugged away from her touch. She smiled a bitter little smile. "Tell David that Absalom ordered a tent to be pitched on the palace roof. The king's concubines were brought there—those David left to tend the palace. There the new young king demonstrated his virility for the gratification of his foolish followers. Say to David that whatever women can do by flirting or flattery to delay a conceited young man, the concubines of David did today. Say to David we were proud to have a part in delaying Absalom's pursuit of our lord." Here Dinah raised her head proudly, while her lips set in a line of bitter anger. "Say also to David that when Ahithophel saw that the rebellion was doomed by Absalom's folly, he went to his house and hanged himself."

Jonathan shuddered, "That poor old man."

Dinah said, "Don't waste pity on Ahithophel. He wanted to rush down to the fords of the Jordan and destroy David. I am glad he is dead. I spit on him."

Ahimaaz said, "What else are we to say to David?"

"Tell him Hushai warns that he must cross the Jordan before morning. No one can tell from hour to hour whether Absalom will hold to his purpose. There is no safety in the open field. Absalom has been preparing this rebellion for many months. His army is young, strong, eager, and much larger than David's."

The runners reached David shortly after midnight. When they had delivered their messages they turned back in order to reach their hiding place in the tombs before sunrise.

The fords of the Jordan were four miles above the point where the river emptied into the Dead Sea. From the top of the Mount of Olives to the fords the distance was twenty miles and downhill all the way. But Joab roused all the company and set soldiers in a long line across the river to mark the ford and to help any who stumbled.

Fortunately it was the end of summer and the river was low. All through the moonlit night the people moved across the ford. When dawn streaked the sky with pink and purple, the long procession was winding northward up the sandy Arabah, the figures silhouetted against the high yellow bluffs of the Gilead plain. Nor did they pause to rest until the last of them had passed over.

They rested for an hour, making a meal of what food they had. Still strong and active at sixty-five, Ira was in charge of the distribution of the food. He doled it out impartially to king and servant, to prince and armor-bearer alike. While they rested, Joab sent runners ahead to the cities of Gilead and to Shobi, king of Rabbah-Ammon, to spread the news that David had fled from Absalom and a rebel army, that he would lodge in Mahanaim, and that he had need of help from all who loved him.

Then Joab roused up the disheartened people and sent them on again. The sun beat down and the people longed for shade, for in the low Arabah the heat of summer is not to be taken lightly. Still Joab sent them on, knowing that in the hottest part of the day they would be forced to rest.

Immersed in despair, David left all planning to Joab and the captains. When Joab fell in beside David to discuss the plans, David listened with an abstracted air. "Do what seems best to you," he said. "But don't forget this is no army marching. Our little ones are with us, and some of the people are old and infirm."

"Now that we have eaten the provisions," Joab said, "we are setting the weakest of the people on donkeys. I have been told that when our ancestors came out of Egypt to make their journey across the desert, a day's journey was ten miles. We came twenty yesterday, and I think we can do twenty today. Our ancestors had their cattle with them and all their household goods. They numbered thousands, while we are only a few hundreds, and without tents or any other heavy truck upon our backs. I want to get our people across the Jabbok before we rest tonight. Then if we can manage to travel another twenty miles tomorrow we will be safe at Mahanaim. A sixty-mile journey made in three days is a creditable achievement for so many, yet I think it is not unreasonable."

David said wearily, "Do what you think best, cousin. We are in your hands."

And so the journey continued.

The sun was low over the green hills of Ephraim when the people came out upon the bend of the Jabbok where it enters the Jordan. And Joab's soldiers, those who marched ahead of the people, took their stand at the stones which marked the ford, and so another river crossing was made.

"We will camp between the rivers," Joab shouted, and the word was passed up and down the lines. For this was a place where the Jabbok wound southward for several miles, before turning west at last to lose itself in the Jordan. On this spit of sand the people would rest, wrapped in their cloaks, for they had no beds to ease the hardship of the journey.

While the people were still crossing the Jabbok there came a braying of donkeys from around the bend of the river upstream, which was answered by the donkeys of David's company. While Joab's men waited with ready weapons, Shobi, son of the old Nahash of Rabbah-Ammon, came into view. David had given his daughter Tamar to Shobi. Now Tamar was here, walking beside her husband at the head of a long donkey train, with gifts of beds and utensils, and abundant supplies of parched grain and ground meal, beans and lentils, honey and butter and cheese, and with flocks of sheep driven behind the donkey train.

Tamar ran to her father and threw her arms about his neck and wept on his shoulder, and David wept with her, since both of them loved Absalom and could not stop loving him no matter what evil he did.

Ira distributed cheese and parched grain to all the company, for he was unwilling that fires should be built to roast meat or make meal into bread. Tamar went to sit on the sand with her mother, Maacah, and all the wives of David. This was the first time they had talked together since Shobi married Tamar and took her away to his own city.

Next morning Shobi and Tamar returned up the Jabbok, but Shobi left behind the donkeys he had brought and many of the servants.

David's company plodded steadily northward. Before the heat of the day came upon them they had left the Jordan behind, following a tributary wadi north and east until they came to the city of Mahanaim. At the gate others waited, men who had come to David in his time of need, bringing beds and cattle and sheep and fruit and grain and cheese. When David saw them he wept, because now he knew which of his friends were faithful in his time of adversity.

41

THE CITY OF Mahanaim stood in wooded country, with abundant springs rising both within the walls and in the ravines below them. The city was fenced with double walls, so that an enemy who managed to scale the outer would be exposed to bowmen on the inner. The very name of Mahanaim meant strength—a place where armies meet. Here in this high, well-watered land, marked by many streams cutting their way down to the Jordan, was the stronghold to which Abner, with Ishbosheth, had fled from the Philistines when Saul and his other sons were slain. From Mahanaim, Abner had marched out to meet Joab at Gibeon, and when the battle ended led the remnants of his army back to the city. When Ishbosheth and Abner quarreled, and Abner went over to David only to be killed by Joab, Ishbosheth lived on in Mahanaim, a king in name only.

The south gate of Mahanaim was a tower connecting the outer and inner walls. To this gate came Ahimaaz and Jonathan after two Sabbaths had passed, bringing word that Absalom had crossed the Jordan, that he would march by way of the Arabah, and that his army numbered twenty thousand men. Since the army with David was small—only three thousand veterans—Absalom's plan was to besiege the city until famine forced the people to surrender David to him.

But Joab had no mind to permit Absalom to shut him up within the city. Instead he planned an ambush in a place of his own choosing, where the Arabah was narrow and choked with forest.

At dawn the army marched out through the south gate. David stood in the gate, giving each unit his blessing. When all were massed outside, David climbed to the tower room and spoke from a window with the loud voice of command.

"God go with you," said David, so that every man among the thousands of his soldiers could hear. "And when you have put down the rebellion, deal gently for my sake with my son Absalom."

And all the men responded with their formal shout, "Long live David! Long live the king!"

Joab raised the ram's horn and sounded the order to march. The battalions moved down the valley and soon the dust they raised hid them from the watcher above the wall.

After an hour or two the marchers came to where the valley divided, with wadies branching off to north and south. Here the battalions separated. Seth led his army into the north fork and Ittai led his into the south fork, while Joab with his thousand marched down the central valley. Where the three wadies entered the Arabah a forest of terebinth trees crowded the opposite shore right down to the water's edge. Here Joab had chosen to set up his ambush. Here Absalom's inexperienced army, taken by surprise, would have no room to recover and reform for attack. If all went well, this one battle could end the rebellion.

Two companies of archers separated themselves from the rest of Joab's battalion and climbed the headland to await his signal. An Ethiopian lad called Cushi was Joab's armor-bearer. He climbed a magnificent oak overlooking the Arabah; when Absalom's army reached the designated spot, Cushi was to yelp like a jackal. Then Joab would mass his men for the attack, and sound the ram's horn. Joab's forces would fall upon the enemy in the center while Seth's soldiers blocked their advance and Ittai's soldiers blocked their retreat. The archers on the bluffs above would rain down arrows into the tangle of trapped men.

An hour passed, while the sun climbed the sky. From the tree came the bark of a jackal. Joab raised his spear aloft, and behind him the captains repeated the signal, and the ranks formed solidly, filling the mouth of the valley. Then Joab sounded the ram's horn, and with savage cries his soldiers fell upon their unprepared and unsuspecting enemy.

Absalom was the first to break for the shelter of the forest across the shallow Jordan. In his pride and folly, Absalom rode at the head of his army on David's mule. He left the river and got in among the terebinth trees while his soldiers were trampling one another into the sand and water in their haste to find cover from the arrows and spears flying all about them. When the melee grew too congested for the archers to tell their own men from the others, they dropped their bows upon the height and leaped down into the Arabah to engage the enemy with sword and lance.

Veteran of many wars, Joab had never fought a battle like this one. Fighting is a business, and anger has no part in it; yet anger possessed Joab now, for these were men of Israel, both the forces of Joab and the forces of the enemy. Under his feet, under his sword, tangled among one another wherever he turned, were men of Israel. Joab's anger was focused not on the men he struck down but on three men only—the three he considered to blame for this frightful massacre of Israelite by Israelite—Absalom the ambitious, Amasa the dupe, and David, who in his foolish love of his evil son had permitted this thing to come to pass. Do not harm the young man, David had said. David had never lifted a sword against an Israelite. David could not know the horror of such a battle. But Joab had learned long ago, while David was king in Hebron, what it meant to strike down men who swear by the God of Israel. And now he had it all to do again, because of David's weakness in all matters that pertained to his own sons. Every blow Joab struck was struck in anger against Amasa, Absalom, and David. Well then, Absalom had vanished into the forest, and David was weeping in the tower at Mahanaim, but Amasa was here somewhere. Joab dodged among the struggling, cursing, dying men, seeking his cousin Amasa who had led these soldiers of Israel against their king. Twice he was close enough to cast a spear, but both times Amasa dodged behind someone else.

Then suddenly Amasa, too, disappeared into the forest. Joab turned and looked at the bodies that clogged the river, and the anger he felt was like nothing he had ever felt before in all his forty-four years.

Now Cushi was beside him, plucking at his sleeve. The boy's dark face was streaked with sweat and the turban he had wound upon his oily black curls had been plucked awry by the thorns of the terebinth trees.

"I have found him," the lad panted.

"You have found Amasa? Where?" Joab shouted to be heard above the savage cries of the attackers and the screams of the wounded and dying.

"Not Amasa. The enemy. The traitor himself, Absalom." Cushi's eyes rolled and his head wagged in horror. "He is hanging in a tree in the midst of the forest. His mule walked right out from under him, leaving his head wedged among branches and his hair tangled in thorns so he cannot work himself loose."

Joab seized the boy's shoulders in a grip of iron. "You saw him there and did not kill him? I would have rewarded you with a hundred shekels if you had brought me his head instead of this news."

Cushi stared at Joab in terror. "The king said we are to take him captive. We are not to kill him! I would not lay a sword on that young man for a thousand shekels!"

Joab shouted, "Then lead me to him."

They ran, both of them, past soldiers locked in battle, past corpses and dying men who begged for help. They dodged trees and crawled under low-hanging boughs, tearing great rents in their clothes, until Joab came upon a cluster of men beneath a tall tree. Absalom, dressed in a short cloak of purple linen and with golden armlets binding his straining arms, hung in the tree. On the ground beneath lay a magnificent shield of bronze and cowhide, and beside it an equally splendid helmet. Blood oozed down Absalom's cheeks where his struggle to free his head from the forked branch only served to tighten its pressure. He was not struggling now. He had hooked both arms over the branches to take the weight of his body. He had closed his eyes against his agony and against the jibes of the soldiers who ringed him round.

Joab said harshly, "Well, cousin, you seem to be at our mercy."

Absalom's eyes opened, and when he saw that Joab was here at hand tears of relief rolled from them. "Thanks be to God that you've come at last, cousin," he said in a voice weak from exhaustion and pain. "Get me down from this cursed tree, will you? Take me to my father." His tears mingled with the blood on his face, forming pink rivulets which ran down into the dark, handsome beard. "Just take your sword," he said, "and cut away my hair where it is tangled in these cursed thorns. Then, by pushing the branch just a little—cousin, for the love of mercy, hurry!"

"Mercy," Joab said, and spat into the dirt near where the dusty sandals hung, less than half a cubit's length above the ground. "Do you indeed ask me for mercy, cousin?"

"In the name of God," moaned Absalom, "don't torture me now. Get me down. I'll serve you as long as I live. I'll wash your feet. I'll tread your grapes. I'll be your slave."

Joab hefted the spear in his right hand. Glancing about at the ring of watching faces he saw mingled emotions of pity and pleasure.

"Mercy," said Joab. He stepped back three paces, and cast his spear so that it entered the muscles below the left armpit, and hung quivering there. "This is the mercy you showed Amnon," he said, and reached for the spear in Cushi's hand.

[241]

Absalom's arm had loosed its grip on the limb above him. He whispered, "Mercy, cousin. In the name of God."

Joab said, "Mercy, cousin. The mercy you showed to Tamar, who is your sister and who would have married Amnon." And he cast the second spear, cutting the muscle under the right arm. And now Absalom hung by his head only, and fresh blood was running down over his eyes, blinding him. He bit his lips but did not speak or cry out.

A nearby Reubenite extended his spear, and Joab took it, balancing it before the throw. "And this is the mercy you showed David your father, who loved you well even when you sought to destroy him."

Joab cast the spear so that it entered below the navel, where death comes most agonizingly. And the bleeding figure in purple linen swung back and forward again and the spears hung quivering, and screams bubbled from the open mouth.

Then Joab turned away, sick of the hatred in himself which had led him to inflict such frightful pain on his kinsman, yet knowing he would never truly repent of what he had done.

His hand swept out, permitting the young men to close round the figure that hung now so near the ground. In a moment the screams stopped. Absalom was dead. And Joab raised the trumpet to his lips and blew the signal which would recall his soldiers from their pursuit of Absalom's fleeing army.

They carried the body of Absalom to a nearby ravine, and each man brought a stone and cast it upon the body. And as other soldiers returned from the pursuit, each in his turn brought his stone and cast it, so that at last nothing could be seen of mangled flesh or golden sandal cords or purple linen. Then Joab sent runners back to Mahanaim to tell David that the rebellion was ended.

Joab did not return to Mahanaim that night. East of the city the huts of his own battalion stood, and Joab spent the night in the hut of one of his captains, wrapped in his cloak. I can never face David again, he thought, as he lay awake far into the night. Against his orders I killed his son. Yet his orders were wrong. David was no king, but only a foolish, grieving father when he ordered us to deal gently with Absalom. Israelites died in battle because of Absalom. More would have died if he had been left alive, for he would never have ceased from plotting so long as there was breath in his body.

But to torture him. Joab had marched against many an enemy who made it a practice to torture the wounded, but such a thing was not done in Israel. Philistines tortured before they killed. Edomites and Amalekites tortured before they killed. But such a thing was never before done by a responsible officer in a Hebrew army. Where can I hide my shame? And yet wherever he had turned during the hours of the afternoon and evening, he had met the covertly admiring glances of his men.

Cushi found him among his soldiers on the third day. Seth had sent the lad to bring Joab to the city. David had shut himself up in the tower above the gate and would permit no one to enter. David had not eaten, and at all hours, by day and night, his lament could be heard.

"Over and over he cries out the same thing," Cushi reported. His youthful face under the fat yellow turban was solemn with anxiety and pity. " 'Oh, my son Absalom, my son, my son Absalom! Would I had died instead, O Absalom, my son, my son!' When he lifts his voice the words are heard throughout the city."

Joab said angrily, "Tell my brother—" Then he paused. He was responsible. Well then, he would do what he could. Why should Seth brave the king's anger because of a deed done by Joab? Surely nothing Joab might do or say could earn him a greater hatred than that which David already bore him. "I will see what can be done," Joab said, nodding curtly to the lad. The soldiers who had risked their lives at his command had a right to expect him to face the king's anger in person.

Joab washed himself and put on a clean tunic and the short cloak of the soldier. He buckled on his sword and shield, and pulled on the worn old helmet with three sword cuts in its crest.

When he came to the gate he turned and climbed the stone steps inside the outer wall. With the wooden shaft of his spear he beat upon the tower door, shouting, "It is I, Joab. Whether it pleases you or not, cousin, I must speak to you."

He heard the shuffling sandals of a tired old man within the room. Then the door was opened.

At sight of David's grief-ravaged face, Joab's heart grew hard with anger. "You cover with shame the men who risked their lives for you—and your wives and your children," he shouted.

David stepped back from the door. "Come in, Joab. What you have to say I will hear, but let us talk in private."

Joab stepped inside the bare, stone-walled room with its slitted windows. A pallet lay on the floor in the corner. Glancing at the rumpled bedding, Joab knew the king had been lying there, alone with his grief, when Joab knocked. The muscles of his jaws and neck bulged with anger.

"Your soldiers have risked their lives for your sake, yet now they creep in and out of the city as if they had lost the battle. Among themselves they are saying that you care nothing for them, that if they were dead and rotting on the earth you would not grieve at all, if only that worthless young man, Absalom, were still alive. If Absalom were to walk up that road out there now, they are saying, you would walk out to meet him and lie down in the highway and wait for him to strike the head off your shoulders."

[243]

David's eyes were steady on Joab. "Tell me how he died," he said.

Involuntarily Joab moved back a step. "You know how he died."

"I heard rumors. I do not believe them. I taught you myself to kill with the single thrust below the fifth rib. I do not believe that my commanding general required three spears to kill a man who hung defenseless in a tree."

Joab shouted, "Do you know anyone who had better reason than I for killing Absalom?"

David said steadily, "Tell me how he died."

And Joab told the story, omitting nothing.

When he had finished, David still stood erect before him, pale but composed. "You brought him home from exile in Syria. You interceded for him, so that I brought him back into my court. He thought you were his friend. I thought so too."

"Did you!" Joab cried. "I would rather believe you gave the order to spare Absalom because you knew it would be disobeyed and you wanted to cleanse your own skirts of his blood. Well then, the guilt is upon me. I can bear the guilt because I have no son to inherit the curses you have heaped upon me more than once. So I say, let the guilt be upon me, for in shedding Absalom's blood I have saved our people much misery. The enemies of Israel must perish. It is for this God raised you to be king. It is for this He gave you a man such as I am, a man unafraid to do what must be done for king and country. I disobeyed you for Israel's sake. If, in my anger, I forgot for a moment that I am a Hebrew—well, I had seen a river choked with dying Hebrews, men whose death was caused by Absalom's ambition. And now, if indeed you love your people at all, you will come forth from this room and sit in the gate and give your people thanks for the wounds they suffered and the comrades they lost and the victory they won for you."

David said quietly, "You must be punished, Joab. As when Abner died, the guilt is yours and you must bear it. Not for my sake but for the sake of harmony in this troubled kingdom. Give me the trumpet. I must find another man to be my commander."

Joab took the trumpet of command from his neck and handed it to David. "Find a commander who pleases you," he said. "I have had enough of war. I shall return to Bethlehem and farm the land and tend the sheep, for I am sick of war and death. As for punishment—" He shrugged and turned away. "I think you cannot punish me more than I have been punished. I must live out my life with the memory of Abner's death, and Uriah's, and Absalom's. It is enough."

David took the trumpet and left the room. He went down the stairway and sat in the gate. When the people saw him they came to him and bowed down, and he blessed them all and gave thanks to them for their loyalty, for all they had suffered for his sake, and for the victory they had won.

But Joab left the city. He spent one more night in a soldier's hut. The next day he set out for Bethlehem.

42

JOAB RETURNED TO Bethlehem in the beginning of the month Tishri. He was not surprised to find that Amasa had not come home. The family in Bethlehem had not supported Absalom's rebellion. Amasa, with the others who had thrown in their fortunes with Absalom, were now in Hebron licking their wounds.

The winter rains were due before the end of the month, and Joab devoted himself to plowing his barley field, turning under stubble and thistles and tares, preparing the ground for the rains. Work on the land helped to heal the wounds of the spirit. Every quarrel Joab had ever had with David had ended thus, with Joab returning to Bethlehem to find solace in familiar faces, familiar sounds and sights, and in the labor which restored the mind and brought sound sleep at nightfall. By the time the plowing was finished Joab was able to say, even of the frightful manner of Absalom's death, "It is done. I will not think of it again."

He did not go to the fields the day before the rains began. He stayed in Bethlehem in the stable yard, whittling out pieces to repair the plow handles. Here Seth found him, having come to Bethlehem with disturbing news. David had not yet returned to Jerusalem. He had sent Seth through the land from tribe to tribe, to bring word of the state of Israel. Seth found the land in turmoil. Absalom, whom they had made their king, was dead. David remained beyond the Jordan. The people were quarreling among themselves in every town and tribe.

"There is a loud-mouthed Benjamite, Sheba by name, of the family of Bichri, who says the time has come to make Mephibosheth their king. Some say Mephibosheth stayed behind when David marched out of Jerusalem, hoping to head up a faction such as this one. Yet Mephibosheth declares he was left behind because he is lame. While he was still trying to get hold of a donkey to ride forth with David, Absalom's troops reached the city and it was too late for him to go out. That is Mephibosheth's story, and perhaps it is true. At any rate, the nation is ready to fall apart at a touch. A powerful leader is needed. David is without strength; he is a man with a broken heart. It will take time for him to recover."

Joab said, "Does he think no one else has been hurt?"

"He needs you, Joab," Seth said soberly. Few were the times Seth had paid tribute to his younger brother's shrewdness and strength of purpose. "He needs you, and Israel needs you. 'Where is Joab?' they ask. 'Why has he abandoned the army?' People are confused. They are ashamed that they became the dupes of Absalom, yet they do not forget the charges he made against David. If you would march among them at the head of an army the people would be content."

Joab said bitterly, "Absalom is dead, and by my hand. Against David's order I killed him. David must restore unity to the kingdom now. The people have been enriched for many years by the tribute and captive slaves he won for them. He has only to stand before them, strong and confident, and they will shout, 'Hail David' ten times louder than ever they shouted for Absalom."

Joab put aside his tools and walked with Seth into the court of the rambling old house which had been boyhood home to both. They crossed to the cistern and Joab took up the heavy earthen bottle and poured water for Seth and for himself. All about them the women were preparing a feast which Eliab had ordered to celebrate Seth's visit. Eliab had sent messengers to the heads of every important family in Bethlehem, inviting them to come.

Clouds were gathering and the rains were due, and the low table had been moved under the shelter of an overhanging balcony. Joab and Seth went under the balcony and Joab spread a striped rug he had taken from Amalekites long ago, when David was king in Hebron. The two brothers seated themselves on the rug.

Joab said, "The people ought to go over the Jordan and bring David home. They drove him forth. It is for them to send envoys to bring him back. Let them respect his pride, for David's pride and his dependence on the love of the people of Israel are the great sources of his strength. He was never able, no matter how desperate his straits, to raise a hand against Israel. How then can he understand or condone their wish to hurt him? Let the people humble themselves and bring him home again to Jerusalem."

"You are right!" Seth shouted, so loudly the women paused in their work to glance at him. "If the people went to bring him home he would come, and they in turn would be eased of their shame."

Joab said, "Men of Hebron should take the lead in bringing him back, since they took the lead in anointing Absalom."

Seth's wide smile threatened to split his face. "They shall do it, if I have to knock their heads together to accomplish it."

He rose and took a turn about the court. "There is a matter I do not like to speak of," he said. "You know David, how prone he is to offer kindness to his enemies instead of executing them. He has sent for Amasa to join him in Mahanaim. David is giving Amasa the trumpet of command he took from you."

"That young whelp!" Joab exploded. "He hasn't a thought in his head that someone else does not put there. He led an army of twenty thousand into a trap set by three battalions, and lacked the wit or the courage to sound the trumpet and rally his forces. Half the men who died that day were killed by sheer panic."

Seth nodded. "I mentioned that when David announced his intention. He replied that Amasa had undoubtedly profited by his error. He says this is the way to prove to the people of Judah that he forgives them and loves them." Seth shrugged. "We are at peace. Unless unforeseen violence breaks out somewhere, Amasa can do us no harm."

Joab said angrily, "This is the Abner affair all over again. David seeks peace by making the leader of the opposition second in the kingdom. He was wrong when he promised the trumpet to Abner, and he is wrong in giving it to Amasa."

"Do not be so sure he is wrong," Seth said reasonably. "You spoke of David's pride. What about the pride of Judah? David knows that peace lies in winning and holding the love of each of the twelve tribes."

Eliab had come in during the conversation. He sat down near them, while a small black-eyed slave boy brought cloths and water and washed their feet. "You say Amasa is wearing the trumpet for David?"

Seth nodded, with a smile more than half apologetic.

Eliab smiled. "It seems a poor choice. Yet we have seen many of David's choices turn out well. I have been an elder in Bethlehem long enough to understand that David is moved by faith, forgiveness, love. The people recognize greatness of soul in David, and some despise him for it, but the better sort love him because his greatness makes all Israel great. We who are David's kinsmen differ from him. Being practical men, we measure in terms of justice and logic. I think it is no accident that the man of faith is first in the kingdom, while his practical, logical cousins are the men who execute his orders."

Joab's anger had left him under the influence of Eliab's reasoning. He smiled. "Can you deny the God of Israel, who is pleased with David's faith and forgiveness and the songs of praise he invents, was also pleased with the service of these practical cousins, men capable of mopping up the blood that flows when David's visions become too visionary?"

The slave boy had finished washing Eliab's feet and was now busy serving Joab. He looked up at Joab with an expression of astonishment, then ducked his head, lest he be punished for presuming to listen to the conversation of the men he served.

Now the guests invited to the feast were beginning to arrive. Elhanan with his sons entered and Joab stepped forward to greet him, forgetting the summer he had fled in terror of him, remembering rather the ten years when Elhanan had commanded a company of archers in Joab's army. Since the fall of Rabbah-Ammon, Elhanan had lived in Bethlehem. His father being dead, Elhanan was now patriarch in his own family.

Lamps of alabaster, of black basalt from Bashan, and of the deep red porphyry of Egypt were set out in niches in the wall or hung from brackets suspended under the balcony. The women brought out roast lamb and fowls, figs and dates from the autumn harvest, raisins and melons and bread and cheese. Wine from the vineyards and wine from the mulberry trees flowed freely. A group of musicians strummed the melodies every shepherd learned to sing from childhood, and an old man famous as a teller of tales entertained the men at the table and the women who sat in the shadows at the other end of the court.

The feast continued into the night. The next morning the sky was cloudy and sullen, as Seth set out for Hebron. Before midafternoon the first of the autumn rains was falling.

The month Heshvan came, and Joab went out with other men of the household to sow the barley, while the boys led the sheep out from their shelter to seek winter forage. The rains increased during Kislev, but when the month Tebet came grain was sprouting in the lowlands. On a day late in the month Joab was out walking beside the barley fields, rejoicing in the sprouting green that colored the earth, when he saw wayfarers traveling north on the highway. He ran across the fields to question them, for no news had come during all the months of the winter.

The men were Hebronites, one of them nephew and heir to Aziel, the wine merchant who had enslaved Joab nearly thirty years ago. He, with other elders of Hebron, were on their way to Mahanaim to beg David to return to Jerusalem and rule Israel again.

Aziel's nephew was a fat, languid fellow who was traveling by donkey, though most of his companions were on foot. He tugged his donkey to the side of the road and dismounted. "Come with us, Joab," he urged. "Plead our cause with David, for we are like wayward children who seek comfort in the arms of our mother. Speak in our behalf, for although we are of his own tribe and kindred, in our folly we listened to the lies of that wicked young man, Absalom."

The sight of this pudgy elder and his small donkey and the thought of these dignitaries likening themselves to wayward children were almost too much for Joab's gravity. Yet he would not say anything to dampen their ardor, since they were doing what was right for Israel and for David.

When Joab still held his peace, the nephew of Aziel inquired curiously, "Is it true that you tortured Absalom while he hung in a tree?"

The others crowded closer, staring at Joab and nudging one another. Joab said sternly, "It is true that I rescued your king from a wicked son who, with your help, would have killed David if he could. Now, do not delay upon the road, lest the rains return and drive you to shelter. Go to David and bring him home to his palace. Do not ask me to intercede in your behalf. Speak for yourselves, for it was you who listened to Absalom, and it is you who must seek David's forgiveness."

Joab strode back to his fields and the men moved on up the highway. Yet Joab could not keep his thoughts in Bethlehem. Whenever he raised his eyes he saw bands of travelers moving north, carrying gifts to the king they had driven forth half a year ago. He longed to go with them and watch the drama of David's forgiveness and restoration. But he could not now go into David's presence. Between them a prince in purple hung in a tree. Would the sound of Absalom's screams echo between them forever?

43

THE MONTH SHEBAT brought blossoms to the fruit trees. Adar passed and the pomegranates flowered along the wayside, and grain was tall in the fields. Messengers came now and then, and in Bethlehem they heard how people of all the tribes had come down to the Jordan, quarreling among themselves over which should show David honor in ferrying him and his people over the swollen waters of the river. And Joab was content to know that David reigned again in Jerusalem, and that his family lived in their own quarters in comfort.

Nisan brought the spring rains. The courtyard of Eliab was filled with the bustle of roasting and baking and seething in preparation for the feast of sheepshearing. Food would be given to the neighbors and hirelings who helped with the shearing, and to all the needy of the region. In the midst of the bustle Seth arrived, coming in haste. Civil war had broken out in the tribe of Benjamin, where Sheba the Bichrite had sounded the trumpet of revolt. Amasa had spent the winter in the Millo barracks in Jerusalem, gambling and gaming and drinking wine with the idle soldiers. Impatient with Amasa's lack of enterprise, David had summoned him and ordered him to go into Judah to raise an army. After three days Amasa did not return. Then David ordered Seth to take charge of the palace police and lead them north in pursuit of Sheba. They were to set out the next day.

Joab was in the shed where sheep were being sheared when Seth found him. He looked up from the ram he held by a horn and the shears in his hand ceased their click. "Why are you here?" he asked. "Did David send for me?"

"It was in his mind. David knew I would not march without you, Joab. Why else would he choose me for this responsibility in preference to Ittai or Benaiah? This is David's way of asking you to march for him once more."

With a quick movement of the bound legs of the ram, Joab flipped him over. The clicking resumed, moving from flank to shoulder. Seth bent to roll the fleece that lay on the floor and stuff it into a bag. "David knows he was wrong to give the trumpet to Amasa. The soldiers declare that Sheba would not have dared to head an uprising if you had been commanding the army. Must David humble himself to bring you back where you belong?"

Joab released the cords that bound the ram's legs. With a shake of his naked body and a bubbling bleat, the creature trotted off to join his shorn companions. Joab flexed his shoulders. "I'm leaving, Eliab," he shouted. "The army is marching and David needs me."

He handed the shears to a servant and followed Seth to the house. There he washed himself and donned once more his battle tunic and over it buckled on a sword. Then he bound on the short, dyed battle cloak and leather breastplate, and into the girdle thrust a second sword, the first being hidden by his cloak. It was not the first time Joab had put on a concealed sword when he armed himself for battle.

Seth smiled grimly as he watched Joab's preparations. "The man with two swords," he said. "You prepare for every contingency."

"Why not?" Joab replied.

The brothers did not wait for a meal, but tucked a loaf and some raisins into the scrips at their girdles. They filled their bottles from the cistern. They reached Jerusalem before sunset. At the barracks occupied by the palace police Joab found Benaiah, and learned that he had just returned after a day in the king's judgment court. Benaiah had orders to turn over all his men to Seth, keeping back only two score for duty in the palace and at the city gates. Benaiah made no reference to Absalom's death or to Joab's quarrel with David, but spoke rather of Mephibosheth, who had been at great pains for many days to convince David that he was loyal in spite of the fact that he had spent the winter in Jerusalem while David had been in Mahanaim. Mephibosheth had redoubled his protestations after Sheba sounded the trumpet of revolt. Sheba had talked of making Mephibosheth king, but Saul's only remaining heir declared Sheba had done this without consulting him. The crippled grandson of Saul protested his loyalty and innocence until David grew weary with listening.

Seth joined them shortly after sunset. He had learned that Amasa was now camped beside the pool at Gibeon, awaiting reinforcements. Word had come from Shechem that Sheba passed there, with a handful of men, heading north. Sheba was trying to enlist men from the tribes he traveled through, but had had little success. Still, given time enough, he might muster a following. David urged haste in pursuing the rebels lest they find a walled city that would give them shelter. When Seth mentioned to David that Joab was marching with him, David had said only one word. "Good."

They spent the night in Seth's house, but set out as the sun was rising with two companies. The soldiers were Philistines, the mercenaries of David's palace guard. Joab's anger was bitter at the necessity that forced him to lead Philistines out against Israelites.

The sun was halfway to the zenith by the time Joab and Seth with their two companies came up over the last hill south of Gibeon. The pool lay blue and deep between the highway and the town. It was full to the brim after the winter rains. Above the town the tabernacle still stood, more ragged than when Joab first came here leading a single company of picked men and fifty archers. It was at this pool that Joab fought the first of his countless battles. Since then twenty years had passed. Of all the battles Joab had fought, the first and the last had been against men who, as they died, cried out to the God of Israel.

Beside the pool sprawled about four companies. The camp was so disorganized one could not be sure as to the number of men, yet even at this distance Joab recognized the battle emblems of groups he had commanded. The earth about the pool was covered with spring green. Some of the soldiers were preparing belated breakfasts over open fires. Others were washing garments beside the pool. Some were playing at dice or engaging in wrestling matches.

At the sight of his army dawdling here while rebellion flourished elsewhere, Joab felt a surge of cold resolution mingled with dread. He had known what must be done when, in Bethlehem, he buckled on his two swords. He had known, yet he had hoped until this moment that the inevitable might by some means be averted. Now he saw his cousin Amasa move out from among the wrestlers, walking sluggishly toward him. Upon his face was a smirk. Amasa's headcloth was gone; his hair was tumbled and his cloak and girdle had been discarded. One item testified that he was a leader of men. He had picked up the trumpet of command and hung it about his neck before he came out to meet the advancing forces.

The sight of the trumpet on Amasa's neck was tinder to the spark of Joab's anger. He had left Bethlehem on business that required haste. There was only one way to get the disorderly army of Israel into swift and purposeful motion. It could not be done while the trumpet hung about the fat neck of Amasa. Joab raised his arm, signaling his Philistines to halt. Amasa moved slowly out toward the highway, grinning foolishly, perhaps fearfully.

He called, "Well, cousins, do you come in peace?"

Joab stepped forward. He unbuckled the sword that hung outside his cloak. It dropped, in its scabbard, to the dust. He advanced toward Amasa while the army of Israel and the palace mercenaries watched.

Amasa cleared his throat. "Welcome to Gibeon," he said loudly. "It will be well to have the sons of Zeruiah sit with us in council this afternoon. Sheba with his clan, the men of Bichri, is somewhere north of here. We are awaiting reinforcements. Now that you have come with these two companies we should be able to start in pursuit in a day or two."

They were close now, and Joab put out his right hand and took Amasa by his tangled beard, and drew his face close as if to kiss his cheek. His left hand reached inside his cloak, gripped the second sword, and thrust it into Amasa's belly. With a twist the deed was done. Amasa's mouth was near Joab's ear as the high-pitched screams began. The sword came away and with it a gush of blood and entrails, warm and wet against Joab's cloak.

Joab's right hand slipped from the tangled beard to the trumpet. He wrenched it up over Amasa's head as he fell writhing and screaming onto the highway. As the encamped soldiers came running toward their fallen captain, Joab raised the trumpet to his lips. Commandingly, he sounded the signal to break camp and prepare to march.

Amasa's screams changed into panted words. Joab bent to listen. "You did not have to kill me," Amasa whispered. "I was no Absalom. I was no Abner. Why should the mighty Joab fear me?" Gasping with pain, Amasa turned his face into the earth and died.

The men from the camp were all around the body. The looks they turned from Amasa to Joab were both admiring and accusing. Seth seized Amasa by the feet and pulled him off the road into the field. He seized the cloak from a nearby soldier and spread it over the body.

"If you are for David," he shouted, raising his mighty voice, "follow Joab! If you are against David, then stay with this dead man. Thus we will know who our enemies are!"

A lad detached himself from the awe-stricken group and ran to pick up the sword Joab had dropped into the road. He ran to Joab and handed it to him. The lad was Cushi, his yellow turban askew on the oiled black hair. Joab took the sword and scabbard and handed the bloody sword to the boy. "Clean it," he ordered. "March with me, Cushi. Be my armor-bearer once more."

Cushi ran to clean the sword in sand and grass. The figure in the field was alone. Soldiers were rushing about the camp, putting out fires, fastening on weapons, gathering up scattered belongings and rolling them for carrying.

Joab stood in the road and waited. I feared Abner for David's sake, he thought. I did not fear Amasa. He lied even while dying, when he said I feared him. He was the victim of one of David's mistakes. I corrected the mistake. It had to be done. And he thought, God of Israel, I will not kill again. It is enough. Except in battle I will not kill again. Before him rose the faces of men he had killed, Abner, Absalom, Amasa—Uriah also, and even the poor fool, Lem. Unable to endure his thoughts, Joab turned to Seth.

"Once we are in marching order, go on ahead. Choose a man to go with you. We must follow the highroads, since the streams are in flood. We will try to reach Bethel tonight. Failing that, we will stop there tomorrow to get supplies. Arrange with the elders in Bethel to have supplies of meal and parched corn which we can carry, and some meat if possible. We will reach Shechem tomorrow night and wait there for word from you concerning Sheba's whereabouts. Pick up a runner in Shechem to go on with you and return with your message. Send us word where to camp from day to day. This whole thing has been so mismanaged that the men are marching without supplies, and we will have to live off the land as we pass through."

Seth laid a hand on Joab's shoulder. "When the elders know you are commanding the army they will cooperate. Do not give any further thought to this carcass here—you did what had to be done."

Seth kissed Joab's cheek, beckoned a soldier to come with him. "God be with you, Joab," he said. "I will be in touch with you day by day." He strode up the highway and the soldier trotted to catch up with him.

Joab sounded the trumpet again. He watched the men as they formed their companies, noting which of the captains were here, judging in his own mind whom he could trust and who would bear watching. And so began the pursuit of Sheba.

Shechem lies in the pass between Mount Gerizim and Mount Ebal. Here by Jacob's well the army camped for a night. Men were waiting to join Joab's army. They were seasoned soldiers, not the young skylarking fellows who had been attracted to Absalom and Amasa. They were men who had fought under Joab in the earlier wars and had gone home afterward to farm their land and harvest their olives and shear their sheep.

Shechem was a place of orchards and gardens and springs. Fruits and vegetables were waiting here for Joab, and a donkey train to carry the supplies. All these things were gifts to David's cause from the men of Manasseh.

Joab marched his army in a single day all the way to Engannim at the southernmost reach of the Plain of Jezreel. He led them on next day, across the plain, moving rapidly. At the base of Mount Tabor Seth was waiting with news that Sheba and the Bichrites had passed through Issachar, Zebulun, and Naphtali without finding a city that would shelter them. Reaching at last the northernmost city in Israel, Abel-Beth-Maacah, which nestled at the foot of Mount Hermon, they had entered and found refuge.

"If the elders of Abel-Beth-Maacah had known it was Joab who pursued the Bichrites I think they would have locked their gates against them," Seth told Joab with an affectionate smile. "Still, the city is strong, and they are within it, and Amasa's delay in the pursuit of Sheba has brought this about."

Joab said, "We will lay siege to the city. Perhaps we will not need to destroy it. Yet if the men of Abel-Beth-Maacah persist in sheltering the enemies of David, we will do what must be done."

They passed up a valley till they came out upon the shores of the Sea of Chennereth, blue and rough with winds, lying like a gem amid surrounding hills. They skirted the sea and followed the upper Jordan until they came at last to where the city lay under the shadow of the snow-clad peaks of Lebanon and Hermon.

Now they busied themselves building a camp of huts and a tower from which a battering ram could be used against the walls. All was done with deliberation, while companies of soldiers patrolled the roads leading out from the city gates. The beams of the tower were mortised with care, and a great stone wrapped securely with ropes and raised aloft, ready to swing upon the wall. And all the while Joab hoped that this show of determination would have its effect upon the men of Naphtali in the city, so that they would cast out Sheba and avoid bloodshed and destruction.

The tower was completed. A line of soldiers laid hold of the rope which was attached to the great stone, and pulled it back and released it, so that it swung with a powerful, crunching noise against the city wall. So heavy was the stone that the wall shook with the impact. The battering of the great stone was repeated only a few times before an old woman appeared upon the wall, shouting Joab's name.

"Listen to the words of your maidservant," she cried. "The people here are peaceable and faithful. You seek to destroy a city which protects the border of Israel. Does it seem to you right to swallow up the heritage of these children of God?"

Joab answered sternly, "I wish to destroy no city of Israel. But a traitor called Sheba sounded the trumpet of rebellion, and you have sheltered him. Give him up to us, and we will return south and leave your city in peace."

The old woman cried, "Behold, his head shall be thrown to you over the wall."

At dawn next day a sack was lowered from the wall. In it, matted and bloody, was Sheba's head. Then Joab stuck the head upon the top of the tower he had built, and sounded the signal to break camp.

Thus the army returned as it had come. Those who had left their farms to follow Joab returned every man to his own place. After five days Joab reached Jerusalem, bringing with him only the palace police and a nucleus of the army. Joab went to the palace, for now he was ready to face David once more.

David sat upon his throne in the court of judgment, wearing purple and the jeweled breastplate as well as the other formal regalia of the king— a jeweled crown upon his grizzled, curling hair, golden bracelets on his upper arms, and upon his thumb a handsome signet ring.

[254]

Joab moved swiftly down and knelt before the dais, bowing his head to shut out the look David turned upon him at sight of the great, crooked ram's horn, the trumpet of command, which hung about Joab's neck.

Benaiah stepped to Joab, drawing him to his feet. David came down the six steps and kissed Joab on the forehead and embraced him.

"You have done well, cousin," David said. "Only half a month has gone by since you marched north in pursuit of our enemy. Now the war is ended and you are again victor, nor was any man's life placed in jeopardy save that of the rebel himself, Sheba the Bichrite. The kingdom is greatly in your debt, Joab."

"You are gracious, cousin," Joab said, and bowed.

David said, "Perhaps, hereafter, if the people will not keep the peace for love of David, they will do so out of dread of Joab. The trumpet is yours to wear while I am king in Israel, for I know you would lay down your life for our people."

Joab left the judgment hall. He knew he might be David's commander as long as he lived, but he would never again be David's friend. That night when Reba came to him, he clung to her, seeking the comfort he could not find in his own strength.

"David forgave me," he told Reba sadly. "I wish I could find it in my heart to forgive David."

PART EIGHT

Adonijah

44

AUTUMN WAS IN the air. Abi knew it the moment she awakened. The wind had changed. Even here in the house you could smell the fresh, moist tang that told you the wind was coming from the west, off the Great Sea. Abi had never seen the Great Sea, but she knew where it was—yonder to the west, beyond Mount Carmel.

This is the day we start our journey to Jerusalem, thought Abi, and jumped briskly out of bed. She took off the long woolen cloak in which she slept, folded it neatly and put it with the other clothes she had laid out to take to Aunt Rachel's house in Jerusalem.

The house Abi lived in had three rooms. She was proud of her home; not many houses in Shunem were so large. You came in through the stable, and you climbed four steps into the main room. To reach the room above the stable you climbed more steps. The roof of the main room was surrounded by a parapet, making it safe to sleep there in warm weather. I suppose there are finer houses in Jerusalem, thought Abi. Oh, she would see many sights in Jerusalem she had never seen before.

She heard a dry cough which announced that her father was awake. She called a cheerful good morning to him.

"Good morning, Abishag," old Bildad replied. His rosy face with its white scar and its frame of white hair and beard appeared at the door. Bildad's blue eyes lighted up as always when he looked upon his youngest child. "The wind has changed," he said, and snorted as he splashed cold water over his face. "It will be a good day to start our journey."

Abi ran down the steps into the stable. The family owned half a score of sheep and cattle, and the animals greeted her with friendly sounds. "I won't see you again for many days," she told them as they cavorted against her on their way out into the pasture. The grass in the pasture was sere and yellow after six months without rain. Abi threw her arms around the bullock which was to be taken to Jerusalem and sacrificed on the new altar there. Bildad had wanted to take Baba, Abi's own pet lamb, since lambs are acceptable for sacrifice and easier to come by than a large, sturdy bullock. But Abi would not agree to part with Baba, even as a sacrifice to the Lord God of Israel.

Now Baba was butting her, pushing her out the door into the autumn sunshine. Baba was six months old and much too big to be carried. But Abi was a strong vigorous girl and she carried the struggling lamb behind the house to the cistern. The cistern was going dry now at the end of summer; the water she brought up for the animals was filled with sediment. Until the rains came to fill the cistern again she would have to bring water from the village well for household use.

She ran up the flight of steps to the roof to get raisins drying there, then got a wide-mouthed clay pot and squatted on her heels to milk the goat.

"Naomi will milk you tomorrow," she told the goat. "And the day after, and the day after, and the day after, for many days. Will you miss me, Izzy?" She named all the animals, even those destined to be sacrificed before they were fully grown. She had named the goat long ago for the tribe of Issachar to which all the people of Shunem belonged.

The thought came, perhaps I shall never milk Izzy again. The thought brought both excitement and sadness, though it seemed to Abi unlikely that she would, as Sarah suggested, find a husband in Jerusalem. Abi had no mirror. For Abi her beauty meant only that everyone was kind and friendly. Eyes lighted up when they looked at her, and she greeted the world with happy confidence because of the pleasure the sight of her gave to others. From Abi's viewpoint the world was populated entirely by very nice people.

Thinking of marriage, Abi giggled, remembering the arguments she had heard, night after night, between Bildad and Sarah in their upper room. Sarah's father had been a thriving merchant, and she did not let Bildad or her children forget it. Her other daughters had married farmers, and she wanted Abi to do better than her sisters had done.

"What have you got against good, honest work?" Bildad inquired mildly. He did not fret about Sarah's opinions. She had been a good wife to him. They had worked hard and prospered, except in times of drought.

Drought was indirectly the cause of today's journey. For three years all Israel had been afflicted with drought. When at last the rains came, to be followed by abundant harvests, David sent messengers to every tribe and village, inviting the elders to come to Jerusalem and bring thank offerings. David had bought a high place within the bounds of the city, formerly the threshing floor of Araunah, king of the Jebusites. Here he had built a new altar to the Lord.

"We will go down for the Feast of Tabernacles," Bildad had announced when the invitation came to Shunem.

Sarah immediately began making her plans. "If we go at all, we will make a real visit," she had said. "We will stay in Rachel's house. We are luckier than most people, having relatives in the city. Abi is old enough to marry," she continued. "She is a beauty. She could marry anybody! I don't want her to settle here and scratch for a living as you and I have done!"

"And who do you think she would marry in Jerusalem? The king? Or maybe you want to marry her to the heir to the throne? I understand Adonijah has not taken a wife yet!"

Sarah ignored Bildad's sarcasm. "There is her cousin Jonathan. He is a friend of Adonijah, and might be a counselor when Adonijah is king. Do not forget, my sister is married to Abiathar, the high priest! Abi could meet all the important young men in the house of Rachel. At least let her be seen by those who are rich and important. Then, if she chooses to return home and marry a farmer, she will know she had a choice."

The arguments went on and on, at night, in the little room above the stable. And Abi listened till she went to sleep, suppressing her giggles at the idea that she might marry somebody as important as her cousin Jonathan. She had never met Jonathan, but Abiathar came by sometimes on his way to Asher or Naphtali or Zebulun, and sometimes he spent a night with his wife's relatives, bringing messages and little gifts Rachel sent.

Abi had finished milking Izzy. She patted the goat. "Now you be good, and give lots of milk for Naomi," she said. Bildad's answer to Sarah was true: "Abishag loves her home. What makes you think she would marry someone far from Shunem?"

Sarah had come out and was stirring up the fire, preparing to bake bread before their journey. Soon the cooking would have to be done at the fireplace inside the house. Abi said, "I dread the rains, and the smoke that fills the room when we cook in the house. I wish we could eat outdoors always." She looked about with pleasure, for all the nearby slope was terraced into vineyards or dotted with fig and olive trees, and the Jezreel Valley stretched away to the west, flat and golden now at summer's end. Abi was sure Jerusalem could offer no sight lovelier than the view on all sides from her own home.

Sarah's reply was grumpy, largely because she was convinced that Bildad and indeed the whole village spoiled her youngest daughter. "I suppose you would like it if we had drought every year, and the blessed rains never came," she said.

Her father only smiled and asked, "Sure you won't change your mind and let me take Baba? If you stay in Jerusalem you will never see him again anyway." Sarah had thought a pair of turtledoves would be offering enough. But Bildad reminded her they were not going for worship alone, but in hopes of gaining an advantageous marriage for Abi. Nothing short of a prime young animal, without blemish, would do to give to the Lord.

Abi said, "I've already sponged and brushed the bullock. I fastened a thong about his neck for leading." She sighed impatiently. "I wish it was time to start."

Sarah had planned their journey to take advantage of relatives who lived in towns along the way, partly for the sake of seeing the relatives, but also to save the cost of staying at inns. At Engannim, a two-hour walk from home, they would join a merchant who had a donkey train; there would be less danger of attack by robbers if they went in company. However, the land was peaceful and had been for many years. Bildad and Sarah could remember more than thirty years back when Philistines had occupied the land. Poverty had been common then, and travelers were never safe from robbers. But David had driven out the Philistines and had conquered all the neighboring nations. Now for twenty years there had been peace in Israel, with tribute and labor levies flowing in from every neighbor. Abi's whole life had been lived in a land of peace and plenty. To be sure there had been a minor rebellion which Abi remembered only because she had seen that fabulous soldier, Joab, when he marched past Shunem at the head of a few hundred soldiers. That was twelve years ago, and Abi was only four years old at the time, but she had never forgotten the strange, light color of his hair and beard, nor the way all the lines in his face seemed to ray out from his gray eyes.

Abi had thought no country could be lovelier than that around the village of Shunem until, on the second evening of their journey, they came into the village of Shechem. Autumn though it was, the country here was green. The village lay in a sheltered valley between Mount Gerizim and Mount Ebal. Streams rose on the slopes of the mountains, and flowed down flashing to spread verdure and fertility in every direction. The whole valley was filled with gardens and orchards and vineyards.

They reached Jerusalem on the fourth day during the midday hours. From afar they saw the city on its high plateau. New, pearl-gray walls gleamed in the afternoon sun. Towers rose on the walls and within the city; the owner of the donkey train was pointing out this tower and that to Bildad, giving each a name.

The north wall of the city was merely a long line of foundation stones, marked by a tall, fortified gate over the Ephraim road where they entered. On their right, barracks for soldiers were built right into the city's northwest wall. On their left the land rose to a peak. This, said the merchant, was Mount Moriah. It was being cleared to make a parkway leading to the top, where stood the tent of meeting and a wide, brazen altar. Building stone of gleaming white was heaped upon the slope, and Abi overheard enough of the merchant's talk to realize that David planned to have a temple built on this mountain top. He was bringing in materials now, though the building had not begun.

Now they were in sight of large stone houses. The first of them was the

[259]

palace, a spreading, great affair, built tall, and with fine doors of cedar opening right onto the street. All the houses were tall, and there wasn't a trace of sun-dried brick anywhere.

"Where do the people put their animals?" Abi asked.

"There are pastures outside the city. Now this house," the merchant continued, "belongs to the captain of the host, Joab. A terrible man. He inherited it when his brother Seth died of a fever last year. A man of devices and tricks. It is said—"

Bildad interrupted with a chuckle, "It is best not to speak ill of the mighty Joab in my wife's hearing. She remembers too well the years when Saul and Abner were over us, and we paid tribute to Philistines."

The merchant shrugged. They continued up narrow winding roads till they came to the street of the fortress Millo. On this street Abiathar had his house.

"I leave you here," the merchant said. "Anyone can direct you to the home of the high priest."

Rachel herself answered their knock. Tears of joy filled her dark eyes as she embraced Sarah.

Bildad explained that he must dispose of the bullock before he could come in, that he could not bring it into the house nor leave it in the street.

A small servant boy appeared and took the bullock from Bildad. "We have a bit of pasture land outside the Damascus Gate," Rachel explained. "He will be safe there. Come in, Bildad, come in. I'm so glad to see you!"

She led them through a fine, large room and on to a sunlit court. Then she turned to them again, this time looking at Abi rather than Sarah and Bildad. Her eyes widened. "It can't be Abishag!" she exclaimed. "What a beauty you are, dear child. Abiathar spoke of you as attractive, but—"

Sarah interrupted. "Now, Rachel, don't spoil the child."

Rachel called servants to come and wash their feet and take their bundles to the room they would occupy here, then said with a happy smile, "Minna has been married for more than a year now. She has a baby. They will be here to share the meal with us. Shephatiah is one of David's sons, next after Adonijah. Now, Sarah, tell me your news. How are your children, and all those grandchildren—Minna's baby is our first grandchild. Jonathan is not married, and if I leave it to Abiathar to find a wife for him he never will be!"

The servants were at work now, preparing the meal, and Sarah looked about at the fine house and the many servants, and Abi saw she was uncomfortable in the presence of all this prosperity. She moved closer to her mother, and took her hand affectionately as she said to Rachel, "I love your house. Do show it all to us."

Whatever Rachel might have said in reply Abi did not hear, for at that moment a tall young man appeared in the doorway, and Abi's eyes had never beheld anyone so handsome. Could this be Jonathan? He wore a beautiful scarlet cloak that swished when he walked. His hair and beard were crisply curling and—they were red! Across his forehead were scattered freckles as large as silver shekels. He was staring at her, and though she felt her face flush she could not take her eyes from him. Her heart was thumping beneath her white linen tunic. If this was Jonathan—and Sarah wanted to marry her to Jonathan—and Rachel had said Jonathan must take a wife before long—

And then Aunt Rachel exclaimed, "Welcome, Adonijah! Have you come to take dinner with your brother Shephatiah?"

Adonijah? Then he wasn't—Jonathan.

Another young man had appeared behind Adonijah, a tall, wiry fellow, nice enough of course, but not to be compared with Adonijah. "I am Jonathan," he said, "and you must be my cousin Abishag. Adonijah, what do you think of my little cousin, eh?"

Abi scarcely heard the introduction. It did not occur to her that Jonathan was watching her with a strange intentness. It did not occur to her that Jonathan must often have been compared with his friend Adonijah in exactly the way she was comparing them. Abi felt alternately happy to be able to look upon Adonijah and miserable because he was who he was, and she knew she had no right to be thinking such thoughts about the king's eldest son, heir to Israel's throne.

Minna arrived with her husband and baby and, after Abiathar offered thanks to the Lord God, giver of all bounty, the meal was served. Everything she saw and heard seemed to Abi to touch her deeply, so that the tears seemed always just ready to fill her eyes. She could not speak at all, but only listen to the blur of sound all about, and Aunt Rachel was the kindest, Abiathar the most profound, Minna the prettiest, Minna's baby the sweetest of mortals. Everything wore a sheen of beauty and the happiness Abi felt was beyond gaiety. She kept her eyes from Adonijah most of the time, but when she did steal little glances at him, he was always watching her. Jonathan was also watching her with dark, brooding eyes, but of this Abi was quite unaware.

Sarah scolded Abi because she was not eating. Rachel reminded her that until after sunset tomorrow no food would be eaten in this house. But Abi had no taste for food.

The meal ended before the light was gone. Now the Day of Atonement had begun. Abiathar sent for a lamp, and Jonathan went to the upper room for a certain scroll. While they sat in the shadows Abiathar read, or as it grew darker recited from memory, Moses' instructions for keeping the great day of national humiliation and repentance. When he finished he said a prayer. Then Adonijah returned to his home and the family and guests of Abiathar went to their rooms to sleep.

The Day of Atonement was for the people a high and holy day. At sunrise the high priests went to sanctify themselves before conducting the service of atonement for the people. Not many had arrived when the family and guests of Abiathar reached the top of Mount Moriah. But family groups, barefoot, with heads uncovered and wearing sackcloth, kept climbing the hill until at last penitents were crowded about three sides of the old threshing floor which now held the brazen altar. On the fourth side was pitched the tent of meeting.

Abi had attended religious ceremonies at home, when the entire village of Shunem climbed to the top of the Hill of Moreh and the elders presided at killing a young animal before the Lord, offering up certain parts on the altar and making a feast for everyone with the edible parts remaining. The skin of the animal was given to whichever of the elders served as priest on that day. Bildad had presided many times, and Abi always thought he performed his part with dignity and decorum. But those occasions paled into insignificance today.

The altar of heaped stones on Moreh was a poor thing compared with the brazen altar with its curving brazen horns. So high was this altar that a ledge projected about midway up on all four sides, where priests could stand in order to reach across the vast bed of coals. Sacrificial animals were tied to the altar horns. Trenches in the stone flooring caught the blood.

The interior of the tent of meeting was lined with curtains of fine linen, embroidered in lovely patterns and colors. A large brass basin on a pedestal stood beside the door of the tent, and here the priests washed their hands frequently during the course of the service.

Zadok and Abiathar wore garments of whitest linen, quite different from the intricate and colorful robes of other ceremonial occasions. Zadok moved with a devout dignity, so that you could not think of things common or secular while he went about the rites.

A bullock was the day's first victim. This bullock had been bought by Zadok and Abiathar and was an offering to cleanse them and their families. Zadok took a knife and slit the throat of the creature. Of the blood which gushed forth he caught some in a basin and sprinkled it all about the brasswork and posts of the altar. The bullock, which had sunk to its knees, was turned over upon its back, and the belly slit open. Zadok took all the fat from within the belly and wrapped it about the liver and kidneys. This was placed among the coals, and the fire flared up with a fragrance which seemed to Abi both sweet and precious, since it burned away the sins of Abiathar and his family. A Levite took the remaining parts of the bullock down from the hilltop to be burned outside the city walls, since the animal was a sin offering.

Then Zadok, carrying a shovel filled with burning coals and a basin containing the bullock's blood, and Abiathar, who had taken up a double handful of incense, went together through the Veil into the Holy of Holies where the ark rested. There Abi knew they would sprinkle the blood upon the mercy seat. When the smoke of incense billowed over the top of the Veil she knew the incense had been thrown into the shovelful of coals, thus ending the service for the high priests.

By this time the Levite choir had assembled and were singing songs of repentance written by David. Abi saw that Jonathan and Adonijah were singing with the choir, and Shephatiah also. Near the tabernacle she saw the king with his wives and daughters.

Abi thought King David must be very old, though she had been told he was about the same age as Bildad, which was between sixty-five and seventy. But the king seemed thin and feeble. His face and hands had a transparent pallor. His beard was snow white, as were his hair and brows. Poor old man! she thought. Her eyes went to the glowing athletic figure of Adonijah. Rachel had said last night that David, when he was king in Hebron, had looked much like Adonijah now. It seemed to Abi terrible that being a king for more than thirty years could so exhaust and weaken a man.

Beside David was a woman who looked younger than the other wives, thirty-five perhaps. Her eyes rested with a glow of pride and devotion upon a dark-haired youth who stood among the Levites. It must be Bathsheba, thought Abi. The boy, of course, would be the youngest of the princes, Solomon.

Abi thought she had never heard anything so lovely as the music and the voices of the men under the autumn sky on this hilltop. "Purge me with hyssop and I shall be clean," they sang. "Wash me and I shall be whiter than snow."

Zadok and Abiathar had returned to the altar wearing clean linen. The two goats used for the atonement were brought forward. Abiathar took from a pouch about his neck two blue stones. He spoke a prayer and cast the stones. That was the way they determined which goat was to be sacrificed and which would bear the sins of the people away into the wilderness.

Zadok took a clean knife and killed the goat designated for the Lord God. He caught the blood in a basin and went again into the Holy of Holies. When he came out, the sight of the blood on his hands held Abi fascinated. Then he sprinkled this blood also upon the brazen altar.

The Levites sang, "Against Thee, against Thee only have I sinned, O Lord."

It came to Abi that this was more than a ritual of sprinkled blood and burned flesh. This rite of atonement had to do with the relationship of each child of Israel with the Lord Most High. "Against Thee have I sinned," she thought, while Zadok cut open the goat, and laid upon the

[263]

altar the fat parts which had been wrapped about the feet and the head and the kidneys and liver. I have been selfish, thought Abi. I would not give Baba to the Lord, though Father wanted to bring him here. I wanted Father to sacrifice an animal for which I cared nothing. And she thought, I have lifted my eyes to the king's son, even though my parents have other plans for me, and I cannot aspire to this prince who is heir to the throne. I have been guilty of pride. I have vaunted myself to imagine that the king's son cares for me. "Against Thee, against Thee only have I sinned, O Lord." Tears rolled down her face as she resolved to be dutiful and obedient, and never again impose her own selfish desires upon her parents.

When she looked up again the lady Bathsheba was staring at her fixedly.

Now Zadok laid his hands upon the head of the live goat, and lifted his face to heaven and said a prayer confessing the people's iniquities, all their transgressions, all their sins. When the prayer ended, a Levite took the tether by which the goat was tied, and led him down from the hilltop. Abi knew that they would pass out through the Damascus Gate, and continue for many hours until they came to the wilderness south of Bethlehem. There the goat, bearing the sins of all Israel, would be set free.

But the edible parts of the goat which had been sacrificed to the Lord were blessed by Zadok, and set apart to be roasted. After the sun set this day, the dedicated priests who were in the city would come here to the hilltop to feast.

45

DURING THE MORNING meal next day Shephatiah mentioned his intention to look at his vineyards. All the sons of King David, he told Bildad, had vineyards in the Tyropoeon Valley below the southwest wall of the City of David.

Abiathar remarked, "You have a vineyard of your own, Bildad. Why not go with Shephatiah and see the irrigation system David contrived by which the vineyards were watered even during the recent drought?"

When Minna suggested that Abishag go too, Abi's bright smile of agreement was purely mechanical. The resolution she had made yesterday rested upon her with a heaviness she had never known in all her sixteen years.

Shephatiah led the way with Bildad beside him. Abi followed, walking between her cousins, Minna and Jonathan. Truth to tell the young man Jonathan had scarcely left her side all morning. Remembering her resolution to be dutiful and obedient to her parents, Abi smiled pleasantly upon him whenever she noticed his presence. He is really very nice, she reminded herself more than once. His eyes were soft and dark and very kind.

Now the five of them walked down through the gate in the old north wall of the City of David. This was the gate, Shephatiah explained, that Joab and his company had opened to admit David's army on a night more than thirty years before. Abi was astonished at the width of the walls—twenty-seven feet thick, Shephatiah said—so that armies could mass upon them.

"What a lot of stone it took!" Abi marveled, thinking of all the captives who had surely died to build the walls.

The paved square inside the north gate contained the bazaars. Minna would have lingered here but Jonathan and Shephatiah hurried her along. They emerged through the narrow Valley Gate into the Tyropoeon Valley. This valley was a breath-taking sight. Everything delighted Bildad: the terraced vineyards and the grassy floor of the valley; the fountain En Rogel with its broad, inviting curb and arched roof; and most marvelous of all, the drainage system David had invented. Potters had made long trough-like tiles of baked earthenware which, laid end-to-end, formed conduits taking water to each terraced plot. The upper plots caught the overflow from the reservoir within the city, and the lower plots were watered from En Rogel.

Bildad marveled at the use of olive trees as vine-posts, for he was constantly replacing his trellises in the vineyards on the slopes of the Hill of Moreh. Abi listened to her father's enthusiasm over these many wonders but could not feel she had a part in any of his plans.

I will not go home again, she thought. Nor will I marry Adonijah. I do not know what will happen to me, but I have sinned in refusing my pet lamb to the Lord and in going against my parents' wishes. I know I will be punished for my pride and selfishness.

They were sitting on the curb beside the fountain when they heard a sound of shouts and running horses. Looking up to the heights across the valley Abi saw a chariot of iron and bronze drawn by two black horses. The driver wore a rust-colored cloak. His head was bare, and hair and beard were copper-red in the sunlight.

Minna cried excitedly, "There goes Adonijah!" She jumped onto the curb, waving. Adonijah drew hard on the reins and his horses slowed.

"We must go and see his chariot and horses," Minna said. "He bought them from an Egyptian trader only a month ago. They are splendid!"

She led the way up to the plateau where the Bethlehem road lay. Abishag was struck dumb at the sight of the magnificent chariot and the grace of the spirited horses. They wore elegantly embroidered cloths over their backs. The harness and bridles were of fine leather, dyed red and lavishly set with turquoise.

Adonijah leaped down from the chariot and stood at the head of the near horse. "Don't come too close," he warned. "They are skittish. They need more exercise than I find time to give them."

He laughed at the amazement on their faces. "You know, this is what people expect of a king's son. I would rather prune my vines and plow my barley fields than go scorching up the highway behind wild horses." He shrugged. "David rides upon a white mule whenever he travels, but he is getting on and is entitled to such comforts."

A strained expression had appeared in Jonathan's face since the dramatic arrival of his friend. Shephatiah cried, "I'd like to drive this contraption while I'm in town."

"Drive it now." Adonijah smiled. "The stable is north of Damascus Gate. I'll escort Bildad and Abishag."

Shephatiah leaped eagerly into the chariot. Minna said fearfully, "Be careful! Don't go too fast or you will turn over!"

Shephatiah smiled down upon his wife as Adonijah handed him the reins. With a shrill whistle to the horses he was off in a whirl of dust.

"I know he'll get hurt," Minna worried.

"He knows how to drive," Adonijah reassured her.

"I hate the sight of a chariot," Bildad said. "And I hate the sound of horses. I fought with King Saul in the battle on Mount Gilboa. The Philistines came tearing down the Jezreel Plain in their iron chariots with their horses in a lather. I tell you, chariots put the fear of God into a foot soldier."

Adonijah looked down into Abi's pensive face. "You haven't said a word about my fine equipage, Abishag."

"It is beautiful," she answered. "But the horses frighten me."

Bildad looked about him at the spreading view visible on this height. "This hill is higher and wider than Ophel, yonder. I wonder why the Jebusites did not build their city here."

"Because Ophel is watered by two springs, one on each side."

Bildad nodded gravely. "Water is everything, in choosing a site for a city," he agreed.

Minna said, "All the houses built in the new Jerusalem section have cisterns, but even so, water has to be carried. That is why only families with servants can afford to live there."

"My father talks of building an elaborate system of conduits down from springs to the north," Adonijah said. "He talks about having underground conduits everywhere, so that every house will have its own reservoir, but that plan is like his plan for the temple—something he expects his sons or grandsons to accomplish. He is not yet seventy, but he has known so much trouble he has aged fast. Every winter he is ill, and sometimes we wonder whether he will survive till spring. Yet he never stops planning for the future of this city. He lives now in the past and in the future, not the present."

Jonathan remarked, "Sometimes I think he expects a lot from you, Adonijah."

He spoke to his friend with affection, and nobody listening could have guessed the pain he felt at the change which had come over Abi from the moment the chariot of Adonijah drew to a stop on the hill. Only a selfless young man could have maintained friendship without envy with Adonijah, who, in addition to all his natural gifts and his prospects, had also become the object of Abi's star-bright glances.

Adonijah nodded. "He is so gifted himself he does not understand that his son might not be equally brilliant in every branch of literature and music, invention and engineering, judgment and war. I often think I would trade places with Shephatiah—settle on a farm away from the city, marry one wife, prune my vineyards and till my fields, and leave to one of my brothers the tasks David has laid out for the next king of Israel." He glanced at Abishag and she felt her cheeks grow hot, for she could not remain downcast and hopeless in the presence of this good and handsome prince.

She thought, He talks to father as Jude did when he was courting Naomi, confiding his inmost thoughts to him, because a man wants to know what a prospective son-in-law is like. He will talk to father and mother both in this confiding way before he asks for me. But the thought brought the sense of shame she had felt in the tabernacle. Surely she was conceited and filled with false pride, as mother had said; too many people had spoken to her of her beauty, both during the days of their journey and since they reached Jerusalem. Beauty is the gift of God. Self-vaunting is evil. And yet when she looked up into the face of Adonijah she could not help reading the message so plainly written there.

"Whether you want to be king, I do not know," Bildad said. "But Israel wants you to be king. During the recent drought there were many who said that David should give you the kingdom, since it is well known that impotence in a king causes the land to lose its fertility."

Adonijah smiled. "My father says that is pagan superstition and has no place in Israel. He says drought is God's punishment, and if the people search their hearts and cast out evil, the rains will come again. It was for this reason that he bought the threshing floor on Mount Moriah, and began laying his plans for the temple which will someday be built there."

Minna said, "We have been away too long. I must get back home and suckle my baby."

It was well after midday when they returned to the house of Abiathar, for they had made a circuit of the old city, passing down the Tyropoeon Valley to where it joined the Kidron at the base of the stairs leading up to the Dung Gate, then up the Kidron to the Gihon spring. Here Bildad had to see the ancient conduit made by the Jebusites, which David's men had repaired. Then on they went till they came out on the Jericho road, following it back into the city through the splendidly broad and well-fortified Damascus Gate. Before he entered the city Bildad wanted to examine the pastures where the residents of the city kept their flocks and cattle. How queer it is, Abi thought, to trust to hired herdsmen something as precious as your animals.

Sarah was waiting anxiously when at last they arrived. "A messenger from the king came, commanding us to attend upon him in the court of judgment between midday and evening. I thought you would never get home," she told them. "There is no time to lose. You must wash yourselves, and put on clean raiment, new sandals and these new chaplets over your headcloths. I went to the bazaar myself, with a servant for company, to buy something fit to wear into the king's presence."

"Now why would David want to see us?" Bildad asked. Then suddenly, with a searching glance at Abi's scarlet face, he clamped his mouth shut, scarcely concealing a broad smile. "Of course," said Bildad. "He has heard that we are the parents of a beautiful daughter, and he wants to rest his eyes upon her."

Sarah cried, "Nonsense! He wants to ask about affairs in Shunem. After all, we are related to his high priest. Why should he not ask for us?"

Midday had passed by the time Abi and Bildad were dressed to suit Sarah's critical eye. As they climbed the cobbled street toward the palace they met people returning from the king's court. "We are late," Sarah scolded. "We will have kept the king waiting. You should have known enough to come home."

"It isn't every day country people have a chance to be shown about the city by the heir to the throne," Bildad replied. And to that remark Sarah had no answer at all.

Abi kept telling herself, It cannot be what I think it is. There are many reasons why David might send for relatives of Abiathar. Yet she remembered the look in the eyes of Adonijah, both at dinner before the Day of Atonement and today on the hill west of Jerusalem; and she thought, he asked David to invite us to come today.

How will it be, she wondered, to live in Jerusalem all the rest of my life, and never again milk the goat or bring water from the village well, or put my bed away in the corner behind the loom? How do the wives of the king occupy their time? They do not cook, they do not tend the animals, they do not fetch water, they do not scrub the flagging. What do they do all day long? And she thought, I would buy a loom and work at my weaving. Sarah wove beautiful cloth but Abi's weaving left a great deal to be desired. If I had nothing else to do, I would learn to weave as well as Mother does. Of course, she thought, while her face grew hot, there would be little sons and daughters to be loved and tended and taught.

I would never see my sisters and brothers again—unless they came to visit me in Jerusalem—I would never see Baba again, or the people of Shunem. But I love him so much I would give up everything dear to me for his sake. I would learn the ways of people who live in the palace. I would learn to like the things he likes, and to move among the great people of the kingdom, and think only of what is good for my husband and the people he rules.

She lifted her head and walked quietly, surely, confidently. I am not afraid, she thought. David is kind, a good king and a good man, and I am not afraid.

The wide gate of polished cedar stood open. A few people were still here, though court was no longer in session. Soldiers guarded the gate, but Bildad mentioned his name and village to their commander and the man stepped back, motioning for them to enter.

Abi heard Sarah gasp as they entered the shadowed room. How beautiful is David's court of judgment, thought Abi, looking at the walls with their embroidered hangings, the dais with its brown and yellow carpet, the throne with its carving and its inlay of gold and amethyst. David stood near the throne, talking with a portly man with grizzled beard. The commander spoke their names, and Bildad and Sarah and Abi bowed low on the carpet at the foot of the dais.

Abi had begun to tremble with nervousness. When a hand took her arm to lift her to her feet she saw that the king had come down to the lowest step, but she could not raise her eyes to his face. While the king spoke to Bildad of Shunem and of the state of agriculture in Issachar, Abi noticed the youth who sat on the top step. He looked to be not much older than herself, and she remembered seeing him with the Levite choir yesterday morning. Solomon, she thought. He had a look of sleek elegance in keeping with the whole appearance of the room. She remembered the simplicity with which Adonijah talked about life on a farm as compared with life in a palace. Elegant, persuasive people surround a king, she thought. Such people could never build a kingdom, but they are on hand to flatter and fawn upon the king once the kingdom is established. The boy seemed harmless enough, but Abi disliked him if only because he was unlike his eldest brother.

Abi glanced at Sarah, and read in her expression the shrinking discomfort she had shown at the sight of the richness of Rachel's home. She touched her mother's hand, longing to reassure her. She longed to whisper, "Don't be afraid, mother. Our three rooms in Shunem contain as much happiness as this palace, and maybe more."

When David turned to speak to Sarah a woman came forward and stood beside him. Bathsheba, mother of Solomon. Why were these two present for the meeting with the family of Bildad? What could they have to do with this affair? Surely if any of David's family belonged here it would be Adonijah and his mother, whose name was Reba. The sight of Bathsheba and Solomon and the interest they took in David's reception of her family filled Abi with a dread she could not understand.

Now David turned to Abi. A thin, transparent hand was under her chin, lifting her face until her eyes met the faded blue eyes of the old king. He smiled as people always smiled at Abi, a smile of pleasure in her beauty.

"How fair you are, my child," he said. "Fairer than I could have believed, even after what was told me."

Abi returned the king's smile. How easy it was to love this kind old man, knowing that he had once been the mighty David, savior of Israel. "My lord David is most gracious," she murmured.

Bathsheba remarked pleasantly, "She is indeed fair, my lord." The words sent a chill over Abi. She was relieved when David finished speaking to Sarah and Bildad. He raised his hands in a priestly benediction and spoke a blessing over them, and they turned and walked back down the length of the room and out into the late sunshine.

On Minna's and Shephatiah's last evening in Jerusalem, Jonathan, Rachel and Abiathar joined with them to sing a hymn after the evening meal. Like all the hymns Abi had heard for the first time during this visit in Jerusalem, this too was a psalm of David.

"He that dwelleth in the secret place of the most High
    shall abide under the shadow of the Almighty.
I will say of the Lord, He is my refuge and my fortress,
    my God, in him will I trust.
Surely he shall deliver thee from the snare of the fowler
    and from the noisome pestilence.
He shall cover thee with his feathers, and under his wings shalt thou trust;
    his truth shall be thy shield and buckler.
Thou shalt not be afraid for the terror by night;
    nor for the arrow that flieth by day;
Nor for the pestilence that walketh in darkness;
    nor for the destruction that wasteth at noonday.
A thousand shall fall at thy side, and ten thousand at thy right hand;
    but it shall not come nigh thee.
Only with thine eyes shalt thou behold and see the reward of the wicked.

Because thou hast made the Lord, which is my refuge,
    even the most High, thy habitation;
There shall no evil befall thee,
    neither shall any plague come nigh thy dwelling.

[270]

For he shall give his angels charge over thee,
    to keep thee in all thy ways.
They shall bear thee up in their hands,
    lest thou dash thy foot against a stone.
Thou shalt tread upon the lion and adder;
    the young lion and the dragon shalt thou trample under foot.
Because he hath set his love upon me, therefore will I deliver him:
    I will set him on high, because he hath known my name.
He shall call upon me, and I will answer him; I will be with him in trouble;
    I will deliver him and honor him.
With long life will I satisfy him, and shew him my salvation."

The song affected all the family of Bildad. The alternating hope and dread which had been with Abi since Adonijah first entered this room two days before settled into a mood of quiet waiting for whatever should come. A smile of quiet peace touched Sarah's lips and she rose to leave the table without a backward look at the servants who were clearing away the remains of the meal.

As they left the court and went into the main room at the front of the house, Bildad said musingly, "David has spent his strength for our people. Before we came here I thought of him as a great soldier and a just judge. Now I see how many and how varied are his gifts. Shall Israel ever see such another man?"

Bildad spent the next day in the upper room where Abiathar kept his scrolls. Abi went up for a time, looking about at the shelves where the scrolls lay on brazen spools, and watching the scribes with their reed pens copying neat rows of script upon new parchment. Now that Minna had gone back to the farm with Shephatiah, taking the baby, Abi was sorely in need of occupation. Sarah had found a loom among Rachel's possessions and was weaving a small cloak as a gift for Minna's baby. The sight of her mother at work made Abi more restless than ever.

As the midday period was beginning a visitor arrived—one of the wives of David, the foster mother of Adonijah. Abi greeted Reba with the greatest pleasure and not a little curiosity. She was a tall woman, clad in a cloak of a bright golden color and with a great deal of golden jewelry on her arms and at her throat. When she removed the blue mantle Abi saw the heavy gray hair, carefully dressed and smooth, and the straight black brows above dark brown eyes. Her mouth was wide, expressive, pleasant. She took both Abi's hands. The two women were tall and they looked directly into one another's eyes.

Reba said, "Adonijah told me of your beauty, but I thought he was exaggerating. I see now that he was not."

Abi laughed, feeling happy and excited. "I have heard more talk about that in three days here than I heard in sixteen years in Shunem."

"Just remember that beauty is from God and you cannot take credit for it," Sarah warned.

Rachel rose and put her arm about Abi. "It is good for us to have her here. Come, let's go out into the court and enjoy the sunshine while it is still with us."

A sycamore tree grew in the court at the back of the house, and the wall and pavement had been built around it. The women sat together in the shade. Reba had brought some sewing with her. Rachel got out a cloak she was making for Jonathan, Sarah's loom was clacking away busily as they talked together. But Abi sat with idle hands, and she wished there were something she could do in this house.

Reba said, "Adonijah asked me to speak to you of marriage, Abi. He is going to speak to David today or tomorrow, if you are willing."

Sarah said firmly, "Bildad will answer the question, not Abi. In Shunem the man is the head of the household."

Abi said, "Oh, mother!" and buried her face in her mother's skirts, too overcome for speech.

Reba smiled quietly. "I am answered. And David will put the question to Bildad. However, when a king puts such a question to one of his subjects the answer cannot be no, and Adonijah does not want a bride his father commands for him. That is why my son sent me here to speak first to your daughter. Perhaps this procedure is irregular, but I do not think either Abi or her mother is offended."

Rachel said, "Then Abi shall be daughter to me when you return to Shunem, Sarah."

"And to me also," Reba said.

Abi raised her face. "How does one learn to live in a palace?"

Reba said gently, "Would you mind if Adonijah should not be king?"

Abi said, "If I could be his wife and still live the life I know, on a farm, with vineyards and sheep and a goat to milk, I would have all I want in the world. But—why do you ask? Adonijah is the heir. It is not a question I have any right to answer." Nor do you have the right to ask it, she thought, but did not say the words.

Reba said, "All Israel assumes that Adonijah will be king. But David has never actually said so. You see, Bathsheba is ambitious for Solomon. If David lives till Solomon is a man fully grown, she may accomplish her aim. Adonijah is not ambitious, nor am I ambitious for him. Bathsheba has influence in many quarters. She has influence with David also. If it were not for Bathsheba, David would have turned the kingdom over to Adonijah during the drought. Now they are saying in the harem that Bathsheba is urging David to take a new wife, someone young and beautiful, in the hope that his vigor will be restored. I doubt she will succeed in this. David is very tired, and there should be a limit on how far Bathsheba can press him."

Sarah's hands dropped from her loom as she turned startled eyes on Reba. Abi jumped up crying, "Father, father!" She ran up the steps of stone which led to the scroll room, stumbling in her haste. Father would know how to save her, how to get her away from this place! For all at once she knew too well the meaning of Bathsheba's presence and Bathsheba's remarks during the audience she had had with King David only yesterday.

Jonathan came down the stairs, and caught her by the arms. "What is the matter, Abishag?"

"Where is my father?" Tears were streaming down her face, and when Jonathan moved as if he would hold and comfort her she turned quickly from him and saw that Reba and Rachel and Sarah were clustered at the foot of the stairs, looking anxiously up at her.

Jonathan said, "He was summoned to the palace. He left an hour ago. I think he will be back soon." His voice was soft and very tender. "Let me help you, Abi. Tell me what I can do."

Abi sank on the step. All her strength was gone and her tears had ceased to flow.

Rachel came up the steps quickly. She put her arms about Abi. "My child, my child," she crooned. She cradled Abi's head on her shoulder. "My poor, sweet, lovely child."

Sarah said, "Something was wrong. I knew it all along. That woman stood there beside David, speaking of Abishag's beauty as if she were selling a commodity in the bazaar. I knew that David was pleased. I would to God my child were pock-marked and harelipped."

Reba said heavily, "I thought after Uriah's death that David had robbed another man of his love for the last time." Her lips were pressed together in a bitter line. "I will go to him. I will tell him to his face if I am killed for it. I will not stand by while my son, my boy, my Adonijah—"

Jonathan's voice was tight with strain. "What is it? What is happening?"

The door opened. Joab came in, wrapped warmly against the evening chill. He went to Reba, looked questioningly at her, then at Sarah. Then he saw Rachel, Jonathan, and Abishag on the stairway. "You must be the one," he said. "I am Joab. Is Adonijah here?"

Reba shook her head. "What brought you here?"

"David has announced to his officials that he is taking a wife, a girl from up in the north country, Abishag the Shunemite. Her father consented. The palace is in an uproar. I came remembering that Rachel had relatives from Shunem visiting here. I want to have a word with Adonijah. You know what this means—Bathsheba has won another victory."

Reba said, "David is taking a girl Adonijah loves. How long can these things continue?"

"As long as there are kings I suppose." Joab came up the stairway and took Abi by her hands. "Do you know what lies ahead of you, Abishag?"

Abi stared dumbly into the keen gray eyes. At the foot of the stairway her mother was sobbing. Above her Jonathan stood motionless, hands clenched. Only Rachel saw how much silent suffering was contained in his hunched body.

Joab said, "It is not for me to tell you—but do not, if you value your life, let Bathsheba guess what you feel for Adonijah. Do not tell David, or let him guess, if you want to help Adonijah. All Israel expects that he will succeed David. Bathsheba alone has arrayed her wits and her influence against him. Do not underestimate her cleverness or her power. You may see or hear something in David's chamber that should be known to Adonijah's friends; if you do, come and tell Rachel. She will know what to do. But above all, protect yourself. Bathsheba is a woman with one thought, and she is ruthless. Do you understand?"

Abi shook her head. "I want my father to come and take me home."

Joab put his arm about her shoulders and led her down into the court. "Not even I could take you home now, my dear child. Be strong, and of good courage. You must play a woman's part. Do you love David at all? Do you have any feeling of affection for your king?"

Abi closed her eyes. When she opened them again she stood very straight. She looked directly into the strange gray eyes of this fearless man. She knew she could speak to Joab of things not even Bildad would understand. "I love David. My father has told me since I was a little girl how good he is and how much all of us owe him. I think he is a great king and a good man."

Joab's hands gripped her arms firmly. "Be of good courage, Abishag. David is old and you are young. A time will come when Adonijah will be our king. He will inherit his father's kingdom and with it his father's harem. You will yet be the wife of Adonijah. And now I think he will be ready to exert himself and fight for his birthright."

46

THE FLOOR OF David's bedroom was checkered with thin-hewn squares of whitest limestone from Naphtali and black basalt from Bashan. Built above his hall of judgment, the chamber was set back from the parapet, leaving a promenade on all four sides. The walls were paneled with polished cedar wood. The windows were large and numerous, affording more daylight than in any other room Abishag had seen. But when the storms came in winter, the windows were closely shuttered and the doors leading to the promenade were tightly closed. Many lamps of porphyry and alabaster gave off the heavy odor of spikenard. Spikenard is a costly perfume, but after three years of it Abi had learned to dislike it intensely.

Abi folded her sewing and put it away. There wasn't any use trying to sew by lamplight, no matter how restless she got with nothing to do. Her loom was down in the harem court. Weaving was too noisy an occupation to bring into a sickroom. She paced up and down, but the checkerwork pattern of the floor gave her a feeling of dizziness so she sat down again. She must not pace the floor in any event, for that would call David's attention to her restlessness. She sat on a rug and leaned her head against the wall and listened to the storm.

The wind whistled about the upper chamber, rattling the shutters. Rain drummed on the roof and on the promenade. Twice this month sleet and snow had fallen in Jerusalem. It had been a bad winter, especially for David. He was coughing again but Hushai remained beside him, talking and talking, as if unaware that David was too ill to be bothered. Everyone was used to hearing David cough when the rains started. Abi had a theory that it wasn't the dampness that made him cough, but the heaviness of the air in a room shut up tight with the odor of spikenard. David's Levite physician declared that the incense-like odor would help David's breathing. But Abi thought if the Levite had to live with the odor morning, midday, and evening and right through the three watches of the night, he might think less of it. She thought of the smell of winter on the Jezreel Plain, clean with rain. Homesickness was not the least of her troubles.

I do nothing for David, she thought, except to give him my gift of cheerfulness. I must not think of home.

The voice of the fat old man on the rug by David's bed went on and on. Whenever David wasn't well enough to go down to the judgment chamber, Hushai heard the petitions and gave judgment. At the end of such days he always came up to tell David every tiresome detail of every case, till Abi was ready to scream from the sheer dullness of the old counselor's recitals. But David listened to all, commenting, asking questions, commending Hushai's wisdom and prudence. When David went into a paroxysm of coughing Hushai waited until the coughing ended, then went right on.

Everyone is the same, thought Abi sorrowfully. Nobody thinks of David's welfare. They come to him about their own affairs, or to persuade him to use his authority to gain their ends. Don't they see how tired he is?

Then the thought came, and not for the first time: What if David doesn't realize his own weakness? Abi had heard Sarah talk about the last illness of Bildad's father. She had watched over him, keeping away the people who worried and annoyed him, forbidding Bildad to talk to him about farm problems—blight in the barley or an attack of worms in the sheep. Is there in Israel a single person, Abi wondered, who has the authority to tell David when to rest, to say to wives and counselors and sons and secretaries, you cannot see David?

The Levite physician would never forbid the mighty in Israel to visit his patient, the king. He liked important people to come in when he was with David. He liked them to listen while he talked learnedly of balms and purges, bleeding, trepanning, and leeches.

Bathsheba would not hesitate to assume authority, but Bathsheba was the worst offender. She put her ambition ahead of David's welfare. If Bathsheba had the opportunity to exclude visitors she would bring in her faction, Benaiah and Zadok and Solomon, and exclude Joab, Adonijah, Abiathar.

At first Abi thought David loved Bathsheba more than his other wives. But now, after three years with David whenever he was in this room, of watching how he received each wife, each son, she knew that David had no favorites either among wives or sons. He loved them all. But he had suffered a terrible sense of guilt because of sins committed with Bathsheba and for her. David was of so noble a nature that he could not realize Bathsheba had not borne an equal sense of guilt. He felt a mistaken pity for this woman. Because of it he yielded to her requests whenever possible.

Abi left this chamber only on days when he went down into his judgment hall or to visit in the houses of his sons. She had spent many days in the harem after she married David, and she knew all David's wives very well now. She knew that in the harem Bathsheba had grown waspish, but in the king's chamber she was smooth as butter. It was Bathsheba who had instructed Abi when she married David in what was expected from her. Abi shuddered whenever she remembered the shock and revulsion she had felt at Bathsheba's words. But David's kindness had healed the lacerations of her spirit. The autumn rains began a week after her marriage, and with the rains David's health deteriorated so sharply there was no longer any question of attempting to rekindle the old man's virility. The problem was to keep him alive till spring.

These brooding thoughts came to Abi because she was idle. She jumped to her feet and softly crossed the checkered floor to where David lay, propped up with pillows on the wide couch. David watched her as she moved about the room, even while he listened to Hushai, and she thought, I could not help him as he had hoped, since he remained impotent. Yet he likes to have me here with him. He has an eye for pretty women, old though he is.

She sat beside the couch and said, with a smile for Hushai, "I have been trying to think who in all this kingdom could say to David, 'You must not have so many visitors.' I have been trying to think who could say to a counselor and friend, 'David is tired. He should have his chest rubbed with balm from Gilead, and be wrapped in warm blankets and try to sleep.' I can think of nobody who has that kind of authority over David. Can you suggest anyone, my lord Hushai?"

David smiled and patted her hand affectionately. "My cousin Joab has assumed authority over me more than once in the past. The painful thing was that when we disagreed he was usually right. That left me with no defense against him. If you want to make me your prisoner, Abishag, consult Joab. He will tell you how it can be done."

Abi pressed his hand to her cheek. "I do not want to make you my prisoner, my lord. I only want you to be well."

Hushai's voice was unctuous and patronizing. "I think the young lady can trust her king and her lord to know what he wants to do and whom he wants to see."

Abi said, "I will bring you clean napkins, my lord David." She went to the alcove which was wash room and clothes closet. As she dropped the soiled napkins in the hamper she noticed blood on them. Twice before it had happened, this coughing up of blood. What can I do? she thought, feeling panic. I must find someone who can tell me how to take care of this kind old man whom everyone uses and nobody protects. And she thought, I cannot go for help. My place is here when David is here.

I will send a servant and ask Rachel to come here to see me, she thought. David would be confined to this room for many weeks.

She paused to look into the mirror David had bought from an Egyptian merchant. David always noticed if there was a flaw in the drape of her tunic or the fold of her girdle. He had given her a wondrous assortment of girdles and mantles and tunics and cloaks of every color in the rainbow, and had taught her how to combine colors. But Abi liked white best, and usually wore a white tunic here in the upper chamber, or in the harem. She adjusted the scarlet girdle, gathered up an armload of clean napkins, and went over to speak to the servant who was always outside the door.

"Go to the house of the high priest Abiathar," she said to him. "Ask for Rachel, his wife. Tell her for me that I must see her today, without fail."

She took the pile of clean napkins to David just as he went into another spell of coughing. She poured water from the alabaster jug beside the bed into a silver cup. When the paroxysm ended she handed the cup to David.

Hushai said, "There is just one more case, my lord David, if I may—"

David glanced at Abi's worried face and said, "I trust your judgment, Hushai. You have never disappointed me. Save this one till another—" He did not finish. He had started coughing again.

Abi gazed pleadingly at Hushai. "He mustn't talk. He slept so little last night. He coughs so hard, and we can do so little to help him."

Hushai had difficulty getting down on the rugs, and even more difficulty getting up again. He turned himself about so that he was kneeling, then crawled over to the wall and grasped the side of the doorway, and so got his legs under him. He did not stop talking to David all the while he was struggling to his feet. He did not stop talking until the curtain that covered the door had dropped behind him.

Abi put towels and a woolen sheet to warm before the fireplace and got a pot of balm made from the sap of the cedar trees of Gilead. It was a favorite remedy of Sarah's. The Levite physician had no regard for it since it was inexpensive and used by the common people. When he attended the king he believed in using rare and costly ointments. But Abi kept the balm anyway and used it to rub on David's chest and back. Then she covered him with hot towels and wrapped him in a warm blanket. Almost immediately David fell asleep.

Abi went to an outside door and opened it a crack and looked out upon the drumming rain. The cold, moist air was refreshing. She breathed deeply of air untainted by spikenard. David has no queen, she thought. In most palaces, Abiathar had told her, there is a wife with authority over the rest. It may be the first wife, or it may be the mother of the eldest son. Or perhaps the wife whose rank is highest, a princess from an important kingdom. If David had such a queen, she would have authority to say who can trouble David in his illness and who cannot. Michal was David's first wife and the daughter of King Saul. Reba is the mother of the heir and the only wife to be called mother of two sons, the first-born and the eldest surviving. But between David and each of these wives there was a wall, as a wall separated forces throughout the kingdom. Joab favored Adonijah and Reba. Yet Joab's army was scattered. Benaiah favored Bathsheba and Benaiah's police force was always on hand, guarding the palace and the gates.

Thinking of all the dangerous rivalries existing in Jerusalem and having their center here in the bedroom of a sick old man, Abi shivered and closed the door. Even the priests were divided. Those who loved Abiathar were with Adonijah. Those who loved Zadok were on the side of Bathsheba and Solomon.

Abi got a jug of oil from the alcove and went from lamp to lamp, filling each in turn, then relighting them with a taper from the fireplace. What if Solomon should become king? What if Bathsheba succeeded in her careful plans? I am afraid of Solomon, young as he is, thought Abi. I am afraid of what would happen to Adonijah if Solomon became king. She shivered. "To Adonijah—and to me."

Adonijah, she thought, my dearest, how long will it be before we are together? He called on his father daily whenever David was confined to his room. However, at present Adonijah was away from Jerusalem. He made trips about the kingdom, giving the people pleasure from the sight of their prince, a young man who was surely a credit to Israel. In every city he talked with the elders and priests and merchants, a minister of goodwill for a continued prosperity and unity in Israel when his father should go the way of all mankind. Joab directed all the activities of this young prince whose strength was with the people.

How careful Adonijah and Abi had been to behave circumspectly whenever he came to this room. Each for the sake of the other rigidly controlled each word, each glance, to keep all on the friendly basis which should exist between the eldest son and the youngest wife of David.

Several times during the past three years Abi had gone with Reba to visit Adonijah in his apartment. When David was well and Abi free to visit Rachel, they sometimes saw each other in the house of Abiathar. They had never been alone together, and both were too fond of David and too loyal to risk behaving in an unseemly manner while David lived. Adonijah had said more than once that he would never be lord of a harem but would marry one wife only, and that one Abishag, else he would go to the tomb unwed.

As Abi was filling the last lamp the curtain at the head of the stairway was pulled aside and Joab came into the room. She went to him, finger to lips, lest he waken David. She led him to the farthest corner. There they sat and talked in whispers.

"When Rachel received your message she was sure your trouble should be told to me, and asked me to come in her place," Joab said. How strong and healthy he seems, thought Abi. He is perhaps twelve years younger than David, but he looks not much over forty. Both Joab and Benaiah seemed young and strong for all their many years of service to David.

"David has been coughing up blood," Abi said with a worried frown. "He ought not to be troubled by visitors, yet there is no one to protect him from such people as Hushai and Bathsheba. She keeps at David to set Solomon on the throne at once—to relieve David of all anxiety about the kingdom, she says. I don't think David can stand up against her much longer. What can I do, Joab?"

"You can do nothing, my child." He looked at her and smiled gravely. "Forgive me for calling you child. You are no child after three years in this palace. You have played your part well. But now it may be time for me to do something." He smiled again. "Nothing suits David better, when he has a troublesome decision to make, than for someone else to make the decision and present him with the accomplished fact."

From the bed came a strangling cough. David struggled to sit up, coughing into a napkin he held crushed in his hands. Joab went over to the bed and looked down with pity and affection in his eyes. Abi knelt and with her arm braced the thin figure erect. When the coughing stopped she held a cup of wine out to David. He sipped a little and handed the cup back to her. He glanced at the blood-reddened cloth in his hand, then thrust it quickly out of sight under the pile of napkins.

He spoke to Joab in a whisper. "Welcome, cousin. How goes the work on the north wall?"

"Well enough. Perhaps it will be finished in my lifetime. Perhaps, like your temple, it will be finished by another. David, I did not come to trouble you. I understand it is bad for you to talk. I will say only what cannot wait till spring comes and you are well again. I wonder if you know how close to civil war our nation is at this moment. On the first day that you sent Hushai to take your place in the judgment court, it became clear to your people that you have not fully determined who shall be your successor. It requires no great cleverness to deduce that if you had made such a decision, your son would be giving judgment instead of your friend."

David moved as if to speak but Joab raised his hand. "Do not try to speak, cousin. A man who is coughing up blood must not do anything to bring on such attacks. Bathsheba came out into the open on the day when Hushai first held court. She has lined up Benaiah and the palace guard on her side, as well as Zadok and the priests and Levites whose loyalty is with Zadok rather than Abiathar. Last week Benaiah sent out couriers to the Philistine cities, asking for double the number of mercenaries he now commands. Cousin, if tonight you should go to sleep with your fathers, tomorrow this country would be bathed in blood. Name a successor. Set your son upon your throne while you are alive to affirm your decision and prevent war. Do not leave us to fight to establish your son."

David lay against his pillows, breathing quietly. "We have come a long way, cousin," he said softly. "Don't push me now. This matter is for the Lord God to resolve. Not you. Not me. Don't try to take this into your hands, for if I live I will stop you." He began to cough. Joab rose with a strong thrust of his legs and walked down the room. When David was quiet he strode back across the checkered tiles.

"I have marched against Israelites three times, David. I have fought battles twice against our own people. You have never shed the blood of Israelites. You do not know what it is to stand over a dying man whose blood is on your sword, and hear him commit himself to the Lord God of Israel. Don't force me to do it again. Place your son on the throne. Give your successor your blessing. The people complain of Hushai. He is old and garrulous. Justice from Hushai is not what our people come to Jerusalem to obtain. Set your heir upon the throne of judgment."

David said very softly, "Which son?"

"Are you serious?"

David's face was suddenly very sad. "It would be a comfort to know that God had deigned to bless my marriage to Bathsheba in choosing our son to be king. Solomon is a brilliant boy. Have you ever listened to the songs he has written? He is young, and will do better when he has lived a little longer. Solomon would build a magnificent temple, Joab. No, no, do not interrupt. I know you think our nation is too small to support a king with tastes as lavish as Solomon's. I think it is possible, cousin, that we have thought too much of Israel's strength, and too little of her glory."

Joab said heavily, "So you have made a choice."

David laid his hand over Joab's crossed forearms. "God shall choose, cousin. It is true Bathsheba has comforted herself all these years with the faith that God would choose Solomon. Where Bathsheba is concerned I am not a strong man. If she is to be disappointed, and I suppose she is bound to be, it will have to come about through the clear leading of the Lord God of Israel. As for civil war—Joab, you have kept this land quiet through many crises. You will keep the land quiet also when I am gone."

"If Solomon reigns," Joab replied somberly, "I will not be here to keep the land quiet." He rose with a fluid ease which made one forget he was nearing sixty.

David looked at Joab with love. "You have been my strength, Joab. You were instrumental in making me king of all Israel. You gave me this city to be my capital. You quelled our neighbors and you put down two insurrections. Let me go to Sheol in peace, without having to say to one of my sons, 'You shall be king,' and to another, equally dear, 'You shall not be king.' "

Joab replied, "Without you, David, I would have been a shepherd and a farmer. I would never have learned to recognize and use the powers in myself which have, as it has turned out, been useful to you and to our people. Not to me alone but to uncounted thousands who, in following you, became a nation—to all these you brought the opportunity to make their lives have more than trivial meaning. For this we bless you, David."

David looked really happy, Abi thought. He had talked more to Joab without coughing than to anybody since the rains began. He was breathing easily and seemed comfortable. He protects all the others, she thought. He feels responsible for them, and so he grows anxious when he talks to them. But with Joab he speaks to a man whose strength he trusts. Sometimes he grows angry with Joab, but he never pities him or feels that he ought to try to do something for him.

She followed Joab out through the curtain to the stairway. "What will you do?" she asked.

"Nothing, for a while."

"I have never before heard him say so plainly what he feels about his sons. He will not make Adonijah king, will he? You will have to do that for him, Joab. Poor old man. Bathsheba would hound him right into his grave if he were to give Adonijah his blessing."

Joab put his arm about her shoulders. "You are a good girl, Abishag. You deserve happiness, for you have been devoted and unselfish and very kind to David. No better thing could come to Israel than for Adonijah to become king, with you as his queen. Well, for the present we will do nothing to disturb my cousin in there. But I learned long ago that it is better to prevent civil war than to win it. You must tell me if there is any change."

47

SPRING HAD BROUGHT no improvement in David's health. The Passover had been celebrated. The wind blew warm and dry from the desert. And it was now clear to everyone who frequented the king's bedchamber that his life must surely be drawing to a close.

When Reba received a message from Adonijah asking her to go with him to the house of Joab she felt a stab of fear. Adonijah came before midday and together they walked down the cobbled street. Abiathar, Jonathan, and Rachel were already seated in the sunny courtyard of this bare, stone house which had known two masters but never a mistress.

Adonijah took his place beside his friend Jonathan in the circle. After Joab welcomed them, Reba burst out fretfully, "I am sure I know why you have called us together, Joab. You think the time has come to set Adonijah on the throne. I dread such an act! I keep remembering the tragic results that grew out of Absalom's anointing."

"Mother," Adonijah protested, "I would never try to become king by force!"

Joab said, "We are not acting against David, as Absalom was. We are against Solomon and the little group that supports his pretensions. Only this month Benaiah increased his police force from two hundred men to a thousand! They go armed with both javelins and swords. Many carry bows. Meanwhile my army is scattered throughout the land, every man on his own farm or in his own city. I could not assemble an army in less than a week's time. There is no question of taking the throne by force. But if we can anoint Adonijah king without Benaiah's knowledge, we believe David will recognize the accomplished deed and give his blessing to Adonijah. Then Adonijah can disperse Benaiah's Philistines and give me command of the palace guard. The real crisis will not come while David lives, and we will use the time to reach an agreement with Solomon, thus preventing armed conflict when David is no longer here to keep peace among his sons."

Abiathar stalked up and down, his linen skirts flapping about his long legs. "I do not like the plan," he said. "I do not want to anoint Adonijah in secret. Such a thing should not be done in Israel. A king's anointing is holy and should be done beside the altar in the sight of all men."

Tears filled Adonijah's bright blue eyes. "Do you think I would choose to be made king in secret? I love my father. And he loves me. Why should I seize his throne while he lies ill and suffering in his chamber?"

Joab shrugged. "I will not urge you to take this step. David says that God will choose among his sons, that God will set the right heir upon the throne. I do not have such faith. I know what I know about Benaiah and his quadrupled guard, and his purpose in bringing these mercenaries to Jerusalem. How many times have I seen the prayers of David answered by means of the sword and the stratagems of Joab! If I know David, whatever turn of events sets one of his sons upon the throne will seem to him as the hand of God, making choice among his sons. If we wait, Benaiah will act. Is there one among you who believes that Solomon would rule in such a way as to strengthen our nation?"

There was no answer. Abiathar's pacing slowed. With his long, knobby fingers laced together he halted near Joab and stood staring down upon him, deeply perplexed.

At last Reba cried, "How can anybody be sure about such things?"

Joab said, "Solomon's tastes are lavish. David himself agrees that this nation is too small to support Solomon's extravagance. Yet I do not see how Adonijah can ever hope to occupy the throne without either a war or a stratagem that will outwit Benaiah and Bathsheba and Solomon. If we do this thing, and David accepts the deed as God's hand moving once more in Israel's history, we will have saved this nation much trouble and perhaps much bloodshed."

Abiathar sighed a gusty sigh. "If only David would inquire of the Lord at the high altar with the Urim and Thummim."

"Have you urged him to do so?" Reba asked.

Rachel smiled ruefully. "Abiathar has urged David on each of his last three visits to do this. David says both Abiathar and Zadok have taken sides and that the Urim and Thummim are valid guides only in the hands of an impartial high priest. Yet I think it is an excuse. I think David is in such dread of Bathsheba's reproaches that he cannot agree to any deliberate act that would bring about a decision in Adonijah's favor."

Adonijah rose. "We will not discuss it further. I can see, Joab, that the time has come to relieve my father of this burden of indecision. You make it clear that otherwise we must either stand like oxen while Benaiah puts Solomon on the throne or else fight a civil war after my father's death."

He turned to the tall priest. "If you are willing, Abiathar—" He went to Abiathar and laid his hand over the interlaced fingers. "If you can in good conscience anoint me king under the circumstances facing us, I am willing to be so anointed. The decision shall be yours, Abiathar. I pray that God will guide you."

"Will you kneel, my son?"

While Adonijah knelt before him, Abiathar placed his hands upon the curling red hair and raised his face heavenward. His lips moved silently. In her heart Reba also was breathing a prayer, lest this dangerous plan bring disaster upon them.

Presently Abiathar turned his face and looked about upon the close, small circle. "I cannot say clearly what the will of God is. But it must be right to put the matter to the test. If I could use the Urim and Thummim in such a matter I would do so. But it is not lawful save in the presence of the king and by his direction, for the sacred stones belong to the kingdom, not to a faction. If you, Adonijah, and you, Joab, believe this thing ought to be done—well then, I will do my part. And may God have mercy upon us if we are mistakenly following our own will and not the will of God."

Reba rose early and put on new garments of green and russet. She wore golden bracelets and at her neck a heavy golden chain which Adonijah had given her for this occasion. All the wives had been invited by Adonijah to a feast in the Tyropoeon Valley beside the fountain En Rogel.

The feast would begin at midday, but Reba was anxious to go early to the valley. She had asked Maacah to come with her at this early hour. Maacah, poor soul, was only too willing to be needed by someone.

The guests at Adonijah's feast included the wives and the sons of David, all except Bathsheba and Solomon. Only Jonathan and Abishag of all who knew the purpose of the feast would not be in attendance. Abishag could not leave David's bedside. To Jonathan fell the responsibility of roaming through the city, observing the actions of Zadok, Benaiah, Solomon, and their friends in order to bring warning if anything went wrong. Jonathan had lived for three years with the secret knowledge that he shared with Adonijah a lonely and hopeless love for Abi. For himself Jonathan had never had any hope. Abi loved Adonijah. What he did for Adonijah he did for her and for Joab and Abiathar as well.

None of the guests had been told the purpose of the feast. Trumpets had been brought under cover of darkness during the first watch of the preceding night and were now hidden, covered over with branches, in a shallow pit behind En Rogel. The signal for the anointing would be given by Joab. He would rise from the feast and go to uncover the trumpets.

When the trumpets had been given to the priests, Abiathar would rise and the ceremony of anointing would begin.

Reba and Maacah left the city by way of Millo Gate. In the Tyropoeon Valley spring had brought green to the twisted branches of grapevines, and thick carpeting grass to the floor and western slope of the valley. Reba had told Abi the purpose of the feast yesterday as they walked upon the promenade where they would not be overheard. Today she told Maacah.

Maacah had been high-spirited when she first came from Syria at the age of fifteen to marry David. As the mother of Tamar, she had had the good fortune to keep one child with her in the harem. Her pleasant good nature had survived Tamar's humiliation by Amnon, Absalom's murder of Amnon and his flight to Geshur, and the marriage of her daughter to Shobi, Nahash of Rabbah-Ammon. But when Absalom made war on David, forcing him to flee over the Jordan, and when Maacah knew of the manner of his death, she had become a mousy creature, quick to agree with those who were kind to her, slow to speak unless spoken to.

Reba dreaded the effect Adonijah's secret anointing would have upon Maacah. She feared it would bring back the agony Maacah had felt when Absalom was anointed king in Hebron.

"Maacah, do you think we are doing wrong?" she asked.

Maacah's eyes were like dark holes in her pale face. "How can I tell? Absalom ruined himself when he made himself king. Many Israelites were with him, yet he was ruined. David has never been the same since it happened."

Reba replied, "If Adonijah thought David would be displeased he would not go through with it. Adonijah will never take up arms against his father. Oh, Maacah, for us it should be the highest point in our lives, to see a beloved son anointed king of Israel. Adonijah wept when he agreed to be anointed in this secret way. Yet Bathsheba and Solomon have so set their minds to steal his birthright from Adonijah that I cannot oppose the plan. Joab has gauged David's mind correctly many times. Joab declares this move will please David and is moreover the only means whereby Adonijah can become king without civil war. Surely we can trust Joab."

Maacah said listlessly, "We must trust Joab, for he is wiser than we."

Reba smiled. "We must contrive to be gay, Maacah. This is a feast. Adonijah is troubled, and if he sees us despondent he will be further saddened. Perhaps for you it would have been easier if I had kept silence, but I feared the shock you would feel when the moment comes. Are you sorry I told you, Maacah?"

"You are the best friend I have in the world, Reba. And this is not like Absalom's anointing. Adonijah is acting against a younger brother, but Absalom was acting against David."

They were approaching the fountain. All the valley wore the clean, washed look that follows the rains. The sun was above the city wall now, shining into the valley. At the fire pits servants bustled about. Shephatiah was with them, overseeing the preparation and the spreading of the feast. Minna and Rachel were here but Minna's two children had been left with servants on Shephatiah's farm. Reba went about the valley, greeting those who had come at the invitation of her son.

Shortly before midday, Abiathar and Joab arrived together. Abiathar wore the handsome regalia reserved for Israel's high priests on the most ceremonious occasions. Every garment was made to specifications laid down in the laws of Moses, from the turban and mitre on his head to the trousers under the long blue coat. The trousers were worn by priests for modesty's sake, for when they stood on the altar ledge and leaned across to lay offerings on the coals, the resulting exposure would otherwise have been scandalous. Over the robe of blue linen Abiathar wore an embroidered doublet fastened with onyx clasps at the shoulders and bound about the middle by a wide girdle of gold, blue, purple, scarlet, and white. A breastplate hung from his neck with twelve precious stones set in four rows. Each stone was delicately engraved with the name of one of the twelve tribes of Israel. Over the turban was a mitre of gold on which the words "Holiness to the Lord" were inscribed.

Tucked into the folds of the girdle was a horn of spiced oil brought from the tent of meeting. Abiathar's beard was snow white, thick and curly. His brows were white and bushy, shadowing deeply sunken eyes. His hair hung about his shoulders, thick, white, curly. Seldom indeed had Reba seen Abiathar look like this. Not even Zadok could make a more impressive appearance than Abiathar made today. Joab too was dressed in his finest robe, but Abiathar's splendor was such that Joab's raiment went quite unnoticed, except by Reba.

Now the sun was nearing the zenith. The sound of horses and the shouts of the driver were heard. From beyond Millo came Adonijah's chariot. The horses gleamed with oil and their harness and harness-cloths were magnificent. The driver brought up the horses with a flourish at the edge of the Tyropoeon slope. When Adonijah stepped down, a whip cracked and the chariot careened away.

Adonijah had come dressed in scarlet from head to foot, with golden clasps and buckles upon the gleaming black leather breastplate and a chaplet of golden cords strung with rubies over his scarlet headcloth. Reba's breath caught in her throat because he looked just as David had in Hebron when Zadok and Abiathar had anointed him king of the twelve tribes of Israel.

What a king he will be! thought Reba. She could not keep back tears of pride. All about Adonijah his brothers clustered, vying with one another to show their pride and admiration. Reba glanced from this display of love to the faces of the wives, for by now all the wives except Bathsheba and Abishag had come. It is no secret, the purpose of this feast, she thought. Adonijah had chosen to wear scarlet rather than purple to safeguard the secret. But for Abiathar to come here dressed in ceremonial vestments revealed the purpose clearly. Still Reba could see on no face any sign of disapproval or displeasure. Even Michal was smiling. Michal was in very poor health, with swollen and painful joints. She had been carried on a pallet by servants. Michal, thought Reba with a smile, would go almost anywhere if the occasion was likely to put Bathsheba out of countenance.

The goodwill of the wives and sons of David, thought Reba, compensates for David's absence. Now Shephatiah was urging his brother's guests to seat themselves for the feast. Strips of white linen were laid on the grass and on them were spread cheese and bread, raisins and winter figs and dates, and the roasted flesh of sheep, oxen, and fat cattle. Adonijah took his place at the head of the improvised table, with Abiathar on his right and Joab on his left. On both sides of the table were ranged the wives and the sons of David. Down at the far end the priests were grouped. When Adonijah reached for a joint of roast lamb everyone fell to partaking of the feast. So abundantly had Adonijah provided that the servants were continually replenishing the great bowls of food, and the feast continued until the sun was more than halfway down the western sky.

Now the time had come, and Joab rose and went to the fountain. One of his servants hurried over to help him, and together they uncovered the trumpets and brought them to the priests. A silence fell, half expectant, half fearful. When Joab returned to his place Abiathar rose, and took from his girdle the horn of oil and removed the stopper and lifted it in his right hand. Adonijah knelt before him with bowed head. Then Abiathar laid his left hand upon the bared head of Adonijah and lifted his face and began earnestly to pray, for Israel, for Israel's King David, and finally for this young man, the heir to Israel's throne, upon whom a heavy responsibility must now be placed.

Lost in his prayer, Abiathar was last to hear the uproar which had begun in the city. Sonorously, earnestly he prayed, while at the table the wives and sons of David, the priests with their trumpets in hand, and even Adonijah began glancing fearfully at one another. They heard the sound of trumpets and shouts within the walls. These sounds of rejoicing grew louder and louder while Abiathar, oblivious, prayed on.

Suddenly Jonathan appeared at the head of the valley, running toward them and shouting. This Abiathar heard. He had closed his prayer and was ready to begin the ritual, "Adonijah, son of David, I anoint thee . . ." when Jonathan was beside him.

"Solomon has been anointed king. He is riding through the streets on the king's mule. He will sit on David's throne in the hall of judgment. David gave the order. The thing has been done! All the palace guard have surrounded the palace and will cut us down if we make a move against Solomon."

The horn of holy oil was knocked from Abiathar's hand as Adonijah leaped to his feet. Joab shouted, "Adonijah, take sanctuary at the high altar. The rest of you—all of you—hurry to your own houses. Change your festive attire. Pretend, if you can, that this was only a feast. Be discreet, if you value your lives!"

Adonijah was running up the valley with all the young princes following him. Reba could not move, but sat weeping beside the scattered remnants of Adonijah's wondrous feast. When at last she looked about, nobody was left but Michal, who lay weeping bitterly upon her pallet, waiting for servants to come for her. Where the priests had sat half a score of trumpets lay broken and trampled on the grass.

In David's chamber Abi scarcely had been able to endure the dragging hours of the morning. She had given up trying to sew. David was resting, half asleep, and she walked on the promenade, straining her eyes for some sight of what was going on in the valley southwest of the city. Now and then she saw members of David's family dressed in fine raiment walking down the street on which the palace fronted.

Shortly before midday she heard the noise of running horses and saw Adonijah racing southward in a gleaming chariot drawn by black horses. She waved her white scarf and Adonijah, distant though he was, noticed her and lifted his arm in a long salute.

She closed her eyes and leaned her head against the parapet. Bless him, Lord God, she prayed silently. Be with him in this hour which is the zenith of his life. He is a good man, she thought, petitioning the Lord God of Israel to take notice of his goodness and protect him from any miscarriage of Joab's plan.

Perhaps an hour had passed when she heard the screams and sobs of Bathsheba inside the chamber. With sinking heart she hurried into the room. Bathsheba stood just inside the door with her garments rent and ashes in her hair.

"Treason!" she screamed. "Joab has lifted up his sword against my lord David and is anointing Adonijah king down beside En Rogel. Abiathar took a horn of holy oil from the tent of meeting and went in his ceremonial vestments to perform the ceremony. Joab is taking your kingdom from you and giving it to Adonijah!"

David, pale as parchment and too weak to stand, lifted himself on one elbow. "It is false! You have invented this tale for your own purpose!"

Abi threw her skirts up over her bowed face, frightened speechless. Her strength as well as her wits went from her.

David panted, struggling to balance himself with his arms, "Adonijah is giving a feast. All my wives and all my sons are there. They would not turn against me!" He was seized by a paroxysm of coughing.

Abi hurried to him and with a napkin wiped away the blood. "Oh, my lord David, do not exert yourself," she cried, and darted an angry look at the distraught Bathsheba.

Zadok came panting from the stairway. His fine linen garments were all awry on his portly figure. "My lord David," he gasped, "one of my priests saw Abiathar leave the tent of meeting dressed for a most sacred occasion. When we looked, half the trumpets used to signal great events had been removed. This is Joab's doing, my lord. Joab has arisen against you as that young man Absalom once did!"

Abi had to bite her lips to keep from screaming. David was convinced by Zadok where he had not been convinced by Bathsheba. His eyes closed, his lips moved in prayer and tears flowed from beneath the closed lids. When Zadok and Bathsheba saw that David was praying they became silent.

Presently David's eyes opened. A trickle of blood rolled unnoticed from the corner of his mouth. "God will not let Joab triumph over us in this thing. God has given the kingdom to Solomon. Now, listen, and do exactly what I say. Zadok, prepare to anoint Solomon at once. Call out the people and the priests. Bring them down to Gihon spring. Get priests to gather up all the remaining trumpets. Call Benaiah to set a guard all about the palace, and to send ample guard also with you for the ceremony. Send messengers to bring all the people in the city to Solomon's anointing. Go, Zadok. Go quickly. Do not waste a moment's time. Solomon must be anointed and the trumpets must sound before Joab and his people have sounded their trumpets or entered the city. Act quickly, quickly!"

Zadok hustled out. When Bathsheba would have followed, with a hasty, "Thank you, my lord! God bless you, my lord David!" David called her back. "Place a robe on Solomon but do not waste time in fastidious ornamentation. Send a servant to order out my own white mule. When Solomon has been anointed, he is to ride through the city on my mule and come quickly to my judgment hall and sit upon my throne, and there receive the people. Waste no time in unnecessary fopperies. Go. Go quickly."

Now at last Abishag was alone with David. She knelt beside the couch and wept and wept and could not be comforted. David patted her shoulder, murmuring words of kindness, touched that she should care so deeply for this affront to his authority. Soon the palace was deserted and the streets were empty. That midday was perhaps the longest Abi was ever to live through, for she could not go to warn Adonijah, nor could she be sure that Jonathan had discovered the disaster in time to warn him. She dared not leave David, for he was trembling from shock and from the effort of making the momentous decision.

When Abi saw that David was weeping she forgot her own tears. "Why do you weep, my lord?"

"I weep for Adonijah. What will I say when he confronts me with what I have done—putting his youngest brother above him in the kingdom and in my affections?"

"My lord David, shall I tell you?"

David turned away his face. "You are a child. I must find an answer, for it is I who have passed by the best son a king could have. Yet what I did was done because I am confident Solomon is God's choice. It came to me while I was praying. Yet how can I ever know that anger with Joab did not also intrude, even as I prayed?"

Abi said gently, "My lord David, Adonijah would not want to be king against your will. If you say to him that Solomon will take no reprisals against him, if you say that he may live in safety on his farm, and that he is to have me as his wife, he will be content."

"You, Abishag?" David looked sadly upon the girl.

"My lord, on the day when you brought my father to the palace and spoke to him of making me your wife, Adonijah, knowing nothing of your plan, sent Reba to me to ask if I was willing to marry him."

David caressed the smooth, dark hair. "And were you willing, Abishag?"

"Aye, my lord David." She met his sadly interrogating look serenely, glad that at last she could speak the whole truth to this good old man.

"Would I had known all this long ago, my child. Though you have brightened my last years more than you will ever fully understand. God bless you, Abishag, and bring you happiness and many little ones. You have lifted a burden from my heart. Now it will be for you to make sure Adonijah understands that God, not David, has chosen today between my eldest and my youngest sons. Let him not forget that he has ever been as dear to me as any son could be."

Abi bowed her head upon the edge of David's couch. Her heart went out in prayer to the strange and unfathomable God of Israel who, for reasons she would never understand, had seen fit this day to reject Adonijah and choose Solomon instead.

Soon thereafter came the sounds of trumpets and shouts of "Hail Solomon! Long live King Solomon!"

"Run to the parapet, Abishag, and tell me what you see!"

Abi hurried to the parapet overlooking the street below. The procession, noisy and joyous, was directly beneath. A company of soldiers led by Benaiah marched at the head of the procession. Then came Solomon, erect and graceful on the king's white mule.

Solomon was wearing a magnificent robe of purple linen and in his dark, curling hair the anointing oil still glistened. Behind Solomon came Zadok in all his priestly magnificence, and behind Zadok came many priests with trumpets. Then came Bathsheba followed by the wives of Benaiah, Zadok, and certain of the priests. Another company of palace soldiers followed, shouting lustily and gesturing with their spears. Last of all came a great throng of people, all of them shouting at the top of their lungs.

Abi watched till the people had passed by, cast a final anxious glance in the direction of Millo, then came back to describe to David the scene she had witnessed. "Surely," she cried, "one of them will come up here to tell you all about it, since you cannot go down." But nobody came. Everybody was busy swelling the clamor of praise to Solomon.

At last there came a clatter of sandals on the stairway. The curtain was flung back and Joab entered. His face was flushed and his gray eyes were dark with anger. He was dressed in a bright blue battle cloak with scarlet bands above the hem. A handsome leather breastplate was buckled on at his shoulders.

"Well, David," he said in suppressed fury, "Bathsheba has indeed triumphed. To such lengths will a guilty conscience drive even a king." The words snapped like a whip's crackling in the ornate and lofty chamber.

Malice touched David's lips. "Do you think, cousin, that you must win every engagement between us?"

"You throw upon the dung heap this nation we carved out of these Canaanite hills at such great cost! You destroy Adonijah as well! Do you do all this merely to defeat me, David?"

David was never one to entertain malice for long. He said quietly, "This nation is in God's hands, not ours. Solomon is God's choice, cousin."

Joab stalked down the chamber and back, striving to control his anger. "So you do not even admit the truth about your own motives," he said at last, low-voiced, standing above David with clenched fists. "I would not have expected that from you, cousin. At great sacrifice and with much labor we contrived to set David on the throne and to keep him there for forty years in spite of his foolish forgiveness of such men as Abner, Absalom, and Amasa!"

David said quietly, "Where is Adonijah?"

"He has fled for sanctuary to the altar on Mount Moriah. Do you think this youth you have set upon the throne would spare his life, knowing how much he is loved throughout Israel and indeed by all of David's own household? Solomon will never be easy on the throne while Adonijah lives."

Abi cried, "Adonijah would not attempt to take the throne against his father's will."

Joab said bitterly, "You must explain all that to Solomon. Explain it

[291]

carefully, my child, for he will find it difficult to believe that any man would not try by any means whatsoever to gain the throne of Israel."

David said, "Bring Adonijah to me, Joab."

"What if he does not live to get here?" Joab paced down the room and back. "What if I do not live to reach the top of Mount Moriah? He took sanctuary there. I took sanctuary here. I tell you, David, Adonijah and I are in danger of our lives."

David turned to Abi. "Go and tell my son Solomon I wish to speak to him."

With a mocking smile Joab inquired, "Does the king summon a prince? Or does a fond old man summon the king? I think Solomon is having a busy day trying the fit of his father's crown and throne. I would like to make a wager with you concerning this son of yours, King Solomon. I would like to wager that it will take him at least three days to recall that he has a father who might care to see him in his kingly vestments, and talk with him about the future of the kingdom and of the eldest son of David."

David passed a transparent hand across his face. "This seems to be my day to learn how little I am loved. I suppose you have known all along, Joab, that Abishag and Adonijah were planning to marry, on that day when I asked Bildad to give her to me. I suppose you've known it was Adonijah she loved, rather than his father?"

Abi pressed the thin hand against her breast. "David, my dear lord, you know I love you and revere you! We all love you, all your family, all your people throughout all the twelve tribes. To know David is to love him."

David looked up at Joab. "And you, cousin. You have thwarted me many times. Well then, today, with God's help, I thwarted you. Do you love me? Or do you say that I am a senile old man, dominated by Bathsheba and with no mind of my own?"

Joab said coldly, "Do you ask me to sign my own death warrant?"

David sighed. "You have ever been a downright, outspoken man, Joab. Perhaps you could have gained your ends more easily if you had used, at times, a courtlier approach. Well, let us not accuse one another. We have both had the same objective, which is Israel's welfare. If, now, you think you and Adonijah are in some danger at Solomon's hands, perhaps you will advise me how to safeguard you?"

Joab paced the room, fighting down the anger that filled his breast. At last he returned to David's couch. "Appeal to Bathsheba's conscience, David," he said. "It may work. If not, I have no other suggestions. At least let us see whether she will bring Adonijah down from the altar and give him a chance to make his peace with Solomon."

Abi called for the servant outside the door. When he came—he had been at the foot of the stairway watching the excitement in the hall of judgment—David gave the order, and Bathsheba joined them, radiant and gracious, ready to make any promise to the husband who had set her son upon Israel's throne.

48

ABISHAG WENT TO the window and pushed back the heavy linen draperies of Damascus weave, letting in the early morning sunshine. Six months had passed and the autumn rains had come again. David's breathing was shallow and harsh, and his Levite physician admitted he could not understand how David had managed to remain alive so long.

From the couch came David's weak cough. Abi ran to lift him, so that he would not strangle on his own sputum. He was so thin that he was as easy to handle as a child. Would he be himself today? Devoutly she hoped so. When David was himself he was kind, gentle, grateful to those who tended him. When he was not himself he lived in the past, vengeful and hating toward those he loved. What a pity, thought Abishag, to see a great man outlive his greatness, saying things that would shame him if he were well and fully aware.

Abi had heard stories of David's deeds which already were legendary. Now she lived in this chamber while he lingered on midway between life and death. She warmed his chilled old body with her warm young one. She breathed air made fetid by creeping death, an odor not even the heavy-sweet odor of spikenard could conceal. She listened to the petulant voice of an old man turned childish.

All day yesterday David had complained of Joab, remembering this thing and that from the past. Abi was ashamed to hear the petty, hateful things the old king said. She longed to give David a cup of wine in which some drug of forgetfulness was buried, but dared do nothing on her own initiative. Well, perhaps today would be better.

She brought a brush and arranged the straggling, lifeless white hair, the sparse, wispy white beard. She brought a robe of soft white cotton. It had been long since David had worn his rich robes which lay folded on the shelves in the alcove. David clung to her hands, and looked gratefully up at her. When all was done, Abi pushed back the curtain at the doorway and signaled to the servant that David was ready for visitors.

Solomon was the first. David had sent for Solomon some time ago, but Solomon had returned a message that he was busy with affairs of state and would come in early one morning before going to the judgment hall. Solomon was exquisitely clothed and jeweled. His hair was oiled and curled and he was redolent of perfume. On his shoulder he carried a small yellow monkey attached by a golden chain to his wrist. But beneath all the regalia,

Abishag could plainly read the insecurity that haunted him. David had made him king, but when David was dead, with the country and all his family favoring his eldest brother, the rightful heir, how would he contrive to hold the throne for himself? What would he not have given to have Joab on his side! Abi knew that Solomon wanted to occupy his throne with credit and dispense justice with wisdom. She felt sorry for Solomon and yet she also felt a desperate fear of what he might do to make himself secure when his father was dead.

Solomon stood beside the bed, touching his nose with a handkerchief that reeked of perfume. No doubt he found the odor of death in this chamber unpleasant. He said, smiling brightly, "Well, Father, how are you feeling today? Well, I hope."

David's voice was cracked and feeble. He began talking of Joab, rehearsing old grievances, the killing of Abner, the torturing and killing of Absalom, the slaying of Amasa. "He must not outlive me," David whispered, while tears rolled down his face into the scraggly beard. "He has had the best of me many times and he will have the best of you if you let him live. He is shrewd, my son, a man of clever devices." David reached up and grasped the wrists of the young king and with a screech the monkey leaped from Solomon's shoulder onto David's arms.

David screamed and pushed the creature away with abhorrence. Solomon gathered up his pet and restored it to his shoulder. "He won't hurt you, Father," he said, laughing.

"Don't bring him into my presence again," David said, his voice a croak, his eyes wild with dread of his son's exotic pet.

Solomon smiled with tolerance for the sick old man. "I thought you might find him entertaining. If he doesn't amuse you I won't bring him again. Do you want anything more from me this morning? Jehoshaphat says there are many petitioners waiting."

"I want your promise," David said earnestly, "that you will set to work on the temple at once. I have purchased building materials and golden vessels. You have been king for a whole summer, but you have not yet turned a spadeful of earth."

Solomon smiled indulgently. "Father, I'll start work when workmen have been found. We no longer have captives to work for us. I have drawn up a plan whereby each tribe will send a hundred men each month throughout the year. The mixed peoples who dwell among us can be sent to mines and forests to get out the materials, but the building should be done by the men of Israel." He spoke proudly, as if he thought his plan ingenious. "As soon as we get the machinery set up for this labor supply, the work of building the temple will begin."

David's response was grief and consternation. "Forced labor," he mourned. "The temple ought not to be built with the forced labor of our people. As for this other plan—uprooting the strangers who have made their homes among us—it is a cruel return for their loyalty when they fought and served with me."

Solomon bent and kissed his father's forehead. "Now, Father, the responsibility is mine. You must not trouble yourself. I will send Mother up to sit with you this afternoon." Walking lightly in golden sandals, the young king left the room while the monkey on his shoulder pawed his curls.

David lay among his pillows, weeping and murmuring. "Forced labor! That is not the way I planned the temple to be built! I am fearful for my people. I must talk with Joab. He will find a way to meet this situation." Abi saw that David did not even remember that he had ordered Solomon to kill Joab. She wanted to run after the young king and assure him David did not mean what he said about Joab, that he was not himself this morning. But she knew she must not accost him in that fashion. Perhaps he will forget, she thought. If I speak of the matter it would only emphasize it.

And she thought, when Bathsheba comes I will talk it over with her. As queen mother Bathsheba was gracious. Now that she had accomplished her prime objective, she was seeking by every means to win the love of David's wives and sons.

Abi sat beside the bed. "Will you play your lyre, my lord David? I will sing for you and you will play for me."

David took the instrument. He held it lovingly and strummed his favorite song of all he had composed, the one he called the Shepherd's Psalm. Abi had sung it many times thus, with David playing on the mellow old instrument which had been his since childhood. Now she sang it again, crooning the words softly. When she came to the lines, "Yea, though I walk through the valley of the shadow of death, I will fear no evil . . ." the instrument dropped from David's arm and he clung to her hands.

"It was so far away—death—when I wrote the song. Now it is close. It is very close, and I fear so much evil for my country and my sons. Abishag, have I talked only of fears and of evil these past days? Have I become a troublesome old man? Will you be glad when the shadow of death falls across me and you are free to marry Adonijah? Oh Abishag, what have I done in my pride and my guilt—to take the throne from Adonijah and give it to Solomon? Joab was right, but I was too proud to let him have that final victory over me. What harm an old man does when he lives too long!"

David was weeping a flood of tears now. Soon he was coughing so hard that he brought up a flow of blood, soiling his tunic and his sheets. Abi sent for a maidservant, and together they changed the bed and put a clean tunic on the king. She sent also for the physician. After he had come and gone, David slept for a while.

When he wakened Bathsheba was beside him.

Bathsheba had taken on weight as well as dignity during the six months she had been queen mother. Her influence was enormous, both in the harem and with Solomon, who often brought her to sit beside him on the dais when he sat in judgment. Bathsheba was first among his counselors. The thin delicacy of her features had rounded into the beauty that goes with contentment. She glowed with happiness. With David she made it her business to be gay and full of cheerful gossip. Today she launched into a tale of one of the concubines who had set out for the Gihon spring. Even though the rains had commenced, the palace cistern was still low and the water filled with sediment. As she went she felt a great deluge of water upon her head and shoulders. She thought nothing of it, since the rain was falling. When she returned to the palace the women twitted her about the fruit stones and peelings lodged in the folds of her mantle. She had caught a pot full of refuse thrown from a window without realizing it. "She was surely fortunate that the refuse she caught was nothing worse than peelings, don't you agree, my lord David?" Bathsheba concluded.

David and Abi laughed together. David asked after the welfare of the ten concubines who had lived in widowhood in a house of their own ever since Absalom had lain with them in a pavilion on the palace roof many years ago. Bathsheba replied airily that now Dinah had grown too old to find waywardness amusing, she ruled them with a hand of iron. Then Bathsheba launched into another gay recital concerning an Ephraimite who had come to Solomon for judgment. The story did not amuse David, perhaps because today he was filled with misgivings as to the justice Solomon would dispense in his kingdom. Before the story was concluded David reached out a trembling, clawlike hand and gripped Abishag's wrist.

"You sacrificed this girl to your ambition," he whispered hoarsely. "Do not deny what everyone knows, that you were willing at any cost to keep me on Israel's throne until your son reached an age to inherit. She served your purpose, and she has been kind to me. When I am gone she is to choose a husband for herself. No matter who it is, even if it is Adonijah, she is to be given to the husband of her choice."

Bathsheba shrank from David's anger and from the fearful odor which grew worse when he became excited. She said softly, "But the law—the king is lord of the harem inherited from his father. It is for Solomon to provide shelter to the widows and concubines. If he gives Abishag to another man, her husband could claim the throne, exposing his people to the danger of rebellion and usurpation."

David's eyes rolled. "Let us hear no talk of usurpation!" His face was mottled and terrible. His grip on Abi's wrist was painful. "This girl has borne with patience the demands of a troublesome old man. She must not go through life bewailing her virginity. She has served you and you will serve her, Bathsheba. See that you show your gratitude to Abishag and that your son does likewise!"

Bathsheba cried, "You are feverish, my lord. You must not exert yourself. Abishag, bring a basin and sponge his face and body."

David's whisper was like a shout. "I am not feverish. Solomon has the kingdom. Give Abishag to Adonijah!"

"Yes, my lord David. I promise to do as you wish. Now, rest, my dear lord, and do not harm yourself. Trust me to show kindness to all who have been dear to you. How can I bear it if the husband who has shown me such love and kindness should go down into Sheol with hatred for me in his heart?" Bathsheba was weeping softly.

"Go away," David said bitterly. "I do not want to see you again. Send Adonijah to me."

"I will, my lord," Bathsheba said, and left the chamber.

Abi bent and kissed David's forehead. "Thank you, my lord David," she said. "I am very glad you have asked for Adonijah. He has waited many months for you to send for him."

But before Adonijah could come, David was taken with a fit of coughing and a hemorrhage which the Levite physician could not halt. "It is the end," he announced, and Abi sent a servant to call together the wives and sons of the old king. So it was that Adonijah never talked with David after his attempt to seize the throne.

While all the wives and sons of David congregated in the upper chamber, Zadok and Abiathar, Benaiah and Joab, Hushai and Jehoshaphat came also to stand beside the king they had loved and served. Zadok and Abiathar murmured words from David's songs and offered prayers.

David did not last out the night. When the wind rose and cold rain beat upon the roof, a final weak effort to cough failed to clear his throat of the strangling blood. His final rasp was heard even above the quiet sobbing in the room. Then Abishag took away the pillows and lowered the thin old body, quiet at last, on the bed. Bathsheba bent to close David's eyes and to pull a sheet up over his face. Sobbing, she turned for comfort to her tall, elegant son. He held her against himself while tears flowed down his face. And all David's sons stood beside the bed on which their father had slept with his many wives for many years and they lifted their voices, and the wives and the officers and the priests also lifted their voices in lamentation for David. They rent their garments and from the dying fire put ashes upon their heads and went out from the room, wailing loudly and beating their breasts. Then the concubines of David came to prepare the body with myrrh and aloes for burial.

Solomon sent runners throughout Israel with the news of David's death. The entire month Kislev was set aside as a month of mourning. So well did

Bathsheba organize the harem that throughout the month wailing for David in the women's court was continuous day and night.

It rained on the day of David's burial. The tomb was in the top tier of tombs excavated in the west side of the Kidron Valley, and was so constructed that it opened onto both the valley and the city. Here an arched doorway had been set above the cavern with steps leading down to the base of the large excavation. All around the sides, one above another, many niches had been cut into the walls. Here lay the body of Abigail, brought from Carmel for burial, beside her little son Daniel. And Haggith, who died in giving birth to Adonijah, had been brought from Hebron and placed in this tomb. Amnon lay here, but Absalom still lay in a pit in the Ephraim forest with a cairn of rocks piled above him.

To this tomb was David carried, wearing a robe of purple over which linen wrappings had been bound with myrrh and aloes. The bier had poles of cedar which the sons of David lifted upon their shoulders, five on each side with Solomon leading on the right side and Adonijah on the left. The wives of David followed the bier and after them came the two high priests followed by the other priests and officials who were close to David. Soldiers followed priests, and last of all came a great multitude of people so that the streets could not hold them all. Everyone marched through the cold rain with bare feet and bare heads, wearing dark cloaks of sackcloth, with their hands upon their heads and ashes and soot disfiguring tearful, swollen faces.

When the body had been placed in its niche in the tomb, the door of the tomb was closed. But all through that day and the days that followed, mourners in sackcloth came from all over Israel to stand in the cold rain beside the tomb and weep for David, who had established their kingdom and won their love, and who now slept with his fathers.

49

THE MOURNING ENDED when the month Tebet came, the coldest of the year, with sullen skies and occasional sleet and snow. On such a day, with the wind whistling among the houses and sleet beating down, Joab came forth from Solomon's council chamber seething with anger that was mingled with fear.

Passing by his own house he strode to the street on which Abiathar lived. Joab's knuckles made a thunder on the door. It was Abishag who invited him to enter. Her manner held such grace and sweetness that Joab found himself softening in spite of his mood.

"Reba told me you had come to visit in the house of Rachel," he said.

"I commend your wisdom. This young king has not yet found time with his many activities to choose a wife. You are much too young and beautiful to remain in that harem of elderly women he inherited."

Abishag cast down her eyes. Adonijah appeared beside her in the narrow entry. "Solomon will know by tomorrow that Abishag is to be given to me," he said. He placed an arm about the girl and led her and Joab into the large room where Rachel waited. "Before my father died he made Bathsheba promise that Abishag and I should marry, but she has delayed. Today I went to her urging that she delay no longer. She promised to go before Solomon in his court tomorrow morning as a petitioner. Of course Solomon cannot refuse his mother." He drew Abishag to him. His bright blue eyes were shining with happiness. "Do you wish us well, Joab?"

Joab looked upon the two handsome young people and his heart ached within him. "I am afraid what I have done this morning will not help your cause, or mine. We must talk together, all of us. Rachel, can you send a servant for Reba? And Abiathar—is he at home?"

Anxiety drove the gladness from Rachel's face. "A servant went for Reba some time ago. I will get Abiathar and Jonathan. They are in the upper room." She went out toward the courtyard from which a stairway mounted to the scroll room.

Joab said, "I wish I did not need to disturb your happiness, Abishag. You have earned the gratitude of this kingdom and its king. Yet we must realize that Solomon derived his security from his father. The people, our scattered army, the entire family of David, and many of the priests wanted Adonijah to inherit. This is a frightening majority. Solomon and his advisers are rightly fearful."

Adonijah's cheeks had grown darkly flushed. "My brother knows I would not overthrow the king my father set upon the throne!"

"Solomon has not your nobility, nor David's forgiving nature. You grew up in a palace where the heir to Saul's throne was kindly received and welcomed among the sons of David. Yet Mephibosheth was a cripple and not the attractive contender for the throne you are. If the people of Israel should rise up against Solomon and set you on the throne, I think you could not refuse."

Abi smiled. "You are expecting trouble that surely will not come. If you had heard the promises Bathsheba made to David just before he died—"

"Forgive me, Abishag," Joab said gently. "Bathsheba is not the king."

Abi cried, "Solomon knows very well he owes his throne to Bathsheba!"

Adonijah's eyes filled with tears. "I would like to be sure of that. A thousand times during the past eight months I have asked myself, why did my father choose Solomon? Why did he reject me? In all the months before he died, he did not send for me. Why?"

Abi took his hand and held it against her cheek. "He was ill and filled with remorse for what he had done. He put off sending for you because he dreaded saying what he knew he ought to say to you. But when he knew he was nearing his end he did send for you, Adonijah. After Solomon told him he was going to build the temple with forced labor—I think that was what killed him. He never spoke of you, Adonijah, except with love."

Adonijah buried his face in Abi's dark, smooth hair. "That is the only way I have ever thought of my father—with love."

Rachel was returning now, followed by Abiathar and Jonathan. Reba also arrived, flushed and breathless from hurrying on the icy, cobbled streets. Her heavy mantle glittered with sleet and her hands were red with cold. She went to Adonijah and Abishag and laid her hands on their shoulders. "Bathsheba has told me she will petition Solomon tomorrow to let you marry," she said. "My dear children, I am so glad for you."

Rachel hung Reba's mantle over a bench near the fire. Joab led her to a seat near him. "I have come with heavy news for us all," he said. He put his arm about Reba, a thing he had never done before in the presence of others. He sighed and turned to Abiathar. "We have given the years of our lives to building this people into a nation. I think Solomon will destroy it. If we give ourselves to his plans and help him destroy Israel, we could live. You, Abiathar, he would not dare kill. But for Adonijah and myself— we must see if there is a way out for us."

Seeing the stunned disbelief on these faces Joab smiled bitterly. "Well, I must not go on making vague and gloomy predictions. Solomon called me to his council chamber this morning and made me an offer of a post in his government. He did not say that I could buy my life and Adonijah's by accepting. He did not need to say it."

Reba stirred restlessly. "What post did Solomon offer you, Joab?"

Joab replied, "First, let me tell you some of the plans he has for his program of construction."

"I have heard strange tales," Abiathar remarked, "concerning palaces, and pavements like jewels—acres of pavements—leading to the top of Mount Moriah and the temple he will build. Also I have heard that every lamp and basin and pitcher made of porphyry or alabaster will be replaced with gold."

Adonijah's smile was grim. "He always had extravagant notions. He used to question traders who came with caravans from Egypt and Babylon concerning the wonders in the cities they had seen. Yet there is a limit even to the king's resources. I think he will realize it soon."

"He has learned it already, Adonijah," Joab said grimly. "David found his income ample—so ample he laid aside a great sum of money in gold talents to be used in building the temple, as well as a treasure in golden vessels and building stone and cedar wood from Lebanon. But that income is not sufficient for David's son. For Solomon much more will be wanted.

He did me the honor today to lay before me his plans for raising money. This Solomon is not the callow youth we had supposed. He is shrewd and practical. Some of his plans will be executed at once; others may take a few years. But this is what he intends to do. First, he will rent out on shares all the lands belonging to himself and all he inherited from David, from Amnon, and Absalom. He will take into custody all non-Israelites living in our kingdom, seize their lands and possessions, and send them as slaves to work in the quarries, forests, and mines from which will come his building materials."

Adonijah exclaimed, "Those people have served in our armies. They have observed our laws. We have treaties with them, some of them dating all the way back to Joshua!"

"He should not break the laws concerning the strangers within our borders," Abiathar agreed. "If I go to Zadok and tell him that Solomon is planning to break our ancient treaties—"

Joab laid a hand on Abiathar's bony wrist. "Zadok would not believe you. Or if he did, he could not stop this king, this youth with his grand ideas. And this is only the beginning. From our own people he hopes to extract certain sums each year in gold talents, tribe by tribe. He also will demand from each tribe a month's supply of foodstuffs for the palace and its guard—cattle and sheep, cereals and oils and fruits. Each tribe will provide a thousand men for one month's labor without pay, year after year. These are the men who will build the temple and palaces, complete the city walls and improve the highways. The task he offered to me is to set up this program among the tribes. I have friends in every tribe, soldiers and captains. To them I am asked to go, and with their help choose officers in each tribe to see that gold, labor, and foodstuffs are forthcoming."

Reba covered her face, shaking with silent sobs. Adonijah's face was red as fire; his eyes were staring and his fists clenched. Abiathar began to pace up and down the room. Jonathan sat silent, looking from one to the other.

Joab continued, "For you, Adonijah, he has plans also. He spoke of treaties with Egypt. He has this thought: that instead of giving foreign merchants permission to travel through our land to trade with one another, he will demand that each—Egypt on the one side and Phoenicia, Syria, Babylon on the other—sell him their goods which he in turn will resell at a profit. This applies in particular to horses and chariots, which the Egyptians sell continually to our northern and eastern neighbors. Solomon envisions a monopoly in the trade that passes through our land. He wants you to represent him, Adonijah, in the capitals of our neighbors, much as Seth used to represent David, but on a much larger scale."

"Why would a man with a wife like Abi spend his time traveling to

[301]

Egypt and Babylon?" Adonijah protested. Joab had never before seen him so angry.

"What answer did you make to Solomon?" Abiathar inquired.

"I was evasive. I said I had served Israel for many years and would like now to retire to Bethlehem to end my days. Yet I think he knows that if I live till spring I will raise an army and drive him from the throne."

"Can we stop him?" Adonijah asked.

Reba lifted a tear-streaked face. "You will lose your lives, and when you are dead and we are left to mourn, he will do all he plans, and without your help. What good can you accomplish by opposing him?"

Joab said gently, "We may not have the choice. Tomorrow in the hall of judgment Bathsheba will petition Solomon to give Abishag to Adonijah. If Solomon was shrewd enough to read my mind aright today, he might take the occasion to order Adonijah's execution, and mine."

Abi cried, "He would not publicly humiliate Bathsheba!"

"Let us hope not. But let us make our plans in case he does. And we must be present in the court tomorrow, to gauge his temper and his purpose."

Jonathan rose suddenly.

"I will go to court tomorrow. You must wait for me to bring you word. If Solomon means to kill you, you will be able to go into hiding."

"Solomon is the king," Adonijah said. "What can we do? Benaiah has a thousand men in Jerusalem. If Solomon orders him to put us to death, where can we go?"

"We can take sanctuary at the altar," Joab replied soberly, "and wait for the army to rise in the provinces and come to our aid."

"Civil war," Adonijah said sadly. "Is my life worth such a price?"

Abi protested, "Solomon won't refuse Bathsheba. She is purposely making her petition in this public way because he might refuse a private request, but he would not humiliate his mother publicly."

"Don't count on that," Joab warned. "Solomon will be forced publicly to choose between humiliating his mother and strengthening his brother's claim by giving him his father's wife."

"I was never David's wife. I was his nurse, nothing more," Abi insisted.

Abiathar said, "It must be put to the test. We will let events take their course, and trust in God to hold us all in His keeping."

"I will go to the court," Jonathan repeated. "Meanwhile, you can go up to the tent of meeting and offer sacrifice. Your presence there would cause no comment, and I will come and report on how Solomon received the petition."

"It would be safer that way," Joab agreed. "Yet I think our presence in court might reassure Solomon concerning our good faith."

Adonijah went to Jonathan, placing his hands upon the broad shoulders of his friend. "Again you offer to risk yourself for my sake. For this I thank you. I would accept your offer if I could. But it was I who asked Bathsheba to make the petition. I cannot skulk about the sanctuary while Bathsheba braves her son's anger for my sake, and Abishag's."

Abi touched Jonathan's sleeve. "You have been our staunch friend, always." She stood on tiptoe to kiss his cheek, and his face went a fiery red.

"We are too fearful," Reba said. "Solomon loves Bathsheba. I think he also knows that Bathsheba is often troubled by her lonely position in the harem. She sincerely wants to win our love, our regard—not just the minimum of respect we now show her. This petition is deeply important to her, and I cannot believe that Solomon will refuse her."

Joab stood alone among these friends. Did any of them understand the extent of the danger? Perhaps it was better if they did not. We have today, he thought.

As if echoing his thought Rachel said, "Let us spend this day together. We will not talk any more of danger for a while."

"I will go to Zadok," Abiathar announced. "Perhaps he can help us. He has influence with Solomon."

"Do what you can," Joab replied. "Ask him to remind Solomon that David forgave even his enemies." A stricken look came over his face. "How can I ask any man for mercy? I never quite understood the true nobility of David until this moment. It would be folly for Solomon to show mercy, for if Adonijah lives, Israel will yet make him king. And if I live and Adonijah does not, I will surely set Shephatiah or some other son of David on the throne."

"Do not say such things!" Reba exclaimed. "Suppose a servant were to hear you?"

Abiathar repeated, "I will speak to Zadok. I will do what I can, for of all men on earth none are as dear to me as Joab and this worthy son of David."

Reba rose and the golden bracelets on her arms jangled musically. She looked from Joab to Adonijah. "We are in God's hands. Let us speak no more of death or danger. Today we are here together, and if we must weep, we will do so another time."

50

ADONIJAH, JOAB, AND Abiathar came separately to the hall of judgment next morning, in the hope that no one of them would endanger another and also because a man alone can slip quietly out of a crowd, while two men together cannot. Abi and Reba had come with all the widows of David, who knew Bathsheba was to petition her son about something this morning, and had argued heatedly as to the nature of the petition. Shephatiah and Minna had come in today, and were attending court with Rachel and Jonathan. Shephatiah was well known to be close to Adonijah by ties of lifelong association as well as brotherly ties, and he had no illusions about the extent of his influence with Solomon. Yet in attending Solomon's court he was placing himself on record as a witness of the treatment one of the sons of David would today accord another.

Joab came into court wearing two cloaks and with another rolled into a small bundle and tucked in his girdle. He was not armed, nor was Adonijah. They did not stand among the officers of the court near the dais but among spectators near the street door. Each was clothed in dark and commonplace attire, yet their faces were known to all, and there was no question of concealment or disguise. Many turned to stare at one or the other of them, but when Solomon appeared he became instantly the focus of all eyes.

His purple robes were stiff with needlework in threads of gold. On his dark curls he wore a golden crown set with gems of many sizes and colors. The dais and the throne and the hangings in the chamber had not yet been changed, but on Jehoshaphat's low table the bell, the cup which held the pens, and the core on which scrolls were rolled were all of gold. A new rug had been ordered from Damascus, and Joab wondered if he would be alive to see it laid. If only I could have ten years to live in Bethlehem with Reba as my wife. We are too old for the wild passions of other years, he thought. But we are not too old to find comfort and companionship together.

Bathsheba had not yet appeared. Solomon heard two petitioners quickly and rendered judgment of a quality that compared favorably with the justice dispensed by David. And Joab thought how attentive Solomon had always been since, at the age of seven, he first began sitting on the steps before the dais while his father received petitioners from all over Israel.

After the third petitioner had bowed himself away, Bathsheba entered. She was dressed in purple, with a golden girdle tied about the long full coat. She wore jeweled bands of gold woven through her dark hair. She is a handsome woman, Joab thought. He saw how proudly and affectionately the eyes of the young king went to his mother, and hope stirred faintly in his heart.

Bathsheba came to the steps and knelt as a petitioner. Quickly Solomon descended the steps. He lifted Bathsheba to her feet and led her to the dais. A soldier brought a low bench and placed it beside the throne, and Solomon seated Bathsheba beside him, on his right.

"Make your request, my mother," he said kindly. "For I will not refuse you."

[304]

In that moment Joab knew that Solomon had had no warning of the nature of his mother's intentions.

She clasped her hands and looked up at Solomon with dark, pleading eyes. "Hear the petition your mother brings, my lord, O King," she said. In the breathless silence of the court her voice rang to the farthest corner. "Give Abishag the Shunemite to Adonijah your brother, to be his wife."

She has what she most wanted, Joab thought, and now she wants an easy conscience as well. He did not for a moment doubt the earnestness of her petition.

Solomon rose, and his hands were tightly clenched and on his face the veins stood out. At his first words Joab began making his way cautiously toward the door. "Why do you ask Abishag the Shunemite for Adonijah? Ask the kingdom for him also, for he is my older brother, and Abishag was wife to King David. You know he has friends in the kingdom who would seize upon any pretext to make him king." He raised his fists above his head and swore a great oath. "God do so to me and more also if this word does not cost Adonijah his life! As the Lord lives who has established me and placed me on the throne of David my father, who has chosen me to be the heir according to His promise to David, Adonijah shall be put to death this day."

Joab paused in the doorway, reconnoitering as an old soldier must before the retreat. He saw Solomon look toward Benaiah, saw the gesture which was the king's command to his chief executioner. Bathsheba stumbled blindly down the steps from the dais, sobbing aloud, whether because of this public humiliation or because of the disappointment of her own earnest hopes, who could say? Against the wall Joab saw the anguished faces of Reba and Abishag. He did not see Adonijah, and hoped fervently that the young prince had already left the room.

Joab slipped through the doorway, crossed into an alley and began to run. Following narrow streets and alleys he made his way toward Millo. Gibeon was his destination.

To Adonijah the altar on Mount Moriah was the most sacred place in the kingdom, for there David had transformed the threshing floor into a place of worship. There Adonijah had stood countless times to sing with the Levite choir while Israel worshiped. But to Joab the ancient tabernacle at Gibeon was more precious. Here he had come with Asa his brother, bringing David's offerings. Here he had fought his battle with Abner. Here he had killed Amasa, shedding another man's blood for the last time, and recovered the ram's horn of command which was never again taken from him.

He had reached the Millo Gate. He knew every stone, every slitted window, and he touched the gate as he walked through, speaking courteously to the soldiers on guard and moving at a deceptively leisurely pace so as not to arouse their curiosity. But as soon as trees hid him from their view he was running again.

The shortest route to Gibeon would have been by way of the Ephraim Gate, but Adonijah was headed that way and Joab knew their chances were better if they fled in different directions. Moreover, the Ephraim Gate stood close to the barracks occupied by Benaiah's police. This way was safer, and now that he was out of sight of the city Joab was glad he had chosen to come this way. With a sharp constriction in the heart he wondered whether Adonijah had got away safely. If he had, he would now be within the sanctuary on Mount Moriah.

Joab reached the last hill from which he could look back upon Jerusalem. The city of David and the city of Joab, he thought. Ah, David, how much we shared! Many comrades have I loved, but none so much as you. I loved you for the wars we fought, for the triumphs we won, but most of all for this pearl of cities we gave to Israel. He looked only a moment longer. He knew every turn, every turret. There was no need to linger.

He walked rapidly, breathing deeply. He was feeling the weight of his sixty-one years. The rapid pace of the forced march did not come as easily as it had when he led the armies of Israel. If I go down now into Sheol, he thought, I will find many there whom I have loved—Zeruiah, Asa, Seth, Amnon my son, and David. Death cannot be so terrible, when so many I have loved have gone by that road. I do not fear death. I have touched the hem of its garment many times. But oh, I would like to have ten years to live with Reba in Bethlehem.

He topped another hill and looked back. He had not been followed. Perhaps he would have some time before they thought to look for him in Gibeon. Perhaps Benaiah would not find him before tomorrow. The night will be cold in the court of the tabernacle, he thought. Especially if it rains.

Adonijah, he thought, will you live to marry Abishag? We made one terrible mistake. We should have brought together the army for your coronation. We trusted too much in David, not realizing how his strength and wisdom had been wasted by illness.

Today was fair, and the sleet that had stung the flesh yesterday was only a memory. The hills on all sides were sere, with outcroppings of gray stone. Olive trees dotted the slopes, their twisted shapes naked against the blue sky. Winter is a good season for a man to die, thought Joab.

He came over another hill and saw the pool of Gibeon below, with the low, gray stone houses beyond and above all the tattered old tabernacle. He reached the place in the road where he had killed Amasa, and looked at his hands. They had shed much blood, much blood. Would the God of Israel deny sanctuary to one who gripped the altar horns with hands stained with so much blood? And then he thought, in all honesty it is not of the God of Israel that I ask sanctuary. Rather I ask it of the men of Israel.

He remembered the day when David had fled before Absalom. On the Mount of Olives David watched while all who fled with him passed by. The priests came, bearing the ark, and David sent it back. "If God is with me," David said, "I do not need the ark. If God is not with me the ark cannot help me."

So be it, thought Joab. And his heart turned in prayer to the God of Israel.

How long ago he had made his vow, saying, I will serve David with my life and let David attend to serving the Lord. Slowly Joab climbed the three-tiered flight of steps to the tabernacle court, conscious as never before that he had made this headlong flight to this holy place for reasons of policy, not worship.

He moved very slowly. Midday was passing. Someone had polished the brasswork on the altar since the morning sacrifice, but no one was here now.

Sanctuary, thought Joab, is the gift of God. The God of David, the God of Israel, the God of Joab—He is one God, and I have not approached Him often in my lifetime. His hand went out, hesitated, then grasped the altar horn above the brass meshwork. Sanctuary is for the man who comes to claim it, not because of his merit but because God gives it. If I die here it will not be because God refused to give me sanctuary, but because Solomon is ambitious, determined, and will stick at nothing.

The touch of the altar, cold though it was, comforted Joab. I am in God's hands, he thought. Whether I live or die, I am in God's hands. Israel is in God's hands. I have lived for Israel, following the promptings of such wisdom as has been vouchsafed to me. Others have also lived for Israel, and still others will be born into this land who will live for Israel. This people will go on, though one by one the men who serve the people die. And all are in God's hands—this people, their king, and I—even I, Joab.

He was weary from turbulent emotions and events, and from the long distance he had come. He sat upon the ledge and leaned against the brazen mesh, raising his arm above his shoulder to keep his grip. While he was alone here there was no need to hug the altar thus. Yet he did not relax his grip because of the comfort he felt from its touch. God is in this place, he thought, and his mind went back over the centuries, back even to the time when Moses stood beside this altar and looked upon this tabernacle. The altar horn is like the hand of God, holding me safe while I reach up to touch it. That is the meaning of sanctuary—to enter upon the unseen presence of God. How peaceful it is, he thought. I should have come here long ago. But there was always much to be done. I gave my life to David. Had I been wiser I would have given my life to God.

He had been noticed. A priest and two Levites were entering by the side gate near the house from which Zadok had come some thirty-five years

[307]

ago to accept the offering sent by David. The priest came near, peering nearsightedly. "You are Joab," he exclaimed. "Why are you here? I never thought to see this sight!"

The priest was an elderly man, a cousin to Zadok. He was plump and kindly, yet Joab knew he would lose no time sending a messenger to tell Zadok that Joab could be found here. To save him any qualms in the matter Joab explained at once that he had fled here from Solomon. "I do not doubt that you will want to let Zadok know where I can be found," he said.

The priest looked anxious. "I am sorry to hear that you are in trouble. I remember when you first came here. You have served our nation for many years. Can I do anything to make you comfortable?"

"Do you have a piece of tent cloth? If it rains in the night I would be grateful for shelter to keep me dry."

Benaiah came before midday next morning. He wore simple battle dress with a worn leather breastplate and a helmet Joab had seen many times. He was followed by a company of soldiers. He left the soldiers outside the court since they were not Israelites, sending a squad to guard the side gate and leaving the rest at the main gate. He stalked across the court with his hand resting on the handle of his sword. Joab noticed that Benaiah rose on the balls of his feet as he walked. Like a young man, thought Joab. Yet he knew Benaiah was older than himself by two or three years.

Joab rose from the ledge where he had been sitting. He flexed the hand that gripped the altar horn, then closed it again. Benaiah's eyes were on him steadily as he came, and in them Joab read a weary kind of grief.

Joab said, "What has happened to Adonijah?"

"He was caught in the doorway of the hall of judgment. Solomon watched as I killed him with this sword." Benaiah half drew his sword, then thrust it back again. "Adonijah was a goodly prince. Too much like David, perhaps, for his own safety."

Joab wept silently, covering his face with the sleeve on his left arm. He was thinking less of Adonijah than of Reba and Abi. Benaiah waited in silence, respecting his grief.

Presently Benaiah said, "I have my orders, Joab. So come away from here. You can't save yourself. You can only make it more troublesome for everybody."

Joab dried his eyes. "However troublesome it may be for others, friend Benaiah, it is a great deal more troublesome for me. Do not ask for my cooperation. You have been executioner for David for more than forty years. Do you never tire of your work?"

"Just now—yes, a little."

Joab's hand tightened on the altar. "Tell me about Adonijah."

"Look you, Joab, I do not care to discuss these things. You cannot stay here by this altar forever. So come down from this holy place and let's get it over with."

"I will not come down. I will cling to this altar until Solomon changes his mind or help comes. I can outwait you, Benaiah."

Benaiah said, "How long have you been here?"

"Since yesterday."

"It will rain tonight. It will rain and it will snow. This is the month for it. You will come down." He bent and picked up the piece of tent cloth, looked at it, then put it back where Joab had left it. "I suppose the priests bring you food?"

Joab said, "I brought money with me. Enough to buy a lamb to offer to the Lord God each morning so long as I am here. The priests have been kind."

"It is their business to be kind. I suppose they make sure the fire is close enough to warm you but not close enough to burn you, eh?"

"Benaiah, old friend, it would do you no harm to spend some days and nights beside this altar. We have been violent men, and godless, and now we meet here where God has met with the devout among our people from the time of Moses until now. Do you think it possible that God might also meet with us, if we stay here quietly for a time?"

Benaiah walked rapidly back across the court. Joab heard him shout to one of the soldiers, "Jeshua, run to the city. Tell my lord Solomon that Joab will not leave the altar. Say that I will remain here and await his orders." One of the soldiers set off running. Benaiah said to the others, "Make yourselves comfortable. Do not leave the gates unguarded, and do not permit anyone except the priests to enter."

One of the soldiers said, "A young man is here; will you speak with him?"

Benaiah walked down two of the three tiers of steps, and talked in a low voice to someone. Joab climbed up and stood on the ledge but could not see who it was. When Benaiah returned he said, "The young man Jonathan, son of the priest Abiathar, came and asked to stay here with you, but I have sent him away."

"It was kind of him to come," Joab said. "Are you going to kill Abiathar?"

Benaiah's eyes shifted and he changed color. "I've had no orders about Abiathar. Look, Joab, sanctuary is for men with private crimes on their conscience. A man sentenced by the king has no right to sanctuary. You know that."

Joab said, "Sanctuary is for whoever needs it. Benaiah, your king may order you to kill me here, but would you do that? Would you strike me down in this holy place?"

[309]

Benaiah said steadily, "Would you, in my position?"

"Do not put it on me. This is your problem."

"I will give you an answer if the problem arises, not otherwise."

"Why do you kill me, Benaiah? Why did you kill Adonijah?"

"I am a soldier. I obey my orders."

"We killed for David, you and I, but always in the name of Israel. We killed enemies who would have destroyed the peace and prosperity and unity of Israel. You cannot honestly believe that my death will help Israel. Why do you kill me?"

Benaiah's face was suddenly twisted with hatred. "Why did you kill Uriah?"

Joab sat down abruptly upon the ledge. When Benaiah stepped quickly toward him he realized he had let go the altar. He grasped it again. He said, "You have struck home, Benaiah. David ordered Uriah's death, and as a good soldier I obeyed my king. I remember that night, on the eve of the battle in which Uriah died. If he had known of the orders given concerning him, if he had come out upon the hilltop that night to argue with me—well, I will not trouble you with any more arguments. It is the son of Uriah's wife who orders my death. This, I suppose, is justice."

Benaiah came close, towering over Joab. "David ordered your death! On the day he died he said to Solomon that unless he put you to death he would not be able to reign in peace. Carry that thought into Sheol with you!"

Joab covered his face and wept. David, he thought, was this your dying wish for me? Yet he knew that David had spoken the simple truth to Solomon. He is not safe on his throne while I live, Joab acknowledged.

When he looked up again Benaiah was sitting on the pavement facing the steps, and beyond his soldiers sat upon the ground wrapped in their cloaks. And Joab thought of life and death, of Reba and David, Abishag and Adonijah—the living and the dead—all seemed equally remote from this altar. He thought also of Benaiah, and of what was to come when the messenger he had sent to Solomon returned.

If I die before the sun sets, he thought, I will yet give thanks to God that I had these hours in this holy place. The code by which I have lived is simple, an honest code. You shall love your friends and hate your enemies. This was not David's code. David forgave his enemies and sought to make friends of them. I have made it my business to kill David's enemies, even those he forgave. Is it possible that I was wrong? If I had held back, is it possible that God would have dealt with them on David's behalf? If I went down from here, forgiven by Solomon, would I find forgiveness in my heart for this youth who is my enemy? He sighed. It seemed unlikely that he could learn so late in life the art of forgiveness. Moreover, who could say whether God had not chosen to deal with David's enemies by providing just such a kinsman as Joab to cut them down? It is all too deep for me, he thought. Yet it is well for a man to ask such questions of himself before his life has run its course.

Evening had come. The worn old tabernacle stood between Joab and the setting sun. But he was not looking toward the west, for the runner was returning. Benaiah walked quickly to meet him. There was a confusion of talk beside the steps, and beyond the soldiers Joab saw that many people were congregating. This was the time when the priests should be busy about the sunset sacrifices, and several priests were waiting, holding back from the altar because of the soldiers.

The talk between Benaiah and his messenger had ended and now on all sides of the court voices rose in protesting wails. Benaiah was returning more slowly than he had gone. From his sorely troubled face Joab knew what Solomon's order had been.

Benaiah came close, hand on his sword. "I must kill you, Joab, whether here or elsewhere. My lord Solomon has ordered me to do it without delay. Will you come down?"

Joab stood erect, feeling himself to be at peace, and gripping still the friendly altar horn. "Let this sin be upon the conscience of that young man, Solomon, then, and may it bring him some warning thoughts concerning himself and this people of whom he is king." He stood very tall, and his eyes met Benaiah's. Fear and grief were on the swarthy face of his old comrade, yet there was no weakness of purpose. "If I must die," Joab said softly, "let it be by your hand and by David's order. I would not want to be killed by lesser men."

He looked into the open door of the tattered tabernacle, to the Veil beyond which the ark had rested long ago. Joab had heard it said that the presence of God was in the ark, and that without the ark the tabernacle had no holiness at all. They were wrong, he thought. Without God there is no sanctuary. I will die in the presence of God. It is a better death than I deserved.

He heard the priests cry out in protest. He saw the horror which sprang into the face of Zadok's cousin. Then the sword of Benaiah struck him, entering below the fifth rib.

He released at last his hold on the altar, yet the hand of God seemed still to grip his hand as he sank onto the pavement, overcome by a strange inertia.

When he opened his eyes he saw bending above him the wavering figure of a tattered outlaw, a bloody bandage in his dark, matted hair. Far away Ira's voice said, "And is that down upon *your* cheeks a beard, Benaiah?"

The words came through stiffening jaws, thick as winter honey. "Bring me—to David." And so Joab died.

[311]

Since the death of Adonijah and Joab, and Abiathar's banishment to Anathoth, the village of priests, Reba's health had been poor. She was tended in the harem by Abishag and Maacah, yet she did not mend. When spring came Abi begged Bathsheba to let her take Reba to Anathoth, suggesting that a change of surroundings and the sight of old friends might comfort and restore her. Bathsheba offered a donkey for the journey and Abishag accepted gratefully. And so, early one morning near the end of the month Nisan, Abishag brought Reba out through the Damascus Gate to the highway that led across the upper reaches of the Kidron wadi. The hills were green with spring, and blanketing flowers rioted in rich and splendid colors on the slopes. Reba's pale face brightened as she inhaled the tangy air.

The journey was slow because they were forced constantly to the side of the road to make way for sledges bearing stone to the city. The men dragging the sledges were the first of Solomon's slave labor groups.

Reba said softly, "Joab lived to see everything he had fought for accomplished. But he did not live to see slavery take root in Israel."

Abi replied, "Benaiah says he met death with tranquility. We cannot grieve forever, Reba. See how beautiful the countryside is today."

It was true. All the undulating Benjamite country spread about them, greener than Judah, terraced and well-tended, with orchards and vineyards everywhere. The lush smell of spring enlivened their spirits as nothing else could.

The village of Anathoth was spread over the top of an unusually high hill. Abiathar's estate was small but thriving, with vineyards and fig trees and an olive orchard and a share in the communal pasture. The house was small in comparison with houses in the northern sector of Jerusalem, yet it was larger than Abi's home in Shunem, having four rooms around its court and a spacious room above the jutting roof.

Rachel opened the door and hurried with welcoming cries to help Reba down off the donkey. She embraced both women, then led them to the courtyard and up a flight of steps to the upper room.

Abiathar met them at the top of the stairway. He had a reed pen in one hand and ink had spattered on his tunic. He had aged during the winter, but the deep-set eyes brightened as he took Reba's hands in his.

"How fitting it is that you should come today," he said. "I have just been writing down the record of how they died." He did not need to name the names. "Benaiah has come several times this winter. He talks of the strange things Joab said to him during the hours they were together at the altar. It is all written here, and I will read it to you presently. He told me also how Eliab came for Joab's body, and took it for burial in the family tomb in Bethlehem. Benaiah is not the man he was. He spoke about retiring to the land, but I reminded him of Joab's wish that above all the country remain unified. That will take a strong man, a man such as Benaiah."

"How much like Joab you sound," Reba said sadly.

Abiathar shook his head. "Joab was a man of action. I live in a world of scholarship, the world of days and years gone by. It is a tremendous thing to realize how much Israel has survived. But enough of that. It is a great comfort to see you both. I can no longer go out into the world. I am happy and grateful when those I have known and loved come to me here. Do sit here in the sunshine with me and talk to me of Jerusalem. Then later I will read the story of David and Joab and Adonijah and all the others as I have written it."

Reba clutched her hands together and walked to the parapet, looking south toward the distant towers of Jerusalem. "David would have been nothing, nothing without Joab. I can never forgive David for ordering Solomon to put Joab to death."

Abi cried, "It wasn't like that at all. David was not himself. He was at the end of his life, and he said only that if Joab lived he would drive Solomon from the throne."

Abiathar's voice was strong and ringing. "Joab would have been nothing without David. Joab himself would be the first to say so. Each of us was nothing, except as David gave meaning to our lives. As for me, no greater glory could be mine than that David lived when and where he did, giving me this matchless opportunity to record his story and Israel's story."

Reba was sobbing. "I never wanted glory. I wanted only my sons, my two fine, strong, beautiful sons who are dead. I wanted only Joab, who was never my husband though we loved one another all our lives."

Abishag asked, "Have you written of how Solomon profaned the tabernacle in ordering Benaiah to kill Joab there? Have you told how the priests of Gibeon did not again offer sacrifice on the altar until Solomon came at Passover with a wealth of animals and compelled the priests to offer them up for him? Afterward it is said he knelt at the door of the tabernacle all through the night, praying to the Lord God for wisdom to rule Israel, and God came to him in a vision and gave him his choice of wealth, victory in battle, or wisdom. As Solomon told it later, he chose wisdom, and God was so pleased with this choice that He promised him all three gifts."

Abi shivered, turning her face away. "I grow sick at heart when I hear Bathsheba talk and talk of the greatness of her son, and of how God chose him above all his brothers, and of how God will bless him and show him honor and glory beyond anything we can imagine."

Abiathar laid his great hands on the girl's shoulders. "I do not trouble myself concerning the acts of Solomon. They will be recorded by scholars who revere him. Yet I urge you, do not be quick to scoff at Solomon and Bathsheba. We think of him as shallow, vain, ruthless. But I was glad to hear how he kept the Passover at Gibeon. It may be that Joab, in dying as he did, brought to this king of Israel the need to seek divine guidance, without which no man can rule well or indeed live well. We are God's people, and Solomon is our king, and I believe that Joab in his death did that for Solomon which no living man could have done."

He paced up and down the roof, while Abi made Reba comfortable with cushions. "As for me, my records are written. Henceforth I will read them over, making copies of such portions as ought to be distributed to priests in the cities of Israel. I do not waste my strength grieving over what has been and what has not been, for these things are in God's keeping. If we had not served David, all of us, we would have no kingdom, no Jerusalem. We lived through great and stirring events. If I do not live to serve the Lord in the temple David planned, you will worship there, all three of you. You will bring your gifts in thanks to God who let each of us, and Joab and Adonijah and many others, do their part with David in bringing all these things to pass."

Abi gazed at him, dry-eyed. "I do not understand very much of what you say. Perhaps it is because I am young and have done nothing at all except nurse David in his last years. I only know that I am twenty years old, that I have twice been widowed though I have never been a wife." She went to Rachel and laid her face against Rachel's shoulder and wept.

There was a shout from the courtyard. She ran to look and saw Jonathan in the courtyard looking up, his face bright with happiness. He wore a short shepherd's tunic and carried a small kid in his arms. The years in the palace slipped away as Abi saw the docile mother goat who followed him. This was a farm, and there was work for her hands to do.

"Wait, Jonathan," she called, and ran to the stairway. "Wait for me. I'm coming."

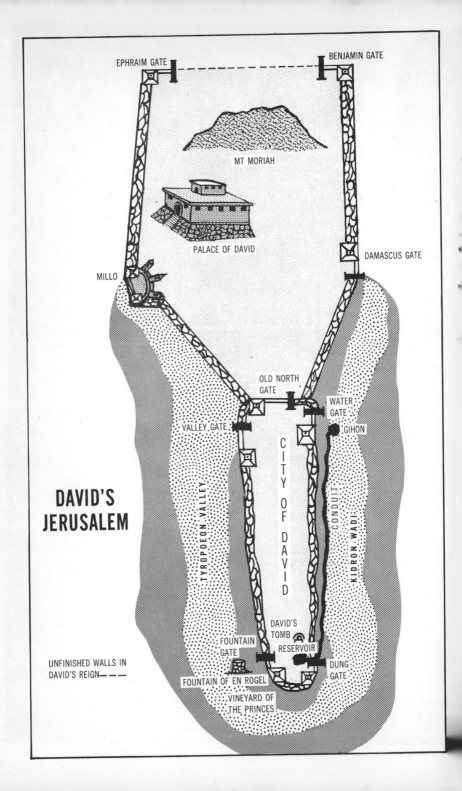

DAVID'S
JERUSALEM

UNFINISHED WALLS IN
DAVID'S REIGN———

EPHRAIM GATE

BENJAMIN GATE

MT MORIAH

PALACE OF DAVID

MILLO

DAMASCUS GATE

OLD NORTH
GATE

WATER
GATE

VALLEY GATE

GIHON

CITY OF DAVID

TYROPOEON VALLEY

CONDUIT

KIDRON WADI

DAVID'S
TOMB

FOUNTAIN
GATE

RESERVOIR

FOUNTAIN OF EN ROGEL

DUNG
GATE

VINEYARD OF
THE PRINCES